A BURST OF SUBMACHINEGUN FIRE SHATTERED THE NIGHT SILENCE.

Curt Carson had his *Novia* resting in front of him, its i-r scope activated and ready. A murky, fleeting image appeared on Curt's goggles. He flipped them up to his forehead and shifted his attention to the rifle's sensor. The rifle's laser range finder got the range data and set the sights. Curt centered the dimly illuminated crosshairs on the computer generated target marker and pulled the trigger.

The three-round burst came so fast it sounded like a single report.

"Got him!" Curt growled and began looking for another target.

G. HARRY STINE

#3: THE BASTAARD REBELLION

WARBOTS

PINNACLE BOOKS
WINDSOR PUBLISHING CORP.

PINNACLE BOOKS

are published by

Windsor Publishing Corp.
475 Park Avenue South
New York, NY 10016

First printing: September, 1988

Printed in the United States of America

To:
Loretta A. Jackson, former Airman, USAF

"It has always taken a while for a weapon to become a fully contributing member of the current arsenal of weapons, to be used in a way that capitalized to the greatest possible extent on its characteristics and potentialities. This is understandable, since experimentation is ordinarily required to see how any new device will perform best, and no peacetime testing—no matter how realistic it may appear—can replace the terrifying environment of real combat. This time lag is further influenced by current models of military thinking, which invariably tend to try to fit a new weapon into existing tactics. Changes in tactics come later only as it becomes apparent that the new weapon permits, or demands, such changes."

—Colonel Trevor N. Dupuy, AUS, Ret.
"The Evolution of Weapons and Warfare"

CHAPTER ONE

The radio receiver's loudspeaker hissed and popped, then barked with an excited male human voice slightly tinged with a German accent, "Headquarters, this is Able Two One! A civil disturbance is in progress on Kaiser Street! Request assistance!"

The Schutzmann Wachtmeister of the Otjomuise Bureau, Feldgendarmerie, Namibian Security Forces, lowered the German sex novel he was reading on watch and quickly stuffed it into the lower desk drawer. Midnight was nearly upon him, meaning his shift was about over, and he was not only lazy but tired. It had been a slow night once the television coverage of the world championship football match between Germany and Nigeria had finished with a close German victory—on which he'd won a fifty quantza bet. "Able Two One, this is headquarters," he spoke languidly at the microphone in a bored tone of voice. "How much of a civil disturbance is it? What is the nature of the assistance you require?" With any luck at all, it was just another street brawl between drunks. A quick look at the status board showed he could probably send patrol wagon Victor Four Six to serve as back-up for Able Two One. He hoped that would take care of it.

But his hopes were dashed. "Started as a fight between some whites and some Bastaards!" came the reply. "Whites were parading down the street celebrating the German football victory. Some Bastaards didn't like it! Couple of hundred people are involved now! More coming in!"

The Wachtmeister sat up. This was going to be a bit of trouble. Maybe he wouldn't be going home at midnight after all. It had been several years since a major race riot had taken place in what had once been called Windhoek, the capital of Namibia. He checked the status board again. "I can get two more patrol wagons there in a minute or so. Will that help you control the crowd?"

"Control the crowd? Wachtmeister, the crowd is surrounding us and trying to turn over our wagon! May we have permission to open fire with gas grenades?"

That was indeed an emergency, because the rules of the military police required that patrolmen obtain permission before using any sort of force or violence to control a mixed-race fight. In the first place, the Army of Namibia wasn't big enough to really control the populace; it could barely handle individual crimes of violence while protecting the government officials, politicians, and bureaucrats, guarding government installations, and providing at least a token initial force-in-being to discourage an invasion by the Republic of South Africa.

And, in the second place, now that the racial tensions of the country had been brought down to a slow simmer, the government really couldn't appear to take any sides whatsoever in a racial confrontation for fear of being overthrown. So the government was almost a passive bystander that operated with the policy, "Go ahead and fight. Let us know who wins."

Ach! Himmel! the Wachtmeister thought to himself in German which, in this multilingual country, happened to be his milk tongue because his ancestors had once been colonial subjects of Kaiser Wilhelm II of the German Empire. He waved his hand over the radio control board and activated all patrol and emergency frequencies. "All units and all personnel! Racial riot in progress on Kaiser Street! Patrolmen in danger! Proceed at once to Kaiser Street and contain the disturbance!"

He then keyed the telephone to report to the Oberst and receive further orders.

It became a night of violence in Otjomuise, and the military police couldn't stop it, much less contain it.

Prudent townspeople—whites, coloureds, Asiatics, Ovambos, Namas, and Damaras included—stayed in their homes, armed and ready to defend themselves. But the native Hereros and the mixed German-Bushman Bastaards turned out in force; they'd been spoiling for a fight now that the weather was getting warmer and summertime was upon them.

But, in fact, both the Hereros and the Bastaards had been spoiling for a fight for over a hundred years—centuries, in some cases. Not all of this was a desire for revenge against the exploitation of the Portuguese, Dutch, German, English, and Afrikaaner colonizers of the past. Some of them just liked to fight because fighting had been a way of life for as long as anyone could remember.

The celebration of the soccer victory of Germany over Nigeria was the current trigger. The Bastaards weren't about to suffer the hated whites celebrating anything, especially a victory over blacks.

They were quickly joined by thousands of Hereros living in Otjomuise.

And the violence rapidly spread beyond the center of the capital city.

By midnight, the Wachtmeister not only didn't get to go home, but he couldn't even get out of the police station. The streets were full of rampaging Bastaards.

And by unfortunate coincidence, the French ambassador happened to be returning from a diplomatic dinner at the foreign ministry at about that time.

A group of several hundred Bastaards saw the sleek Citroën limousine with its diplomatic license plates and the French tri-color flags flying from staffs on the front fenders. It didn't take more than a dozen brawny Bastaards to stop the car and turn it over with the French ambassador and his wife and chauffeur inside. Then they set fire to it.

None of the occupants of the limo were permitted to get out. They were roasted alive inside, their screams and entreaties for mercy drawing only laughter and shouts of derision from the crowd.

Thus fired-up by their success at humiliating and killing a hated foreigner—Namibia had been growing more and more xenophobic as it fought to keep foreigners from dominating the new country as had been done in the past—the Bastaards moved on to the diplomatic compound. En route, no shop, bank, or office of any foreign firm was spared. Fire, broken glass, looted interiors, and smashed facilities were the lot of the new offices of Royal Dutch Shell, Phillips, General Motors, Renault, and Mitsubishi. The Bastaards even looted the neighborhood *kondieterei*.

Any white found on the streets was slaughtered. Some murders were particularly slow and painful.

It went beyond that point. After a white Namibia family was dragged from their small home and murdered in the street, other whites, coloured, and Asiatics began fighting back with firearms that had been carefully and secretly sequestered in their homes, never reported to the government or confiscated.

But there were thousands of Bastaards accompanied by more thousands of Hereros . . . and far fewer whites, coloureds, and Asiatics.

By dawn as the already hot sunlight struck the city, a thousand of these unfortunate people—unfortunate only because their skin possessed a low concentration of melanine pigment—were fighting a withdrawing action and retreating into the only defensible location in the city: the walled diplomatic compound where the embassies of nearly fifty countries had been forcibly located by the Namibian government in a sort of ghetto. The compound had been intended to keep the foreigners sequestered so that the government could keep better track of their comings and goings.

Now the diplomatic compound was converted into a walled and defensible bastion.

Quite contrary to Namibian regulations and quite covertly, the various embassies had developed a common defense and managed to accumulate a rather large cache of weapons, ammunition, food, and other supplies in the diplomatic compound itself. The Namibian government suspected that this had been going on but had taken no action because of the general weakness of the political situation and the normal diplomatic courtesies on non-search and non-entry. The spies planted in the compound by the Namibian government had been quickly detected by the high-tech capabilities of the major world powers. The Namibian Secret Service learned only what the diplomatic security teams wanted them to know.

More than five thousand Bastaards and Hereros surrounded the compound by the time dawn broke over the city. When the first assault on the compound came shortly thereafter, the United States Marines added another battle banner to their colors and another verse to the "The Halls of Montezuma" as they stood shoulder to shoulder with their counterparts from Great Britian, France, Germany, Italy, Spain, Australia, India, Pakistan, Japan, and other countries, some of whom had serious disagreements elsewhere in the world which didn't seem to matter now that their people were under seige by the Bastaards and Hereros.

Some embassies had war robots modified for use as guards; these were quickly pressed into service in the defense of the compound because they could provide heavy fire and be deployed into the most hazardous and dangerous locations.

But there weren't enough warbots to really defend the compound. And some nations with embassies there had eshewed warbots, maintaining regular human soldiers as their major military component.

Apparently, the beginning of the Bastaard Rebellion that night caught even the Namibian government by surprise.

But the Namibian government did little to discourage the Bastaards.

In reality, the Namibian government was powerless to take action. The Namibian Army was only 8,700 strong and—with the exception of small contingents of military police in Otjomuise, Swakopmund, Tsumeb, Rehoboth, Mariental, and other towns—deployed to defend the country.

Due to the strength and power of the tribal chiefs and kings of the Ovambos, Hereros, Damaras, and Namas, the Namibian government had never been powerful enough to be anything more than a general housekeeper. So it stood by and watched the Bastaard Rebellion . . . and did nothing.

Because there was little or nothing that it could do. The trigger had been stroked. The conflict had been started. It was now beyond their control.

But they kept a wary eye cast in the direction of the Republic of South Africa. The government was acutely aware of its only real purpose and therefore its only strength: to act as a focal point of defense for the country.

Thus, no Namibian troops were moved into Otjomuise from their positions elsewhere in the country. They couldn't be moved without creating a weak point that might encourage South Africa to invade and reclaim its right to rule Namibia. The Bastaard Rebellion quickly took on international implications.

Nothing is ever as simple and straightforward as it appears, however, especially on the international levels of national interests expressed in terms of diplomacy and its military support.

The South African Defense Forces were totally capable of overrunning Namibia in a matter of days any time they wanted to try . . . provided the RSA was willing to risk leaving weak points along its own borders. The RSA feared that this would invite a resumption of the violent Colour War which was still in a state of truce after years of uneasy stalemate.

The South African Defense Forces were again large, strong, well-armed, and highly motivated. They had an indigenous defense industry behind them and were held in check only by international diplomatic pressures. They could prevail in Namibia if they could move faster than Zimbabwe, Mozambique, Zaire, and Angola. If their

Namibian offensive was fast enough, they could take the country and move back into defensive positions before an invasion could be mounted. But their military planners weren't sure. It could be suicidal to trigger a resumption of a bloody war, and South Africa wasn't totally prepared yet to continue to fight the Colour War. So South Africa didn't move. But they didn't announce their intentions to hold fast.

By dawn of the following day as the blazing sun of the high desert began to beat down on the city, it became apparent that the Otjomuise diplomatic compound would survive at least for a few days or weeks. Embassy guards and armed civilians within showed they could hold against attack after attack by Bastaard and Herero irregulars. But there was no way out. More than a thousand men, women, and children were trapped. Sure and certain death awaited them if they surrendered or if their defenses did not hold.

The Otjomuise diplomatic compound could defend itself because the defense was a matter of twenty-first century technology and weaponry against twentieth century and even Stone Age weapons. And because of twenty-first century technology, embassies in the compound could also communicate at will with the outside world.

And they did so immediately.

The rest of the world knew of the Bastaard Rebellion at once.

The message from Otjomuise was "Help! *Au succor! Hilfe!*" and the same pleading request in a dozen other languages.

There was no other way that more than a thousand people could possibly get out of the compound alive.

Someone was going to have to come and get them out.

Soon.

And with military forces.

Which caused certain problems.

CHAPTER TWO

It was cold. It was wet. Snow was on the ground and on the drooping branches of the ponderosa pines. A dry, sharp wind blew through those pine trees, making a mournful sighing sound.

The only saving grace insofar as Capt. Curt Carson was concerned was the sun shining brightly in a clear blue sky overhead.

One of the nice things about Arizona, he thought, *is the fact that the nearest cloud is usually in Iowa . . .*

Curt wasn't cold; his heated body suit kept him warm under his soft body armor and camouflaged coveralls. But he was dirty because he was lying flat on his belly in a little gulch where the early winter snow had been melted by the sun, turning the footing into sticky mud laced with dead pine needles. His FABARMA M3A2 combat rifle—now bearing the Army designation M33A1 Ranger, but no one called it anything but the "sweetheart," which was its original Mexican name—was covered with mud and water. Since he wouldn't be firing live rounds out of it on this field exercise, he didn't worry about it. But he knew it would work as well dirty as it did when it was clean.

Not so with some of his other equipment. The new helmet-mounted comm gear wasn't working worth a damn. The Signal Corps had plunged into the development of a "Mark C152 Mod O unit, communications, field helmet, mountable, body-powered, and neuroelectronically activated," with the usual fervor of engineers and technicians enamored with the latest state of the art.

Operation Steel Band on Trinidad had revealed the urgent need for human-portable tactical communications gear that was as rugged as a brick. So the Signal Corp technerds and their commercial contractors had delivered an experimental product that was anything but rugged. But, boy, did it have all the latest possible bells and whistles! Right then, Curt would have been happy with any communications gear that worked.

He'd lost radio contact with Manny's Marauders who were somewhere over on his left flank with orders to provide a fire base for Carson's Companions with whom Curt still had visual contact. Out there somewhere in the piney woods were Ward's Warriors and Kelly's Killers, the two companies making up opposing Yankee Force of this regimental field exercise. Without communications to the Marauders, half his Zulu Force, Curt was at a distinct disadvantage. He only hoped that the Mark C152 units of Yankee Force were performing as badly as his. That would give both forces an equal disadvantage.

But Curt had become combat-wise over the past months. Once a pure warbot brainy like every other person in the United States Army Robot Infantry, he and his company had had to abandon the existing procedure of commanding warbots by remote neuroelectronic linkage from the comfort of an armored and hidden command vehicle at the rear, allowing the warbots to be exposed to the hazards of the battlefield. He and his people had been forced to get down and dirty in Zahedan in order to pull off the hostage rescue. When the high brass in the Pentagon analyzed the mission, they came to the conclusion that some of their Robot Infantry troops would have to put their pink bodies back on the battlefield for many types of missions. Thus, the Special Combat or "Sierra Charlie" forces had been born, and Carson's Companions had been the first company unit to work out the new doctrines and tactics of fighting in the field alongside directly commanded warbots who assumed the role of the heavily armed infantry soldier of the past while the humans provided the versatility and mobility that always separated mankind from machines.

He'd given a set of contingency orders to Capt. Manny Garcia. "If we lose communications and you make contact, immediately pin down the enemy with heavy fire while continuing to advance; I'll hear it and move to flank them from the right. If I make contact first, I'll shift to the left while engaging so you can take over as fire base." Curt didn't want to let Manny's Marauders act as the maneuvering element yet. Warbot brainies had no trouble assimilating the roles of fire support, but it took more training and experience before they grasped the principles of mobility under fire because it involved the possibility of actually getting shot, something warbot brainies had never had to face before. For some of the officers and NCOs of the Washington Greys, who were converting to become the first Sierra Charlie regiment, this was taking some getting used to.

It didn't bother Carson's Companions. They'd been under fire on Trinidad. So they were serving as the instructors.

Curt lay there in the mud and listened. He heard nothing. He poked his helmeted head above the lip of the gully and cautiously looked around. Pulling his portable scanner from his pack by reaching over his shoulder, he set it first to scan for infra red radiation and brought it up to his eyes. Nothing. Too many trees. The same result from the radar scan mode, although he let it scan for only one sweep lest the pulse be detected by the Yankee Force ELINT detectors. Nothing. He set it to scan for odors, especially those chemicals exhuded by human beings.

Hunching sideways, he came alongside M. Sgt. First Class Henry Kester who was operating the Zulu Force ELINT. Keeping his voice low, he asked the veteran combat soldier, "Henry, you picking up anything?"

"Thought I got a radar sweep a few seconds ago, but it ain't there now."

"Any drones out?"

"Negative. Yankee's maintaining low profile just like us. Waiting for us to reveal ourselves."

"Well, shit, we can lie here in this cold mud all day long waiting," Curt suddenly decided. "Damn! I wish we had some recon birdbots! It would help if we had some intelligence that told us where Yankee Force is. A birdbot might not tell us where Sierra Charlies were crawling around in the bush, but we might get some data from the visual and electromagnetic signatures of their warbots which are harder to hide."

"Wouldn't count on it, Captain," Kester advised. "And we don't have the direct linkage capability anyway. Small unit operations of battalion size, it's better to let the regimental intelligence unit do it."

"You're right. Okay, let's go offensive."

"Damned good idea. Keeping a low profile don't win battles, sir."

Curt toggled his Mark C152. "Lima One?" he thought into it, asking for confirmation of communications from First Lieutenant Alexis Morgan on his right.

It was still working at close range and on the company tactical frequency. "Lima One here," came her voice in his head.

"Lima Two?"

"Lima Two here," replied 1st Lt. Jerry Allen on the left.

"As skirmishers, forward!"

As if by magic, eight other human forms clad in gray cammies erupted silently from the surroundings accompanied by twelve M60 "Mary Anne"* Mobile Assault warbots in the right and a dozen M44 "Hairy Fox" Heavy Fire warbots on the left. Two M33 General Purpose "jeeps" accompanied Curt and Kester. All were mildly stealthed in dirty shades of gray and emitting only the bare minimum of electromagnetic radiation. The humans made the best possible use of speed, mobility, and cover as they dashed sporadically forward. In spite of the fact that the Mary Annes and Hairy Foxes were the most mobile warbots yet developed, they were essentially miniature armored vehicles and therefore slower. But their weight

* See *Glossary of Robot Infantry Terms and Slang*, p. 429.

also allowed them to carry heavier armament—25mm rapid-fire cannons on the Mary Annes and 50mm semi-recoilless tubers on the Hairy Foxes—and more ammo. Thus, the warbots had the firepower while the humans had the mobility. Curt had developed experimental tactics that tried to make the best use of the strengths of each to cover the weaknesses of the other.

Three bright red, scintillating spots suddenly appeared on one of the Hairy Foxes.

"Incoming!" was the cry that sounded through Curt's C152.

Other red laser spots appeared on rocks and trees.

"Our Mary Annes have it pinpointed!" came the voice of Alexis Morgan.

"Lima Two, aim on Lima One's data," Curt snapped the order to Jerry Allen. "Lima One, to the left flank. Move!"

"Shaggin' ass!" came the cryptic reply from the female platoon officer.

"Lima Two, follow Lima One! Don't stop and dig in!" Curt warned his youngest officer. "Marching fire! Move left!" A moving target is hard to hit.

Curt knew that getting hit with a laser fire designator isn't the same as taking a round in the body armor over your chest, and this tended to make these nonlethal field exercises somewhat less realistic than real shooting combat. He would have preferred pellet guns which left a bloody-looking splash when they hit plus a stinging impact which wasn't pleasant, albeit far more comfortable than taking a 5.56mm round in your body armor. But the Army was still overly concerned about the welfare of the human soldier on the battlefield. It was impossible to change overnight a policy more than twenty years old that said, "Don't let humans get hurt in warfare."

Curt knew where his fire support, Manny's Marauders, had to be located on the basis of his last communications. He tried to confirm this as he swung to the left flank with his company, catching snatches of data from his portable scanner as he dodged from tree to rock to fallen log.

Goddam it, Manny! he silently cursed at the other company commander, *We're taking fire, and you can hear it, so for chrissake move up and join the fight!*

The company's left flank suddenly lit up with the red spots of laser fire . . . but from *behind* the Companions!

"Captain! We're taking fire from the rear! From the Marauders!" came the cry in Curt's C172 helmet comm.

Curt switched to battalion frequency, hoping it might work at this close range. "Lima Three, this is Lima Leader! Do you read?"

Silence.

Damned thing is less than useless! Curt thought. He switched back to company tac freak. "Lima One, Lima Two, turn about! Back where we came from. Divert all your fire to the right!"

He was too late.

Sensing that the Companions had been caught in the crossfire from the Marauders, Capt. Marty Kelly decided to charge. Curt heard the man's whooping yell, followed immediately by accompanying yells from his company. But where were Ward's Warriors, the other company in Yankee Force?

Curt discovered this soon enough. He ran right into the Warrior's company headquarters unit consisting of Capt. John Ward, M. Sgt. Marvin Hill, and two jeeps. They'd worked their way around behind the line of Alexis Morgan's platoon and now had the Companions boxed between the Killers and the Warriors with the Marauders unknowingly firing into their own troops.

Reaching into his pocket, Curt withdrew an ancient Army signalling device, a whistle. He put it between his lips and blew. The shrill warbling whistle resounded through the piney woods. It was the signal to end the exercise.

But he also yelled at the top of his voice, using the old West Point trick of driving the command by a rapid exhalation action of his diaphragm, "Cease fire! Exercise is over! Pass the word! Assemble on me!"

The sparkling spots of red laser light slowly stopped

dancing off the trees and rocks. One by one, units and their warbots came out of the woods.

Marty Kelly was ecstatic. "Goddammit, Carson, whupped your goddammed ass good that time!"

"Bullshit!" was the uncharacteristic reply from Capt. Joan Ward who rarely vented profanity. Curt saw her walking through the trees. Her round face was flushed, and there was an unusual excited look in her blue eyes. Curt also saw the same expression on the face of one of her platoon leaders, Lt. Claudia Roberts. "Manny, we had 'em flanked, and we would have wiped them all out in two minutes! Killed them all!" And *that* statement was unusual, too.

"Not all of us, Captain." It was Lt. Alexis Morgan. Strange, but Curt had never noticed that excited look on his platoon leader's face before, either. Maybe he'd overlooked it in the past. "I was ready to smear you all over the landscape when the Captain called the game."

"Hold it, hold it!" Curt admonished them. "Calm down." He wasn't so calm himself. "Manny, where the hell are you?" he called to Capt. Manny Garcia.

"Right here." The little captain came into view. "Sorry, Curt."

"Sorry?" Curt exploded. "For chrissake, Manny, you fired on your own forces! Why the hell weren't you on your feet and advancing by marching fire like I told you to do?"

"On our feet? Hell, Curt, that would have been sheer death! We'd have been hit for sure! I told my troops to fire from cover—"

"And as a result they didn't see that they were firing into their own forces!" Curt fired back. "Manny, I've told you the same as I've told everyone else in the Greys: If you're advancing while firing, you'll keep the enemy's heads down and keep them from shooting back . . . or if they do shoot back, their aim will be spoiled . . ."

Garcia shook his head. "It didn't seem to work. There was a hell of a lot of fire. Damned dangerous situation."

The four companies were clustered around now, and Curt backed off. He didn't like to chew out other officers in public. He'd have words privately with Capt. Manny Garcia after the critique later that afternoon at the Diamond Point Casern. So he just looked squarely at Capt. Marty Kelly and said, "Yankee Force won this exercise. No question about it. You maneuvered well, outflanked Zulu Force, and caught us when we made a mistake. That's the sort of initiative that wins battles. Congratulations. Who's got a working tacomm so we can call in transportation back to Diamond Point?"

First Sgt. Carol Head of Manny's Marauders had a working C172 comm unit, and he was the one who called in the aerodynes for pickup.

First Lt. Jerry Allen eased up to Curt. "Captain, I've never seen you so pissed-off before . . ."

Curt breathed slowly. "Captain Garcia knew his orders and had an operating C172 comm unit. If my transmissions weren't getting out, that's one thing. If I wasn't hearing his transmissions, that's something else. But the mere fact that he didn't identify his targets and opened fire on his own forces is something I'll discuss with him later . . ."

"Sort of looks like he got cold feet about marching fire, too—"

"Lieutenant," Curt snapped, "you are not privileged to criticize a superior officer!" Then he calmed down a bit and added in a lower voice, "But you're right, Jerry."

CHAPTER THREE

It was a strange, blank-walled room in which the president of the United States sat in a simple chair before a simple table. Numerous aides and staffers viewed the scene through one-way windows in the bare walls. The president was alone in the room.

Across the table from him sat the prime minister of Great Britain, the president of France, the prime minister of Australia, the president of India, and prime minister of Pakistan, the president of Germany, and the prime minister of the Republic of South Africa.

These individuals looked as real and solid as if they'd actually been there. But they were holographic projections that originated in similar rooms in London, Paris, Melbourne, New Delhi, Islamabad, Bonn, and Pretoria.

It would have been easier and faster to hold the international conference by means of neuroelectronic linkage. The images of the other heads of state would have then appeared in the president's mind. But security measures wouldn't allow it. There was continual fear, especially in the minds of the Asian leaders, that the computers and intelligence amplifiers required for direct mind-to-mind linkage might either be tapped or could possibly be reprogrammed during the conference to read the minds of any leader present. In addition, the Asiatics objected to neuroelectronic linkage for religious reasons.

So a holographic conference was the next best thing and the only way to get all of the various heads of state involved.

Even at that, some had declined to participate.

In fact, had it not been for the fact that the prime minister of the Republic of South Africa had been tendered a special invitation accompanied by diplomatic messages that it would be in the best interests of his government if he were indeed present, he would have boycotted the conference. Namibia was right next to the Republic of South Africa and the RSA government still had strong economic and defense interests in its former province.

The president of France had been the one who'd initiated the work necessary to hold this holographic conference. Therefore, as soon as the images solidified, he took command of the situation. Contrary to his usual demeanor when he spoke publicly or for the media, he spoke English this time because it was the one language everyone understood—he longed for the days when French had been the universal language of diplomacy.

"I thank you all for participating. You have received via telefax all the latest information on the situation in Otjomuise," he began. "Does anyone here have any additional information that might be of help?"

"Henri, why don't you tell us why you called this teleconference at this ungodly hour?" the prime minister of Australia broke in. It was 4:00 A.M. in Melbourne, and he hadn't adjusted his biological clock so that he was fully alert yet. Therefore, as those who knew him could confirm, he was a bit testy under such conditions.

"The Republic of France intends to mount an immediate emergency military operation to rescue the besieged legations in Otjomuise. France solicits the help of other nations whose embassies and citizens are in danger there. From each of you, we need at least a regiment of ground troops, naval support for logistical and intimidation purposes, and air support in the form of transport aircraft as well as tactical strike aircraft." He was uncharacteristically direct and blunt in his request.

"We cannot permit such a military operation in an area of national interest to the Republic of South Africa," said the prime minister of the RSA.

"The prime minister of the United Kingdom furrowed her brows and merely asked, "And you expect us to allow RSA troops to enter Namibia, Johan?"

They were all known to one another and on a first-name basis because of high-tech communications such as this meeting. "The South Africa Defense Forces are ready at this time to send a relief column from both Walvis Bay and Upington."

"I'm sure you are, Johan, and I'm sure you could do the job quite well," observed the prime minister of Germany. "But we had the devil's own time getting RSA troops out of Namibia the last time they were there, and I understand that your country hasn't yet given up its territorial claims to the area—"

"The government of South Africa has no territorial claims to Namibia," Johan Cruywagen insisted. "The 1978 election results still hold; the people themselves said then and still maintain that they wish to be part of the Republic. My government was forced to withdraw from Namibia by the Geneva truce agreements, since we were heavily involved in defending our country against the invasions of the Colour War."

The prime minister of India folded her hands on the table before her and turned on the exotic charm that masked the enormous power of the woman who was called the "Steel Kali," but never to her face. "Johan, we all know your government's policies and desires, overt and covert. This is not a forum to debate them. It is my understanding that you have been invited to participate in this teleconference only because this Bastaard Rebellion is occurring in your region of the world and the rest of us wanted you to be aware of it, so that your government would not react in a way that would lead to further conflict in the area. Do I make myself clear?"

"You do. You want my government to stand by while our legitimate territory is invaded."

"Johan, I believe you have no other choice in this situation." This was said quite sweetly by the prime minister of the United Kingdom who, like her counterpart in New Delhi, could charm the socks off the strongest military dictator in the world while at the same time enforcing economic sanctions against him supported by blockading naval forces.

"Geraldine is right, Johan," the president of the United States added. "I consider it quite unusual that you were invited to sit in as an observer in the first place. Let's find out what Henri apparently has in mind with his military rescue operation."

"I do not have to stay in this conference and be insulted!"

"Of course you don't," the prime minister of Pakistan told him. "But, if you do not, your intelligence agencies will have much trouble and take much time to discover what you can learn by continuing to remain here. And you, Johan, are not less intelligent than any of the rest of us here today . . . Henri, proceed. Tell us what you want to do, and I will then be able to tell you to what extent I may be able to assist you, if at all."

"Thank you, Ahmad," the French leader said, bowing his head momentarily. "France needs from each of you a regiment or more of warbots or soldiers, naval ships to provide rear echelon logistical support, tactical strike aircraft to assist the ground troops, and transport aircraft to evacuate people from Otjomuise. Because our ambassador was killed last night in the beginning of the Bastaard Rebellion, France intends to lead the rescue mission to uphold our honor."

The president of the United States inwardly cringed at the mention of French honor. To him, that was an excuse liberally used by the French many times in the past to justify almost anything the French wanted to do. Sometimes the results had been disasterous. Before he'd been elected president of the United States, he'd often flown back and forth to Europe on financial business, and he'd made it a habit never to fly a French airline. He believed that one day a French hypersonic transport would thunder down the runway and lose two engines, but that the French pilots would attempt to make the craft fly anyway because their personal honor was at stake, a strange form of *machismo* unique to the Gallic mind. "Have you worked out a plan yet, Henri?"

"The French general staff has spent all night developing a plan," the French president replied. "The mission, which we are calling 'Operation Diamond Skeleton' because of the Diamond Area and the Skeleton Coast unique to Namibia, will be under the overall supreme command of Gen. Franchet Maurice Lanrezac, twice recipient of the Legion of Honor for his valor commanding the *Legion Robotique* in the Levant. His staff is similarly decorated for heroism."

"If we're supplying troops and equipment," the British prime minister reminded him, "Great Britain would expect to be represented as deputies to the supreme commander in chief."

"Geraldine, I would anticipate that the United Kingdom would have equally experienced and valorous people available as deputy commanders in chief," the Frenchman told her smoothly, aware of her powerful negotiating manner. "General Lanrezac is prepared to offer such positions to the United Kingdom not only because we hope that you will provide land, sea, and air forces but also because the nearest staging base for Operation Diamond Skeleton is the island of St. Helena which the United Kingdom still occupies."

"I believe we can offer the use of St. Helena," she told him flatly. "What French forces will you commit?"

"General Lanrezac will use the *Legion Robotique* to be airlifted to Otjomuise by the *Armee de l'Air* and covered by the valiant *Groupe Cigognes* for tactical support. He requires naval support for off-shore launching of tactical and logistical aerodyne flights because Otjomuise is nearly two hundred and sixty kilometers inland from Swakopmund and Walvis Bay."

"We do not give anyone premission to enter South African international waters or to violate South African air space, especially over Walvis Bay and the Restricted

Diamond Zone," said Cruywagen.

"Your hospitality is touching, Johan," the president of the United States snapped sarcastically. "Have you considered the bad press you'd get if you shot down one of the rescue aircraft?"

"It would be no worse than the bad press we continually get from the rest of the world . . ."

"Did you ever wonder why you get it in the first place?" the Australian prime minister asked testily.

The British prime minister looked down at a terminal screen recessed into the desk top in front of her. Apparently referring to it, she announced, "The United Kingdom offers the Royal Scots Fusileers to enter Otjomuise with the *Legion Robotique*. We shall also have available for General Lanrezac's use Number 222 Squadron of the Royal Air Force for tactical air cover and Number 525 Air Transport Squadron. I shall ask the Royal Navy to put together a suitable task force from available ships. In view of this committment plus our permission to utilize St. Helena, I shall want the British government to have its military leaders in deputy command of land, sea, and air operations—"

"Hold on!" the president of the United States interrupted, looking at what his advisors were telling him on his own recessed terminal screen. "The United States' embassy is also under siege in Otjomuise—Why don't they pick names we can pronounce?—The United States has a regiment available, the Washington Greys, that can break off its training schedule. As you may recall, the Greys performed in an outstanding manner on Trinidad—"

"Please don't bring that matter into this discussion!" snapped the French president. The major involvement of Americans in the invasion of Trinidad had had political as well as economic reverberations in various countries.

"I apologize, Henri. I'll commit the Washington Greys, the 55th Tactical Fighter Wing, the 60th Tactical Airlift Wing . . . and the 375th Aeromedical Airlift Wing. I believe we can also move Task Force 44 out of the

Caribbean this afternoon."

"*Merci*, George. As usual, the Americans can be counted upon. Walter, can we count on German involvement? Many of your businessmen are in Otjomuise as well as your legation—"

"Henri, we cannot participate. The *Bundeswehr* is now maintained at minimum strength to defend our eastern borders. We may thank the warbots for that because we no longer need as many men to perform border defense. But I cannot withdraw any units at this time. Any weakening of our border defense at this time may invite East Bloc skirmishes testing such critical points as the Fulda Gap . . ."

"Very well, Walter, but I know you will be with us in spirit." The French president was diplomatic. "Ahmad?"

The Pakistani prime minister shook his head sadly. "We have had continual pressure on our western border with Iran ever since the American rescue mission to Zahedan caused the Iranian government to attempt to push the Jerhorkhim Muslims eastward into our country and the Afghan. I am afraid I am fully committed at this time."

"India will be there!" said the beautiful prime minister of that subcontinent. "I am proud to offer the First Assam Regiment."

"Well, we won't be left out, either," said the Australian prime minister. "Will the First 'Kokoda' Regiment help?"

"Although both the First Assam and the First Kokoda are non-warbot regiments, yes, both will be of help although they may not be useful in the assault on the Bastaards in Otjomuise," the French president responded.

"Henri," the American president broke in, "our Washington Greys are organizing around our new mixed-force, Special Combat doctrine which is a combination of warbot and non-warbot operations. In view of that, may I suggest that General Lanrezac might welcome our most experienced general officer in the non-warbot and mixed forces area, Maj. Gen. Jacob Carlisle, as perhaps the deputy supreme commander?"

This was a bit of political give-and-take. The French expected it. The British had already exercised it. It was time the Americans got their people in the high command loop, too, because it would be the Americans who would supply most of the air capability and a great deal of the naval support. No one but the United States Navy had the monsterous new *Raborn* class of carrier submarines which could be critical in this operation which depended upon a staging island 2,420 kilometers from Otjomuise, far beyond the range of most unrefuelled aerodynes and tactical strike aircraft.

Besides, the sight of the hulking black shape of the huge *Raborn* or its sister ships paying a "visit" to the harbor of Walvis Bay during Operation Diamond Skeleton might do a great deal to temper the impulse of the South Africans to get involved . . .

"I believe that can be arranged," the French president muttered. "I'm sure that General Lanrezac and General Carlisle know one another . . ."

"I'm certain they do."

"Then is it agreed concerning our various countries' participation?"

A chorus of affirmatives came from the heads of state of the United States, Great Britain, India, and Australia.

"Sorry we can't participate this time," the Pakistani added.

"Give us a little more time, and we'd be there," the German president said.

"And, my dear friend Johan, we do not want South African participation," the French president went on. "But we will keep you constantly advised concerning Operation Diamond Skeleton. We will have strong forces in the area; you will know their location and intentions at all times. We anticipate no interference from the South African Defense Forces. Operation Diamond Skeleton will withdraw from the region as quickly as we can effect this rescue."

"We shall be watching carefully," Johan Cruywagen

said flatly.

"And we must move quickly," the Frenchman concluded. "As quickly as humanly possible.

"Better get your people on St. Helena ready, Geraldine," the American president remarked.

"We'll be ready for you, George."

CHAPTER FOUR

Col. Belinda J. Hettrick, commanding officer of the 3rd Robot Infantry Regiment, the Washington Greys, looked disappointed and glum as Capt. Curt Carson stood before her desk.

"Captain Carson reporting as requested, Colonel," Curt remarked formally, saluting.

Hettrick returned the salute and observed, "Hell of a day to be outside."

Curt was wondering why the regimental commander had called him to her office just as he'd returned from the field exercise on the Rim. He'd sent his company on to chow, but he didn't dare take the time to eat, not with a request from Hettrick to come to her office. "Colonel, we can't control the weather, and Sierra Charlies must be ready to fight in any weather . . . if we can teach them how to operate in the field in the first place."

"Sit down, Curt," Hettrick offered, indicating the chair alongside her desk. Curt accepted her invitation, leaning his *Novia* assault rifle against the chair's back and securing it against falling with its forward swivel hooked over the chair. "The troops having problems with the new American-made FABARMAs?"

Curt shook his head. "No, m'am, the M33 is one fine rifle. My problem isn't with the rifle; it's with the head-mounted computer and calibrated eyeball behind it . . ."

"The troops don't like it?"

"Not exactly," Curt tried to explain. "Some of the old warbot brainies are—how can I put it?—sort of the military equivalent of tech-happies. They love the technology of warbots and they treat robot warfare like some kids treat linkage games. But they never thought they'd ever be in actual combat shooting at other people and getting shot at themselves."

"Never try to teach a pig to sing; it wastes your time and it annoys the pig," Hettrick observed. "If they can't convert, don't force them. We'll transfer them out. The Seventeenth Iron Fist can absorb them, to say nothing of the other three RI divisions. We've got no shortage of people who want to be Sierra Charlies. I'm turning down requests for transfer to the Greys from other outfits. So keep the training on schedule and don't be afraid to recommend wash-outs."

"Yes, m'am." Curt didn't like the idea of being the one who would break up the Washington Greys; he didn't want to be that ruthless. He told himself he'd give people like Capt. Manny Garcia every possible opportunity. After all, he thought, part of the problem could be the instructor. But he said nothing. Instead, he added, "But that's not the real problem."

"Oh?"

Curt tried to explain, "For the first time in their lives, some of our troops are having to deal with fear."

"Fear is nothing new to a soldier," Hettrick pointed out. "I was scared to death the first time I went into linkage with a warbot. It was like surrendering myself to a machine . . ."

She'd described perfectly in those few words the recruit's first reaction to going into neuroelectronic linkage and thus allowing nonintrusive sensors on the skin of her head and back to detect her neural impulses, translate them into computer commands, send them by radio and laser links out to war robots, and then have the warbots send back sight, sound, and kinesthetic information which the computers transmitted through other skin sensors to her nervous system so they appeared in her mind to be her own sensations. It took months of training before a warbot brainy—soldier slang for a military warbot operator—was comfortable in linkage.

But it was a relatively safe operation in comparison to being on the field of battle itself. The worst thing a warbot brainy had to worry about was being "killed in action"—having the warbot shot-up or destroyed to the extent that linkage with it was suddenly and abruptly terminated. This was a traumatic shock to a person's nervous system, a phenomenon probably the most closely akin to actually dying. But it was the sort of risk the Army accepted in lieu of classical combat where the human being was placed in actual physical jeopardy.

This high-tech form of warfare didn't work in all circumstances. And in retrospect, this should have been apparent when the neuroelectronic warbots had been introduced. But history showed that the military realities of new weapons and technologies usually never were apparent. The machine gun, the tank, the airplane, and other high-tech weapons of their time had been shoehorned into existing doctrine and tactics, often to the detriment of the individual soldier.

When robotic and neuroelectronic technologies had developed to the point where neuroelectronic robotic linkage was possible, the Army had adopted warbots to counter the mass armor and motorized infantry tactics of the Soviet Union and the People's Republic of China. The United States Army and its NATO allies had anticipated being outnumbered by as much as five to one against such opponents. Neuroelectronic warbot technology allowed a human being to control warbots remotely from a distance using computers and intelligence amplifiers.

But even such early warbots as the Mark 15 Close In Weapons System, called Phalanx, had to be monitored by human beings. It and the warbots that followed had enormous firepower. It was discovered that a warbot could operate automatically if a human being got "inside its computer" occasionally to check it out, tell it to do or not to do something, and instruct it to move if necessary. By jumping from one warbot to the next, a human being could operate many extensions to his or her ability to deliver fire to the enemy. This seemed to be the high-technology solution to the overwhelming numerical superiority of Soviet and Chinese forces. And it took the human soldier off the battlefield and put him in a position of relative safety while he fought.

But World War III never took place. The army never had to fight Round Three against the Big Red Tide. Instead, world affairs had required the Army and the Marines (who were less completely roboticized) to engage in extensive patrols and guard operations protecting valuable national interests, mostly facilities and resources in the Middle East oil patch. Neuroelectronic warbot doctrines and tactics worked reasonably well in most of these activities. Warbots were considered "cheaper" in accordance with the prevailing philosophy: "What price the human life?" And guard duty has always been abysmally boring.

So the Army—along with Congress and the American public—was happy with the idea that human beings no longer had to be physically exposed to the hazards of actual combat.

Until the Army ran up against situations where warbot tactics were inappropriate. In embracing the Robot Infantry, the Army had exchanged surprise, mobility, and shock for mass, firepower, and economy of force.

The dawning realization that something was wrong was fuelled by the near failure of some missions. Such activities as guerilla warfare, counter-insurgency or COIN warfare, and counter-terrorist operations, especially hostage situations, couldn't be handled with warbots. Warbot brainies had been forced to abandon their warbots and do their own fighting in person. In short, the Army learned the hard way that although the warbot was probably effective against mass tank and motorized infantry assaults—but this had never been tested in actual combat—no warbot could replace the human soldier in most of the combat situations the Army actually became involved in.

Even with the increasing social pressures to reduce the lethality of war and get the human being off an increasingly hostile and dangerous battlefield, and with all the obvious shortcomings of the neuroelectronic warbot system, some critics often wondered why the Army had gone exclusively to warbots in the first place. Engineers couldn't design a compact robot that would crawl on its belly across a muddy field, shooting at enemy targets as it went, then swim a raging river, then climb the slippery rocky cliff on the other side, for example. A robot capable of doing these things was technically possible, but it would be big, clumsy, and expensive. On the other hand, as a robotics engineer once pointed out, a human being was compact, versatile, and could do all of that and more. Furthermore, a human being could be easily mass-produced by relatively unskilled labor.

Fortunately in the meantime, the technologies of robotics and electronics had progressed to the point where small "smart" warbots or "smartbots" became feasible. The smartbots could serve as "stupid grunt infantrymen." They didn't need all the circuitry required to link themselves remotely with a soldier's nervous system; they could accept verbal or radio orders and then carry them out. A soldier who was right there with them could monitor them better and more quickly while doing all the things a human being can do that a warbot cannot—which is ninety percent of everything.

Thus was born the Special Combat forces, the Sierra Charlies—units whose soldiers actually fought in the field alongside their warbots. The Sierra Charlies brought surprise, mobility, and shock back into the combat equation.

"Linkage fear is different from the sort of fear a Sierra Charlie has to deal with," Curt pointed out. "Getting out in the open where your pink bod is exposed and vulnerable to being chewed up by pieces of scrap metal even wearing body armor . . . Well, it's different. It's partly a fear of death. It's the fear of pain. It's the fear of being dismembered or disfigured. It's the fear of not knowing what can happen to you. It's the fear of the unknown."

"You seem to have it all pegged down," Hettrick observed.

Curt shook his head. "Wish I did. Would make my job easier. When we started this Sierra Charlie thing, I read up on some of the old books. Best one was a novel about the Civil War written by Stephen Crane, *The Red Badge of Courage*. It was made into a pretty good two-d motion picture just after World War Two."

"You're using it as part of the Sierra Charlie training, aren't you?"

"Of course. I'm using several others, too. *All Quiet on the Western Front* about World War One. Some others about World War Two and Vietnam." Curt paused, then added, "Some are pretty damned graphic and explicit."

"So the women are having trouble with that aspect," Hettrick concluded.

"No."

"No?"

"The men are having most of the problems converting to Sierra Charlie operations," Curt reported. "Our women troopers in the Greys find the blood and guts aspect distasteful at first but seem to adapt to personal combat easier than most of the men."

"Really? I find that fascinating. How do you explain it?" Hettrick put in.

"Capt. Tom Alvin in the biotech unit told me he thinks the female penchant for violent fighting is genetic in mammals," Curt replied.

Hettrick found that objectionable. "Ridiculous! Ivory-tower thinking! Women have always been noted for their compassion and desire for peace!"

"So have most male soldiers, too," Curt countered. "But look around, Colonel. Among *all* the mammals, ourselves included, the females are always ready, willing, and able to fight with extreme violence, intensity, and viciousness to protect themselves or their young; they attack valiantly and fight doggedly."

"But men have always been the warriors throughout history," the Colonel pointed out.

"Not always. Only in the cultures where women weren't considered to be the property of men," Curt pointed out. "That's beside the point, anyway. Men fight for different reasons. Males fight to protect turf, territory, or property if they have to, but they prefer to scare off a potential enemy. War, combat, fighting, all are ritualistic to males. Tom showed me a couple of Medical Corps' studies done since women were allowed into combat as warbot brainies . . ."

When Curt paused, Hettrick prompted him, "And?"

"The fighting trait is stronger in some people than others . . . strong enough to make a person psychopathic."

"We've got a couple of Greys who border on that," Hettrick said.

Curt nodded but didn't comment. Instead, he went on, "The psych people have used neuroelectronic technology to get inside the minds of both the insane as well as 'normal' people. What they've learned has confirmed a lot of things we've had gut feelings about. For instance, some psychopathic males will go spoiling for a fight—especially the ones whose social restraints go awry under the influence of alcohol. But most men who become professional combat soldiers like the exercise of power and the erotic stimulation of fighting . . ."

"How about women? What did the studies say about women in combat?" Hettrick wanted to know. She could ring up Major Alvin and get the study herself, but she might not have time to assimilate it even through a high-speed data dump in linkage . . . if she could understand all the terminology.

"Women join and re-up because of the interesting men, the erotic stimulation, and because the female psychopathic enjoyment of a fight isn't protected by as many social barriers . . ." Suddenly, Curt remembered the strange expression on the face of Capt. Joan Ward and several of the other women after the field exercise earlier that morning.

Hettrick laughed. "Really, now!" she said. "I find that hard to believe!"

"Well," Curt replied slowly, "I've been in combat with several women. I can vouch for what was said by Rudyard Kipling who knew a lot about soldiers and women: 'The female of the species is more deadly than the male.'"

"So he was the one responsible for that!" Hettrick exclaimed. "And in an era when women were considered to be weak and defenseless, too!"

"That's what the Victorians liked to think, but we've found out differently now that the biotechnologists have managed to get all the hormones under control . . ." Curt observed.

Hettrick suddenly turned serious. "Not everyone has changed their minds about women in combat, Curt. The Army's catching hell right now for letting women fight in Trinidad—"

"I know. Damned news media people were all over me and the girls after that operation."

"Thanks for keeping quiet."

Curt shrugged. "If I hadn't, would I be sitting here now?"

"No, you'd have been allowed to resign your commission with honor."

"Colonel, I have no intention of doing that. The Army's my life. I'm an Army brat. Six generations of us now. So it's something that's probably in my genes. I'm staying in if I don't get passed over . . ."

She swung the terminal screen around so that Curt could see it. "Speaking of that, here's the real reason I wanted to see you. The new make sheet is out, and you didn't get promoted to major, Distinguished Service Cross for Trinidad notwithstanding . . ."

CHAPTER FIVE

This surprised Curt. The recent Operation Steel Band, the invasion of Trinidad, had been a ball buster. He and his company, Carson's Companions, had been the first of the new Sierra Charlie units, and they were tested under fire there. Every member of Carson's Companions had come out of Operation Steel Band with a decoration for valor and bravery in combat. He controlled his disappointment and disgust. "The board pass me over?"

Hettrick shook her head. "No, the promotion board recommended you for upgrade to major."

"Don't we have slots in the TO for two majors as company commanders?" Curt asked.

"We do. But Manny Garcia didn't make the cut to major, either. And I wanted Ed Canby to get his silver leaf, but he didn't because technically his MOS isn't a combat position, and promotion is slower for non-combat specialties. Different make list."

"Ed got shot at in Trinidad," Curt reminded her.

"We all did."

"So what's the problem, Colonel?"

"The three of you got caught by the Officer Grade Limitation Act of 1998," Hettrick explained. "Only twenty percent of the Army's strength is authorized for officers with the rank of major. All the slots are full right now. Peacetime Army, you know."

"Peacetime Army, my ass! Sorry, Colonel, but you couldn't prove it by me! Just because Congress doesn't get shot at in Washington doesn't mean that we didn't catch incoming in both Zahedan and Trinidad!" Curt grumbled, recalling the two most recent combat skirmishes—the latter was actually a small war—that the Washington Greys had been called upon to fight.

"We'll just have to wait for someone to retire or resign," Hettrick pointed out.

"Or get killed in the next little brush fire we're called on to put out," Curt remarked darkly, then added, "Well, I'm glad Jerry Allen made first lieutenant."

Hettrick nodded. "Well, he's got enough time in grade to be promoted without regard to vacancies," she explained.

"And I don't."

"That's right. Another two years before you reach that point."

"I know." Curt sighed. "Okay, I'll just have to hang in there. Did Joan Ward get her permanent promotion to Captain?"

Joan Ward had been a warbot platoon leader when Capt. Samantha Walker, her company commander, was killed in combat on Trinidad, the first and only casualty in the Washington Greys in decades. Walker's Warriors had taken the sobriquet of Ward's Warriors at once, keeping the Warrior designation in honor of their deceased commander. "Yes, she did," Hettrick affirmed.

"Good!" Curt exclaimed. At least the Army had taken care of that matter. Joan Ward had stepped in and managed to maintain the high morale of a close-knit company that had lost its commanding officer, and she'd led Ward's Warriors with verve and zeal in the battles of Rio Claro and Sangre Grande on Trinidad. "Is that all you wanted to see me about, Colonel?"

"No. I also want you to see this." She keyed her terminal and another piece of text came up on the screen. "Because you've already cleared the promotion board, you're eligible for the temporary rank of major. So I've written this letter to the selection board in Washington. It invites attention to your outstanding record, your impressive leadership abilities exhibited in establishing the new

Sierra Charlie doctrine, your distinguished and courageous combat record, and your decorations and citations. I've highly recommended your promotion to the temporary rank of major."

As Curt read the text on the screen, Hettrick had indeed done that, using far more glowing adjectives in her letter. "Thank you, Colonel."

"It's the best I can do under the circumstances," Hettrick remarked. "In any event, this letter will go in your one-oh-one file. And I've put the ball squarely in the Pentagon's court now. But don't get your water hot or buy gold oak leaves yet. It may be several months . . ."

She didn't add that she hadn't written such a letter for Capt. Manuel X. Garcia or Maj. Edward R. Canby. It was none of Curt's business, although she suspected that Rumor Control would soon be circulating something at the Club.

She knew Manny was a good company commander, but he was a warbot brainy. Hettrick knew from reports that he seemed to be having some difficulty, along with others in the Greys, in converting from the standard neuro-electronic warbot operations to the new Sierra Charlie procedures. He was technically competent and an excellent leader. But generations of ancestors who were peasants and migrant farm workers seemed to have bred into him a distaste for personal violence. He was a good and valiant officer when he was working warbots by remote control. However, only his Latino desire to project a *macho* image appeared to be driving him hard to become a Sierra Charlie company commander. Along with Curt, Hettrick was watching him closely. She hoped he'd make the grade in this difficult transition. But a temporary promotion to major wouldn't help him at this point; in fact, it might remove some motivation for him to succeed in changing from a warbot brainy to a Sierra Charlie.

Maj. Ed Canby, on the other hand, was a good, solid, reliable staff man who also deserved promotion and was more than satisfactory as the commanding officer of the regimental headquarters company. But Ed Canby was a detail man; the real leadership in Headquarters Company rested with the chief of staff, Capt. Wade Hampton, and Regimental Sgt. Maj. Tom Jesup. Canby kept them together, signed all the documents, and saw to it that all the nits were picked and the morning reports entered. But he wasn't an outstanding officer like Curt Carson, and she wanted to encourage outstanding officers. Besides, she didn't want to use up too many of her perks recommending too many of her officers for tempromos.

"Well, when it comes through, it comes through. 'The wheels of God grind slowly . . .'" Curt began.

". . . But they grind exceedingly fine," Hettrick finished.

Curt nodded. "If that's all, Colonel, may I be excused? I need to clean up and debrief the troops. We're falling somewhat behind the training schedule."

"Because of the problems we've just discussed?" Hettrick wanted to know.

"No, because being a Sierra Charlie means being in a hell of a lot better physical shape than a warbot brainy who lies there on a couch and lets warbots do all the work. The Greys are soft," Curt observed. "Getting everyone into good physical shape is taking time we hadn't anticipated. This damned winter weather here keeps us in garrison and out of the field where we've *got* to be in order to train properly and get in condition. And especially to learn how to use this new gun properly," Curt explained. He turned and took his M33 in hand. Looking at it, he remarked, "Fortunately, the Sweetheart is a sweetheart to use." He called the rifle by the English translation of the name originally given to it by its Mexican designers, *Novia*. The Army-given name of "Ranger" hadn't been picked up by the Sierra Charlies; they preferred "Sweetheart."

"But easy as it is to use and clean," Curt went on, "a Sierra Charlie has got to be so familiar with the Sweetheart that using it is second nature. As we found out, you can't stop to contemplate the whichness of what in combat; you've got to *know* because so many other things occupy your thinking processes if you're going to stay alive. So I'm having trouble getting the troops into shape, physically and mentally. Cold weather slows us down. I may ask you to get us airlift down to Fort Huachuca."

"As you remarked," Hettrick put in, "Sierra Charlies must be ready to fight anywhere. As warbot brainies, we've fought in the desert in Tunisia and Zahedan, and we fought in a forested urban environment at Munsterlagen. We fought as both warbot brainies and Sierra Charlies in the tropics in Trinidad.

"In spite of the heat and humidity, Trinidad was a piece of cake compared to where we might have to fight," Curt pointed out.

"I agree. So I suggest you continue here in these pine forests where Sierra Charlies are really effective," Hettrick advised him. "If the balloon goes up again, we'll probably have to fight in the Arctic. But nothing's really hot anywhere in the world at the moment, so the training schedule isn't super-critical."

The news hadn't reached her yet, so she was wrong on all counts.

But it did so with suddenness.

Colonel Hettrick's communications terminal chimed to get her attention.

"Betty Jo," Hettrick addressed her computer vocally, "I told you not to disturb me."

"Yes, Colonel, I know. However, General Carlisle has just posted an urgent message for you. It's an emergency Code Scarlet situation," the female voice of Hettrick's computer said.

"Stay with me," Hettrick said quickly to Curt. "Code Scarlet. Probably affects all of us." Then she turned her attention to the communications terminal. She keyed it for receipt of Carlisle's soft-copy message, a restricted bulletin board technique used when the commanding general of the 17th Iron Fist Division (RI) had to contact a lot of people very quickly.

But the message that came up on the screen wasn't directly from Carlisle. The lead tags indicated it had come directly from the JCS to Carlisle and that he'd forwarded it with comments.

"CODE SCARLET. CODE SCARLET. CODE SCARLET. TOP SECRET EQUALS BRITISH MOST SECRET . . ." it began.

"Multinational force situation," Curt remarked, seeing the British security equivalent reminder.

The message went on, "TO CO 17 DIV FROM CHAIRMAN JCS. VERIFICATION CODE AND PASSWORD SLAKE*CORRAL. ASSEMBLE ONE REGIMENT YOUR DIVISION ASAP FOR IMMEDIATE AIRLIFT ST. HELENA UK BASE SOUTH ATLANTIC AS AMERICAN CONTINGENT OF MULTINATIONAL DIPLOMATIC RESCUE FORCE FOR OTJOMUISE NAMIBIA UNDER CODE NAME OPERATION DIAMOND SKELETON. UNIT TO REPORT TO SUPREME ALLIED COMMANDER GENERAL FRANCHET LANREZAC FRENCH ARMY AND/OR MAJOR GENERAL SIR JOHN HERBERT MAITLAND-HUTTON BRITISH ARMY. AMERICAN ACTION BRIEFING AT 2100 ZULU. JOINT COMMAND ACTION BRIEFING AND REPORT FOLLOWS AT 2200 ZULU. AUTHORIZED BY PRESIDENT UNDER PROVISIONS OF JOINT ASSISTANCE TREATY AND ARMED FORCES COMMITMENT ACT. SS/HOWARD RANDOLPH E GENERAL AUS CH JCS."

This was followed by Carlisle's forwarding endorsement:

"TO CO 3RD RI REGIMENT (SC) FROM CO 17 DIV. FORWARDED. YOUR REGIMENT HEREBY DETAILED TO ACTION AS INDICATED. SENDER HAS BEEN APPOINTED DEPUTY SUPREME ALLIED COMMANDER. MY BACKGROUND BRIEFING AT 2030 ZULU, DIAMOND POINT SNAKE PIT. BRING REGIMENTAL OFFICERS. SS/CARLISLE JACOB O MAJOR GENERAL AUS 17 DIV COMMANDING. CC 17 DIV STAFF AND SUPPORT COMPANIES AND BATTALIONS. ACKNOWLEDGE RECEIPT."

"You said something about the world being quiet at the

moment?" Curt said. "Where the hell is this Otjomuise place?"

"Namibia. South West Africa," Hettrick replied curtly as she keyed in her acknowledgement. "Here we go again. Hope to God you've got the regiment whipped into shape . . ."

"Colonel, we're only at Stage Three readiness state," Curt pointed out, reminding her that the Washington Greys were prepared to carry out only part of their combat responsibilities.

"And the Cottonbalers, Can-do, and Wolfhounds are months behind us," Hettrick reminded him as she named the other four regiments in the 17th Iron Fist Division. "They're at only Stage Four. They're not ready to carry out any of their combat responsibilities because they're in early transition to Sierra Charlies . . ."

"Damned good thing our motto isn't *Semper Paratus*," Curt muttered, recalling the US Coast Guard's famous boast, "Always Ready."

"No, it's *Primus in Acien*, First In Battle," Hettrick reminded him. She got to her feet. "At least we've got the right motto. Now we've got to live up to it. Gather your company officers while I get my staff and headquarters people rounded up. Snake pit, thirty minutes. Shag it, Captain!"

CHAPTER SIX

Curt didn't have time to take a shower, much less change uniforms. But Lts. Alexis Morgan and Jerry Allen had done so, although they'd been forced to rush things.

"I'll hear no comments about the dirty job the Sierra Charlies have to do," Curt told them when they showed up at the divisional briefing room, the "snake pit." The mud on his cammy field uniform had dried, he'd managed to wash his face, but he was still filthy.

"Not a word here, Captain," Jerry replied.

Alexis made a wry face in mock disgust at Curt's sweaty, dirty, mud-splattered combat uniform, but she could get away with it. In the Army of warbot brainies which they were slowly leaving behind them in the transition to Sierra Charlie operations, there had been very few problems with mixed gender units, and it was a foregone conclusion that some men and women warbot brainies would become more than just "buddies." However, Army Regulation 601-10, "Rule Ten," prohibiting physical contact between personnel on duty was carefully observed and enforced, mostly because the troops didn't want to screw up a good thing.

The traditions of the mixed gender warbot units were carrying over into the Sierra Charlies. This made personal relationships in a mixed gender, physical combat company something different than the United States Army had encountered in the past. It flew against the face of tradition. Curt and his company knew that higher authority was watching this transition very carefully.

Considerable opposition had surfaced among the general public and in Congress that reflected the historical reluctance to allow the armed forces of the United States to place women in combat positions.

"The "historical" opposition to women in combat overlooked two things. First, the armed services had never had any compunction about putting women in situations or positions near front lines or combat activities where they could be killed without being able to defend themselves; women clerks, specialists, electronics operators, nurses, and other "non-combat" specialties had been permitted so close to the action in the past that the women had been killed in combat actions. Secondly, the Army had forgotten the old American frontier tradition when women fought alongside their men . . . and performed with a zeal and bravery that often turned the day.

Some Pentagon staff officers—male, of course—had started to refer to the women Sierra Charlies of the Washington Greys as the "Molly Pitchers" until the Army's adjutant general, Lt. Gen. Fredrika McAuliffe, put a very quick and firm stop to it.

"Damned good thing I can't put you on report for an insubordinate facial expression, Lieutenant Morgan," Curt remarked quietly.

"Yes, Captain. Mind if I sit upwind of you, sir?"

"As you wish, Lieutenant. But let me say to you what I heard our venerable master sergeant tell a new squad leader the other day: 'Wipe that smile off your face, throw it on the ground, and step on it'!" An easy-going tolerance born of close cameraderie existed between the officers and NCOs of Carson's Companions. Discipline was always there and could be tight when necessary, but Carson's Companions had pride in their unit and in the Washington Greys. Curt could be a stern taskmaster, but he was no martinet. His people knew when he was being laid-back and when he wasn't. Obviously, right then he was very laid-back, although he knew that things were probably going to get very tough very quickly.

They found three briefing couches and settled in.

Some of the officers and NCOs of the Washington Greys had ceased shaving their heads because it was no longer necessary to do so in order to interface intimately with the skin-mounted sensors and electrodes of the neuroelectronic warbot system. As a result, the appearance of the old "snake pit" had changed subtly. The neuroelectronic hook-ups were still available for those diehards—mostly division staffers—who continued to shave their heads. However, in response to the Sierra Charlies who had elected to reverse the symbol of the unique badge of the warbot brainy by allowing their hair to grow, most of the stations had been converted to a combination set-up with low-resolution neuroelectronic equipment: skin-mounted sensors and electrodes that would work through skin hair. These stations also had terminals and screens.

"Ten-HUT!" General Carlisle's aide stepped in the door and shouted. It was a traditional order; those in the briefing room who'd already settled into briefing couches merely stopped talking and did what the order demanded: gave their attention. Those who were still standing now stood erect and faced the door.

Maj. Gen. Jacob O. Carlisle hadn't let his hair grow. In the first place, he didn't have much of it left, so he continued the warbot brainy tradition of scalp shaving. However, his aide, Capt. Kim Blythe, obviously hadn't shaved her scalp lately.

"As you were," Carlisle automatically said.

Jerry muttered to Alexis, "Hey, I like Kim's appearance since she started getting fuzzy on top."

"You men just like a woman with a high velcro factor," she replied quietly, referring to the fact that newly grown stubble felt at first very much like hook-and-loop fabric fasteners.

"Yeah, you've gone past that stage," Jerry observed.

"Knock it off!" Curt told them.

Because of the transition to Sierra Charlie operations, briefings had changed in the past several months. They were now more personal. Although holographic cameras were picking up General Carlisle's image and projecting it both in the holo tank in the center of the snake pit as well as through the intelligence amplifiers into the minds of those in full neuroelectronic linkage, Carlisle himself stood in the pit while his huge and ghostly holographic image followed his every move.

"The Washington Greys have a new mission," Carlisle began. "I know that the regiment is only in a Stage Three state of readiness, but this is an emergency. And, if things go as planned, we may not see combat at all. The Greys will form the land contingent from the United States participating in the multinational diplomatic rescue mission to evacuate the legations from Otjomuise, the capital city of Namibia on the southwest coast of Africa."

A murmur ran around the snake pit. Those who'd remained in the Diamond Point casern that morning had picked up the news of the Bastaard Rebellion on the news media. But others such as Curt and the personnel of the combat companies who'd been out in the field on the Rim since dawn hadn't heard a thing.

The first order of business after that preamble was a discussion of the lay of the land, the theater of operations. The general allowed one of his G-2 staffers to describe Namibia and the events leading to the present situation.

The dapper little major briefly reviewed the violent history of southern Africa going back into the twentieth century, reminding them of how the Karoo Uprisings of the Civil War of the Republic of South Africa had so weakened the RSA that it had been invaded by Angola, Zambia, Zimbabwe, and Mozambique in what was called the "Colour War" (always spelled the British way). One result of the truce agreement had been the forced relinquishment of Namibia by the RSA. The resulting self-government of Namibia hadn't improved the situation there at all. The RSA continued to occupy Walvis Bay and had recovered militarily to the point where they reoccupied the so-called Restricted Diamond Area along the South Atlantic coast. The Namibian government, ostensibly a parliamentary democracy, was in reality nothing more than a tribal debating society—often violent—of chief and faction leaders, each of whom refused to relinquish power in the areas of the country they controlled.

"The current crisis had been brewing for at least a century," G-2 reported. "It has its roots in the colonial days when the German empire attempted to commit genocide on the Hereros. While they were in Southwest Africa, the Germans fathered a race of mixed German-Bushman ancestry called the bastars or Bastaards. Those were the people who led the rebellion that killed the French ambassador in Otjomuise yesterday.

"Something more than a thousand people—mostly diplomats and their embassy staffs along with an unknown number of whites, Asians, and 'coloureds' or mixed-racial people—are trapped inside the walled diplomatic compound which was built by the Namibian government, a legation ghetto as it were. The Namibian government is powerless to stop the Bastaards, the Hereros, and the other tribes who have besieged the compound. An invasion by South Africa is feared, and this might lead to a sure and certain slaughter of those people trapped in the compound by the irregulars. That's the current situation," the G-2 major concluded.

Carlisle took the stage again. "The government of France is mounting a rescue mission and called upon other governments to support this," the commanding general of the 17th Iron Fist Division explained. "Great Britain, Australia, and India have joined the rescue mission. So has the United States. Time is of the essence. The diplomatic compound can't hold out for more than a week or so. Therefore, when the Army looked around for an available regiment that might be assigned to Operation Diamond Skeleton, the Washington Greys was the only one available . . . Question, Colonel Hettrick?"

"Yes," replied the regimental commander. "We're only Stage Three. We're not ready to go into combat."

"You may not have to fight," Carlisle replied, and there was a tone of distaste in his voice. "The French demanded overall supreme command of Operation Diamond Skeleton; the participating governments agreed because it was the French ambassador who was killed yesterday. As a result, the Washington Greys will play a secondary role. Yes, Colonel Hettrick?"

"General, they keep pulling the Greys out of training to put out brush fires. In the past two operations, Zahedan and Trinidad, we went in without reserves and without proper prior planning. I will gladly follow whatever orders are issued to the Greys, General, but I want to go on record that, if the United States government intends to continue this apparent trend of emergency military responses to international incidents, the Greys should be organized and trained like the British Commandos, the old Rangers or Green Berets, or the Navy SEAL teams."

"Your concern is noted, Colonel, and I will personally pass it along because I share your opinion. However, we have orders. And my operations staffer will now brief you on the part the Greys will play in Operation Diamond Skeleton . . . and it's far from what you may think it may be." Carlisle relinquished the stage to a lieutenant colonel—Curt could never keep the division staff straight; unlike the regiment which was held together as a team with few reassignments or regular replacements, the divisional staff changed almost weekly.

"All leaves, furloughs, and training activities are hereby suspended. The regiment will deploy from Diamond Point via transport aerodyne at eighteen hundred hours local time today," the staff man informed them.

Christ on a crutch! Curt thought savagely. *We don't have time to do much except pack an extra pair of shorts . . .*

"The regiment will proceed to the Operation Diamond Skeleton staging base on St. Helena Island in the South Atlantic," the operations staffer went on as a map was projected in the snake pit as well as on the terminal screen in front of Curt. "At D-minus-one day, the 60th Tactical Airlift Wing of the Air Force will airlift the regiment into the city of Swakopmund on the Atlantic coast just north of Walvis Bay. Only one company of Namibian military police is in Swakopmund; the regiment should have no trouble obtaining their 'cooperation' if the air landing is swift and the element of surprise is exploited. The regiment will be the first unit to enter Namibia in Operation Diamond Skeleton. The purpose of the occupation of Swakopmund is two-fold. First, the presence of the Washington Greys in Swakopmund will pin down the South African infantry regiment in Walvis Bay and prevent them from occupying Swakopmund and invading Namibia to move toward the main rescue mission in Otjomuise. Secondly, the presence of the regiment in Swakopmund is intended as a diversionary feint to throw off-balance the Bastaard and Herero irregular forces in Otjomuise. The main thrust into Otjomuise will take place twenty-four hours after our landing at Swakopmund. The regiment will be evacuated from Swakopmund as quickly as the air rescue mission into Otjomuise is successfully completed. Supreme Allied Command estimates we'll be in Swakopmund no more than sixty hours. Again, the 60th Tactical Airlift Wing will provide your airlift."

"What units are going into Otjomuise?" Hettrick wanted to know.

"At D-day zero-hour, the French *Legion Robotique* will be airlifted into Otjomuise by the *Groupe Transport de Pasteur* with additional air support from the *Groupe Cigognes* of the French *Armee de l'Air.* At D-day plus six hours, the British Royal Scots Fusileers will be airlifted into Otjomuise by Number 525 Air Transport Squadron of the RAF," the G-3 colonel explained.

"Both those army units are warbot units, aren't they?" Hettrick asked.

"Yes, Colonel."

"General, can someone get the word to the Brits and French that we've had more than a little experience with warbot units in a hostage rescue mission similar to this . . . and warbots didn't work?" Hettrick pointed out.

Curt could hear Carlisle's sigh of frustration. "Colonel, I've been appointed Deputy Supreme Allied Commander of Operation Diamond Skeleton," he explained. "I've been on the net all morning with the Supreme Allied Commander, French General Lanrezac. He and British Major General Maitland-Hutton, the Deputy Supreme Commander, Land, are obstinate. I couldn't convince them to send in regular infantry. In the first place, both countries have switched almost exclusively to neuro-electronic warbot operations because warbot units are less expensive to maintain; they don't have any grunt infantry left."

"So we're the only Sierra Charlie type forces involved?"

"No, the Australian Kokoda Regiment is dropping into Rehoboth to provide a show of force and keep the South Africans from moving in. They're a regular infantry unit with no warbots at all. And the Assam Regiment from India is also a mud-slogging outfit; they'll be in Tsumeb to the northeast to deter any of the Ovambo tribes from coming into Otjomuise to take part."

"So the three of us, the non-warbot outfits, are essentially the reserves," Hettrick concluded. "General, should we be prepared to trek inland from Swakopmund to Otjomuise if necessary?"

Carlisle shook his head. "General Lanrezac doesn't anticipate that will be necessary."

"Sir, I do; and I believe the Greys had better prepare for that contingency," Hettrick muttered, but everyone heard her. She knew the French, having spent three years on an exchange assignment with the French army. She asked the G-3 colonel, "What sort of weaponry do the the RSA troops or the Bastaards have?"

"Small arms. Lots of old AK-74s; about twenty million of those still about. Probably some old Soviet RPV-7s of various marks. Maybe some mortars. But no armor, mobile artillery, and no heavy artillery bigger than fifty millimeter weapons. And no warbots."

"I'd like to have a complete intelligence run-down so we can all study it during the airlift to St. Helena," Hettrick said. "That includes the best maps available, socio-economic briefing material, and the full estimate of the situation that the French used to develop their strategic plan."

"That's a tall order on such short notice, Colonel," the division staff man pointed out.

Hettrick didn't waste any more time talking to staffers. She addressed the division command directly, "General Carlisle, we may never get out of Swakopmund, but I'm not willing to bet my regiment on that. We've got only six hours until departure, and the Washington Greys will be ready. But I believe I need that information for contingency planning purposes."

Carlisle didn't bat an eye. Hettrick was one of his best regimental commanders. She led her regiment with not only a large measure of charm but also with firm decisions and hard orders; she'd shown herself to be an outstanding tactician, and Carlisle had learned he should listen to her. So he simply looked at her and said flatly, "You'll have that information by the time you depart Diamond Point."

"Thank you, General. May I ask that the regiment be dismissed? We have a hell of a lot of work to do and only about six hours in which to do it. And if we get caught in the middle of the Namibian Desert without something we need, we're likely to have a hell of a time getting it then . . ."

CHAPTER SEVEN

"Warm clothing, Captain? Isn't that part of Africa a desert?" Platoon Sgt. Edwina Sampson remarked as Curt was briefing them on what they should pack aboard the Armored Command Vehicles. "It's summertime in the southern hemisphere, isn't it?"

"Deserts can get very cold. And the Namib Desert is about as dry and desolate as you'll find anywhere in the world," Curt explained. "No rain. No clouds. Very low humidity. The cold Benguelan ocean current comes up the coast from Antarctica. In spite of the fact the Namib has ground fog, it also gets lots of radiation cooling at night. S-2 says take warm clothes. We may sweat like pigs during the day in light desert cammies, but we can freeze our buns off at night if we don't have something warm to wear."

"Sounds like a great place," Platoon Sgt. Nick Gerard muttered. "But we always get sent to the garden spots of the world . . ."

"You mean you didn't enjoy Trinidad?" Edie Sampson needled him. "I recall you wandering off into the night at a great party near Rio Claro—"

"Trinidad was an exception," Nick fired back. "I was thinking of Tunisia and Zahedan."

"With all due respect, Captain," M. Sgt. Henry Kester advised, "I don't think you meant for us to take winter gear, did you?"

"No. It won't get as cold there as it is out on the Rim right now," Curt admitted.

"I'd suggest we pack layered clothing rather than heavy clothing," Kester remarked.

"Oh?"

Henry Kester, now with an additional rocker on his chevrons signifying his promotion to master sergeant, first class, only one rocker below Regimental Sgt. Maj. Tom Jesup, had been around in the field before the warbots came along. He advised, "Then I'd suggest we each take two light desert combat outfits, thermal underwear, soft body armor, a thermal windbreaker, and a couple of pairs of both light socks and thermal socks to wear under our sloggers." Kester was referring to the new ankle-high boots recently "invented" by Quartermaster for the Sierra Charlies.

"You're suggesting that we can dress more warmly at night by layering?" Curt asked, not unwilling to listen to the input from his master sergeant who knew more about field survival than any of them and had proved it recently during training exercises.

"Yes, sir."

"Well, Sarge, I'm going to take extra clothing beyond what you've suggested," Lt. Alexis Morgan said. "No laundries out in the field, and I don't relish the idea of spending a week in the same undies . . ."

Kester knew that women soldiers, like women everywhere tended to take far more in their baggage than they really needed "just in case." But he diplomatically replied, "Lieutenant, if we've got water, we can do laundry. If we haven't got water for washing clothes, I'll show you how to do a sand wash. We'll also have lots of sunlight, and that's real good for cleaning purposes."

"Come on, Sarge!" Sgt. Jim Elliott retorted with disbelief. "Since when can the sunlight clean things?"

Kester merely looked him up and down critically. "Waal," the old soldier drawled, "seeing as how you're from Alabama where you didn't get much sun that wasn't already filtered through a lot of gunk in the air, I wouldn't suspect you'd know about real bright sunlight. You haven't been in Tunisia or the Persian Gulf oil patch. But, tell me, Elliott, have you ever seen an Arab with a dirty while khaftan?"

"No, but Arabs stink," Elliott replied.

"They sure do, but that's because they like to stand close to you to see your eyes and feel your breath. And because they eat things we don't. We're also spoiled by having good sanitation facilities," Kester explained. "Doesn't mean the Arabs ain't clean. Where do you think the Europeans learned to take baths?"

Tracy Dillon, one of the other sergeants, answered for him, "The Crusaders picked it up . . . Or was it the British in India? Anyway, speaking of baths, Elliott, why don't you take five and get a shower? It's gonna be maybe a couple of weeks . . ."

"Showered when I came in off the range."

"This time, take your clothes off—"

"Knock it off." Kester admonished them. He never raised his voice, and his tone was even and not sarcastic. But when M. Sgt. Henry Kester spoke to the other NCOs, they listened . . . carefully and reverently. Kester didn't have to display the twenty-two years of hash marks that marched up his sleeve of his dress uniforms. "If you clowns haven't learned already, in this outfit you don't insult the other guy unless you don't mean it . . . and, Elliott and Dillon, you ain't been here long enough for me to know whether or not you mean it . . . And no Companion picks a fight with another Companion on duty. What you do off behind the rocks is something else. To give you an example of what I mean, want to take five with me and work up a little sweat along with a few lumps?"

"That's enough!" Curt snapped. "We haven't got time for a bitch session. We load in three hours. Kester, will we be ready?" he asked his master sergeant.

Henry Kester nodded slowly. "Yessir, even if I have to kick some ass to do it. But I'd feel a lot better if I had more hot skinny about this Operation Diamond Skeleton."

"What do you mean?"

Kester could be brutally frank at times, and this was one

of them. "Captain, I've dealt with the French and Brits before. I can get along with the Brits and their ability to 'muddle through to victory,' as they're fond of saying. But I have a little trouble with the French habit of taking absolutely idiotic risks to maintain their personal honor."

"I share your feelings, Sergeant," Curt told him, "and so does the colonel, which is why she insists we be prepared to go to Otjomuise and save their butts if necessary. So the Washington Greys will be prepared to move by any means possible from Swakopmund to Otjomuise—"

"Sheesh! Supply Section must be going nuts," Nick remarked.

"Naw, Nick," Edie Sampson told him, "they'll just comandeer everything they can get their hands on, stuff it in an aerodyne, and hope to God it's something we'll need out there in the land God forgot—"

"That's the wrong name for the place," Lt. Jerry Allen corrected her. "According to S-2, the Bushmen call the place, 'the land God made in anger.'"

"I thought that referred to the terrain around Zahedan," Alexis put in.

"Well, this is no Zahedan operation where we've got to be lean and mean," Curt reminded them all. "We've got to move fast, but we can and should take as much as we can carry. If you think you're going to need it, stuff it in." Curt paused, then added, "Unless you want to depend on the Air Force or the Navy to try to bring it to you if you need it . . . Or worse yet, the Frogs or the Limeys . . ."

It was a busy three hours. The Companions stuffed everything they could think of into their three ACVs, the four Robot Transport Vehicles, and the two "Saucy Cans" Light Artillery Mobile Vehicles.

The Companions packed too much.

Fifteen minutes before they were scheduled to board the transport aerodynes, the company mustered in the ready room of the top floor flight deck of Diamond Point along with the other members of the Washington Greys. The long-range, heavy-lift Air Force transport aerodynes scheduled to take them to St. Helena weren't there yet.

This didn't surprise Curt. He knew damned good and well the truth of the old saying, "Three-quarters of a soldier's life is spent in aimlessly waiting about."

Two sergeants walked up to him and saluted. One was a short, round-faced young man with blunt, hard hands who carried a tool satchel slung over his shoulder. The other was a short, small, and rather thin dark-haired young woman wearing a white tabard with the red cross of the biotech unit and carrying a biotech field kit.

"Sergeant Robert Vickers reporting, sir!"

"Sergeant Shelley Hale reporting, sir!"

Curt returned their salutes. "Reporting for what? My company's at full strength—"

"Sir," the little biotech sergeant tried to explain, "this is a little new to us, too. All combat companies are supposed to get a maintenance tech and a biotech. And we've been assigned to the First Company, yours."

"Major Benteen explained that the regimental reorganization schedule calls for it, and we were supposed to implement it two months from now, according to the reorganization schedule. But this operation sort of forced him to speed it up," Vickers added.

"We're under your operational orders but we report administratively to our respective service company units, Captain."

Curt should have asked them for hard-copies of their orders from the regimental adjutant, but he didn't because none of them had hard-copy orders to do anything; there wasn't time even with computer assistance to cover all the paperwork. Headquarters Company could spend their waiting time in Swakopmund catching up. But to Curt it made sense to have a warbot mechanic and a human mechanic both assigned to the company to take care of possible combat damage in both areas. But he hadn't planned for them and he didn't have the foggiest notion where he'd put these two supernumeraries.

"Sergeant Kester!" he called.

Kester popped up between the vehicles standing ready. "Yessir?"

Curt explained the situation. "Sergeant, where the hell can they ride?"

Kester took off his helmet and scratched the thin white thatch on his head. "Captain, we can shake down our gear once we're aboard the aerodynes; we'll probably all congregate somewhere in the cargo hold anyway because it's gonna be a long haul. But where these two can ride while we're embarking the vehicles . . . Well . . ." He looked around. "Hate to say this, Sergeants, but until we can get some gear shoved around, you'll have to ride in the RTV with the warbots. I'll see if we can't rearrange things while we're en route to St. Helena . . . Sorry about that."

Vickers managed a slight smile. "I'll use the opportunity to get acquainted with your warbots."

"Sergeant Kester, will you have time to reprogram the warbots so they'll respond to Sergeant Vickers' voice?" Curt wanted to know.

Kester shook his head. "The aerodynes are due any time."

"That's okay, sir. I'll just check their basic AI circuitry and articulations until we get the chance to reprogram. I may even have time to get into them and tinker with the programming myself," Vickers replied. Curt got the distinct impression that this young man was a natural mechanic, one who probably knew and liked machinery better than people.

Sgt. Shelley Hale was just the opposite. "I'd rather ride with people, Sergeant. Although I've got your medical records here," she said as she held up the grey box of a high-density computer file, "I'd like to be able to match faces with records." Except for the fact that she was rather plain, she reminded Curt of Sgt. Helen Devlin, now the chief NCO of the biotech unit. She had the same empathetic aura about her. Curt knew she cared about people and not about machinery, and this made him feel good because far too many biotechs considered human beings to be "soft robots," biochemical machines that were "jellyware" in contrast to the robotic "hardware" of the sort that apparently fascinated Vickers.

"I'll ride in the RTV with Vickers, Captain," Kester volunteered, "and that will give Sergeant Hale an opportunity to ride with the rest of you. I can give Vickers the rundown on our hardware."

Even through the walls of the Diamond Point casern, the sound of large aerodynes could be heard as they touched down on the flight deck above. The muffled thunder of their engines was overpowered by a sound like a hurricane blowing over the building as the downwash from their lift surfaces roared outwards around them. As quickly as the sound and fury subsided, the loudspeaker on the wall announced, "Stand by to board aerodynes! First Company, mount up!"

The huge doors to the flight deck opened to allow the vehicles to move out and up the ramps of the waiting saucer-shaped aerodynes. A cold wind blew in. Curt was glad he'd layered his clothing. He stepped up to his ACV and called out, "Carson's Companions, mount up!"

But before he stepped into his vehicle, he took one last look at the hills and mesas and trees beyond the flight deck. He liked this part of the world. Every time he had to leave it on a mission, he bid it farewell. He hoped it would be a short time before the Washington Greys returned to it.

What he didn't know for certain, of course, but suspected deep in his gut, was that some members of the Washington Greys would never see it again.

CHAPTER EIGHT

"No naval support? *Por quoi?*" General Lanrezac asked incredulously.

It was another telecommunications conference, but this one was being held neuroelectronically with the Supreme Allied Commander, his staff, his deputies, and the commanders of the various land, air, and sea contingents also in linkage. Lanrezac himself was in Paris; because of telecommunications and the need for rapid response, he decreed that neuroelectronic communications would be the mode for staff meetings. So everyone was in linkage couches with sensor helmets and in place, their individual AI computers and intelligence amplifiers plugged into the telecommunications network that brought them all together electronically.

Not all the allies of Operation Diamond Skeleton agreed with this procedure. Col. Siraj Kasim Mahadaji of 1st Assam Regiment was in the conference only through the good graces of the military attache of the American embassy in New Delhi who was an experienced warbot officer and knew how to handle linkage.

The Aussies didn't like it either because their military forces were non-robotic. With their particular defense situation, they'd opted for less expensive and smaller non-warbot military forces, their island continent not being faced with the overwhelming hordes of Soviet forces feared by the USA and its European allies. But they did have a few officers who'd been trained in linkage in the United States as a result of the Aust-Amer Pact.

In response to the Supreme Allied Commander's question, Vice Adm. Sir John William Unwin, Deputy Supreme Commander, Sea, replied, "Sorry, Franchet. Sir Ian reports that Task Group Four will require three days to reach St. Helena at sixty knots. They're under way, of course. And, as Admiral Spencer will confirm, the Yanks have to gather their task force from Norfolk as well as Bahrain, and that's a matter of a little more than three days for them as well, even at the higher, classified maximum speeds they're able to travel . . ." The way Unwin said that implied that he knew full well exactly how fast the American ships could travel.

Maj. Gen. Sir John Herbert Maitland-Hutton, Deputy Supreme Commander, Land, muttered, "That means, of course, that we must pull it off as an air-land operation."

"Difficult," was the comment from Air Vice Marshal Sir Alen Moorhouse of the RAF. "The *Legion Robotique* and the Royal Scots will have to take the two airfields at Otjomuise within the first few hours. *Groupe Transport*, Number 525 Squadron and the 60th Tactical Airlift Wing all will be able to make the round-trip from St. Helena, but not the tactical air support craft. They can get into Strijdom or Eros from St. Helena, but that's the limit of their aircraft ranges. They'll land dry. They'll need refuelling before they can participate in air support. Does anyone have any aerial tankers around these days?"

"I've found an aerodyne-equipped air refuelling unit," came the blunt reply from Col. William Barnitz of the 60th Tactical Airlift Wing, the ranking USAF officer in the conference. The USAF no longer needed the huge fleets of air tankers once required by the limited-range SAC bombers of old. Most tactical support aircraft had operational ranges of about two thousand kilometers, more with external tanks slung beneath them which drastically reduced their performance and were therefore used only for ferry flights. No tanker aerodynes were operational with the USAF. "It's a National Guard outfit, the 161st Air Refuelling Wing. They can operate out of St. Helena, but they'll spend a lot of time shuttling fuel back and forth from Laejes and Naparima. It would be helpful if one of the various navies could provide a sea-going tanker or two at St. Helena."

"Sir John?" Moorhouse asked his Royal Navy counterpart.

"Alan, our ships have been all-nuclear for decades. Even North Sea petrol is far too expensive these days, and nuclear is cleaner. But you Yanks have some fleet oilers around, I believe," the Royal Navy Vice Admiral observed.

"General Carlisle," General Lanrezac interrupted, addressing his Deputy Supreme Allied Commander, "we have a logistics problem here. Your American Army regiment, being an experimental unit that is only partially robotic at this time, will be involved only in holding Swakopmund. However, your Air Force is a critical element in this operation. And fuel is critical to the air support and airlift segments. Please assume the authority for solving this problem."

This would effectively take Maj. Gen. Jacob O. Carlisle out of the command loop for the next twenty-four hours, which were critical in the deployment of the American contingents of Operation Diamond Skeleton. And Carlisle knew it. He didn't like it. He didn't like the way the Americans were playing second fiddle in this operation when they were the ones who'd had the most experience lately in conducting quick-response, remote, shock-type military activities.

In addition, USAF tactical strike forces would be operating deep in the southwestern interior of the African continent under the command of the French and with the South Africans definitely ready, possibly willing, and certainly able to shoot at them. Carlisle didn't like that, either, and the spooks of DIA were rather solid on that intelligence data.

Finally, when the United States Navy got there three days' hence and the Operation was ready to withdraw the land tacair contingents—if everything went as planned, which it sometimes didn't—Task Force 44 would be cruising off the coast and could provide both fuel and emergency aerodyne landing facilities in the form of the huge *Raborn* class carrier submarines which were unique to the United States Navy. It would also be under the guns of the South African Defense Forces which had a firm history of controlling the sea-going choke point of the Cape of Good Hope; if the South Africans had become involved by that time . . .

Yet in the face of all this, the United States had been given only a minor carrot in the form of one of their general officers, far outranked by all the others on the staff, holding down the position as Deputy Supreme Allied Commander, Number Two man, second in command to a commander who obviously didn't intend to give up command.

Maj. Gen. "Jumping Jake" Carlisle was almost angry enough to live up to the sobriquet he'd been given as a young infantry officer right out of West Point with a temper that had taken years to get under control. Carlisle had learned some diplomacy now, a form of social intercourse in which one could insult another person face to face and make it sound like a compliment. He studied the neuroelectronic image of General Lanrezac in his mind, kept his thoughts under control without broadcasting them as long years of training had taught him to do, and decided that he'd be the one who'd have to take over from this old, white-haired French general with the snowy white Van Dyke beard and frail form. Undoubtedly, this was going to be Lanrezac's last assignment before the French government retired him. As it was, the French president had to pull Lanrezac out of his teaching assignment at the *Ecole Militaire* at St. Cyr.

But Carlisle knew he could do nothing at this point except follow orders. So he'd do what good soldiers have always done in similar situations: He'd salute, go do what he was ordered to do, and in the meantime use his authority as Deputy Supreme Allied Commander to make damned sure the whole operation wouldn't go toes-up if the French plan failed, which he also felt was a strong possibility.

Carlisle knew the soft spot in the strategic plan. It was far too complex and too dependent upon warbots. The French and the British were counting on their neuro-electronically controlled warbots to break through to the embassy compound in Otjomuise, fighting against a horde of lightly armed irregulars. Carlisle had had some recent experience with standard warbot operations under those conditions; he'd had to muster-out to retirement an old friend whom he'd placed in charge of the Zahedan operation, a man who thought in Lanrezac's ancient fashion and had blown it. Carlisle knew that friendship is important among military leaders, but he also knew from painful experience that friendship couldn't be allowed to override military reality.

So he told the white-thatched French general who obviously hadn't commanded a warbot in linkage for years, "Yes, sir! I'll do what I can, sir! Can I count on the cooperation of the *Armee de l'Air*?"

"Of course, if equipment and manpower are available. There is, as you know, a strike in France at the moment which—"

"General," Carlisle snapped, his temper finally getting out of control much to the astonishment of the British general officers who knew him, "this is an emergency operation. Your nation organized and is directing it. The United States is making available every resource not irrevocably committed elsewhere. I suspect that all cooperating nations of Operation Diamond Skeleton are doing the same!"

"I have told you that you will have available all that France can provide."

"Good, because we're stripping our military capabilities to the bone for this, and some of our units elsewhere in the world will have to go on short rations and long watches until we wrap this thing up," Carlisle said testily, aware that he may have blown his chance to possibly salvage this operation if it went to worms . . . as it already appeared to be doing even in this early planning meeting. And he thought to himself, carefully shielding it from linkage, *Goddam it, and I asked Randy Howard for this job! Why? Because my Washington Greys are involved, that's why! And I wasn't born an Eisenhower or Marshall . . .*

"Jacob, old chap," General Maitland-Hutton put in diplomatically, trying to keep this impulsive Yank from disrupting what was turning into a very sensitive international military operation, one about which he, too, had considerable reservations because of the initiative and leadership of the French that had historically gotten the UK into trouble insofar as he was concerned, "we're all stretching our resources quite thin. After all, this is peacetime, you know, and we're all on short rations as usual. Our national leaders have told us to go do a job. So, as usual, we shall have to pull it off with what little they've given us. Now, shall we settle down and try to determine how we can make this nasty little operation work with what we've got? And so that we don't lose anyone and yet pull about a thousand people out of a very sticky situation not of their doing?"

"Sorry, gentlemen, let's get on with it. We haven't got much time," Carlisle said in apology.

"We haven't got *any* time, General," said Col. Phil Glascock of the USAF 55th Tactical Fighter Wing. "My squadrons are deploying right now to St. Helena—"

"And so are my troops," Carlisle added. He addressed the Deputy Supreme Commander, Land and the Deputy Supreme Commander, Sea, "Sir John, both of you, I hope the facilities on St. Helena are up to what's going to take place there in the next twelve hours . . ."

CHAPTER NINE

"This place is a goddamned zoo!" That was M. Sgt. Henry Kester's evaluation of the mass of people and equipment that covered the Deadwood Plain on the northeast side of St. Helena. The leaden gray of the low cloud deck and the intermittent and alternating periods of rain and drizzle didn't seem to help at all. The early evening skies were filled with the roaring, rushing sounds of aerodynes landing by the dozens. People on the ground were running around, some with small flags on short staffs, waving aerodynes into landing spots. It didn't appear to be organized at all. "These Limey trash haulers are running it like a Chinese fire drill."

The aerodynes of the 60th Tactical Airlift Wing, which had transported the Washington Greys non-stop from Diamond Point, were scattered about where they'd been directed to land by personnel of Number 525 Squadron, the RAF unit that had just airlifted the Royal Scots Fusileers to the British-owned island only hours before. It was obvious that the Brits didn't yet have the situation fully in hand.

"Yeah, Napoleon himself couldn't have gotten this mess whipped into shape," Lt. Jerry Allen added. The soggy ground held the mass of the aerodyne from which they'd just debarked, but the young lieutenant was wondering if some of their vehicles might bog down if they unloaded them.

"Knock off the nationalistic references," Curt told them as he tried to gather the company under the lip of one of the USAF aerodynes to keep everyone out of the rain and drizzle. "I don't think any of us could do any better. Nobody here has run a big multinational operation like this before—"

"Except General Carlisle," Alexis Morgan pointed out. "The Department of Defense did a pretty good job with Operation Steel Band. I can't understand why the French didn't let our experienced people run this one."

"Personal honor," Curt reminded her.

"Yeah, sure, of course."

A rather harried young RAF officer scurried up to Curt and saluted. "Captain, I'm Flight Officer James Burton. I'm your liaison here on St. Helena. But you won't be here very long, I'm afraid."

Curt returned the salute. "Mister Burton," he acknowledged, "I'm Captain Curt Carson, Carson's Companions, Washington Greys."

"Ah, yes, you Yanks have finally reverted to our British system of naming units rather than assigning them barren numbers. Well, please don't unload your gear."

"Oh?"

"As quickly as we can get these ships refuelled, you'll be on your way," Burton explained. "We've put together whatever comfort facilities—loos and the like—we could manage to scramble together in a few hours, and the Royal Scots have established a field mess if you wish to join them for a spot of tea and some biscuits."

"Thank you, sir," Curt replied. He noticed that the young Britisher seemed a bit uncomfortable because his eyes kept darting around the American troops. "You seem a bit out of sorts. Can our biotech help you?"

"Oh, no, sir! It was just the unusual nature of your troops. You see, the British Army and the RAF haven't allowed women to be assigned to combat positions."

"Relax, Mister Burton," Alexis Morgan told him gently. "We're not going to be fighting you."

"Well, yes, I realize that, but it's just so unusual—"

"Your forefathers didn't seem to get upset when they came up against the Marathi women soldiers in India."

Alexis reminded him.

This information was a surprise to Burton. "Good heavens, I didn't realize women troops had been used in India!"

"A lot of things you probably weren't told. Check with the officers of the First Assam Regiment," Alexis suggested.

"Thank you, miss, I may do that if there's time. Now please excuse me. I must check in with one of your other companies . . ." And he dashed off into the misty drizzle.

Whereupon the cluster of Carson's Companions was suddenly set upon by a television news team complete with soggy anchor man, female camerman, assistant cameraman, audio man, woman microphone technician, two people who were running the satellite link equipment, the key grip, and the director . . . all of whom were required by the union. "Captain! I'm Todd Andrews, American Network News!" the anchorman said with a toothy smile that spread across his whole face. He was unbearably handsome, even soaked by the St. Helena drizzle. He shifted the microphone to his left hand and thrust out his right. "We'd like to interview you and your soldiers . . ."

The news vultures had gathered. This wasn't going to be a gagged operation as the Trinidad venture had been. But Curt took the man's hand, shook it in a perfunctory manner, and replied coolly, "We haven't got much time, Mr. Andrews, and I can't talk at all about Operation Diamond Skeleton."

"Oh, I didn't have that in mind at all!" Andrews shot back quickly with a smile. Always the smile. "The American public is interested and concerned over the fact that the Army is now allowing women in combat. So I want to interview the girls of your unit."

"That's up to them," Curt told him. "I presume you have press clearance to be here?"

Andrews flipped a plastic-laminated press badge. "Of course!"

"If Lieutenant Morgan and Platoon Sergeant Sampson

wish to be interviewed, they'll talk to you. It's completely up to them," was Curt's decision as he indicated his officer and NCO, both of whom didn't look very feminine in their body armor, cammies, lack of cosmetics, and head-covering helmets. "Lieutenant? Sergeant?"

Without waiting for Curt's permission, the crew had started moving into position, setting up portable lights under the protective lip of the aerodyne and positioning cameras.

"Glad to," Alexis replied.

"Sure thing," was Edie Sampson's comment.

"All right, girls, if you'll just move over here," the director said, suddenly stepping in to take charge, urging both women into a position all by themselves next to the aerodyne's loading ramp. "And take your helmets off so we can see how beautiful you are—"

"In the first place, we're not girls," Edie snapped. "So don't make that mistake again, mister!"

"And we're soldiers, not glamour girls," Alexis added. "These helmets are part of our combat gear, we're proud of being combat soldiers, so our helmets stay on our heads . . ."

The mike specialist clipped tiny units to the front of their cammies. The lights glared, causing both to squint. "Make-up? Where's the make-up kit?" the director wanted to know.

"We don't wear make-up going into combat, mister," Edie told him flatly. "Unless you want us to smear on some of our cammy grease—"

"Okay, girls, okay! Didn't mean to upset you," the director told them.

It took a few more minutes for the TV crew to get set up. Finally, the anchor reporter picked up his mike, said a few words into it, and smiled. "How's the lighting?"

"You look great, Todd!"

"Okay, roll it!" the director barked.

The reporter looked at the nearest camera, smiled, and began, "Todd Andrews here on rainy St. Helena island in the South Pacific where the American army is joining the British, French, Indian, and Australian troops for the assault on Namibia. Only the American units have women who will be fighting in deadly combat. I'm talking here to Lieutenant Alexis Morgan and Master Sergeant Edith Sampson, two women in the Washington Greys regiment now staging on St. Helena. Tell me, Lieutenant, how do you feel about going into combat?"

Alexis shrugged. "No different than Zahedan or Trinidad."

"You were on Trinidad?"

"Both of us," Edie put in. "I was held captive by the Jehorkihms in Zahedan."

"Doesn't the thought of going into combat and possibly being killed bother you?" the reporter persisted.

"Not any more than any other person would be bothered," Alexis said nonchalantly.

"But you're a graduate of West Point, aren't you?"

"I graduated from the United States Military Academy," Alexis corrected him.

"So apparently they hardened you to combat there?"

"No, I—"

But the reporter didn't let her finish; he turned to Edie Sampson. "Sergeant, how about you?"

"Sure, I get scared. Every soldier in the world is scared before and during a fight. But I'm a professional—"

"Do you ever cry when you think you might not come out alive?"

Curt thought that Edie's redhead's temper would burst forth at this point. But she merely hoisted her rifle right in front of her face and growled, "Naw. Tears would spoil my aim so I couldn't kill the bastard who's trying to kill me!"

This took Andrews back for an instant, but he was fast on his feet and recovered. "If I understand you right, both of you think you're as good as the men in your outfit . . ."

But it wasn't Alexis or Edie who answered that. Nick Gerard, Jerry Allen, and Tracy Dillon stepped up behind the two women and their reply came almost in chorus: "Damned right they are!"

"Mister," said M. Sgt. Henry Kester, stepping in and making sure that the TV crew saw the chevrons and rockers of his rank, "don't ever belittle the women soldiers of the United States Army! It took them decades to get where they are, they're good, and they're damned proud of it. And so are we."

"Well, these girls can certainly count on the gallant help and support of their male comrades," Andrews said more to his unseen audience than anyone else.

Alexis took this opportunity to take the initiative. "The warbots let us into the combat roles, then we had to fight without them, and we're just as good as any other soldier in the world! And we know it!"

"And that, ladies and gentlemen," Andrews suddenly said, turning to face the camera, "is what is known as *espirit de corps* or plain old self-confidence. This, then, is the new Army where men and women fight together. It's no longer, 'women and children first.' Times have changed. Women are back in battle like Molly Pitcher of old—"

"Molly Pitcher, my ass!" Edie Sampson finally erupted.

"Cut! Cut! Cut!" yelled the director. "That's good, Todd! It's a take! New York got it all. They'll edit that last comment . . ."

Curt was enjoying this because he knew that Alexis and Edie wouldn't let this smooth media man get the better of them. He would have liked to have seen the wrap up, but it was apparently all over. And his helmet comm signalled. The readout on the underside of his helmet visor told him it was Colonel Hettrick calling a meeting of her company commanders.

"Lieutenant," he told Alexis, "the Colonel wants to see me. Assume command while I'm gone." It was a formality, but Curt followed protocol nonetheless. It was especially important to maintain as much discipline as possible prior to combat, and formality was part of it. Formality meant that you didn't have to think about giving the proper response to a given situation; it was preprogrammed and could be run as an automatic program, giving one time to think about the things that couldn't be reduced to procedure.

He'd also said it for the benefit of the TV crew.

But the crew was packing up. They'd got their story here, and perhaps it would appear as a twenty-second snippet on one of the newscasts in the States. They had other people to interview, perhaps ones who might be more cooperative in getting a story about women in combat, which was the primary purpose of their assignment. After all, the new Sierra Charlie doctrines would put women back on the battlefield for the first time in recent history, and the American public was fascinated by their new "amazons" as well as concerned. The old tradition that "a woman's place is in the home" was still deeply ingrained in the American psyche, and decades of women in the workplace, female equality, and "women's lib" really hadn't made too much of a dent in that basic feeling. And when it came to letting American women be shot at and possibly killed in combat, the American people—and their politicians—were both proud and concerned. It wouldn't take much to push the issue either way.

On Trinidad, only one company had been Sierra Charlies, and Carson's Companions had come through it without injuries. The only casualty had been Captain Samantha Walker who'd been hit quite accidentally. Yet it had caused an uproar that was dampened only by the overwhelming victory of the American and Caribbean forces.

Operation Diamond Skeleton was something else. There were now twenty-six women in the Washington Greys. The chances of some of them being killed or wounded were much greater. And the numbers would influence whether or not women would be allowed to continue to hold combat positions.

Curt hoped that the women of the Washington Greys would continue to be there. They were good soldiers. They did their jobs well. They were hard as nails when they had to be, and Curt was frankly willing to admit that it was nice to have them around, Rule Ten notwithstanding. They weren't always on duty.

CHAPTER TEN

Curt found Colonel Hettrick thanks to her use of a very ancient rallying symbol: she'd erected the regimental field colors (without their battle streamers, of course) on a three-meter staff next to her aerodyne. The dark blue flag with the regimental coat of arms was easy to locate as the damp wind blew it out in folds and furls.

Curt saluted her when he arrived and stood where she indicated.

"Good flight?" she asked.

"About as good as could be expected, Colonel," he told her. "No windows, so there wasn't anything to see. Uncomfortable as hell, but military air transport has never been comfortable anyway. Gave me time to go over the maps, and my company checked all its equipment. Our new supernumerary from maintenance worked with Kester to get the warbots in shape and programmed. So we're ready to go."

"Well, the next leg is only about three hours," Hettrick remarked. "But it will be the longest three hours . . ."

"It always is," Curt agreed. Going into possible combat always caused the hours to drag out.

Once everyone had gathered, Hettrick announced in a loud voice, "We don't have time for a more formal conference and briefing in a comfortable snake pit out of this lousy weather. No snake pit in these aerodynes anyway. So let's get it over with. Got your maps, everyone?"

Curt did what everyone else present did: pulled from his

pack the 1:100,000 printed chart of the Swakopmund-Walvis Bay area. An identical chart plus others as well as satellite images had been loaded into the RAMS of the tactical command computers in his Armored Command Vehicle which was aboard the aerodyne at the moment. But in addition to these usual computer tactical graphics, all officers of the Greys had been supplied with printed maps and charts as well, much to the dismay of the high-tech staff people who considered printed charts and maps to be Stone Age technology. But Trinidad had taught the Greys that a printed map can save the day if the satellite links go away or if the nanochips of the computers suddenly become food for fungi, causing blank terminals to greet the user at a critical moment in a fight.

"We're landing at Swakopmund one hour before dawn, just at first light," Hettrick explained. "The Air Force is taking us in subsonic on the deck fully stealthed. That sort of precaution isn't considered necessary by our Supreme Commander. He tells us the South Africans know our every move, thanks to the diplomats and politicians who didn't want the Afrikaaners to get antsy and start shooting at what they might construe as an invasion force. *But* General Carlisle—who's Deputy Supreme Allied Commander, by the way—sort of sees it our way: Don't be a sitting duck, regardless of what someone else says. We're the ones who'll catch the incoming if some dumb sonofabitch doesn't get the word and the Afrikaaners at Walvis Bay start shooting. Cover the contingencies, *all* the contingencies if you can. Never forget it when you're commanding troops.

"Gee-Two says the Afrikaaner infantry regiment at Walvis Bay won't interfere as long as we don't intrude on their airspace or territory," she went on, "So we're coming in from the north and being very careful about going over the line. Gee-Two also says that there's only one company of Namibian military police in Swakopmund with a couple of armored vehicles, some light automatic weapons, and the usual complement of submachineguns and pistols. They also say the unit won't give us any trouble. If you believe it, I want to talk to you about some land I own in northern Arizona . . . Anyway, be prepared for this military police outfit to resist.

"Curt, you and your Companions have the most experience in this sort of urban fighting because of Zahedan and Rio Claro. Your aerodynes will land on the old parade ground—or maybe it's a soccer field now, but who cares? Marty, you'll go in behind Curt as usual to provide cover, and I'll give you thirty seconds to bitch about it as you always do."

Surprisingly, Capt. Marty Kelly of Kelly's Killers replied without rancor, "We follow orders, Colonel. What are our rules of engagement? Can we shoot to kill if we get shot at?"

"No. Shoot to suppress fire, then capture and disarm. We're going to be in Swakopmund only as long as it takes the *Legion Robotique* and the Royal Scots to get the people out of Otjomuise."

Curt could almost hear Kelly's supressed mutter of dissent, but he had to hand it to the man: Kelly might be a bloodthirsty sonofabitch who loved to pick a fight, even in the bars of Payson on a pass, but he could also follow orders and was a good man to have at your back in an alley.

"The Marauders and the Warriors will land astride the Swakopmund—Otjomuise railway and highway on the eastern side of the town," Hettrick went on, "and then move into Swakopmund. *Be sure to stay on the north bank of the Swakop River!* The Walvis Bay territory of South Africa is on the south bank. You'll probably have Afrikaaner troops keeping an eye on you to make sure you don't cross into their turf. They may pop a few at you anyway to see if they can provoke you. Don't shoot at them unless you get a direct order to do so from me. Understand?"

"Yes, Colonel," Capt. Joan Ward replied.

"Will do, Colonel," said Manny Garcia.

"The regimental command post and Headquarters Company will land to the north of the Warriors and Marauders and move into town with you. Once we take

Swakopmund, our orders say that we sit there and look mean. Period. Our purpose is to pin down the Afrinaaner regiment at Walvis Bay by our presence and to keep them from moving up to Otjomuise to take advantage of the confusion. And our second purpose is to serve as a feint for the French and British landings at Otjomuise. So we're going to make a lot of noise and look like we're the advance guard for a seaborne invasion force. Hopefully, we'll draw some forces out of Otjomuise to defend against what we hope will be perceived as an invasion by sea." Hettrick looked around. "Any questions?"

"That's it? No combat?" Marty Kelly asked.

"That's it," Hettrick confirmed. "No combat foreseen. Unless the military police unit in Swakopmund decides to fight, which they probably will. But, judging from the way the police unit is armed, it should be a walk-through. Nothing we can't handle. We outnumber them by at least five to one. We're just a diversionary and quite temporary occupation force that's supposed to look like an invasion force. That's the total role of the United States Army in quelling the Bastaard Rebellion."

"Which means the French and the British are going to get all the credit," Joan Ward muttered.

"So? It's the French who thought of this operation, and it was their ambassador who got killed . . ."

"But that compound also contains Americans."

"That it does."

"Colonel, you don't sound very upset about our minor role in this," Manny Garcia interjected.

"No, I don't, because, frankly, I have the very strong feeling that the French and British are going to screw up," Hettrick admitted. She looked around to make sure only her company commanders and staff were within listening range, then added, "But I keep my mouth shut. So does General Carlisle, who thinks so, too. And we've talked a bit about this on the way over today. This is the way it scopes-out by our estimation: The *Legion Robotique* and the Royal Scots are both full warbot outfits like we were when we went charging into Zahedan all full of piss and vinegar. And the situation in Otjomuise is similar. So there's a high probability they'll screw the pooch. Therefore, we have Carlisle's Plan B—unknown to the French, by the way—which says that the Washington Greys will be ready to move out of Swakopmund to Otjomuise either by land or by air to get the French and the Brits out of either a furball or a knife fight. Or utter disaster."

She put her map away and looked around. "Why do you think you were all issued those extra maps? And why additional data was uploaded into your tactical computers? And why I told you to bring everything you could stuff into your vehicles? We may not be able to get airlift, the air situation being what it is, and we may have to trek three hundred kilometers through some of the most desolate and hostile terrain on this planet before this is over."

Hettrick was interrupted by a shout, "Colonel Hettrick?"

She turned to see a short, stocky, round-faced man in quasi-military dress—cammies, boots, and a fatigue cap—with a huge pack on his back slogging across the wet grass of Deadwood Plain around the aerodynes and people and machinery. She waved her hand. "Right here!" Then she added to her troops, "What the hell—?"

The man came under the shelter of the aerodyne's lip and presented documents carefully protected in a plastic sleeve. "Good! Rougher than hell to find someone here today! I'm Leonard Spencer, New York *Times*."

"How do you do, Mr. Spencer?" Hettrick responded formally, taking the plastic-covered documents. "You wouldn't happen to be *the* Leonard W. Spencer, the *Times*' military analyst, would you?"

"One and the same, Colonel."

As Hettrick opened the documents, she smiled and asked, "And what can I do for you, sir?"

Spencer was handsome in his own way with a pleasant round face and an animated, lively manner. "State Department and the Pentagon gave me permission to accompany the Washington Greys during Operation Diamond Skeleton and make daily reports."

Hettrick's face fell. She didn't like having a media snoop, even one as well-known as Spencer, bird-dogging the regiment through good and bad . . . and it could get bad.

But the letters, invitational orders, and all the other paperwork were there in his packet. Hettrick couldn't deny the man anything he wanted to do, not with his hard-copy of a letter from Gen. Randolph E. Howard, Chairman of the Joint Chief of Staff, to which was appended a forwarding endorsement by General Carlisle in his capacity as Deputy Supreme Allied Commander.

However, she could and had to put Spencer where he'd have the least probability of getting hurt . . . and that wasn't with one of the Sierra Charlie companies in the line. "Mr. Spencer—" she began.

"Call me Leonard, please."

"Mr. Spencer," she went on, ignoring his request, "I don't have very much room to stuff another person and his personal effects into our aerodynes for the assault. But I'll make room in mine, and you'll be at the center of the action when we land on Swakopmund at dawn tomorrow."

Spencer immediately sensed the twinge of resentment emanating from both Hettrick and her company officers gathered around. He was a stranger in their midst, and they were all comrades about to go into possible combat. He knew better than to try to elbow his way into the inner circle of a tight-knit unit at a time like this. There would be time later on to do what he wanted and to get the kind of story he was after. No need to rush it. He'd been a green cub during the Munsterlagen operation; he'd pushed when he shouldn't have pushed. And he'd learned the hard way that soldiers in combat tended to get touchy about little things when they were pushed by a civilian. That experience had cost him a potential award-winning bit of reportage. He wasn't about to make the same mistakes again, and this was a unique and once-in-a-lifetime situation. Several years of close reporting not only during maneuvers in the States but with the Petro-Fed Patrol forces had taught him how to get along very well indeed with the military. He was going to do just that. He was going to become one of the Washington Greys. At least, that was his plan.

So he merely said smoothly and graciously, "Whatever is convenient, Colonel. Since you've read my stuff, you know I can rough it with the troops under the worst conditions. The most important thing to you and your officers right now is carrying out a successful mission with the lowest casualties. I'm a professional, so I'll stay the hell out of your way and just watch how you professionals do it."

The man's charm worked on Hettrick. Curt saw her transform from the military martinet to a cooperative commander. Curt was also studying Spencer. Sure, he'd read Spencer's reports and articles about the Army, about its trials and tribulations, about its transition to the Sierra Charlie doctrine. The man was a good writer and reporter, his writing was accurate, and he seemed to be fair in the way he presented issues and laid out their pros and cons. But he was also very, very smooth and polished. That worried Curt. He was concerned that Spencer might be the sort of man who could get whatever he wanted from most people, especially women, even if it took him a long time to build up another's confidence in him.

Hettrick looked around at her officers. "Very well, stick with me, Spencer. The rest of you know what the plan is. You know what must be done and when. Brief your companies, get some chow, check your people and their equipment, and be prepared to lift out of here no later than midnight. Dismissed!"

CHAPTER ELEVEN

First light appeared over the Khomas Hochland hills more than eighty kilometers to the east, outlining their barren ridges against the fading stars of Scorpio and leaving only the bright red Antares visible. As usual, low-lying ground fog along the Swakop River reduced visibility there to nearly zero, and it wasn't possible to see Walvis Bay. But the fog would burn off in a matter of an hour or so once the blazing sun climbed into the cloudless sky.

It was the *scheiss schift* for the Feldwebel and his partner as they sat atop their lightly armored patrol wagon and quietly enjoyed a cup of tea in silence while the city around them grew brighter. No one would be arising yet for hours. It was the middle of the summer season, and Swakopmund was still favored as the watering hole for those in Otjomuise who could get away from the high desert heat to this seaside resort.

Back in the days when the German empire had ruled Sudwestafrika as a colony, Swakopmund had been the place to be in the summer, and the entire colonial government moved in from October to May. The town still retained the same Germanic flavor of more than a century ago. In spite of the relatively short colonial tenure of Kaiser Wilhelm's people, they'd left an indelible mark on the place. Swakopmund looked more like a German Baltic village than an outpost on the rugged African seacoast.

The Feldwebel was pissed. The Feldgendarmerie had

been put on twenty-four-hour alert by the Otjomuise headquarters yesterday because the Bastaards and Hereros had gotten out of hand. Nothing like that could possibly happen in Swakopmund. The place was too laid-back, a typical tourist town. Most of the commerce of the area went through nearby Walvis Bay, and few tourists from elsewhere in the world ever bothered to stop in this out-of-the-way backwater . . . and that's just exactly the way the Feldwebel liked it. It made his job a snap.

But he'd be glad to see the sunrise. It meant he'd soon go off-watch and head for home and his *frau*.

But his reverie was suddenly and abruptly broken by the howling, roaring whine of turbofans blowing the slots of transport aerodynes whose saucer-like shapes quickly appeared over the treetops to the north. In the dim first light, he didn't know if they belonged to the South African contingent across the river at Walvis Bay or had come from Angola. His first thought was Angola because it lay to the north.

But he didn't have much time to do more thinking than that because three of the aerodynes squatted down on the huge soccer field that once served as a parade ground for the grey-clad, Mauser-carrying troops of the Kaiser's *LandWehr*.

He grabbed for the microphone of the communications gear but before he could key it, ramps dropped from the bellies of the landed aerodynes and the strange, dark shapes of warbots trundled out.

"Drop your weapons!" came the order from the nearest warbot. "We're American troops and we're here to help rescue the people trapped by the Bastaards in Otjomuise!"

The Feldwebel's companion, a lowly corporal fresh from Ovamboland, raised his submachinegun and aimed. But before he could get a burst off, the lead warbot swiveled its 7.62mm automatic and fired a three-round burst less than a meter over his head. The sharp *crack-crack-crack* of the shock waves were more than intimidating. "I said, drop your weapons, get down from your vehicle, and surrender! The next shots won't go high.

ose were warning shots. Our warbots can shoot a hell of lot better than that!"

It was, of course, Curt Carson's voice projected through the audio transducer of his M33 General Purpose Robot.

Other warbots—M60 Mary Annes and M44 Hairy Foxes—were also rolling down the ramps of the other two aerodynes.

They were followed by human soldiers.

"Scheissdreck!" cursed the Feldwebel. "Otijo, we've been invaded! They're stronger than we are! Put down that submachinegun before you get us both killed!" But he keyed the mike anyway and reported, "Swakopmund Central, this is Fox Able Four! We're under attack! Three American aerodynes loaded with warbots and troops have landed on the soccer field! I see three more coming in from the north! We're out-gunned! I'm surrendering! Out!"

A sleepy voice came back from the schutzmann, "Say again, Fox Able Four?"

But the Feldwebel had dropped the mike by then and was clambering off the patrol wagon to the ground.

Carson's Companions had poured out of their aerodynes ready for trouble. They found none, which was a good thing because they'd spent the last three hours cramped in the cargo holds of the aerodynes sweating in their body armor and checking and rechecking their weapons. There were no windows to see out of and no indication of where they were. M. Sgt. Henry Kester, who was probably in better shape than any of them, moved in a way that told Curt the man was stiff from the flight. But at least Henry was moving and Curt had other things on his mind right then.

In the dim pre-dawn light, the houses and shops ranged about the soccer field were dark, and the two military policemen were now standing in front of their patrol wagon, their hands held high in surrender.

Curt trotted up to them, his rifle at the ready. "Where's your headquarters?" was the first thing he asked them.

The Feldwebel remained silent, partly out of sheer terror. This soldier was bigger than any he'd ever seen,

wore strange clothing, had a huge helmet that shaded h
face, and even his face was covered with a fierce design c
dark war paint. It was obvious from both the battle gear
and the speech that this was no Afrikaaner but someone from a long distance away.

Getting no answer to his question in English, Curt switched to German which he'd been told was one of the many languages spoken here. *"Wir sind Amerikaner! Wo ist sein Stabsquartier?"*

"I understood you the first time," the Feldwebel replied in English. "It's in town."

"Take us there!" Curt snapped.

But before the Feldwebel could move, the sound of a siren came from the houses and buildings to the west.

Curt keyed his helmet comm. "Companions, that's the alarm! They've been alerted to us. Move out, keep spread out, form as skirmishers, warbots in the lead. Get to the west edge of this field fast. Companion Alpha, move down the street toward the sound of that siren. Companion Bravo, drop behind Alpha and form your fire base. Killers, you don't have tacair strike capability, so get on the ground here and sweep around to the north of us to the beach. Move fast before they have a chance to get organized! Snap to!"

The aerodynes that had lifted the Companions into the soccer field had now disgorged their cargo and lifted off, leaving room for the three aerodynes carrying Kelly's Killers to move in and touch down. The place was a malestrom of sound that shattered the pre-dawn silence.

Curt then turned his attention to the two terrified military policemen who were by now completely overwhelmed by what had happened on their watch. "You've got a choice," he told the Feldwebel. "You can come with us as prisoners and guide us to your headquarters, or we'll lock you in your vehicle, snap off the antennae, empty the fuel tank, and blow off the wheels. That'll keep you out of our hair while we get our job done."

The Feldwebel looked again at the eastern sky. The sun would be coming up within minutes. Inside the patrol gon, it would get hotter than an oven within an hour. could get shot for helping these invaders. But, on the other hand, he figured the Ritter would surrender the company very quickly . . . and excuses wouldn't be required. It was plainly obvious that these American invaders far outnumbered the military police company stationed in Swakopmund. It was the task of the Swakopmund Feldgendarmerie to maintain law and order in the town, not to defend it against an overwhelming invasion force.

"I have no choice if you take us with you at gun point," he replied with a shrug. "And you're going to need a local constabulary anyway. The Afrikaaners will keep your troops busy . . ."

Curt grinned. "Maybe they will, and maybe they won't." He hoped that Hettrick had been right and that the fix was in. They hadn't violated South African territory or airspace on the way into Swakopmund. "I want you to go ahead of me . . . only about five steps ahead of me. I want you to tell your commander to surrender, that we're Americans, and that we don't intend to change things while we're here . . ."

The Feldwebel snorted derisively. "Hah! Invaders always change things! Why are the Americans invading? Are you going to fight South Africa? Or is it because of the Bastaards in Otjomuise?"

Curt waved his M33 toward the sound of sirens. "You've got a lot of questions. Maybe I'll answer them. Maybe I won't. But we haven't got time to screw around now. We're here because of the Bastaard Rebellion in Otjomuise. Now, march!"

"If I go out ahead of you, I'll be shot," the Feldwebel complained. "You're wearing body armor—"

"But I'm not walking ahead of you, Feldwebel," Curt snapped. "It will be an incentive to help you talk your fellow gendarmes out of shooting at us. We don't want any violence. Understand?" He poked the man in the ribs with the muzzle of the *Novia*. He wasn't very worried . . . provided G-2 was right and all he faced was 9mm sub-

machineguns. All SMGs were short-range weapons a
didn't carry enough kinetic energy to penetrate his bo
armor at ranges in excess of thirty meters. He just had t
keep from being ambushed at close range.

But Curt didn't walk unaided down the streets of Swakopmund. Even though the Feldwebel preceeded him, Curt was flanked by the two jeeps with their 7.56mm machineguns and M. Sgt. Henry Kester bringing up the rear, dancing from side to side of the street, making maximum use of cover. Behind this point unit came Lt. Alexis Morgan with her platoon and their Mary Annes, while Lt. Jerry Allen brought up the rear with his platoon and their Hairy Foxes.

They entered what was undoubtedly the town square. It was laid out just like the small towns of Germany. Facing them across the square were two Feldgendarmerie armored patrol cars and about a dozen uniformed men carrying submachineguns.

Crack! Pow! The supersonic shock wave of the bullet passing overhead arrived before the muzzle report of the submachinegun across the square.

"Don't shoot! It's Feldwebel Schmidt! Let me talk to the Ritter!" called Curt's prisoner, his hands in the air. His partner, the Ovambo corporal, stood beside him, visibly shaking in fear.

In the dawn light, a man appeared in the doorway of what was apparently the Feldgendarmerie casern. He appeared to have dressed hurriedly. The early sunlight glinted off his lapel insignia and the Namibian crest on his garrison cap. "Well, Schmidt, what is this?" came the question. The Ritter or police captain already knew what it was—an invasion—and he'd already passed the word to Otjomuise by radio. He hadn't liked the reply he'd gotten which amounted to orders to fight to the death against the invaders. He had a wife and three children in Swakopmund, it was a nice family town, and he wasn't about to pay too much attention to a powerless headquarters two hundred kilometers away that usually ignored him anyway. He'd decided he'd handle the situation as he saw fit; the Oberst in Otjomuise had his hands full with the Bastaards and Hereros anyway, and by the time this all got sorted out, who knew what would happen?

"An entire American division of warbots and soldiers has landed in and around Swakopmund," the Feldwebel replied. It was a total fabrication on his part, but he didn't want to give the impression that he and his partner had been overcome by anything but a vastly superior force. As usual with surrendered troops, the enemy strength was deliberately exaggerated. Who wanted it known that he'd surrendered to only a few people and a couple of intimidating warbots of highly unusual design? "We are greatly outnumbered. They have air support and heavy artillery. They can destroy the city. Even as I speak, they are surrounding the city square."

"I cannot surrender the city," the Ritter replied. "That is the mayor's job. It is my job to protect and defend the citizens! That I shall do!"

Curt guessed that the Ritter was talking around the subject of surrender in order to save face among his own troops gathered outside the casern. So Curt spoke up, "Feldwebel Schmidt speaks the truth, Ritter! I am Captain Curt Carson of the Iron Fist Division of the United States Army. We have been ordered to occupy Swakopmund because of the Bastaard Rebellion in Otjomuise. We will be in Swakopmund only as long as it takes to put down this rebellion and rescue the foreigners trapped in the embassy compound in the capital. If our troops are not attacked or otherwise provoked, I will guarantee that the citizens of Swakopmund will not be harmed and may go about their daily lives . . . without firearms, of course. The same holds true of your feldgendarmerie company. Surrender your firearms, and you may continue your police duties armed with night sticks . . . and I assume you still know how to use night sticks."

There was silence for a moment while the Ritter thought this over and figured the odds and consequences. Finally, he called across the square to Curt, "Do I have your word as an officer?"

"You have my word as an officer," Curt told him, giving him the strongest of all binding promises of the military profession.

"May my men be permitted to put up a token resistance?" came the next question.

"What will that consist of?" Curt wanted to know.

"We may later need to show that we have fired our weapons and expended ammunition in the defense of Swakopmund. However, I estimate that we shall need to fire at the extreme range of a thousand meters . . ."

"We'll help you justify that defense," Curt replied. Then he toggled his helmet comm and told his company, "Companions, take cover! Don't return fire unless I give you a direct command to do so. Let these people save a little face. Companion Alpha, have your Mary Annes put about a dozen twenty-millimeter rounds into the casern over the heads of the policemen."

"Roger. Wilco," came Alexis' reply.

Two of her Mary Annes opened up with their 25mm cannon firing light ball rounds high across the square into the facade of the casern.

Her fire was immediately returned by a fusilade of 9mm SMG fire that went all over their heads.

In the ensuing pause, Curt called out, "Surrender your forces!"

But before the Ritter could answer, the square was filled with heavy fire coming in from the north. From the streets feeding in from the right rolled Mary Annes and Hairy Foxes accompanied by Kelly's Killers yelping their battle cry.

Curt switched frequencies on his helmet comm. "Marty! Knock it off! Cease fire! Call off your Killers! These people have just surrendered!"

But it was too late. Half a dozen men fell in front of the casern before Marty Kelly got the cease-fire order out.

"What the hell, Marty? Did I give you the word to open fire?" Curt asked his backup man via helmet comm.

"Heard you firing," came Marty's reply. "Figured a fire fight had started and you'd need help from your backup!"

"Well, we don't, for crissake!" Curt snapped back. "Hold your Killers where they are! Companions, forward! Sergeant Hale, for God's sake get in there and see if you can't help some of those wounded men! Kelly, get your biotech forward! Goddammit, what's the regimental frequency? Okay, there! Grey Head, Grey Head, this is Companion Leader! We've taken the town! Do not open fire. Repeat, do not open fire! Send in the biotechs. There are wounded!"

Then, without waiting for a reply, he boldly walked into the square and directly toward the Ritter who'd stopped tying a white handkerchief to the tip of his ancient sabre and was instead in the process of drawing his 9mm P.38 from its holster and pointing it at Curt.

"You gave your word!" the Ritter screamed in anger.

"The other captain didn't hear it!" Curt yelled back. "Put down that pistol! I've ordered a cease-fire, and our biotechs are on their way to help!"

"You are a disgrace to officers everywhere!" the Ritter bellowed, pointed the pistol, and pulled the trigger.

But he was shaken up. The bullet went harmlessly over Curt's head. Curt knew that an excited man will always shoot high with a pistol. Even when he wasn't excited, the chances of hitting the target were slim. Curt had seen only five people hit with round fired from a pistol; four of them had been friendlies shot by their own weapons. And one of those had been Henry Kester whom he'd shot himself by accident in Zahedan.

So it completely baffled the Ritter when Curt knocked the pistol to one side with the barrel of his M33 and simply said, "Ritter, it's over. And you fought bravely and honorably. Now let's go get a cup of coffee or tea while my biotechs patch up your policemen."

CHAPTER TWELVE

"Colonel, Lieutenant Frazier was on point and heard firing as his platoon entered the town square," Captain Marty Kelly pointed out. "He saw the military police unit and two armored cars drawn up in front of the casern, saw them firing, and saw the twenty-millimeters from Morgan's Mary Annes hitting the building. He assumed that the Feldgendarmerie was putting up stiff resistance, so he ordered his own Mary Annes to open fire. Lieutenant Messenger then opened up with the fifties on the Hairy Foxes. My platoon sergeants and squad leaders followed up by opening fire with their M33s. This is standard urban combat doctrine!"

Col. Belinda Hettrick was trying to get the facts on what some were calling the Swakopmund Massacre. It didn't help that Leonard Spencer of the New York *Times* had come into the square with Hettrick's command vehicle shortly after the fiasco had taken place. It had been all that Hettrick could do, turning on all her charm, to prevent Spencer from sending back a video satellite report on the action. He agreed to withhold transmissions until the full story could be sorted out, but he insisted that he be allowed to sit in while Hettrick received the reports of the incident.

She'd heard Curt's report, and she'd interrogated the enraged Ritter Hoffmann. Now she was learning Capt. Marty Kelly's side of the story. She didn't like what she was hearing. "Your orders, Captain, were to shoot only to suppress fire, then capture and disarm."

"Those military policemen were firing at Carson's

troops!" Kelly maintained.

"That didn't mean you had license to shoot to kill, Captain," Hettrick admonished him, biting off every word. "You killed a policeman, not just a soldier. You wounded four more, one seriously, and Doctor Logan still has him in surgery at this time. This is going to cause me all sorts of trouble in dealing with the local populace during our occupation of Swakopmund. Why? If you studied your briefing material—and I must assume you did—you know that the Namibian government doesn't have a separate police force like we do; their army also serves as an internal security force, and the local units are manned by local people. The military police here are local citizens."

"When someone's shooting at our troops, he's an enemy and he gets shot at by my outfit," Kelly maintained.

"Not under the rules of engagement you were given, Captain," Col. Belinda Hettrick insisted. "Were you monitoring the regimental tactical frequency?"

"I was in a potential combat situation. My helmet comm was tuned to the company tac freak. So was Lieutenant Frazier's," Kelly admitted.

"In Sierra Charlie operations, Captain, I don't have an override to blast through your company communications as I would have in full warbot linkage," Hettrick reminded him. "That fact was part of your Sierra Charlie training. So all officers must monitor the frequencies downward to their command and upward to higher command as well."

"Colonel, this was the first time we've gone Sierra Charlie," Kelly admitted, still maintaining his aggressive defiance. "In the heat of battle, I reverted to the old procedures."

"And apparently Lieutenant Frazier did the same. If he'd been monitoring the tac freak as he should have—and as you should have, too—he would have known the Feldgendarmerie was merely letting off a few rounds in a ritual resistance before surrendering to Captain Carson as Ritter Hoffmann had already agreed to do."

"Fortunes of war and the haze of battle," Kelly tried to rationalize.

"Probably. But that doesn't excuse it. We're supposed to be trained, disciplined officers, Kelly." Hettrick was about as angry as Curt had ever seen her. She continued dressing-down Kelly in front of her other company commanders, something Curt had never seen her do before. "By rights, I ought to strip you of your command and bring you up on a special court martial—maybe Frazier separately as well—for failure to obey orders. And I'd damned-well do it, too, if we weren't stuck out here in the middle of nowhere with the Afrikaaners staring over the river at us. Plus the fact we also face the possibility the Brits and French might need us to save their asses if they screw up."

She sighed and Curt could see that she was trying hard to get herself under control. "Unfortunately, Kelly, because of the tactical situation, you and your outfit can't be spared right now. So I want you to listen carefully. Get that outfit of yours shaped-up. Do the same for yourself while you're at it. Take appropriate disciplinary measures with Frazier and his platoon. I want a little less enthusiastic, gung-ho overreaction and a lot more judgement under fire. I want you to pay a hell of a lot more attention to what you and your outfit are doing. Or I'll for-sure bust up your outfit and convene that special court martial when we get our butts out of this sling. Understand?"

Kelly nodded.

"Understand, Captain Kelly?" she repeated loudly.

"Yes, Colonel! Understood!" Kelly snapped, coming to attention and saluting.

"Good! Now, we aren't an occupying enemy force engaged in a war here. We're part of an international operation whose purpose is to rescue diplomats and other people who cannot be protected by the existing government. We expected to encounter some armed resistance because of the nature of our activity. We'll be mistaken for South Africans by those who don't get the word, or we'll simply be shot at because we're strange soldiers. Or the

Afrikaaners may decide to have a go at us for any number of reasons. So we've been given specific orders on how to handle this situation with the minimum of destruction and bloodshed . . . and we did it very well here in Swakopmund until that last moment when orders were not followed.

"Therefore, we do not consider ourselves an enemy occupation force but an international police force, if you will. So, Captain Kelly, you and Lieutenant Frazier will accompany me to pay our respects and present our condolences to the Mayor of Swakopmund and Ritter Hoffmann. You will personally apologize to both the Mayor and the Ritter. Then you and the Lieutenant will accompany me to the home of the dead policeman to console his widow, his three children, and other members of his immediate family. Kelly's Killers will wear a black brassard over the company patch and the regimental patch beginning at once, and your company will participate in the service and burial of the policeman with your rifles unloaded, unlocked, and reversed." Hettrick was now deadly serious, carrying out a task she obviously did not want to do and that was highly distasteful to her.

She then announced to her officers, "The regimental colors will *not* be cased because of this, but the regiment's battle streamers will be surmounted by a black burgee until this operation is completed or until Kelly's Killers cause said burgee to be removed because of courage and valor by the company in combat, if and when we see any. The actions of Kelly's Killers have not dishonored the regiment but they have brought shame to us . . . and their future actions can rectify that situation." She turned to her second in command. "Major Canby, please see to it that Captain Wilkinson, the regimental adjutant, takes the proper steps to publicize this to the regiment."

Canby saluted. "Yes, Colonel."

She looked around at the somber faces of her five company commanders. "No one expects us to be perfect. But insofar as I'm concerned, we're allowed one and only one bad screw-up like this in a campaign. Well, we've had it. As far as I'm concerned, we don't get another one. If it happens again, someone will get his or her knickers ripped pretty bad by me. Accompanied by a notation in their one-oh-one file. And a report up the line to Carlisle at division. Companions, Warriors, Marauders, you all did a good job; you have nothing to be ashamed of. But this isn't over yet. I want everyone on their toes and ready. We may tangle assholes with the Afrikaaners across the river, or we may have to shag ass into those hills out there to save this whole frigging operation." It wasn't often that Col. Belinda Hettrick's speech lapsed into rough slang. But she was speaking only to her company commanders. And she was angry, anxious, and under personal pressure. "General Carlisle has seen the possibility that the Brits and the French may not be able to cut it, and he's told me to stand by. I only wish we'd been dropped in a lot closer to Otjomuise . . . We may not be here very long in any case. Your off-duty people might as well enjoy this seaside resort, such as it is, while they can."

Having said that, Hettrick's face was both hard and sad as she snapped the order, "Return to your companies! Carry out your specific orders concerning the occupation of Swakopmund. Dismissed!"

Leonard Spencer attached himself to Curt as the meeting broke up and Curt began to walk back to where his Companions were deployed down by the beach where the Swakop River joined the sea. "Captain, do you mind if I tag along with your outfit for a while?"

Curt did, but he couldn't tell the journalist no. "Frankly, Spencer, after that mess in the square, I do mind. But you can tag along if you don't get in the way."

"Oh? Why do you mind? What upset you so much about what happened in the square with the police unit?" Spencer probed, falling into step alongside Curt.

"I think the Colonel said it pretty well. We're professionals, and what happened there wasn't very professional and reflects badly on all of us."

"Come now, Captain! Soldiers are supposed to be able to kill."

Curt shook his head. "Spencer, I'm surprised at you!"

"Surprised? Why?"

"With everything you've written about military affairs, that statement from you is flat-out ludicrous!"

"Why?"

"We're professional *soldiers.* We're not professional murderers."

"Can you amplify on that, Captain, for someone who may be a little confused right now?"

"Well, I wouldn't think you'd be confused, but . . . A soldier's job isn't killing. It's the application of physical force to bend another person to the political will of one's country. You're a pro; you bend people's wills with words and pictures."

"Wup! I'm not so sure I buy that!" Spencer objected.

"I don't care whether you do or not. We're professionals, yes. We're fighters, true. But our job is to win, and we try to do it without killing if possible. Killing the enemy is the last resort when all other methods fail."

"Sounds vaguely familiar," Spencer admitted.

"It should . . . if you've read Sun-Tzu or Clausewitz . . . and I presume you have. Now, why do you want to hang around the Companions?" Curt suddenly asked, changing the subject.

"I chose to be with the United States Army troops in this operation," Spencer admitted, "not only because they're Americans but because this is the first regiment to put human troops into the battlefield alongside warbots. It heightens the perceived danger of war in the eyes of our readers."

"I can understand why," Curt put in, not breaking stride. "Death and destruction, murder, rape, slaughter . . . those things have always been high priority news items. Bad news is good copy."

"Not always. I'm following what our research polls tell us."

"Chasing statistics again, eh?"

"Don't be so antagonistic, Captain," Spencer suddenly said. "The pollsters are damned good. Give them a random sample of two thousand American adults, and they'll predict national moods and opinions with less than two percent error. If I didn't pay attention to these opinion polls, I'd be shooting from the hip in the dark."

"So what do your polls tell you?"

"That Americans are in favor of their soldiers going back on the battlefield . . ."

Curt stopped when he heard that. "The American people are in favor of us getting our asses shot off? For God's sake, *why?* When I was commissioned, people were damned glad that neuroelectronic warbots were taking the soldier's place on the battlefield!"

"Opinions change, Captain," Spencer pointed out. "Americans always want heroes. But it turned out to be impossible to hero-worship a warbot. If Americans are going to spend the money to have an Army, they've decided they want to be proud of the people they pay to get shot at."

"I'll be a sonofabitch!" Curt muttered. "The feedback we've gotten said the politicians and the public were worried about the possibility of the Sierra Charlies getting hurt when the warbots could take the incoming."

"That was before Trinidad."

Curt thought about that for a moment. "Yeah, I had a little trouble with the media bothering the hell out of us after Sangre Grande . . ."

"You and the Companions were heroes, Captain, the first military heroes we'd had in a quarter of a century—"

"So that's why you want to attach yourself to us, huh?" Curt asked him bluntly.

"Yes," Spencer replied just as bluntly.

"The action is likely to be with the French and the Brits in Otjomuise," Curt pointed out.

"That'll be just another warbot operation," Spencer observed. "And I agree with General Carlisle and Colonel Hettrick. The *Legion* and the Royal Scots are going to get their knickers ripped for the same reasons you nearly got your shorts shot off in Zahedan. So I'm taking a calculated risk. I figure the Greys are going to make the trek to

Otjomuise. If I'm wrong, I've still got a story. If I'm right, I've got a *hell* of a story. It'll be even better because more than a dozen American women are going to be involved . . . and you should see what the polls have to say about the American public's opinions about women in combat—"

"I thought so! But spare me the details," Curt snapped. "The women in my outfit don't like the thought of being reassigned to non-combat duties . . ."

Spencer looked up at Curt and grinned with an impish look. The man's round face and broad mouth were puckish. "They won't be," he announced confidently. "The trend has been inexorable for the past two centuries. It's been moving from women as property to women as separate but equal members of the human race. I intend to help them put the final piece in the edifice of women's rights and equality, Captain. The combat infantry was the last bastion to be tackled by women, and the neuro-electronic warbots gave them a toehold. Now that the pendulum is swinging back to the human infantry soldier, I know your women aren't going to give up what they've got. They shouldn't. They did well in Trinidad. I think they'll be outstanding in Namibia. I want to be there to see it and report it. The opinion polls are too close to call at the moment, so people can still be swayed. Since the United States' population today has more women than men, I know what the outcome *has* to be. I'll see to that."

The newsman suddenly paused, then added thoughtfully, "Or did I misjudge you, Captain?"

"Misjudge me?"

"You've served in combat with women as superiors and subordinates," Spencer told him. "On the basis of your record, Captain—which I've taken the trouble to look up and study, by the way—you are indeed a professional. You would not and could not have done what you've done if you had any reservations about women in combat roles."

Maybe this guy isn't so bad after all. Maybe he's one of the few honest newshawks, Curt thought, then he replied, "I have no reservations at all, and I'm damned glad to have

Lieutenant Morgan and Sergeant Sampson. You've met Colonel Hettrick. You'll find that Lieutenant Morgan and Sergeant Sampson are not only top-notch professionals, but they also help make soldiering a whole hell of a lot more interesting than it used to be—even with Rule Ten! Come along; I have work to do, and you'll want to meet the Companions . . ."

CHAPTER THIRTEEN

The guard/watch area assigned to Carson's Companions stretched for two kilometers along the southern edge of Swakopmund inland from the point where the normally dry Swakop river bed joined the South Atlantic Ocean. In this desert climate, the river had no running water in it above ground, although the presence of underground flow was evident from the jungle of vegetation along its bed.

Inland of the Companions were Ward's Warriors, covering yet another two kilometers of river bank.

Curt found his ACV parked at the lip of a small, low bluff along the river bank about a kilometer from the ocean. As usual, M. Sgt. First Class Henry Kester had everything shaped up and in order as his captain walked up with the newsman.

"Company is deployed, sir, and the guard has been set." Kester greeted him with a salute.

"Thank you, Sergeant," Curt replied, returning the salute. He indicated his companion. "Mr. Leonard Spencer will be accompanying us. Spencer, have you met Master Sergeant Henry Kester, my chief NCO?"

Spencer thrust out a hand to Kester. "No, but I saw you on St. Helena, Sergeant."

Kester shook hands with him. "Let me know if there's anything I can do to make you comfortable, Mister Spencer."

The reporter looked from Kester to Curt. "Please call me Len. I want to get to know you both as friends."

Kester had a long-time suspicion of news reporters, so with a bland expression on his face, he replied, "As you wish, Len. You can stash your gear in our ACV if you wish. I think I can find room somewhere."

Spencer shifted the pack on his back and picked up the two cases he was carrying. "I understand that Lieutenant Morgan commands Alpha Platoon. I'd like to meet her and make her platoon headquarters my base of operation . . ."

"I'll take you down there, Len," Curt told him, "but Morgan has far less room than we do and she's pretty busy with her platoon. And if we move out—as you and the Colonel seem to think we will—Lieutenant Morgan will be our point platoon with her Mary Annes. I'd rather not have you up on the point." That was a lame excuse, and Curt knew it. Was his reluctance to let Spencer headquarter with Alpha Platoon and Alexis Morgan prompted by a twinge of jealousy or mistrust? He didn't know or didn't want to admit anything to himself at this point. Spencer was just a tad too friendly. And Curt wasn't precisely certain of the man's motives yet in spite of their conversation during the walk from the town square.

"As you wish, Curt," Spencer replied diffidently, assuming that he could use Curt's first name on the basis of his own insistence that he be called by his. Curt recognized this as a typical newshawk ploy to gain the confidence of those who were to be interviewed or reported about. "But I do want to interview Lieutenant Morgan . . . and I know I'll need your permission as her superior officer."

"No problem there," Curt told him, then added, "as long as you also interview Platoon Sgt. Edwina Sampson of Bravo Platoon."

"Equal time for both girls, eh? Well, I certainly don't want to be accused of playing favorites among your women."

Curt ignored him for the moment. He had other things to worry about. "Sergeant," he addressed Kester, "give me a report on our deployment. Who's where, and what's the situation?"

"I can show you on the tac display inside, sir," Kester indicated the open ramp of the ACV.

Curt looked around in the bright morning sunlight. The ground fog along the Swakop River had burned off, and the air was crystal clear. "Give it to me in real time-space, Henry. If I need to see something on the display that's not visible from here, we'll go inside."

"Alpha Platoon is deployed between here and the beach," Kester reported, indicating the direction with his right arm. "The highway and rail bridges to Walvis Bay are about three hundred meters to our right, and Lieutenant Morgan has deployed Alpha Platoon to cover them as well as to provide surveillance over approximately one kilometer eastward from the shore to here with one warbot and/or a vehicle every twenty meters. She's located her Mary Annes so they have the best fields of fire, maximum cover, and the best opportunity for movement if necessary, particularly near the two bridges."

"Has she set up a border guard post to control the traffic flow to and from Walvis Bay?" Curt wanted to know.

Kester shook his head. "Negatory, sir. A Feldgendarmerie unit's already there. They have a normal border guard post, if you want to call it that. It looks like more of a formality than anything else. Not much road traffic. The feldgendarmes say there's two trains a day in each direction. Their NCO is cooperative and it seems they don't get paid unless they're manning their guard shacks, so Lieutenant Morgan decided to let them continue as border guards. She says there's no need to use our people to do it if we can keep an eye on the feldgendarmes."

"Sounds reasonable, but I'd feel a little better with tighter control over that border crossing," Curt remarked, scanning the bridges with binoculars he extracted from his equipment belt.

"Oh, I wouldn't worry too much about that, Captain. The Lieutenant assigned Sergeant Gerard to oversee border security at the bridges. Nick is properly suspicious, and I've talked to him about it." He turned and indicated the river bank to the east. "Bravo Platoon is deployed one kilometer to the east of this position along the bluffs and hills of the river bank. Lieutenant Allen has positioned his Hairy Foxes with their best field of fire focused on the bridges. Same deployment interval."

Jerry Allen had done a good job; Curt had trouble locating the Hairy Foxes, and Allen's manpower blended into the scenery well. "Any trouble with the locals?"

Again, Kester shook his head. "It's kinda like Germany except for the mixture of races here," he admitted. "We haven't occupied anyone's house because we've got room to deploy. And we haven't even trampled anyone's prize rose bushes, either. So the locals are sort of nonchalant about us. Very subservient to authority, just like Germany. We're soldiers and they're used to having a few soldiers about in the form of the Feldgendarmes. So no big deal and life goes on."

"No repercussions from the killing of the policeman?" Spencer wanted to know.

"Not that we've detected," Kester admitted. "The word's out that it was an accident, the sort of thing that can happen when military forces are involved. I get the feeling that these people have seen a lot of South African soldiers come and go through here; this hasn't exactly been a very peaceful part of the world for a hundred years or so. Everyone we've talked to seems impressed by the fact that the Colonel and Captain Kelly apologized in public and then went to see the man's family. Seems like that's something totally new to them, at least from soldiers." The master sergeant paused for a moment, then went on, "I think we're also something new to them. We're Americans. They've heard a lot about us. They don't have any reason to dislike us. On the other hand, they got no love whatsoever for the Afrikaaners across the river." Kester indicated the white stucco house behind them. "The *hausfrau* there came out a few minutes after I'd set up here and brought me a plate of homemade chocolate cookies like the ones they make in northern Germany. I put them inside the ACV to keep them out of the sun.

Pretty good. You hungry, Captain? Len?"

"What did you swap for, Henry?" Curt asked.

"Sir?"

"I know you. You always stash away some sort of goodie to trade with the locals. I don't know how many kilos of junk jewelry you loaded, but I know from past experience you've got something like that in the ACV." Curt understood his old master sergeant.

"I didn't swap for anything, Captain!" Kester objected. "She gave me a gift of a plate of cookies. I returned the favor by giving her one of those Arizona copper ash trays I bought up in Payson a while back . . ."

"Come to think of it, it's been a long time since breakfast," Curt suddenly said, looking up to where the bright sun was climbing into the northern sky. It had been a busy morning thus far and, although noon was a couple of hours away, his own circadian rhythm had been thoroughly screwed-up by the rapid trip from North America through ten time zones in the last day or so. "Yeah, I'll snitch a goodie before we go inspect the company. Len, this is the Army; you eat when you get the chance."

"Don't have to tell me that," the reporter replied. "Sometimes news work is the same way."

Curt looked at the man's stocky form. "Maybe, but it doesn't look like you've missed many meals."

"Too many Army chow lines," the reporter replied.

"And those New York restaurants with a company credit card . . ."

Alexis Morgan had positioned her platoon ACV a hundred meters from the bridges in partial defilade so that its turret sensors could maintain surveillance for her tactical computer and the 15mm machinegun could sweep both the highway and the railway. Curt noticed but didn't remark to Spencer that she'd also positioned her LAMV with its 75mm Saucy Cans where it bore-sighted down the highway bridge.

But Len Spencer did notice what Morgan had done to the railway. "Nice touch," he remarked as they stepped over the rails. "Four M3 moldable plastex grenades with remote detonators, two on each rail. Your lieutenant doesn't take chances, does she?"

"Morgan leaves very little to chance," Curt agreed.

Curt had warned Alexis by tacomm that he was coming over to inspect and bringing Spencer with him. It shouldn't have surprised him, therefore, to find the Lieutenant in a fresh set of cammies and without her body armor, which Hettrick had decreed might be taken off while they were on guard duty in Swakopmund. She'd also replaced her hulking battle helmet with a garrison cap perched on the side of her head. And, quite out of character for her in a combat operation, she'd applied just a slight bit of cosmetics to her eyes, cheeks, and lips. Right off the bat, Curt knew it hadn't been for his benefit because Alexis had never done that before in the past.

But Curt introduced Spencer to her, rationalizing to himself that Alexis had gotten gussied-up because of the possibility of a satellite television interview or at least a videotaping where a girl should look her best and give a good impression of the United States Army and a West Point graduate.

Len Spencer was unusually gallant. In the European fashion, he not only took her hand when she proffered it to him, but kissed it as well. Alexis blushed as any woman will when a man unexpectedly kissed her hand.

"Captain Carson remarked to me earlier," Spencer told her, looking her directly in the eyes, "that the women officers and NCOs of the Robot Infantry were not only very good but also made soldiering a great deal more interesting. Now I know what he meant."

Alexis' eyes flicked to Curt then back to Spencer. "We're only soldiers, Mister Spencer, and I must agree with him from the other side," she replied coyly.

To see Alexis Morgan being coy with a man was somewhat of a shock to Curt. Alexis was anything but coy; she was one of the most direct women he'd ever known.

"I think a lot of people wonder how male and female soldiers manage to get along in the Robot Infantry and, now with the Sierra Charlies deployed, how it affects the Army's fighting capability," Spencer observed.

Alexis knew very well what Spencer alluded to. "You mean, how do we manage to keep this from turning into a military orgy at the taxpayer's expense? Let me tell you something I learned at the Military Academy: 'To every thing there is a season, and a time to every purpose under heaven . . .' "

Spencer picked it up, " ' . . . A time to kill, and a time to heal . . . a time to embrace and a time to refrain from embracing . . .' Ecclesiastes, Chapter Three, if I recall correctly."

"You do. But the Army says it differently in Regulation 601-10 . . . or Rule Ten as we know it . . . and God help the soldier who busts Rule Ten!" She was no longer coy; she was a deadly serious officer of the United States Army.

"Can I interview you and talk about that just the way you did it now?" Spencer wanted to know.

"No." Alexis Morgan was blunt and adamant. "It's not a proper subject for discussion insofar as I'm concerned!"

"Why do you say that, Lieutenant?" Spencer was curious. This would have made an outstanding interview.

"As far as I'm concerned, it falls in the same category as discussing the possibility that one might panic and break under fire . . . or even desert one's comrades in the face of the enemy," she told him in no uncertain terms.

He saw he wasn't making the sort of headway he wanted, and certainly no woman had ever before turned down a chance to be interviewed on a subject of his choosing. "Well, the American public often wonders—"

"I believe the American soldier, male or female, would rather be judged on loyalty and performance of duty," Lieutenant Alexis Morgan interrupted him in a sharp tone of voice. "I have no control over the fantasies of the American public. If some people with teen-aged minds want to fantasize about the erotic side of Army life, let 'em enlist and learn about it first-hand! And, by the way, a lot of them have done so. And some of them have been mustered out because this is a volunteer outfit and the sex maniacs can damned well go somewhere else!" Then her tone became softer and more feminine. "But I'd be happy to talk to you about how well both men and women of the Sierra Charlies have done working together on the battlefield . . ."

Spencer figured he'd better get set up and get whatever sort of interview he could with this outspoken and attractive young lieutenant. Maybe he could direct the interview around to the subject again and get her extremely strong viewpoints on record. "Yes, let's do that," he told her in far more friendly tones. "Will you give me a few minutes to unpack my gear and set up my satellite relay?"

"Certainly," Alexis told him sweetly. "And, while you're doing that, Mister Spencer, I'll let the Captain inspect the deployment of my platoon."

As Curt and his lieutenant walked together toward the border patrol shack at the end of the highway bridge, Curt remarked privately, "Nice work, Alexis."

"Damned newshawks are all the same," she replied. "I felt I had to set him straight right at the start. If he tried that on Edie Sampson, she'd hand him his head. And his gonads, too."

"Don't prejudge Len Spencer. He's different," Curt tried to explain.

"I've read his stuff," she replied. "I agree: he's good. That's why I popped off. From what I've gathered from his writing, he learns quickly. So I think we've got that subject behind us. I'm tired of it. If I said something I shouldn't have, Curt, I apologize. It's been a long day, and it isn't over yet—"

"And you didn't get prettied-up for nothing."

"You noticed?"

"How could I help but notice? One of these days, we ought to talk seriously about strategic planning for a joint life mission."

"Not if all it takes on my part to get you to bring up the subject is a little face paint. And not while you still outrank me."

Platoon Sgt. Nick Gerard was at his post outside the border guard shack at the end of the highway bridge. He wasn't standing guard; he was comfortably settled in a chair, his M33 across his knees, and his eyes scanning the far side of the bridge through binoculars. Thus, he didn't see the two officers approach until the Feldgendarmerie corporal in the hut stepped out, slammed the door, and shouted, *"Achtung!"*

Gerard arose, slung his *Novia,* and saluted. "'Morning, Captain, Lieutenant."

"Any problems?" Curt wanted to know.

"No sir. But they can serve chow any time they want to. It's been a long time since we chowed down those emergency rations in the aerodyne," the platoon sergeant said.

"I'll check into it," Curt promised. "Lieutenant, an early lunch might be in order. You might want to call in your troops singly or in small groups for chow."

"Yes, sir . . . *Captain!"* Alexis suddenly pointed across the bridge.

Three South African soldiers—officers from their uniforms—were marching straight across the bridge toward them on the center line of the roadway.

accompany the Washington Greys during Operation Diamond Skeleton and make daily reports."

CHAPTER FOURTEEN

"Lieutenant, alert your platoon," Curt told her and toggled his helmet tacomm. "Kester, Companion Leader here! Afrikaaner soldiers! Three of them! Crossing the bridge! Alert the company and report this to Grey Head!"

"Roger, Captain," Kester's calm voice came in Curt's brain from the neurophonic pickups of the helmet. "I've got them nailed in the long-range sensors here. Three officers of the South African Defense Forces—a colonel, a major, and a lieutenant. They're armed only with holstered pistols, probably nine-millimeter Sanna one-fifties. I have them targeted by the fifteen-millimeter on top of our ACV. Lieutenant Morgan's ACV has also acquired and laid its fifteen-millimeter on them. Other sensors are scanning the river bed and the opposite bank to check for activity there. Negative contact so far."

"Report it to Grey Head."

"Reported, Captain."

"Get your jeep here," Curt told Alexis, then keyed his helmet comm again and called for his own general purpose robot, "Companion Action Jackson, this is Companion Leader. Join me immediately."

Company commanders don't rate an aide de camp, but Curt had programmed his M33 General Purpose Warbot, his jeep, to track him constantly and to be able to join him in less than thirty seconds if called. A jeep carried a 7.65mm rapid-fire gun with a prodigious quantity of ammo and was not only heavily armored but could provide sensor data from the radar frequencies up through ultraviolet.

By the time the three Afrikaaners got within thirty meters of the three Americans, the jeeps had joined Curt and Alexis and waited quietly behind them.

The Feldgendarmerie corporal and private who were manning the border post shack had retrieved their submachineguns and now were standing passively alongside and slightly behind the shack, not totally willing to expose themselves fully to whatever might be coming across the bridge in the way of high-velocity rounds. Insofar as they were concerned, this was the American's show, and they were happy to let it be that way.

The leading South African officer stopped about five meters from them and saluted. "Captain," he said, correctly reading Curt's insignia of rank, "I am Colonel Theo van Wijk, commanding officer of South African Defense Forces posted at Walvis Bay. I am accompanied by my second-in-command and my aide. I would like to pay a social call on the regimental commander of the Washington Greys regiment of the United States Army currently occupying Swakopmund. Would you please so inform your commanding officer?" The man spoke excellent English, which didn't surprise Curt because both English and Afrikaans were the official language of the Republic of South Africa.

What did surprise Curt was the fact that Colonel van Wijk knew that the Washington Greys were in Swakopmund. Good intelligence.

Curt had left the audio pickup of his helmet comm activated. This had been heard at regimental headquarters. Hettrick's voice came back in his head, "Orgasmic! Captain, tell them I'll be there in my ACV in five minutes!"

Curt returned the salute, introduced himself and Lieutenant Morgan, then relayed Hettrick's message to Colonel van Wijk.

"Captain Carson! Lieutenant Morgan! Sergeant! Allow me to present my second in command, Major Swart, and my aide, Lieutenant Du Preez. Since we are quite alone, is it totally necessary for your warbots to continue to train their pieces on us? This is, after all, a purely social call."

Curt gave the mental order to Companion Action Jackson through his helmet comm.

Van Wijk then stepped up to Alexis Morgan, took her hand, and kissed it gallantly as Spencer had done. Alexis blushed again. Having her hand kissed twice in one day was quite stimulating as far as she was concerned, and she wondered if she'd ever get used to this sort of treatment. It would certainly tend to spoil a woman, she thought.

But Colonel van Wijk was indeed a charmer. "I have heard a great deal about the fine young women of the American Army's Robot Infantry," he told Alexis, "but this is the first time I've had the honor of meeting a lady combat officer. I certainly hope your stay in Swakopmund remains tranquil because it would be such a pity if the situation became such that you might be exposed to harm . . ."

"Thank you for your kind thoughts, Colonel," Alexis replied diplomatically then added quite bluntly, "I've taken a five-millimeter to my helmet in another action, and I resolved then that I wouldn't get in the way of another one, no matter where I might happen to have to fight. And we certainly intend on our part to keep our stay in Swakopmund as peaceful and tranquil as possible. However, that may not be totally within our control."

"Well said!" Colonel van Wijk replied with a smile. "We certainly don't intend to intrude on your peaceful and temporary occupation as long as there is no breach of previous agreements."

"And as long as we're evenly matched, regiment for regiment," Curt added a little less diplomatically, signalling that even the American company commanders in Swakopmund were completely aware of the situation with South Africa in Operation Diamond Skeleton. Curt knew that the colonel had only one regiment of regular infantry in Walvis Bay.

"Well, of course, a discussion of that sort goes beyond the bounds of social conversation," the colonel remarked, attempting to dismiss the subject from further consideration.

Meanwhile, Len Spencer was getting all of this on tape with a long-focus lens and a shotgun mike that intercepted every word.

True to her promise, Colonel Hettrick showed up in her regimental ACV within five minutes. She debouched with Maj. Ed Canby and Capt. Wade Hampton. Confidently, she strode up to the end of the bridge where the South Africans were conversing with her Greys. Saluting smartly, she introduced herself, "Colonel van Wijk, I am Colonel Belinda J. Hettrick, commanding officer, the 3rd Robot Infantry Division known as the Washington Greys, of the 17th Iron Fist Division, United States Army." Since it was apparent that van Wijk knew which American outfit she represented, she felt no need to maintain security about it.

Van Wijk returned her salute and smiled. "I was aware that the Washington Greys had a famous lady regimental commander, but I did not expect you to be so attractive!"

"Flattery will get you a lot of things in this world, Colonel," Hettrick told him. "But not in my regiment. May I present my second in command, Major Edward Canby, and my chief of staff, Captain Wade Hampton? I see you've already met several members of my command."

After a round of salutes and handshaking and echoes of "Colonel—Captain—Major—Colonel," Hettrick remarked, "I apologize for not having occupied a building where we might hold a meeting, Colonel, but my orders compel me to refrain from disturbing the life of the people of Swakopmund to any greater degree than necessary during our temporary visit here."

"I see. When do you intend to depart?" van Wijk asked.

"As quickly as the people besieged in the Otjomuise diplomatic compound can be evacuated. The sooner that's accomplished, the sooner I'll depart. As you well know, Colonel, all soldiers want to get home as quickly as possible without engaging in combat." Hettrick was both blunt and diplomatic at the same time.

"The Republic of South Africa stands ready to assist you in your effort to succor the diplomatic personnel in Otjomuise," van Wijk put in. "Perhaps we should trek there together."

"It might be interesting, Colonel, but my orders do not contain latitude to allow me to do that," Hettrick told him cryptically. "However, as you are paying a social call, I can offer you only the hospitality of the interior of my armored command vehicle. It's almost lunch time. Would you care to join me and my officers for lunch?" She'd cleared the tactical displays and sequestered all of the classified and sensitive material and information, anticipating that these Afrikaaners would accept her invitation in order to see the inside of an American command vehicle.

But Colonel van Wijk took her by surprise. "Swakopmund is a resort town, Colonel, and we often come here for relaxation. R-and-R, I believe you Yanks call it. Would you allow me to show you a very nice little restaurant on the beach front where it would be my honor to have you and your staff officers as my guests for lunch?"

"That would be very kind of you, sir," Hettrick replied. "Is it within walking distance, or shall we ride in my vehicle?"

"It's about two kilometers, Colonel. Perhaps we should ride because the sun may be getting a bit hot for you."

"Colonel, it may be winter in our hemisphere at the moment," Hettrick reminded him, "but my troops and I are physically capable of doing very well in places like Iran and Trinidad. I doubt that your summer heat will bother us very much. But ride we will. Please come aboard." She turned to Curt and told him cryptically, "Keep the channel open and stay on your toes."

"Yes, Colonel." As a junior officer with occupational guard duties and a company to look after, Curt didn't expect to be included in the luncheon invitation. Besides, the formal courtesy that went on between people who might be fighting one another a few hours later often bored the hell out of him. He was a combat officer, and he didn't really look forward to the rest of his career where, if and when he was promoted to field-grade, he'd be expecte to spend far more time involved in social and diplomatic affairs than in combat.

Besides, he had to inspect Lt. Jerry Allen's deployment.

But, since he'd told Alexis to see that her troops were fed, he passed the order through Henry Kester to Allen's Bravo Platoon to chow-down and decided he'd eat with Alexis and Len Spencer.

The newsman was ecstatic. "Goddam, but that was good stuff there on the bridge, Curt! I fed it right to New York. They're happy as hell. And they want me to get that interview with you, Alexis."

"Fine, as long as you follow my ground rules," Alexis warned him. "Or have you got any idea of what a glob of cammy grease will do to that super lens of yours?"

"My, my!" Spencer chuckled. "My dear, for your sake, I'll follow whatever rules you establish. I am at your command, Alexis!"

"That's better! I'm glad we've arrived at a mutual understanding at last," Alexis told him as they ate.

The guy's a charmer, Curt thought. *But I'll bet my ass the only thing he really cares for is an award-winning story! I'll have to talk to Alexis about this possibility. Otherwise, he's likely to sweet-talk her right off her feet.* He wasn't ready to admit to himself that there was also slightly more than a twinge of jealousy motivating him. He thought very highly of his lieutenant. They went well together both on and off duty. They were considered A Couple in the Club at Diamond Point casern. Rumor Control occasionally featured some juicy tidbit about them. Sure, there was no formal arrangement between them, and they enjoyed each other as often as they each enjoyed someone else. But Curt knew he'd hurt her a little more deeply than usual on Trinidad where the women were both beautiful and willing. Jerry Allen was still in nearly daily communications with Cadet Cpl. Adonica Sweet at the Military Academy.

But Curt sensed no real interest in Spencer on Alexis' part, so maybe he was just worrying about nothing, he d to tell himself.

After lunch, he made the rounds of Jerry Allen's platoon, followed dutifully by Action Jackson at the usual discreet distance. The young lieutenant, now sporting his silver bar, explained to Curt that he'd already taken the time to compute laying his guns in on Walvis Bay 32 kilometers away. "It's just about maximum range for my Saucy Cans, but I think I can worry them a little bit if they start playing hard ball."

"How about the highway and railway?"

"Hell, Captain, my Hairy Foxes can take out both bridges here in a matter of less than a minute," Allen pointed out. "I've targeted the mid-span butresses. Bridges are more difficult to fix than roads or railways. But I can give that highway a neat set of big pot holes, and I can bend a few rails here and there."

"Good, but keep it as an option," Curt warned him. "And tone it down a bit, Lieutenant. You're beginning to sound like one of Kelly's Killers."

"Sorry, Captain."

"How fast can you pull it all together and put it on the road?" his company commander asked him.

Allen thought a moment. "Which direction, Captain?"

"East."

"Otjomuise? Thirty minutes, Captain."

"Good. Keep that option open."

"Yessir, I know the prevailing thinking on that one. When will we know?"

"Tomorrow is my guess," Curt mused. "We were put in here primarily as a feint, secondarily to hold down the Afrikaaner regiment in Walvis Bay. The Namibian government, the Bastaards, and even the Afrikaaners need some time to confirm that we're here, figure out that we may have landed merely to secure the town as a staging base for an overland mission or as an aerodyne refuelling point, and maybe react to it. They knew we were coming; the Supreme Allied Command passed the information along to the South Africans so they wouldn't react to us as an invasion force. God knows what else the French or the

Brits passed along to the Afrikaaners. My guess is t
the *Legion* and the Royal Scots will be air-landed
Otjomuise tomorrow at dawn. So we ought to know by
tomorrow noon whether or not this whole operation is going according to the way the French have laid it out."

"Captain, why do I sometimes get the feeling that we're sitting ducks?"

Curt shrugged. "Do ducks sit? And why do they sit when they know there's a hunter out there in a blind? Hell, I don't run the strategy behind these things, Lieutenant. And this one is a French operation. Sometimes I can't figure out our own. Don't ask me to figure out the French, too!"

A raucous sound like that of a klaxon went off inside Curt's head, fed in by the neurophonic transducers of his helmet tacomm. It was the signal of a Yankee Alert, the next step down from a full Zulu Alert. The voice of Lt. Hensley Atkinson's, regimental S-3 operations, followed. "Companion Leader, this is Grey Ops!"

Why was Hensley calling him instead of Colonel Hettrick? He toggled the helmet comm. "Companion Leader here. Go ahead, Grey Ops."

"I can't raise Grey Head. You're the ranking officer I can reach. Do you know the location of Grey Head and why she might not be answering the Yankee Alert page?"

"She's on the beachfront at a restaurant having lunch with the South African commander from Walvis Bay," Curt explained. "Probably has her helmet off. What's up?"

"New data and an ops request, Captain."

"Tell me about it. I wouldn't want to interrupt the colonel's lunch unless it's pretty important," Curt said.

"I think it's pretty important, Captain, and so does Lieutenant Gibbon," she replied, referring to the regimental communications/intelligence officer. "Came in by satellite from St. Helena. General Carlisle requests immediate teleconference with Colonel Hettrick. Apparently, the *Legion Robotique* jumped the gun. They were supposed to go into Otjomuise tomorrow at dawn with the Royal Scots and all the tacair support available. Instead, the *Legion* tried a vertical envelopment of Strijdom International Airport at dawn this morning, twenty-four hours ahead of schedule and all by themselves with only the *Groupe Cigognes* for support. And they're in deep yogurt, Captain . . ."

CHAPTER FIFTEEN

"Holy shit!" Curt breathed, then realized he'd had his helmet comm mike toggled hot.

"Yes, sir, that's what I think, too," Lt. Hensley Atkinson's voice replied.

"I'll find the Colonel," Curt promised, "and have her report to you ASAP. Companion Leader out!"

Lt. Jerry Allen was white-faced. He'd overheard in his own helmet tacomm. "What the hell are those Frogs trying to do?"

"Vindicate their national honor!" Curt snapped. "They thought they could pull it off alone . . ."

"Then why did they ask us to tag along?"

"Ostensibly for diplomatic reasons. In reality, to extricate their asses if their honor wasn't enough to cut it," Curt said and switched his tacomm to company frequency. "Companion Alpha, this is Companion Leader!"

No reply.

"Curt tried again. "Companion Alpha, this is Companion Leader!"

Still no reply.

Curt was off like a shot, headed toward his own ACV parked nearby and waiting for him. He tossed over his shoulder to Allen, "If I don't check in from my ACV in five minutes, assume command of the company, Lieutenant!"

Jerry Allen didn't know what was up, either, but he was well-versed in the procedures that Curt had established for emergency assumption of command of Carson's Companions. No shots had been fired; at least, he hadn't heard any. But the fact that Curt couldn't raise Morgan could mean anything.

Curt's ACV was only about a hundred meters away, and as he ran up the inclined rear ramp, he told it, "Companion One, this is Companion Leader. Confirm recognition of my voice!"

"Companion Leader, I see you, I hear you," the ACV reported to him.

"Move out at once! Proceed to Companion Alpha ACV! Pick up Companion Action Jackson following me."

"Roger! One is in action." The rear ramp swung up; the ACV would pick up Action Jackson in its warbot retrieval clamps like a sanitation truck grabs a garbage can—although Army Ordnance would never admit they got the idea from that prosaic source. "Where do you wish to take the conn, sir?"

"Top turret hatch. Where's Master Sergeant Kester?" Curt asked his machine.

"Casual inspection of Alpha Platoon."

Well, it wasn't necessary for Henry to cool his heels all day inside the company ACV; Curt's policies encouraged his first sergeant to move out among the troops, especially on guard details like this, to make sure everything was running smoothly in the ranks.

The top hatch swung open, and Curt clambered up, banging his helmet several times on protrusions as the ACV swung around bumpily and began to head for Alexis Morgan's ACV. He got his helmeted head just out of the turret hatch as the ACV went past the railway bridge and bounced over the rails. He saw that Nick Gerard was still on duty at the border guard shack which terminated the highway bridge. Then Curt saw the Alpha Platoon ACV parked up ahead. Its ramp was down and it was quiescent. And Lt. Alexis Morgan's helmet was perched on the lip of the turret hatch.

Lt. Alexis Morgan, her hair blowing in the wind, was seated on the bank of the Swakop River talking intently with Len Spencer.

Curt didn't even wait for the ramp to flop down. He

erupted out of the turret hatch and slid down the side of the ACV to the ground, disdaining the use of the hand holds and stirrups. "Lieutenant Morgan!" he bellowed. Curt didn't bellow unless he was upset. He was upset right then.

And Lt. Alexis Morgan suddenly knew it, too.

She scrambled quickly to her feet, smoothed her cammies, and saluted. "Yes, sir!"

She really did look pretty with cosmetics applied, Curt decided. He had never seen her this way in the field before. But he didn't allow that to temper his anger. "Why aren't you monitoring the company tac freak?"

She suddenly realized that she wasn't wearing her helmet. Her cheeks flushed. "Sorry, sir!" she apologized. She knew better than to profer the excuse that she was being interviewed by Len Spencer; Curt could see that, and Curt didn't like excuses unless he asked for them.

"Return to your Platoon ACV," he told her sternly. "Assume temporary command of the company! Maintain a guard on both the regimental and the company tac freaks. I've got to find Colonel Hettrick. Where's Sergeant Kester?"

"Down by the beach inspecting the right flank," Alexis reported. The fact that he hadn't reprimanded her wasn't lost on her; she knew she'd neglected her duty, but the afternoon sun was so warm and the surroundings so peaceful and Len Spencer so interesting . . .

"Call him in; I want him with you in the temporary company command post," Curt ordered. "I want Kester to monitor all the sensors that are keeping an eye on the other side of the river here."

"Something wrong, sir?" she asked.

"Damned right! Spencer, you come with me, because you've got yourself one hell of a story," Curt snapped.

"Care to bring me up to the same level of ignorance and confusion that Lieutenant Morgan enjoys at the moment?" Spencer responded lightly with a smile.

"It's not funny, and we may have to fight . . . as we figured we might," Curt said briefly. "The French *Legion*

Robotique jumped the gun and landed at Strijdom airport outside of Otjomuise at dawn this morning—twenty-four hours ahead of schedule! They were supposed to go in tomorrow morning with the Royal Scots and lots more air support. Now they're in trouble. I've got to find Colonel Hettrick; she went off to lunch somewhere with the South Africans. So, Spencer, climb aboard and let's get cracking!" He paused, then added, "Spencer, you may have a handle on the hottest story of this fracas, if things go like I think they may. But, in the meantime, if you breathe one damned word of this to Colonel van Wijk or the South Africans when we find them, I promise you won't be buried in this godforsaken place; I'll personally see to it that your remains are shipped home in a body bag, even though they might be full of seven-millimeter rounds from my *Novia*. Understand?"

Spencer was deadly serious now. "Understood, Captain!"

"Oh, my God!" Alexis breathed. "Those poor French warbot brainies! What's this going to do to the whole operation?"

"Screw it up beyond all recognition . . . and maybe even beyond saving," Curt told her.

"General Carlisle must be pissed—"

"I don't know. I haven't talked to him. But he's got every right to be," Curt said, then began to climb back into his ACV.

Spencer dashed around, retrieving his equipment, while Curt opened the rear ramp for him. When Curt glanced down at Morgan again, she'd put on her helmet. She looked and acted quite professional once more. "Shall I get the company ready to move out, Captain?" she called up to him.

"Lieutenant Allen is already getting his own platoon into that condition. Suggest you do the same with yours. Allen's got a fifteen minute head start on you."

"That won't last—"

"But don't abandon the company's present positions," Curt warned her. "The Companions are to remain deployed on guard until we get orders to the contrary."

"Understood, Captain! We'll be ready to move if necessary."

Curt turned his attention to his task. "Companion One, display the street map of Swakopmund on the tactical display and indicate our present position."

Almost instantaneously, the terminal showed what Curt had requested.

"Indicate the most direct route from our present position to the road or street paralleling the Atlantic Ocean and the beach."

A yellow line snaked through the street map.

"Follow the yellow brick road," Curt told his vehicle. "Set sensors to recognize and report verbally to me upon sighting Colonel Hettrick's ACV, code name Grey Head One. And open the auxiliary turret hatch." He motioned to Spencer. "Grab your videocam and come up alongside me. No sense in making you sit on your ass inside this thing. You've got to get your story too."

"Thank you, Captain. I appreciate your understanding."

"I just want to make damned good and sure I don't get pilloried by you as a blood-and-guts martinet before this thing is over. I'll give you every chance to get good coverage; people at home need to have a better idea of what this is all about . . . and especially how the Sierra Charlies operate." He paused, then added, "But, don't worry. If you get in the way, you'll get kicked in the ass."

"Fair enough," Spencer replied and joined Curt in the aux hatch of the top turret on the other side of the 15mm gun with his camera on his shoulder. "You know, you're reverting back to the days of Patton, aren't you?" the newsman asked as the ACV began to wend its way through the streets of Swakopmund toward the shore.

"I've read Patton . . . and others," Curt admitted. "But we're plowing fresh ground here with the Sierra Charlies and the new non-neuroelectronic warbots."

"I don't think you are, Captain. Not really," the military reporter remarked. "Maybe you don't know it yet, but what you've got is the good old grunt infantry assisted by the speed and firepower of miniaturized, artificially intelligent tanks—your warbots."

"Where'd you get that idea?"

"Your First Lieutenant Morgan recognizes it but hasn't been able to get the concept down to that level of simplicity yet," Spencer explained. "This is not to say that she isn't a very intelligent young lady, Captain. And a very attractive one, too. I can now understand your earlier remark that the mixed-gender Sierra Charlie infantry makes Army life a lot more interesting than it used to be—"

"Don't try to monopolize her time and attention, Spencer," Curt suddenly told the man. "She's my second in command, and I count on her."

"I can understand why," Spencer replied somewhat cryptically."

"Grey One in sight!" the ACV reported via its voice circuits as it rounded a corner onto the beachfront street.

"Pull up alongside it and stop," Curt ordered.

He found Hettrick, Maj. Ed Canby, and Capt. Wade Hampton seated inside with the South Africans. Since Curt was under arms with his *Novia* slung over his right shoulder, he didn't uncover on entering the little restaurant. The place was quaint and Teutonic, yet it was rendolent with the flavorable smells of freshly cooked seafood. Curt really hated to interrupt Hettrick's meal in a lovely place like this. He told himself that he'd like to have a meal in the place himself; already he was growing tired of field rations.

Stepping right up to the table where the six officers were seated, Curt saluted. "Colonel Hettrick," he told her in unemotional tones, "regimental headquarters needs to speak with you at once, and they sent me to find you."

Hettrick returned his salute from her seated position. "How'd you find me?"

"You parked your ACV outside, m'am."

"Of course!" She rose to her feet. "Gentlemen, please excuse me for a moment."

Curt followed her. Once outside, she told Curt in a low

voice over her shoulder, "This had better be damned important! I haven't had such good seafood since Trinidad . . ."

"It is important, Colonel," Curt assured her. "I didn't want to mention it in front of the Afrikaaners, but General Carlisle desires an immediate conference."

She gave a little start. "Oh? Really? Any reason given, Curt?"

"Yes, Colonel. The French jumped the gun and put the *Legion* into Strijdom at dawn this morning . . . alone."

"Ohmygawd!" It came out as one word. With surprising agility, Hettrick clambered up the stirrups to the turret of her ACV and dropped inside without bothering to tell it to lower its ramp. Then she stuck her head up out of the turret hatch and told Curt, "If that's the case, I'll need Canby and Hampton, too. Curt, go in and get them, make an excuse to the South Africans, and escort them to the Swakop bridge. Be diplomatic. But don't tell them anything, understand?"

"Yes, Colonel." Curt clambered up to the turret and told his ACV, "Zero all screens and displays, store the defaults, and prepare for uncleared visitors."

"By your command, Captain," his ACV replied.

Curt turned and re-entered the restaurant.

When he approached the table, he saluted the South African officer. "Colonel van Wijk, Colonel Hettrick has asked me to thank you for a most delightful lunch and requests that she be excused. Official duties require her attention, and she requests that Major Canby and Captain Hampton join her at once. I am to escort you back to the Swakop bridge."

Colonel van Wijk didn't look the least surprised, although he appeared to be disappointed. "Really? Very well, I regretfully accept the fact that duty calls . . . but that's a cross that regimental commanders often must bear."

Chairs scraped back as Canby and Hampton got to their feet. "By your leave, Colonel," Canby said, saluting. "It was enjoyable while it lasted."

"Indeed it was," echoed Hampton. "Gentlemen, thank you."

Together, the two of them left the restaurant quickly but not in any way that would indicate they were in a hurry.

Curt stood quietly until they'd left, then reminded the South Africans, "Colonel Hettrick asked me to escort you to the Swakop bridge, Colonel."

Van Wijk waved his hand. "Never mind, Captain. It isn't very far, and we'll find our way."

"I'm sorry, sir, but both courtesy and duty require that I escort you. Swakopmund is under military occupation at the moment."

Van Wijk smiled. "But of course! I'm so used to visiting here under normal conditions that it seemed natural for me to stroll back to the bridge with my officers." He looked down at his unfinished plate of seafood. "Pity to waste it, but I suspect you'll be wanting us to go now, Captain?"

"Colonel Hettrick didn't ask me to escort you back immediately," Curt explained. "I see no reason to further interrupt what appears to be a good meal. Field soldiers seldom get the chance to eat this well."

"Would you care to join us?"

"I've already had lunch, but thank you, Colonel." Curt slipped into a chair, neither removing his helmet nor unslinging his *Novia*. The waiter was quickly at his side. Curt ordered a cup of *schlag* because he noticed that the Colonel had one and it had been a long time since he'd had something like that in Germany. When it came, Curt sipped it and remarked, "Just like Munsterlagen!"

"You've been to Germany, Captain?" Van Wijk asked.

"I've had the honor to serve there, Colonel. Frankly, I'm amazed to discover that Swakopmund has retained so much of its German colonial heritage. After all, the German empire ruled this colony for only about seventy-five years . . . and that ended over a century ago . . ." Curt remarked, trying to make polite social conversation.

"It's a combination of German, Dutch, and Afrikaaner culture, Captain," van Wijk corrected him. "But I suspect it would seem German to you."

"Very much so," Curt came back, "even to the language and customs."

"You mentioned Musterlagen," van Wijk remarked. "That was strictly a robot infantry operation, as I recall. Apparently, you've been in the RI for quite a few years . . ."

"I'm a qualified warbot officer and operator," Curt admitted.

"The American Army seems to have altered its operational doctrine," the South African colonel observed. "I notice that you serve in the field with the warbots now. That's quite a change."

"Yes, sir, it is," Curt told him but offered no further information of Sierra Charlie doctrine or principles, which is what van Wijk was apparently trying to ferret from Curt.

"Is it working out well?"

"I'm sure you've read the military analysts' reports of Trinidad."

"That's right! Then it was your company that was the only non-warbot unit in that operation."

Curt nodded. "We were, and we learned a great deal."

"Really?"

"To satisfy your whetted curiosity, Colonel," Curt told him respectfully, "we learned how to combine the good features of the old infantry soldier with the good features of the warbot so that the combination overcame the shortcomings of both. And, in due course, once this operation is over, you'll also be able to read a great deal in the professional military literature about how we did it. Otherwise, sir, I'm not at liberty to discuss it right now."

Colonel van Wijk saw that he'd get nowhere in further attempts to interrogate this disciplined company officer. So he glanced at his watch and remarked, "Duty also calls in my case, Captain. Please escort us back to the bridge, since those are your orders." And he rose to his feet with his companions and walked toward the door.

"Thank you, Colonel," the *matre d'* remarked to him as

he passed.

"Send me the bill as usual, Heinrich."

"Of course, Colonel."

It became apparent to Curt that the so-called "border" between the South African enclave at Walvis Bay and the non-independent nation of Namibia was probably nothing much more than a line drawn on some maps. The Feldgendarmarie certainly didn't take it very seriously at the border post. And neither did anyone else, so it seemed.

There was practically no conversation on the short trip back to the Swakop bridge. Upon debouching from Curt's ACV, Colonel van Wijk saluted Curt and shook his hand. The two other officers did the same. The Colonel remarked, "I look forward to meeting you again, Captain."

"Under similar social conditions, of course," Curt added. "I'm sure we will. We're both professionals."

"One may certainly hope so," Colonel van Wijk remarked cryptically, turned on his heel, and marched back across the bridge to Walvis Bay. His two officers accompanied him; neither had said a word to Curt during the entire visit.

Platoon Sgt. Nick Gerard had watched this silently from his position near the guard shack. He sauntered over to his company commander and remarked, "Captain, I may be just an old street fighter from Jersey, but that was no simple social visit those Afrikaaners made."

Curt watched their backs as they marched away. "You catch something I maybe didn't, Nick?"

"Yessir, With all due respects to that Colonel, sir, the sonofabitch is lying in his teeth. He's set up to do something, and I think he probably was here to do a little snooping."

"So do I," Curt agreed. "But I don't know what intelligence data he picked up. At least, he picked up the tab for lunch. He tried to probe me, but I was pretty tight-lipped. Let's hope his snoop was successful."

"Let's hope we never have to find out, Captain . . ."

CHAPTER SIXTEEN

Col. Belinda Hettrick noted that it was only a partial audio-video teleconference with no neuroelectronic hookup at all. It occupied six video screens in her big Operational Command Vehicle, the nominal regimental headquarters van which would accomodate her staff and their equipment in the new non-neuroelectronic, non-linkage warbot command environment.

Maj. Gen. Jacob O. Carlisle was on one screen with his two aides, Capt. Kim Blythe and 1st Lt. Colleen Collins.

Another screen which showed the same OCV located on St. Helena contained the images of the other Deputy Supreme Commanders for land, sea, and air, along with their staffs.

Surprisingly, the satellite communications from the 1st Australian Kokoda Regiment in Rehoboth to the south of Otjomuise was excellent, but there was some horizontal tearing and color wash-out in the satellite transmission from the 1st Indian Assam Regiment's mobile headquarters at Tsumeb.

Conspicuous by their absence was General Franchet Maurice Lanrezac or any of the French unit commanders.

Hettrick thought she knew why.

Carlisle opened the conference by announcing, "As Deputy Supreme Allied Commander, the task of overall command has fallen upon my shoulders at this time. General Lanrezac went into Strijdom airport with the *Legion Robotique* this morning. The *Legion* and the Supreme Allied Commander are out of communications with Supreme Allied Command at this time."

The situation was worse than Hettrick had thought. On the other hand, now that an experienced commanding officer, General Carlisle, was in charge, maybe things could be salvaged. But she didn't yet know how bad it was.

Apparently, neither did Carlisle because he then asked, "We're eight hours into Operation Diamond Skeleton at this point. Only one activity hasn't proceeded according to schedule. Before launching into an operational reprogramming session, I'd like each of the units involved in Operation Diamond Skeleton to report their present situation and capabilities, please. Colonel Birdwood, what is the situation with the First Kokoda?"

The Aussies had combat hardhats to wear, but by tradition they still wore the folded-brim campaign hat when not in action. Col. Aylmer G. Birdwood had removed his and set it on the table before him. It was obvious he was in his own regimental command van. "General, the First Kokoda is on the ground successfully at Rehoboth and in total control of both the highway and the railway to Otjomuise. We encountered no effective resistance from the local military forces. They were primarily military police as suspected. Our recon troop has reconnoitered as far south as Kalkrand and our recon drones have reported back from as far away as Keetmanshoop. We have no information at this time that South African units are moving from Upington or in from the coast at Luderitz. In all respects, we are prepared to carry out our duties of preventing any possible South African incursions from the south."

"Keep your recon eyes open, Birdwood," Carlisle advised him. "Strategic reconnaissance satellites have reported South African military activity along the Orange River starting about three hours ago."

The Aussie made a note on a pad in front of him. "Yes, sir."

"Colonel Mahadaji, the status of the First Assam Regiment, please?"

The Indian officer looked properly British. In spite of

the fact that the British Army had been gone from India for several generations, the British traditions lingered on persistently. "Sah, the First Assam Regiment is deployed as ordered in Tsumeb!" Col. Siraj Kasim Mahadaji reported briskly. "Upon being landed by the Americans on time and on target, my forces encountered sporadic resistance from several large groups of Ovambo tribesmen attempting to move toward Otjumuise from their homeland to the northeast. I dispatched my Ghurkha battalion with orders to push the Ovambos back to the northeast while my Sihkh battalion dealt with the local military establishment. At this time, my Ghurkhas have inflicted serious losses on the Ovambo horde while sustaining no casualties of their own. We are defending Tsumeb successfully against the Ovambo hordes and have completely secured the defenses of the town against any movement of indigenous personnel toward Otjomuise. The First Indian Assam Regiment holds Tsumeb and its environs as ordered, sah!"

"Do you believe it would be possible to move toward Otjomuise while defending your rear against the Ovambos?" Carlisle asked.

"We are still fighting on the Ovambo front, so we could not easily move at this time, General!" Mahadaji seemed to speak in sharp exclamations.

"Colonel Hettrick, the status of the Washington Greys, please?"

"We've occupied Swakopmund as ordered and have secured the Swakop River railway and highway bridges as well as the town," Hettrick told him brusquely. "Company light artillery is zeroed against Walvis Bay, the highway and railway leading from Walvis Bay to Swakopmund, and the Swakop River bridges. We've sustained no losses of equipment or casualties. Minor resistance, some of it caused by over-anxious troops of my command, resulted in one death and four injuries among the local Feldgendarmerie. Col. Theo van Wijk, commander of the South African Defense Forces at Walvis Bay, paid a social call at noon."

"Have the South African forces at Walvis Bay deployed against you?"

"Not to my knowledge, General. Our guard outposts along the Swakop River report no activity."

"Royal Scots? Colonel McEvedy-Brooke?"

"We're still on the ground in St. Helena, ready to be airlifted into Strijdom as scheduled tomorrow morning," came the disgusted reply. "If I'd been aware that the *Legion* was going in early, I might have been able to muster to assist them. But I had no warning."

"None of us did," Carlisle remarked. "General Maitland-Hutton, as Deputy Commander, Land, I want you to keep the entire ground forces situation thoroughly under control." It was apparent from Carlisle's tone of voice that he was more than a little bit upset over the fact that the man in charge of the ground forces apparently hadn't been when the *Legion* and General Lanrezac took off on their own.

Maj. Gen. Sir John Herbert Maitland-Hutton, V.C., K.B.E., and D.S.C., was well aware of this, and it was also apparent from his visage on the screen that he was less than totally happy with the situation. Unfortunately, he didn't outrank this Yank general, and he'd been unsuccessful in his social attempts to discover Carlisle's date of rank as well, so he'd been unable to pull any Allied rank and take over as he felt he should do under the circumstances. After all, he was an old warbot brainy and thought he knew exactly how to handle the Strijdom situation since he'd been forced to operate with the volatile French before. Therefore, he tended to be quite informal in an irritating manner with those he considered to be slightly beneath his lordly class. Maitlands and Huttons had served Their Brittannic Majesties for uncounted generations, and he didn't like being subordinate to an American upstart. Particularly when he knew damned good and well he'd dropped the ball by letting the French bypass St. Helena by bringing the *Legion* in through Chad. "That you shall have, Jacob, old chap! I'll keep very close tabs on the situation as it develops from now on, and you can be sure that no troops will move without proper authorization . . ."

"I don't want them frozen in position like chess pieces, Sir John," Carlisle fired back. "We've got a war of movement on our hands here if we can gather up the means to move troops. Admiral Unwin, how goes it with the naval forces? Can we count on any offshore air or logistical support. And, if so, how soon?"

The Vice Admiral of the Royal Navy was quite precise, and he harbored none of the rank consciousness or guilt of the Deputy Commander, Land. "The naval contingents are proceeding at full speed toward the Namib coast, General," he reported. "The Royal Navy's Task Group Number Four with six jump-jet and aerodyne carrier vessels will be on station off Cape Cross in thirty-four hours. The four *Raborn* class submersible carriers of the United States Navy will be on station off Swakopmund in forty-two hours. We shall have sufficient aircraft fuel to permit the land-based tactical air unit to refuel if their pilots are capable of shipboard landings. We shall also be able to mount some tactical missions with the limited number of strike aircraft on those ten ships. By the way, a battalion of Royal Marines will be available from the H.M.S. *Glorious* and the H.M.S. *Redoubtable* if General Maitland-Hutton needs them."

"Sir John, old chap," Carlisle told the British Army officer, deliberately mocking the man's informality, "I want to use those Royal Marines as a mobile reserve."

"I agree. One of the problems always encountered when working with our French compatriots is their penchant for doing battle with insufficient reserves," Maitland-Hutton replied. "Pity. They don't seem to have learned much since Waterloo . . . Or Dien Bien Phu, for that matter."

Carlisle brought his fist down on the table before him. The report overloaded the audio channel. "Gentlemen!" he snapped. "I will tolerate no further degrading or insulting references to any of our allies in this operation! We are professional soldiers! We were given orders to work together as an allied team because our people and those of other countries are in mortal danger in Otjomuise! Regardless of the political machinations that resulted in our present allied command, I must insist that we work together and get this job done!" He stopped to catch his breath, then went on in his usual quiet tone, "The admiral mentioned the air situation. Sir Alan, what is the present situation?"

"Grim, General," replied RAF Air Vice Marshal Sir Alan Kenneth Moorhouse. "The *Groupe Cigognese* accompanied the *Legion* into Strijdom under the assumption that the *Legion* would quickly occupy the aerodrome so that the *Groupe de Transport* would be able to follow them in to refuel and re-arm the *Cigognes* strike aircraft. Obviously, that didn't happen. The *Legion* is pinned down on the aerodrome, which is useless for air operations because it is under heavy small arms fire from the insurgents. The *Cigognes* were forced to divert to the small airport at Grootfontein near Tsumeb. The *Groupe de Transport* didn't know where the *Cigognes* had gone and was forced to return to St. Helena as the closest known friendly base. I've ordered them to be refueled and to proceed to Grootfontein, but they can't get there soon enough to put the *Cicognes* back into operational status before nightfall. Grootfontein isn't very big and it's at high altitude, which will limit both fuel and ordnance loads. Unless the Royal Scots can take Eros aerodrome or pour in enough force to secure Strijdom tomorrow morning, we won't be able to count on much air support of any sort until the naval contingents arrive on station off the Namib coast."

"You don't paint a very rosy picture, Sir Alan," Carlisle observed.

"I'm sorry to disappoint you, Jake, but those are the facts."

"The operation seems to hinge on whether or not the Royal Scots can manage to take Strijdom tomorrow morning, doesn't it?" Carlisle mused.

"Our chances of doing that now are a lot less than they

ould have been if both the *Legion* and my Scots had gone n there together tomorrow morning as planned," Colonel McEvedy-Brooke said. "We've lost the element of surprise. The Bastaards are ready for us."

"Are they expecting anyone to drop into Eros aerodrome?" Carlisle wondered.

"If I were to suggest anything right now," General Maitland-Hutton put in, "I'd recommend that we drop the Royal Scots right into the middle of Otjomuise in Hendrik Verwood Park."

"And right in the middle of about ten thousand Bastaards and Hereros, General?" the Royal Scot colonel asked incredulously.

"You're going to be in the midst of them no matter where you land in the Otjomuise area," the British general told him.

"With all due respects, General," the regimental commander responded cautiously, "if we're going into a hot fire fight, I'd rather do it where we already have some friendly troops . . . and that's out at Strijdom where the *Legion* is pinned down. With any luck at all and a little surprise—the Bastaards may not be expecting us as well—our additional warbots can break through and put this operation back on schedule. I'd like to try that, sir, if I may. The Royal Scots are briefed up for it, and we have our operational plan already worked out. I'm perfectly willing to modify that plan in the field when we learn what the real situation is."

"Sir John, do you approve?" Carlisle asked his Deputy Commander, Land.

Maitland-Hutton shook his head. "I'd rather see them go directly into Otjomuise and try for the embassy compound."

General Carlisle thought for a long moment before he finally replied, "We had to hold this conference because one of our allies and our Supreme Commander jumped the gun and got into trouble as a result. We've got thousands of people, warbots, ships, aircraft, and vehicles all lined up and ready to go with a plan most of us worked several nights putting together. We all agreed it was the best possible plan, given the circumstances. The premature French action compromised surprise. But I don't see that it really alters anything else that greatly. To make a major change in plan right now would be contrary to all military logic. Minor changes, yes, they make sense, and every good general in history has had to make minor changes in his overall plan as the operation progressed. But every time a general lost, it was because he threw out the old plan and tried to improve with a new one . . . and ended up confusing his own forces."

He looked around, seeing his own staff gathered in the conference van on St. Helena and the others in his video displays. "We'll proceed as planned. The Royal Scots will go into Strijdom at dawn tomorrow. By noon tomorrow, we'll know whether or not we have to fine-tune the plan. If I have to put more troops into Otjomuise, the only ones available are the Washington Greys in Swakopmund. I'm willing to leave our rear unprotected at Walvis Bay if I have to because the Royal Marines can go ashore there in about forty-eight hours to re-establish our coastal security. Sir Alan, see if you can work out the logistics of airlifting the Greys from Swakopmund to Otjomuise at any time after tomorrow noon. Colonel Hettrick, can you be ready to go if necessary?"

"General, the Washington Greys are ready right now to move out of Swakopmund," Hettrick reported. "It would be nice if we could be airlifted to Otjomuise, but we're also prepared to make the overland trek if we have to."

Maj. Gen. Jacob Carlisle always knew he could count on Col. Belinda Hettrick and her Washington Greys. They'd come through before. "Good! I hope you can ride there on a soft cushion of air."

"Yes, sir, so do I. It looks like it's pretty damned rough country for about two hundred kilometers, but mobility and speed are the sort of characteristics the Sierra Charlies are supposed to have. I'd rather fly, but we'll trek it if we have to."

CHAPTER SEVENTEEN

"No airlift?" Capt. Curt Carson asked with disbelief in his voice.

"No air lift," Col. Belinda Hettrick confirmed in a discouraged and somewhat bitter tone. "But we anticipated the possibility."

A quiet murmur ran through the officers of the Washington Greys who had congregated on the green grass of the Swakopmund soccer field once trod by the jackboots of Kaiser Wilhelm's colonial German troops. The sun beat down mercilessly from an absolutely cloudless sky; Curt had seen such a sky before in the desert areas of the world—Arizona, Tunis, Chad, Zahedan—but never totally cloudless this close to the ocean whose breakers could be heard in the distance washing up against the beaches of Swakopmund. The cool sea breeze moderated the sun's warmth, which was one reason why Hettrick held the conference on the greensward. The other reason was that even her regimental command van wasn't large enough to hold comfortably all twenty-five officers, and she wanted every officer to be in on this briefing.

"The French *Groupe de Transport* is fully occupied trying to keep the *Legion* alive by air drops of supplies and ammo," she went on to explain. "Our Tactical Airlift Wing and the RAF Air Transport Squadron have been committed by General Carlisle to the establishment of a defensible strike and supply base at Grootfontein, which is the only airfield in our hands not under attack by the local tribes. Grootfontein was allowed to degenerate into a

Class Four airport—one runway full of pot holes, a ram, with more weeds and grass than concrete, and ancient fuelling facilities that are probably contaminated and leaky. The Deputy Supreme Commander for Air says that it will take at least twenty-four hours to get the place in shape to support tac strike aircraft, and that's been given top air priority by General Carlisle . . ."

Len Spencer was videotaping the conference but had acceded to Hettrick's request that he not make a direct broadcast of it because of security. She was sure—and so was the regiment's satellite communications expert, Sgt. Bill Hull—that the Colonel van Wijk's comm specialists and their equipment at Walvis Bay couldn't read his antenna's side lobes, but the South Africans and the Namibians could certainly monitor the news network's satellite down-link at their Washington embassies because the signal code wasn't *that* difficult to break.

On the other hand, Spencer wasn't acting out of respect for Hettrick or the security of the operation; he knew he'd be involved in any forthcoming disaster that might result from his newscasts compromising the regiment's operational plans, so he was protecting his own anatomy. He wanted to come out of Operation Diamond Skeleton with the top story . . . and that story lay in the strong possibility that the Greys would have to rescue the *Legion* and maybe even the Royal Scots.

"Since that's the case, if General Carlisle tells us tomorrow that we trek from here to Otjomuise, we go overland," Hettrick concluded. "So make sure you, your troops, and your equipment are all in shape for a two hundred kilometer dash across this desert and up into those hills to the east. It's a seventeen-hundred meter climb to Otjomuise, and the weather en route is going to be a hell of a lot hotter than it is here. Time is critical, so we'll move around the clock with five minute rest stops every hour. When and if General Carlisle gives the word, we'll move out at once . . . and I don't think there's any 'if' associated with this. Unless the Royal Scots have some warbot tactics that we don't know about, and I doubt that, too. Questions?"

Capt. Joan Ward stuck up her hand. "Colonel, I take it something's happened to the French general who's Supreme Allied Commander? Is General Carlisle now in charge of Operation Diamond Skeleton?"

"General Lanrezac and his personal staff," Hettrick told her with some disgust in her voice, "apparently decided they could run Operation Diamond Skeleton from Strijdom, so they went in with the *Legion Robotique* at dawn today . . . and they've been out of communication since shortly after landing. No satellilte comm. No long-wave earth transmission. Nothing. Zero. Zip. As a result, General Carlisle took over command."

Ward shook her head sadly. "The General inherited another can of worms with this one, didn't he?" was her comment.

"Yes," was Hettrick's brief reply. "Anyone foresee any problems with the overland trek?"

Second Lt. John Gibbon, the regimental S-2, raised his hand. When Hettrick nodded at him, he pointed out, "Colonel, are you planning to follow the main paved highway up to Karibib and then to Otjomuise?"

"Yes."

"May I suggest we develop Plan B?" the regimental intelligence officer said. "We're getting some indication that the South Africans at Walvis Bay are up to something. I'm not sure yet exactly what it is. Lots of radio traffic, mostly in code, and mostly since Colonel van Wijk returned to Walvis Bay about two hours ago."

"Any troop movements yet?" Hettrick wanted to know.

"No, Colonel, not yet. But Colonel van Wijk doesn't have to move any unit very far," Gibbon explained. "His main force is less than thirty-five kilometers away and the Walvis Bay enclave isn't very large. He could move any unit anywhere in less than an hour."

"Do you have any indication yet of his intentions?" Hettrick asked.

Gibbon shook his head. "No, Colonel, as I just reported, we're picking up only heavy radio traffic. No sensor scanning yet. No troop movements that we can detect."

"What's he up to? I'll entertain speculation," Hettrick offered.

"Colonel, Lieutenant Gibbon's unit still has neuro-electronic warbot capability," Curt spoke up. He'd worked hard to maintain a standard, remote, warbot linkage capability in the regiment for two purposes: first, to allow the regiment to take advantage of the outstanding reconnaissance and surveillance abilities of the new birdbots that had first been tested at Zahedan; and, second, to give the regiment a rudimentary fall-back potential to use the old linkage warbots if they somehow became available and were needed in a pinch. Nearly all the officers and NCOs—with the exception of the new squad leaders—were trained and experienced warbot brainies, and it would be tragic if the regiment found itself in a position where neuroelectronic warbots from another outfit became avaliable for use . . . and the Greys had no linkage command vehicle from which to operate them. "I'd suggest we get some birdbots up ASAP. One of our functions here is to keep an eye on the Afrikaaners at Walvis Bay, and it might also be healthy for us to make sure they don't keep us from moving when we're ordered to do so. We're in such a tight box here that Colonel van Wijk could block the main highway to Otjomuise . . . or decide to move that way himself."

"I'll have Sergeants Kent and Wheeler get birdbots up on recon at once," Gibbons said, keyed his helmet comm, and silently transmitted the command to his unit.

"If the main highway is blocked, what are the alternate routes to Otjomuise?" Hettrick asked.

It was Maj. Ed Canby who answered, "Three roads—the paved main highway and two 'secondary' roads of rather dubious condition—are shown on the charts and on the satellite images. But the charts don't match the satellite pics."

"How old are our charts?"

"The latest ones from the Defense Mapping Agency are twenty-seven years old," Canby admitted.

"What? That's ridiculous!" Hettrick exploded.

"Yes, Colonel," Lieutenant Gibbon put in, "but we must remember that Namibia wasn't considered an important part of the world in which American armed forces would become involved. And decades of satellite images had shown that nothing in this part of Africa—and a lot of other places, too—has changed very much over the years. Certainly not like in North America, Europe, or China where things change almost weekly. So DMA reviews charts of places like this once every five years or so, and, if the satellite views aren't greatly in variance with the existing charts, nothing gets changed. Takes a lot of work to map the world to less than a meter resolution . . . and keep everything current to that specification."

"Colonel, we probably won't need charts," said Capt. Marty Kelly. "All our vehicles have inertial positioning systems so we know where we are, and up-dated satellite photos are available—"

"Captain," Gibbons informed him, "the equipment for downlinking the latest high-resolution satellite images exists only at divisional staff level. We have only rudimentary weather satellite capabilities with one-kilometer resolution."

"That's ridiculous! The Iron Fist should never have sent us out here without that capability!" Kelly complained.

"Well, they did, Captain," Hettrick snapped. "We weren't supposed to do anything but hold Swakopmund while the French and the British got the people out of Otjomuise. Didn't work that way, of course, but few military operations come off exactly as planned. Or get all the equipment they think they need. The Egyptian archers of Pharaoh Thutmosis at Megiddo probably didn't have enough arrows to suit them. However, in our case, Congress decided it would be too expensive to give every regiment a high-res satellite down-link. They would have had to take the money out of the foreign aid budget or something . . ."

"Millions for tribute and pennies for defense," someone muttered.

"I didn't hear that," Hettrick remarked. "We're here, and if we march we'll make do with what we have and what we can manage to scrounge in the classic manner of soldiers everywhere and everytime. Canby, is there a library in Swakopmund?"

"Probably, Colonel," the headquarters company commander said. "Anywhere the Germans went, they put in good libraries, schools, museums, and the like. They've always been a high-context culture in which everyone was supposed to know as much as possible about everything imaginable."

"Very well, find it! See what maps they've got. Or aerial photos. Anything covering the terrain between here and Otjomuise," Hettrick told him. Then another idea occurred to her. "Schools, you said? I don't suppose this place has a college, does it?"

"Not likely, Colonel, but probably a very good school system."

"You also mentioned museums. What kind and where?"

"I don't know, Colonel, but I'll find out. What are you looking for other than maps and charts?"

"I had in mind," Colonel Hettrick remarked thoughtfully, "that there is *bound* to be someone in Swakopmund who's been up in those hills between here and Otjomuise. I want to see if we can hire a native guide!"

"Ritter Hoffman seems to know everyone in town," Canby said. "I'll ask him."

"Get on it, please," Hettrick ordered him. "If we have to move out, and if we can't use the main road for some reason, I want good maps or a good guide . . . or both. Anything else?"

No one raised a question. They were all thinking of what they would have to do and what might occur during the trek.

"Very well, dismissed!"

Curt spent the rest of the warm afternoon with the Companions, checking and inspecting while at the same time attempting to give no indication that they might be moving out at any time. His outfit was road-ready, having never come down from the Yankee Alert status they'd been under during the landing that morning. However, Curt was beginning to feel the fatigue beginning to set in, a combination of several days of tension, the circadian desynchronization of crossing too many time zones too quickly, and the stress of being, in effect, an occupying military force in a strange country with a potential adversary across the river.

He saw the same thing in the nine other people in the company. So he switched the guard to four-on and four-off while he alternated with Henry Kester keeping overall surveillance of the situation.

Biotech Sgt. Shelley Hale tried to be helpful. "Captain, I've got a couple of relaxant biofeedback units that will allow people to get some deep rest off-duty," she suggested. The same technology that permitted remotely-controlled, neuroelectronic warbots also allowed small, compact electronics units that were preprogrammed to induce relaxing signals into the nervous system and thus promote rest.

"Sergeant, if the rocket goes up and I need everyone on the firing line, I don't want them fighting something like delinkage," he told her brusquely.

"I understand, sir. But this is different. It's nothing as deeply intrusive as warbot linkage. No warbot brainy should have any trouble coming out of it within seconds with no effects. It's like taking a quick nap."

"Very well. I'm in no mood to argue," Curt snapped. Hale was a professional in her field, and Major Ruth Gydesen of the Biotech Unit wouldn't have given her the biofeedback units and authorized their use under semi-combat conditions like these if they might interfere. Curt remembered how rested he'd been in Zahedan when that

Eurasian bioengineer—what was her name, Dr. Rosha Taisha?—had failed to preprogram him as a prisoner because his mind and nervous system had already been trained as a warbot brainy. "But only to volunteers, Sergeant."

"Of course, sir. Except that I'd like to recommend that you volunteer, Captain. I don't think you've gotten any sleep for at least the last forty hours or so. At least, you've gotten none since I joined the Companions back on St. Helena . . ." Shelley Hale was far more cognizant of the exhausted condition of the company commander than he was. "Twenty hours of continuos task performance is considered by the Biotechnical Corps to be the maximum allowable in precombat and combat stress situations."

"I'm doing fine, Sergeant," Curt snapped at her somewhat testily. "I'm the company commander. I'm not expected to be rested. If I am, it means I'm not doing my job—"

"Yes, sir, but I must remind you that my duties require me to report back to Sergeant Devlin and Doctor Gydesen that you're showing symptoms of extended fatigue." There was no nonsense about this young field biotech, a combination nurse and medic. "Your medical record shows you didn't even go this long without rest on Trinidad—"

"What the hell are you doing with my medical record?" Curt wanted to know.

Hale held up her data communications box. "I have the medical records of everyone in Carson's Companions in here, Captain. It's my job to know the medical histories of the people I have to serve." She opened the black cloth equipment kit she carried and took out a small electronic unit attached to a headband. "Captain, believe me, you're bushed. You're already exhibiting a little bit of fixation, and you may begin to experience mild fatigue-induced hallucinations within several hours. Your first sergeant is on watch for the next three hours. The company's functioning properly. So go lie down over at the side of the ACV, slip this over your head, and I'll give you a call in two hours. I promise."

Curt knew she was right. He knew he was on the ragged edge of fatigue. He knew it had been a long and stressful day, and he also knew it would be a long day tomorrow because there was little doubt in his mind that the Washington Greys would have to pull up stakes tomorrow and strike out for Otjomuise through what Jerry Allen had called "the land God made in anger." So he didn't argue; Sgt. Shelley Hale was perfectly within her rights and duties to report his fatigued behavior back to the Biotech unit. And she was also right about his condition.

"Very well, Sergeant," he muttered, took the biofeedback unit from her, and lay down on the cot arrayed along one side of the ACV's tac display compartment. "But if you don't call me in two hours, I'm going to report *you!*"

CHAPTER EIGHTEEN

The big, sandy-haired, middle-aged man almost filled the access door to Col. Belinda Hettrick's regimental command van. He looked somewhat disheveled and held his battered broad-brimmed cloth hat in his hand. He was accompanied by 1st Lt. Nelson A. Crile, the chaplain of the Washington Greys.

"Colonel," the chaplain said in deferential tones, "if you have a moment, I'd like you to meet someone who may be able to help us as a guide . . ."

Hettrick was engrossed in a study of the terrain features portrayed on a map labelled "Namibia and Walvis Bay" that also carried the starred shield and severed eagle head of the CIA. Alongside were various satellite images. She was trying to make sense of the discrepancies between the two sources, assisted by Maj. Ed Canby, Regimental Sgt. Tom Jesup, and Lt. John Gibbon of S-2. They weren't getting anywhere. Father Crile's announcement immediately buoyed Hettrick's spirits as she straightened up. "Come in, come in, please, Father!"

"Colonel, may I present Doctor Paul von Waldersee?" the chaplain introduced the big man. "Doctor, this is the regimental commander, Colonel Belinda Hettrick."

The big man seemed to be momentarily taken aback for some reason, but reached out to shake Hettrick's hand and reply in a deep, well-modulated voice just slightly tinged with a South African accent, "Colonel, a pleasure to meet you." He didn't sound totally sincere.

"Sit down, please, Doctor von Waldersee," Hettrick told

him after she'd introduced Canby, Jesup, and Gibbon. She addressed her chaplain, "Father, where did you meet Doctor von Waldersee and what prompted you to bring him here?" The easiest way to get up to speed, Hettrick knew, was to get the chaplain to explain the situation to date.

"After your briefing earlier this afternoon, I made a social call on the local minister of the Evangelist church here. I'm Lutheran, you know, but I felt it would be diplomatic to call upon the leading cleric of the town. Besides, the church is a historic landmark and . . ." Crile started to explain, then brought himself up short and indicated Dr. von Waldersee. "When I mentioned our need for a local guide, Father Kruger called Doctor von Waldersee. The doctor is with the anthropology department of the University of Windhoek and summers in Swakopmund. After a preliminary discussion with Doctor von Waldersee, it became evident that he might be interested in the task because of his familiarity with the region between here and Otjomuise."

As Lieutenant Crile gave this background, Gibbon was quickly and silently entering data into a nearby terminal keypad. The intelligence officer was querying the world database via satellite to Georgie, the Iron Fist's computer at Diamond Point, who was on line to the master databank computer in Geneva. Doctor Paul Marais von Waldersee's biographical data from Who's Who and the world university database began scrolling on the screen almost at once. Gibbon dutifully downloaded the data stream into the regimental computer's RAM. And he watched it as it scrolled. Hettrick glanced at the scrolling data from time to time, artfully and discreetly dividing her attention between von Waldersee and the display.

"Doctor, I see that you're a professor of anthropology in Otjomuise," Hettrick remarked to the big man.

"At the University of Windhoek, which the Chancellor and the Trustees have refused to rename in spite of governmental pressures," von Waldersee added. "I suspect you've pulled up my *curriculum vitae* on your computer there. May I add anything to what it's already told you?"

"We have indeed retrieved your bio, Doctor," Hettrick admitted. "To be honest with you, we like to know with whom we're dealing, especially in a semi-combat situation in a country that's shown itself to be somewhat hostile to outsiders in the past few days . . ."

"Oh, Namibia has been turning more and more xenophobic since the Colour War," von Waldersee observed pendantically. "Actually, the roots of the trouble can be traced back to the attempted genocide of the Herero tribes by the German empire. It failed, of course. But the basic distrust of foreigners initiated by the early colonial problems has never abated. The Bastaard outbreak did not surprise me at all. Racial tensions have been growing constantly. Actually, there has never been a time in the past five centuries when there weren't racial tensions here . . . and my time estimate is quite likely to be somewhat conservative. Population pressures have caused the tribes from central Africa to migrate southward for centuries, putting a great deal of stress on indigenous inhabitants . . ."

The anthropologist was obviously a university professor, Hettrick decided. He'd slipped into his academic mode almost at once on the slightest of provocations. Hettrick guessed that he would and could talk steadily for fifty minutes—the length of a usual lecture period—so she brought the lecture to a halt by interrupting, "Do you know the terrain and roads between here and Otjomuise well enough to be able to serve as a guide for me?"

"Of course, dear lady! I've been through both the Swakop and Kuiseb river valleys many times. I'm not one of those indoor anthropologists who simply interprets the work of others and then churns out endless papers replete with pages of references from whence he's taken all his information! I go into the field! How do you think I got into the Explorers Club?"

"Do you speak the local language?" Hettrick interrupted him again. She could see from his bio that he was who he claimed to be.

Von Waldersee sighed. "There are over a hundred different tribal languages and dialects spoken in this part of Africa. I can understand all of them and speak most of them, including the 'click' language of the Khoisans." He stopped momentarily and gave an impromptu demonstration, saying something in a tongue that was full of clicks and glottals. "Afrikaans is, of course, almost a second language to me, although one rarely hears it in Windhoek since the Colour War. Strangely enough, in spite of the hatred of the German colonizers, you will hear a great deal of German spoken in Windhoek. Of course, proper British English is by far the most common language that is either used or understood by nearly everyone in the capital . . ."

The man had a tendency to lecture and speak down to his listeners, and Hettrick knew this probably was his German heritage. But she was curious about something he'd said, so she asked, "Doctor, I've noticed you continue to refer to the capital city as Windhoek rather than Otjomuise. May I ask why?"

"It's real name is not the quasi-native 'Otjomuise' given to it since the Colour War led to independence," von Waldersee explained with a touch of bitterness in his voice. "It was *never* a native town or village. It was founded by the Germans as the colonial capital, 'Windhuk.' The Afrikaaner spelling is a quite acceptable alternative because the pronunciation is the same. I have never approved of the pretentiousness that made the government rename the city. It's rather a similar situation that you might experience if an Amerindian name were applied to your capital city of Washington."

Hettrick didn't argue with him, but the conversation told her that the man was somewhat of a bigot. She expected that sort of thing from any white intellectual in the southeren part of this continent. She also began to see the glimmerings of the answer to one of her major questions about the man and his motives, so she cut right to it by asking him, "Doctor von Waldersee, you hold a reasonably high tenured faculty position at the university in Windhoek—and I must agree with you that it's easier to say than the tongue-twisting 'Otjomuise.' If you guide foreign troops—and that's what we are—into the seat of your country's government, aren't you likely to find yourself *persona non grata* or worse after we evacuate the diplomatic compound and leave the country?"

"Possibly," the academician replied without hesitation. "But I do not like our current powerless government-in-name-only . . . and they know this. I cannot respect any government that will not maintain law and order even in its own capital city to protect not only foreigners, whites, and coloureds who are legitimate citizens but also the diplomatic delegations of other nations. I am inalterably opposed to the growing xenophobia I see in this country. It can lead only to a blood bath—which appears to have started—or to occupation by foreign troops for a decade or more until a proper educational system can bring the ignorant tribesmen and blacks up to the point where they can make a democracy work. You see, it takes a tremendously high level of education to make a democracy work . . ."

Hettrick interrupted the start of another lecture. "Which would you rather see? Blood bath or occupation?"

"The latter, dear lady. We've seen enough killing here."

Hettrick nodded. "So you expect that the current rescue mission forces will stay in Namibia?"

"If not you, then someone, perhaps even the South Africans again. But I would rather not see a return to South African dominance over this country. We deserve the chance to try to make it on our own. After all, Namibia has some of the world's richest deposits of uranium, copper, diamonds, and petroleum—"

"Petroleum?" John Gibbon, the intelligence officer, broke in upon hearing that. "Our database says nothing about petroleum reserves—"

"I wouldn't expect that it did," von Waldersee countered. "Texarco and Shellexxo have done some recent prospecting in the northeastern part of the country and have made some major finds. The present government has done its best to keep the news of this discovery very quiet while they try to work out how they will control and tax it. It is my understanding that negotiations are in progress with the multinational petroleum companies . . . quite discretely, I understand, because of the possible reaction of the other oil producing nations—"

"Interesting," Hettrick broke in, then added, "but hardly germaine to our immediate situation, Doctor, although it's quite apparent that you are indeed a virtual walking encyclopedia."

Hettrick wasn't precisely sure of this man. Perhaps it was his manner toward her—somewhat haughty, very elitist, and definitely chauvinistic. She decided that had been the reason for his sudden start when he first saw her; he wasn't quite willing to accept a woman in command of a regiment. And she was worried, too, about his real motives. Did he really believe that his academic position would protect him from the Namibian government once the Operation Diamond Skeleton troops left the country? Or did he have powerful friends in the detested government? Was he really in the pay of the South Africans, a definite possibility knowing as she did the powerful desire of the RSA to occupy what they'd considered to be part of their country since 1915?

But she had to make the decision. She needed a guide. The charts didn't agree with the satellite images. The regiment could very well become lost in the rugged hills between Swakopmund and Otjomuise without a guide, even with their inertial positioning systems.

It's quite possible with inertial systems to know where you are and where your destination is, but getting from Point A to Point B on the ground isn't as easy as it is in the air where a pilot can simply point an aerodyne along the proper compass heading of a great circular route. The terrain they'd have to traverse if they couldn't take the main highway—and Hettrick didn't want to bet the farm on being able to do that; she wanted to have an alternate, a Plan B—was some of the most rugged on earth. It wouldn't be possible to go from Point A to Point B directly. One had to know the lay of the land, the best route free of gullies, canyons, cliffs, mountains, and other impassible terrain elements.

"I'd like to retain your services as a guide for the regiment," Hettrick suddenly told him, making up her mind. "What do you want?"

"Nothing," Dr. von Waldersee simply said.

This surprised Hettrick. "Nothing? I'm not so sure I want to obtain your services for nothing. Something that costs nothing may be worth just that—"

"Not in my case," von Waldersee said bluntly. "I am only interested in my anthropological studies of the Khoisan tribes, the original inhabitants of this part of Africa, the people you might call Hottentots or Bushmen. I don't need your money; I'm well-off, thank you. I have no family to worry about; never married, you see. I have a secure and tenured position at the University, and the government isn't likely to want to upset the Chancellor and the Trustees who are power symbols of their own over the student body, quite contrary to university situations elsewhere. As a matter of fact, I don't anticipate any negative reaction whatsoever from the government. It would have fallen anyway if this military operation had not been mounted to rescue those the government was powerless to protect. What you are doing will serve only to strengthen the existing government. Once you get to Windhoek, they'll welcome you with open arms, believe me . . ."

It was apparent to Hettrick that von Waldersee either didn't know about the abortive French assault that morning, or that he did know and knew other things that Hettrick didn't.

She wasn't totally satisfied. She wasn't sure she liked this big, rumpled man. But he had information she knew she was going to need.

Hettrick looked at her intelligence officer who'd been engaged in a routine analysis of the man's speech patterns by means of the computer, searching for patterns and inflections that would indicate stress levels which, in turn, might indicate untruths in what he'd said. Gibbon had also been checking CIA, DIA, British Code M, and French *Securite Militaire* databases, looking for any information on Dr. Paul von Waldersee. Gibbon had a pretty good video image of the man sitting there in the command van, and had transmitted this via slow-scan to make a match-up with existing photo images of the man in the databases. He'd also scanned the files of the London *Times,* the New York *Times, Die Burger, Le Monde, Pravada,* and *Beeld.* The computer found nothing negative about the man. He'd carried Explorers Club Flags Number 17 and Number 34 on two expeditions into the northwestern region of Namibia and had presented numerous scientific papers at anthropological meetings in Europe and America. Von Waldersee was no scientific heavyweight, but he seemed to be for real.

Gibbon knew what his colonel's look meant in the way of a question. He simply said, "Nothing negative, Colonel."

Hettrick looked around the van. Neither Canby nor Sergeant Major Jesup gave any indication of a down-check. Neither had said anything; both had concentrated on evaluating the anthropologist.

"If you want the job, you've got it, Doctor," Hettrick told him. "And you will be paid. Captain Wilkinson will see to that after we reach Windhoek."

"Sounds like it might be interesting," was von Waldersee's reply.

Hettrick put out her hand. After a moment's hesitation, von Waldersee took it and they shook hands.

"No written contract?" von Waldersee asked. "You Americans always seem to be infatuated by written documentation and agreements."

Hettrick just looked at him. "Doctor, a contract is only as good as the character of the people who sign it. When I shook hands with you, I gave you my word of honor as an officer of the United States Army. In our social group, that's the ultimate seal on any agreement. And I assume that your handshake was in the same vein."

"It was, Colonel."

"Good! Father," she said to the regimental chaplain, "thanks for finding Doctor von Waldersee. Would you take him back to his quarters, see to it that he gets his kit packed for the trek, and bring him back here? Doctor, I'd like to have you with the regiment as quickly as possible so that we all become better acquainted." Actually, she didn't want to take the chance that he might simply telephone Colonel van Wijk and report. "Does this cause you any difficulty?"

"Not at all, Colonel. It will take me about an hour to close up my summer house here, and I always keep a kit ready for the field. One never knows when one might get the chance to get out and do something new."

CHAPTER NINETEEN

"Dammit, Sergeant, I *ordered* you to wake me in two hours!" Curt was furious. Under the relaxing influence of the biofeedback unit given to him by Sgt. Shelley Hale, he'd slept through dinner. It was now nearly 10:00 P.M. local time. "Do you want me to put you on report for insubordination and failing to follow orders?"

"Captain, I was told by Doctor Gydesen to allow you to sleep and relax," the no-nonsense biotech NCO responded calmly but respectfully.

"But *my* orders were to wake me!"

"Yes, sir, but your orders were overruled by Major Gydesen, and she checked with Colonel Hettrick before she told me," Hale reminded him. The commanding officer of the regimental biotech unit, a medical doctor, had both the right and the duty to override even the orders of the regimental commander when it came to the health and fitness of personnel. Doctor Ruth Gydesen had apparently sought higher approval of her order to allow a company commander to get some additional rest, and this told Curt that his anger at Shelley Hale was misplaced. Gydesen was also apparently feeling out the limits of her authority because the biotech unit had been expanded and its mission changed as a result of the conversion of the regiment to a Sierra Charlie outfit; prior to this time, it had been primarily concerned with the psychological problems that occurred with soldiers in remote linkage with warbots and the physical problems associated with them; now, as a result of the Trinidad experience, it was a small regimental field hospital specializing in combat trauma medicine.

Sergeant Hale therefore wasn't cowed by Curt's outburst; she'd expected it. She put her fingers against the aorta on the side of his neck to check for pulse. "From a medical point of view, you look and act refreshed now, Captain. Feel better?"

"I feel pretty good," Curt had to admit. The crushing burden of fatigue that had pressed down upon him like a heavy yoke was gone, but his concern for his company remained. Hale had been right, but he felt he should warn her that an understanding beyond the scope of the new medical field manual had to be developed between a company commander and his biotech. "You shouldn't have allowed me to oversleep, Sergeant. I had things that *had* to be taken care of with Carson's Companions."

"Captain," she pointed out to him, "your second in command, Lieutenant Morgan, and your outstanding first sergeant have everything in order. You've got very good people in Carson's Companions, Captain. They do what they're supposed to do when they're supposed to do it . . . and they do things they see need doing and know you'll call it to their attention if they don't. You've got an outstanding unit. I'm proud to be your biotech, and I'll take my cue on how to interface with you from the way your company personnel behave. We'll get along, don't worry."

Curt realized he was up against a formidable young woman who, in spite of being small, cute, and dimply, had an iron will of her own, knew her profession, and also knew what she could and could not do under the regs. In a way, he was pleased to have her in Carson's Companions. He already felt that he could count on her to do her job under pressure because she hadn't caved in to the mild pressure he'd just tried to exert. He also realized then that part of his behavior had been stress-induced and he hadn't recognized it.

So he broke off the engagement and began to fumble around the interior of the ACV in search of his helmet, *ovia* rifle, and accessory harness with its extra ammo clips, grenades, standby tacomm set, and other personal equipment for field combat. "Where's Sergeant Kester?" he wanted to know.

"Up here, Captain!" Kester's voice came down through the turret hatch.

Curt strapped on his harness, fitted the helmet to his head, picked up his rifle, and stuck his head up through the turret hatch.

M. Sgt. Henry Kester was sitting in a relaxed position atop the ACV in the cool night breeze, his back resting on the immobile barrel of the ACV's 15mm gun. Clipped to his helmet was a high-resolution infra red night vision sensor through which he was slowly scanning the eastern horizon.

"Our biotech let me sleep in," Curt muttered.

"Yes sir, I know. Came up here because you were making a lot of noise, sir."

"Noise?"

"Captain, you snore when you've got the biofeedback unit activated."

"The hell I do!"

Kester shrugged and continued to scan to the east.

"So report! What's the situation, Sergeant?"

"Everything copasetic, Captain. The company is deployed for guard duty as it was earlier today. All posts are manned and quiet," M. Sgt. Henry Kester reported formally.

"Any unusual activity showing around Walvis Bay?" Curt wanted to know.

Kester replied easily, "Seen a couple of trains. Bunch of trucks on the highway which Sergeant Gerard reported to be normal commercial traffic. 'Course, I can see only about three klicks with these because of the vegetation over there. But if anything big in the way of a military-type vehicle was moving where there wasn't a road, I'd see it. And the computer can recognize the thermal signature of any South African military vehicle if I did happen to pick up anything. Or if it saw something I missed because of its faster scan . . ."

"Is the company ready to move out if necessary?" Cur asked.

"Yes, sir! When we get the word, we crank up and get these suckers moving right quick now. Everyone knows which vehicle to head for when the move-out sounds," Kester told him. "Lieutenant Morgan established the drill after supper and we went through a dry run while you was sleeping."

"Dammit! I should have been in on that!"

"Captain, we've got it worked out just fine. Don't worry about what to do; you just jump any vehicle moving by, no matter where you are," Henry Kester instructed him. "I'll have an ATV bring you here within minutes. Everybody else knows exactly what to do. Lieutenant Morgan got it all worked out, sir. Don't sweat it."

"Where is Lieutenant Morgan?"

"With her platoon between the bridge and the lighthouse," the master sergeant told him, pointing westward to where the flash of the Swakopmund lighthouse beam cut through the darkness at regular intervals, followed by its flashing Morse code identification signal.

Curt flipped the night vision goggles down over his eyes. "I'm going to wander down that way. I'll be monitoring tac freak if you need me."

"Yes, sir. Careful, sir. Understand there's a lot of snakes out there at night. Want to take an ATV?"

"No, it isn't that far, and I probably need the exercise. I'll keep my goggles on, Sergeant," Curt promised as he dropped to the ground.

Kester went back inside the ACV to inform the computers and warbots that Curt was out there. The company commander's ident beacon flashed its IFF code on the tactical display. Satisfied, Kester went topside and resumed his infra red scanning. It wasn't that the old soldier didn't trust the computers; he wanted to make sure for himself and he wanted to keep from becoming bored.

Curt thought that perhaps he should have taken Kester up on the suggestion to take one of the small ATVs; it ould have been quicker. But after his forced rest, he felt stiff and a little achy in the joints. A brisk walk in combat gear would work that out of him.

When he stepped over the railway tracks at the northern end of the bridge, however, he was challenged not by a warbot but by squad leader Sgt. Charlie Koslowski serving his turn on watch at the bridgehead. "Halt and be recognized! Password?"

"Password my ass! Kester didn't tell me!" Curt growled.

"Pass, friend . . . sir," Koslowski replied.

"Sergeant, that was a stupid damned thing to do. I didn't have the password. You should make me come forward to be recognized. I could have been anyone."

"No, sir, you aren't just anyone. I know your voice," Koslowski told him, his outline appearing on Curt's infra red goggles. "And, besides, the company computer's tac display on my helmet visor told me you were there and your IFF code told me who you were."

All of the new Sierra Charlie computer programming was taking some getting used to. Curt often felt—and this incident reinforced his gut feeling—that the Washington Greys had once again been thrown into action before they were ready for it. But few military outfits are ever fully ready for the job they're assigned to do. Curt was relearning the fact that being a soldier involved mostly on-the-job training. Where's the lieutenant? I don't see her beacom code on my helmet display."

"Should be down by her ACV, Captain.

Something might be wrong, Curt decided. She should have her beacon on at night if she was outside her ACV. So Curt muttered. "Carry on, Sergeant."

"Yes, sir. Have a good evening, sir."

Curt knew where the Alpha Platoon ACV was parked because of his afternoon inspection. He headed in that direction. It wasn't long before he picked up its looming bulk on his infra red goggles. The vehicle was still warm from the constant sunlight of the cloudless day and was therefore hotter than the background; it showed up plainly in his i-r goggles. He could also see someone sitting atop the vehicle much as Henry Kester had been.

"Hello, Companion Alpha Leader," Curt said into his tacomm unit, not wanting to surprise whomever was atop the turret. "This is Companion Leader approaching."

"Password, sir?" It was Sgt. Jim Elliott's unmistakeable hillbilly drawl.

"Sergeant Kester didn't bother to give it to me. Call him on tacomm and confirm my presence here as well as my beacon code."

"Yessir. I already knowed it was you, Captain. Computers said so."

"Computers can be wrong, Sergeant."

"Only when somebody don't program them right . . . and these have been done right. I saw to that myself." In spite of his rustic and rural demeanor, Jim Elliott was at home with computers and had turned out to be an outstanding programmer . . . although there wasn't much programming for him to do in a user situation such as a combat company. But Curt knew Elliott had checked every program in the Alpha Platoon ACV computer, looking for bugs; he hadn't found any . . . yet.

"Where's Lieutenant Morgan?" Curt asked. "Her beacon doesn't show on the display."

"Wait one, sir. Lemme get a last-known position out of the computer." Elliott dropped down into the ACV and popped back out again after less than ten seconds. "Try ninety meters on a heading of zero-niner-zero, Captain . . . and mind the terrain; there's a bluff out there that drops off to the crik bed . . ."

"Thank you, Sergeant. Carry on."

Curt began moving in the direction indicated, scanning carefully with his i-r goggles as he went. He finally "saw" by infra red the heat radiation of what appeared to be two humans up ahead on the lip of the bluff.

As he grew closer, he lifted the goggles from his eyes and secured them atop his helmet visor. He got an immediate visual identification.

"Lieutenant Morgan, what the hell are you doing out here on a guard position without your helmet?" Curt ɔked her.

Alexis Morgan got to her feet, leaving Len Spencer sitting there. She immediately turned to Curt and replied, "Sorry, Captain. Things were so quiet and the breeze so nice that I took it off. I shouldn't have." She lifted it in her hands and placed it on her head.

"All right," Curt continued to remonstrate her, "let me now rephrase my question: What the hell are you doing out here on a guard post? And with a non-combatant to boot?"

"We were talking, Captain." It was Len Spencer who replied as he got to his feet.

"Oh?" There were many questions implied in the one word Curt used and the way he said it. He didn't like the idea of his lieutenant, his best officer, sitting out on the edge of a bluff, possibly in the line of fire, with a handsome male newsperson. Primarily, he didn't like the last part but he wasn't willing to admit it right then.

"Swapping war stories," Spencer added.

"Len has had some fascinating experiences," Alexis Morgan added.

"I imagine he has," Curt said. "Lots of experiences in lots of places with lots of different people, men and women alike. Most newspeople do. Where's your rifle, Lieutenant?"

"In the ACV a few meters to the rear, Captain."

"Lieutenant, you're still in command of Alpha Platoon, and Alpha Platoon is on guard duty in a potentially dangerous situation where you could get shot at," Curt started to chew her out.

"Captain," she retorted immediately, "we've been on station for more than fourteen hours, and the only excitement we've had has been a social call from the South Africans who behaved like civilized people. Our scanners and sensors are constantly probing across the Swakop, and we've seen absolutely zero, zilch, zip activity of any kind within our sensor range. You know and I know that the Washington Greys were put into Swakopmund on a make-work guard detail so the Air Force—and the Navy, when they get here—could be used by the Brits and the French to pull off the big show up in Otjomuise. This whole operation thus far has been a hurry-up-and-wait show followed by letting us sit around on our asses . . ."

She was dead wrong, and Curt knew he had to set her right. But how to do it in the presence of this newshawk was something he didn't know how to do without the possibility of the confrontation between a company commander and his junior officer being blown all out of proportion in something Spencer wrote and sent back.

"Lieutenant, we have orders," he reminded her sternly. "If we have to sit on our asses in Swakopmund for six months—which I doubt will be the case—that's what we will do and we will do it well. Return to your command."

"Yes, sir." Alexis had expected more chewing out than she'd gotten. She suspected that Curt would reprimand her more severely when Spencer wasn't around.

"As for you, Mister Spencer, I'd like you to return with me to the company command post. You can cover this boredom just as well from there," Curt went on to tell the newshawk.

"Captain, I'd prefer to be in the front line where the shooting will be . . . if it starts. Besides, you have some fascinating people in your outfit that I'd like to talk with."

"I'm not so sure you want to be in the open if the shooting ever starts, Spencer. This isn't warbot combat where people can't be hurt or killed," Curt reminded him. "And as for fascinating people, I concur with you, but—"

A burst of 9mm submachinegun fire shattered the night silence.

CHAPTER TWENTY

Sparks flew from a nearby M60 Mary Anne as the rounds were deflected by the warbot's passive layered-sandwich armor.

Curt and Alexis immediately dropped to the ground in an action that was almost a reflex. But Alexis had to reach up and pull Len Spencer down with her because he'd reacted as a civilian might; he'd whirled around, trying to locate the source of the fire, and was standing there motionless, frozen by surprise.

"Companion Command, this is Companion Leader," Curt said as he toggled his helmet tacomm. Actually, he didn't have to say it; the neuroelectrodes in the helmet picked up his thought and transmitted what he wanted to say.

The M60 that had been hit swivelled its 25 mm gun around in the direction from which the submachinegun fire had come. It had *not* come from the direction of the Swakop River but from *behind* the guard line of Carson's Companions and from a direction somewhere between the line of Swakopmund houses and the lighthouse that marked the northern cape of the Swakop delta.

"Companion Alpha Leader, may I have permission to commence firing?" the warbot asked in both verbal English and in Curt's tacomm receiver.

More 9 mm rounds bounced off the Mary Anne's armor.

"This is Companion Alpha Leader! Commence firing!" Alexis yelled.

The responding fire from the Mary Anne was shattering

in its sound, but there was no flash from it's well-shroude muzzle.

Whomever was out there had heard Alexis shout and fired in that general direction. Submachinegun fire went overhead.

Curt flipped his infra red goggles down over his eyes and looked in the direction the Mary Anne was shooting. His helmet visor display showed the azimuth and range of the unknown attackers on its display plot.

"Companion Leader, this is Companion Command," Kester's voice came back. "We see you under fire."

Another submachinegun gave vent to a burping burst of bullets. Curt could see both the muzzle flash and the heat radiation from the weapon. It had come from a different place than the first several bursts.

The world was suddenly full of gunfire. Several automatic weapons opened up on the Companions from the northwest.

"Is Bravo Platoon under attack?" Curt asked.

He got his first i-r target on his goggles screen, a human form dashing in a crouched position in front of the houses that lined the riverbank bluff.

"Negative!" came Kester's reply. "Do you want Bravo to lay in Hairy Fox fire on the location of the firing?"

That wouldn't work. Locals were sleeping in those homes, and Curt was not willing at this time to assume that they were the ones who were attacking. If anything, he thought, the attackers might be South Africans who'd managed to sweep around their western flank in small boats out to sea or a unit that Colonel van Wijk had sequestered somewhere around Swakopmund. Unless he uncovered data to the contrary, he was going to assume that the Swakopmund Feldgendarmerie and the townspeople weren't the ones assaulting them. So he didn't want to subject them to fire at this time.

"Negative! Too close to the houses," Curt responded. "I want all personnel and warbots to open fire only when their sensors have zeroed a target. No firing at will or at large. How much of our rear is under attack?"

When the attackers saw that their submachinegun fire was having little effect on the armored Mary Annes, the firing subsided slightly. But bursts continued to snap over the heads of Curt, Alexis, and Len Spencer as they lay there in the short, dry grass.

"Seven hundred meters of the west end of Alpha Platoon from the lighthouse eastward," Kester's voice reported.

A spate of bullets hit the ground about five meters in front of them, kicking up dust, sand, and chunks of grass. Curt's i-r cut through it. He thought he identified a fleeting target. "Roger! Keep the existing units covering the bridges. I want only our jeeps and our Mary Annes involved here right now. Flank the attackers if possible. If Ward's Warriors can spare the people and warbots, send them in on the east flank of these goons."

Curt had his *Novia* resting in front of him on the ground now. Its own i-r scope was activated and ready. With its muzzle resting against a small rock, Curt waited until he could see the target again.

"I'm going to my ACV!" Alexis snapped.

"The hell you are! You're staying right here until we get this situation scoped-out and under control!" Curt told her firmly. "Bad enough you came out here without your *Novia.*"

"Got my helmet i-r on and scanning."

"Good. Identify targets. Nail down azimuth and range of anyone firing, then feed the data to Kester," Curt told her unnecessarily. She would know to do that anyway, but Curt wasn't sure how she was reacting to being under fire at night. This was something new to all of them. He wanted to make sure she did what she was supposed to.

A murky, fleeting image appeared on Curt's goggles. With a quick nod of his head, he flipped them up to his forehead and shifted his attention to his rifle's sensor. The form was still there. The rifle's laser range finder got the range data and set the sights. Curt centered the dimly illuminated crosshairs on the computer-generated target marker and pulled the trigger. The three-round burst came so fast that it sounded almost like a single report.

But, unlike the submachineguns of the adversary, Curt's *Novia* was far more accurate and long-ranging.

"Got him!" Curt growled and began looking for another target.

The Mary Annes of Alpha Platoon were now under Morgan's command through her helmet tacomm to her ACV. They weren't wasting their ammo now. One to three shots at a time came from the ones to the right and left of them. They were in sharpshooting mode, but their 25 mm rounds were almost too big for antipersonnel work.

"My Mary Annes have hit three," Alexis reported.

Curt saw another target, his rifle ranged it, and he dropped it with a single shot this time.

As with most nighttime fire fights, this one had lasted less than half a minute thus far. Thanks to the light firearms of their attackers, all of Alpha Platoon's warbots were operational, and Curt had gotten no reports of wounded personnel. Whomever was attacking them had already had their assault blunted by the rapid response of the warbots and the accompanying return fire of Alpha Platoon's personnel . . . except Lieutenant Morgan who was under fire without her rifle.

Curt thought he knew what would come next. "Stand by for a mass night assault," he warned on the tacomm.

Almost as he said it, a dozen human forms appeared on the infra red sensors, their hot submachineguns standing out starkly. A chorus of yells split the night as the attackers gave vent to warbling, fluttering battle cries . . . and attacked *en masse*.

It was all over in less than five seconds. The sheet of precise, laser-targeted 7.56 mm fire from *Novia* rifles and jeep machineguns, plus the pinpoint targeting of the 25 mm cannon on the Mary Annes simply mowed down the attackers.

"Cease firing!" Curt ordered over the tacomm when it became abundantly obvious that no further targets were left standing out there.

Silence fell.

There wasn't even a cry of pain from the battlefield.

A few lights came on in the houses to the north.

"Okay, Morgan, now you can go back to your ACV," Curt told her. "While you're there, get your rifle."

"Yes, sir," Alexis Morgan replied without further comment, got to her feet, and began moving quickly in the direction of her ACV.

Curt stood up and looked at Spencer. "It's all over now, Spencer. You can get up. You okay?"

"Yeah. Scared, but okay."

Curt ignored him and toggled his tacomm. "Henry, we can use some biotech help here. None of us seem to be hit, but I don't know if any of the attackers are still alive. If we've wounded any of them, they'll need medic assistance."

"Sergeant Hale's coming," the first sergeant reported. "I've asked for biotech help from the Warriors. And Colonel Hettrick's on her way."

"I expected that." He kept his *Novia* at the ready and put his infra red goggles down again as he started forward. "Pass the word for the Warriors to resume their guard posts; we seem to have the situation under control here now . . ."

"Roger, Captain. Will do."

Everyone in the Companions had their identification beacons turned on now, Curt saw on his helmet visor display. "Companions all, this is Companion Leader," he said into his tacomm, "Bravo Platoon, hold your positions and stay on guard; this could be a feint to draw you away from your guard posts. Alpha Platoon, we'll take care of what mopping-up needs to be done. Use your flashlights only when you're sure you won't draw fire; stay on passive infra red. Don't assume that any of these bastards are dead when you first come up on them. If they're only wounded, take them prisoner. If they try to attack you, blow their ass off. Let's see if we can't find out where this suicide outfit came from . . ."

Curt stumbled over something slippery and wet. When he flipped up his i-r goggles and flicked on his flashlight, he turned it off again just as quickly. Whatever or whomever it had been, there was very little left; the person had apparently taken one of the 25 mm rounds from a Mary Anne. Curt couldn't even locate the person's weapon.

The next body he came upon didn't have much of a chest left. He remembered that this body was located at about the azimuth and range of a target he'd given a three-round burst. This time, Curt could identify the dead man as a black African wearing Soviet-style cammies, no shoes or boots, and various designs of face-mutilating tattoos. A Chinese K-97 9mm submachinegun lay beside him. Curt squatted down beside the body and began to search for any form of identification, papers in pockets, or other indication of where the man had come from. There was nothing.

Within ten minutes, Alpha Platoon had located the bodies or remains of twelve African blacks dressed in Soviet-style cammies, all barefoot, and all with similar facial tattoos. All were carrying Chinese submachineguns.

Colonel Belinda Hettrick showed up in her ATV with Dr. von Waldersee and Major Canby.

"Came at us from the rear, Colonel," Curt reported, saluting as she disembarked from the ATV. "Either they were a suicide squad or just plain stupid. They were dumb enough to open fire on one of Morgan's Mary Annes who alerted us and returned their fire under Lieutenant Morgan's orders. We suffered no casualties or warbot damage, although some of our Mary Annes took nine-millimeter rounds in their armor. We've found no survivors of the attack, and I've been unable to identify them."

Hettrick looked down with distaste at the body on the ground. "Doctor, can you identify them from those facial tattoos?"

Von Waldersee knelt down alongside the dead man and examined the facial tattoos with his flashlight. "Himbas," he finally announced, "a small tribe of the Kaokovelders. They live up on the steppes of northwestern Namibia next to the Angolan border . . ."

"That's a long way from here, isn't it?" Hettrick observed.

Von Waldersee nodded. "More than five hundred kilometers."

"Which means they were in this area," Hettrick concluded. "No one can travel five hundred kilometers in less than twenty-four hours—"

"Unless someone flew them in," Curt pointed out.

"Who? The South Africans? Why would they bring in a dozen tribesmen armed with Soviet and Chinese weapons just for a raid?" Hettrick asked aloud.

"I presume, Colonel, that the rest of the regiment is on Zulu Alert now?" Curt asked rhetorically in a way that was intended to remind the regimental commander that there might be more Himbas and their ilk ranging around Swakopmund that night.

"Yes," Maj. Ed Canby replied curtly for the colonel in a tone indicating that he'd taken care of the matter. The deployment of the regiment with the combat companies ranged on picket duty along the Swakop River hadn't been changed, but Canby had relocated both the headquarters and service companies, normally considered to be support units, from their bivouack on the old drill field to a picket line ranged around the north side of Swakopmund. Regimental policy dictated that when necessary the whole outfit could become a combat team and everybody was expected to fight—the commanding officer, the staff, and even the supply personel, everyone except the chaplain and the people in the biotech unit who wore the tabard with the red cross on it.

"Colonel van Wijk may be a convenient scapegoat," von Waldersee interjected. "These guerrillas were dressed in Soviet clothing and carried Chinese weapons. And I rather doubt that the South Africans are on such good terms with the blacks in Namibia that they could get any of them to do this sort of thing. Certain death, and all that, you know. I suspect they may be nothing more than one of the typical hit-and-run terrorist groups sent into Namibia quite often by Angola. And I'd suggest that your biotechnicians get some blood samples and check for drugs; that's a time-proven method of motivating native suicide forces in these parts . . ."

"Strange as hell . . ." Hettrick started to say. Then she straightened. "Another possible motivation for this attack might be to gain the sympathy of the local blacks. Major, have Captain Hampton call on the mayor and Ritter Hoffman; I want them down here to see what happened and to be able to explain this to their citizens. I don't want to get blamed for shooting up part of the town. If we have to go through the diplomatic hoops the way we did this morning with the unfortunate Fedgendarm, we'll do it. *Noblesse oblige* and all that. Costs us little or nothing, but may be worth a great deal. I don't want the blacks here to start something like the Bastards did in Windhoek . . . and they did it there with a whole hell of a lot less provocation."

"Yes, Colonel." The regimental second in command stepped back and lifted a portable tacomm unit to his face, a larger transceiver that operated on the encrypted regimental command net. He began to give quiet orders into it.

"This is the first person-to-person night assault we've encountered. How did your company react and respond, Captain?" Hettrick asked Curt.

Without hesitation, Curt replied, "In an outstanding fashion, Colonel. There was no panic. Everyone took cover until the situation could be assessed and sources of enemy fire could be located. Shots were carefully targeted by both the troops and the warbots. I doubt that we'll find any bullet or shell impacts in those houses back there." Since the outcome of the fire fight hadn't been affected by the fact that Alexis Morgan had failed to adhere to combat doctrine by not having her firearm with her, he deliberately didn't mention it. He'd discuss the oversight with his senior lieutenant privately. He went on, "But I don't think any of us are really cool-headed at the moment. I suspect that some of my troops have rather itchy trigger fingers right now, so I'd hate to be any other Himba squad that tried to attack us tonight . . ."

"Good! Well done!" Hettrick told him, then added pensively, "I still don't like this. Too many unknowns. Too many unanswered questions. Why were they here? Why did they do this? What did they have to gain? Or who stood to gain from it? Who sent them? Who's behind it? And why?"

"Impossible to determine, Colonel, on the basis of the information we have," von Waldersee remarked.

"That doesn't mean I won't lose a lot of sleep over it tonight," she retorted. "Agreed, it could have been a fluke. An accidental encounter. But I doubt it. These things don't happen accidentally. I'll talk with Ritter Hoffman about whether or not there have been any Angolan raids this far south. But again I'll be talking to someone other than an ally, and one should always treat that kind of intelligence data with more than a modicum of suspicion. Dammit, I'm going to be paranoid as hell about this until I learn what's behind it!"

CHAPTER TWENTY-ONE

"I won't make excuses, Captain. I did a stupid thing," 1st Lt. Alexis Morgan admitted.

She was alone with Capt. Curt Carson inside her ACV. Although Len Spencer had objected, he'd returned to Curt's ACV.

"It's the stupid little mistakes that get people killed in combat, Lieutenant," Curt told her sternly.

That wasn't the real reason he was upset with her. She and Len Spencer had spent a lot of time together that day. He knew Alexis Morgan, and he felt she might become enamored of that suave, charismatic newshawk whose military writings were well known in the profession. Spencer had the grudging respect that the professional warrior gives to another professional who's in a different line of work but still seems to understand those who get shot at. It's important for a soldier to have friends in the news media, especially during peace time. Kipling had put it well in his *Tommy Atkins* poem. Others had commented also on the common disrespect given a soldier during peace time. Spencer, in his powerful position with the New York *Times*, had served to blunt many attacks on the military by pointing out that they were out there doing a job so well that it often seemed commonplace and certainly not newsworthy.

"Yes, sir, I know-stupid mistakes kill people; I've seen it happen," Alexis replied. She was a strong woman, however, and didn't respond meekly to her Captain's reprimand. She'd made a mistake, she'd admitted it, she wouldn't do it again, and she also knew full well what the reason behind it was. She'd found Len Spencer to be a fascinating man. It was obvious to her that Curt knew that.

"If I hadn't happened to find you and Spencer, you could have been killed in that skirmish," Curt reminded her.

"The possibility of getting killed always exists in combat, Captain," she reminded him. "However, if I may say a few words in my own defense, I was rather well covered by my Mary Annes and my jeep. I didn't lose command capabilities during the skirmish. I was in control of my unit."

"That you were," Curt conceded. He paused for a moment before he added, "But before the fire fight started, I'm not so sure you were in full control of yourself as a professional officer should have been under the circumstances."

"Ah! Now I believe we're getting to the heart of the matter, Captain!" Alexis exclaimed. "Yes, I find Len Spencer a fascinating man to be with and to talk with."

"I know that," Curt told her. "However, I expect you to conduct yourself in such a manner that whatever relationship you might have with him does not impair or affect your performance as an officer leading a platoon in *de facto* combat."

Quite stiffly and formally, Alexis stated, "In the absence of regulations concerning the conduct of military personnel in their relationships with non-military personnel, I shall do my best to behave in a manner befitting an officer of the United States Army. I am fully aware that Rule Ten does not apply to this particular situation, as we discovered in Trinidad. Therefore, I take my example from my company commander," she retorted.

This took Curt aback. He knew very well that Lieut. Jerry Allen's torrid love affair with Adonica Sweet during the Trinidad operation had been kept under control only by the expedient of having the pretty young guide brevetted to third lieutenant. On the other hand, Curt himself had found himself in a situation with the beautiful Zeenat Tej in which Rule Ten didn't apply and could not be shoehorned to fit the situation.

Now the shoe was on the other foot. And the shoehorn was unavailable.

With equally stiff formality, he replied, "Lieutenant, you may do anything you wish in off-duty time insofar as it does not conflict with your position and duties as an officer."

Alexis thought about this for a moment, then asked, "Request permission to speak candidly and frankly, sir."

"Permission denied!" Curt snapped.

"What?" She'd never known Curt to act this way.

"Permission to speak candidly and frankly denied, Lieutenant." he repeated, "because that still implies formal and official communication between us." He turned his head and addressed the computer terminal in the ACV. "Companion Central, this is Companion Leader through Companion Alpha."

"Go ahead," the computer voice answered him, having determined that someone with Curt's voiceprint was addressing it.

"Please log me temporarily off duty but available at this location," he instructed it. "Please also log First Lieutenant Alexis M. Morgan off duty on the same basis."

"Order complied with!"

He turned back to face her. "Now Rule Ten, official protocol, and regulations don't apply! Alexis, you're too damned important to me not only as a platoon leader and a member of my team, but personally as well."

"Well! I'm pleased to hear you say that, Curt," she replied with equal candor, "although there has never been any question about that sort of thing as I'm concerned."

"That's good because I know it sometimes seems that it goes without saying . . ."

She held up her hand. "Don't get me wrong! I don't take it for granted! Not in this man's Army! But I will tell you that I have a tendency to get damned upset when the rules aren't applied and enforced reciprocally. Maybe I should have raised a little hell of my own inimitable sort right from the start on Trinidad—"

"Look, what happened on Trinidad happened—"

"And what happened in Swakopmund happened . . . except it hasn't happened yet like it happened on Trinidad."

"Goddammit, Alexis, you went out on a moonlight trist with Len Spencer and you forgot your personal weapon and you damned near got killed!" Curt objected.

She shrugged. "Problematical. I was certainly covered by my warbots. Now let's stop talking around the subject like a couple of fourth class kay-dets, Curt! I got upset with you on Trinidad—"

"Well, I certainly made up for it later, didn't I?"

"True. You did. And no complaints. But now you're upset because I've paid attention to another man over whom you have no military authority," Alexis reminded him. "Right?"

"Damned right, but I told you why, and—"

"And you were just reacting in a way to cover up your own emotions in a way I couldn't in Trinidad. I could have gone all female and vengeful and spiteful on you after Rio Claro, couldn't I? And I didn't. Right?"

"In your own inimitable way, you—"

"And in your own inimitable way tonight, you took your own macho path to solving the problem," she told him bluntly. "Well, Curt, I don't like that. In particular, I don't like the way you did it. And are doing it."

"Little difference here," Curt tried to explain to her. "I happen to be your commanding officer and responsible—"

"Bullshit!" Alexis said softly, then smiled. "Dammit, Curt, you're *jealous!"*

Curt took a deep breath, let it slowly out, and then told her, "I do not intend to have this sort of semi-domestic squabble with you or any other female officer. I'll leave that for those happily married domesticated husbands on their nine-to-five jobs engaging in pillow talk about sex or money at night with their wives."

"I'm beginning to think in this outfit we're going to need armored pillows . . ."

"No. Not at all. No pillows of any type. There is *no place* for this sort of squabbling between two officers in a military outfit, and *I won't have it in my outfit!* You know what discipline entails, and I intend to maintain and enforce discipline in Carson's Companions!" Curt didn't raise his voice, but it was obvious that he was more than a little resolute on the subject.

The force of his voice almost overwhelmed her. She didn't reply when he paused.

"I have no authority to prevent Len Spencer from being with you," he went on. "Your behavior is initially a matter of your own discretion, your dedication to your profession, and your deportment as an officer of the United States Army. I won't interfere again unless I believe you've stepped beyond the bounds of honor and duty. Then I have the option of personally reprimanding you or forwarding an official report up the line. What I do will depend upon the circumstances. Understood?"

"Understood as always. Tell me, are we still officially off-duty?" Alexis wanted to know.

"We are."

"And have you finished?"

"I have."

There was pure, crystal ice water in her tone. "Then I respectfully request that I return to duty, Captain."

"Don't you have anything else you want to say?"

"Yes, Captain, I do," came her icy and very controlled reply, "but I shall refrain from saying it to you in the interests of the good of the outfit. You need not remind me that we're in a combat situation. You've already reminded me that discipline is paramount for the success and even the survival of the outfit under such conditions. I fully agree. So be it. You have my complete support and my total committment. May I be excused, sir? It's been a very long day."

This last came as very much of a surprise to Curt. He knew then that he'd pushed his lieutenant too far in spite of the fact that he was still somewhat angry and frustrated. The problem hadn't been solved. But they weren't going to get this settled tonight. They might not get it settled for days. Or weeks. But he knew they'd have to get it settled, perhaps under less stressful circumstances. It wasn't the best time or the place to have it out right then. They'd both been shot at and missed in the past several hours; adrenaline and other hormones were still coursing through them. Curt knew from experience that personal judgements were greatly warped under those conditions. And he suspected his own thinking wasn't very clear and logical right then, either.

In fact, the outcome of the conversation served to confirm that.

Good God, I hope I haven't blown this relationship for good! he thought savagely to himself. *What the hell kind of leader are you, Carson? You've been continually warned for years not to become too emotionally involved with your troops! Get your gonads disconnected from your brain and start functioning as an officer and a gentleman again!*

"No, Lieutenant, you're not the one to ask to be excused," he told her charitably. When she looked surprised in turn, he added, "This is your vehicle and your command post. Resume your duties." He addressed the voice-actuated terminal, "Companion Central, this is Companion Leader returning to duty with Lieutenant Morgan."

"Order complied with," the female voice of the company command computer replied in flat tones.

Curt got to his feet and picked up his rifle and helmet, placing the latter on his head. "Good evening, Lieutenant," he told Alexis Morgan. "Let's hope we don't have any other little fire fights tonight. I think we could both use the rest."

"Good evening, Captain," she replied in pleasant, formal tones. "Yes, I think we've had enough fighting for one evening. I envy you the nap you were able to get under biofeedback."

"You haven't gotten any sleep since we landed, have you?"

"No, Captain."

"I thought so. Get some sleep, Lieutenant. I'll be in my ACV and I'll keep an eye on Alpha Platoon for you until dawn."

"Captain, I—"

"That's a direct order, Lieutenant—"

"Yes, sir!"

"If my guess is right, we've got a long way to go tomorrow . . ."

"Yes, sir. We do have a long way to go. Good night, Captain . . ."

CHAPTER TWENTY-TWO

"Here's the operational plan for Trek," Colonel Belinda Hettrick announced. It was a post-breakfast briefing following a very quiet night in Swakopmund after the brief fire fight with the Himba suicide squad. "It's got to be done quickly with as little fuss as possible. I don't want to stir up Colonel van Wijk; I don't want him to discover that we've left Swakopmund until we're well past Rossing on the main highway to Karibib. Lieutenant Atkinson, if you please."

The Regimental Operations Officer or S-3 was a big English-type blonde, a substantial woman who was always on a diet and complained that Army chow was far too fattening . . . but who never failed to miss chow call. She ran S-3 in an efficient, no-nonsense professional manner. Curt had all but given up trying to teach her how to shoot the M26 Hornet submachinegun, the personal weapon carried by staff and support troops in a Sierra Charlie outfit; the Hornet was hard to shoot accurately anyway, but Atkinson used it like a garden hose to spray bullets over the entire vicinity of the target. Obviously, 1st Lieut. Hensley Atkinson wasn't a fighter, but she was an outstanding manager and administrator. She might have been descended from a long line of British nannies and housekeepers in that regard, and Curt had the feeling she'd have no trouble running a big house full of her own kids one of these days if she ever decided to leave the Army.

"Simple movement to the left flank eastward," Atkinson explained. "If anyone needs a picture of it, it will be on your tactical display when you get back to your ACVs. The original plan of putting the Companions on point with the Killers following turned out to be too complex. It might have tipped our hand to the South Africans in Walvis Bay. So the Marauders will be on the point, Killers behind them, followed by Headquarters Company. The Warriors will swing in behind Headquarters, and the Companions will bring up the rear. Questions?"

"First objective?" Marty Kelly asked.

"Rossing. Thirty-six kilometers up the road."

"Lieutenant Gibbon, did your aerial recon reveal anything out there that should cause us to worry?" Hettrick asked her intelligence and communications staff officer.

"We made one sweep with birdbots at twenty-one-hundred hours last night and found nothing out to fifty kilometers," Gibbon reported. "We repeated the sweep shortly after dawn and detected no change from the previous sweep."

"Orgasmic!" Hettrick exclaimed. "Looks like Operation Trek is clear for a straight shot into Otjomuise via the highway."

"Will you still be needing my services as a guide, Colonel?" Dr. Paul von Waldersee interjected.

"Yes, but perhaps for different reasons than I originally thought. If we don't go overland, we'll still need you if we encounter any of the tribes en route. And your knowledge of the terrain around Otjomuise will be of enormous assistance when we get there," Colonel Hettrick explained. She paused for a moment, then went on, "Leave Plan B in the computer. I always like to have a contingency plan. And, Doctor, I want you to accompany me in my ACV."

"The Navy and Marines on schedule to cover our rear when we move inland?" Curt wondered. "When are they due to arrive?"

"Tomorrow, maybe, barring screw-ups," Gibbon replied. "Late in the day, if then. Early the following day for sure. The Third Battalion of the Eighth Marines is scheduled to land and occupy Swakopmund."

"Do we wait until they arrive before we move out?" Marty Kelly asked.

"Not necessarily, Captain," Hettrick told him.

"When do we move out, Colonel?" was the question from Capt. Manny Garcia.

"When I give the order to do so," Hettrick said brusquely. "Remember, Operation Trek is only a contingency plan if the Royal Scots don't cut it in Otjomuise today."

"How are the Royal Scots doing?" Joan Ward asked.

"Lieutenant Gibbon, any recent updates?" Colonel queried.

"The Royal Scots warbot regiment went in to Strijdom at dawn. They've joined up with the *Legion Robotique*. It's been only three hours, but the reports I've received thus far on the Diamond Skeleton net merely say that heavy fighting is taking place."

"How about the air strike? Did it do the job?" Curt wanted to know.

Gibbon shook his head. "Initial reports confirmed our estimate: Too little. In a word, ineffectual. The tac strike aircraft were operating at extreme range and couldn't lay enough ordnance on the targets to make much of an impact. That plus the fact there's a lot of smoke in the air around there and the warbot units are scattered in small pockets. The radar and infra red had trouble getting through it to identify and mark targets, and sometimes they missed the enemy targets just enough to put the ordnance on the French and Brits. The strike aircraft had to land at Grootfontein, and that place isn't quite up to operational status yet so they can refuel and re-arm."

"In a situation like that where the fighting is in tight quarters with no really prominent landmarks to use for references and pockets of fighting," Curt pointed out, "air strikes can be damned near as dangerous to your own troops as the enemy."

"Yeah, it doesn't take much of a miss to lay ordnance on

friendlies," Marty Kelly added. "The Double Deuces learned that the hard way on Trinidad."

"The Double Deuces?" Manny Garcia asked rhetorically. "Hell, we took it in the shorts ourselves south of Sangre Grande when the Air Force got their coordinates screwed up! Warbots are vulnerable as hell to air strikes!"

"Toughest job in all military operations," Hettrick pointed out, "has *always* been the proper coordination of weapons and tactics . . . especially in combined operations. Any further questions? Comment? Very well, if not, this briefing is dismissed!"

Len Spencer had been listening to the briefing. He'd walked to the soccer field from the Companion's position, carrying all his gear. That had been about an hour ago when it was still cooler and pockets of fog still lingered in low spots. Now the sun had climbed higher in the typical cloudless blue sky, and the temperature was much higher . . . and going higher all the time in the brilliant sunlight. Curt walked over to him and asked, "You going to switch over to Manny's Marauders?"

"Why should I?" Spencer replied.

"They'll be out on point," Curt reminded him. "That's where any action is likely to be."

"Matter of fact, Captain, I plan to stick with the Companions."

"Oh? Why?"

"You're the rear guard."

"Rear guards don't get much action," Curt tried to point out. "They stay busy trying to look in two directions at once—ahead to keep from tailgating the main body and backward to cover their anatomy."

"In this case, Captain," Spencer observed, "the main body is going to be hauling ass for Otjomuise up the main highway. In the point vehicle, I can shoot a great travelog going through deepest, darkest, dankest Africa . . . except this isn't dark and dank around here. On the other hand, the situation being what it is with the proximity of Walvis Bay, Carson's Companions in the rear guard are likely to be the ones to see action if the South

Africans come charging up that road behind us."

"Is that the only reason? I thought you newshawks were interested in the so-called 'human stories.' Since when are you interested only in the action?"

Spencer looked up from packing his equipment. He had a bland expression on his face. "Captain, the human angle is *always* there. The action isn't. It's my job to guess where the action is likely to be and then to be there when it happens so I get the story. Sure, there's all kinds of human interest stuff about the troops of a United States regiment standing guard in an obscure African seacoast resort. There's a story in the mistaken attack on the police station yesterday that killed a local man; great stuff for the bleeding heart reporters, which I am not. There's a story in the skirmish last night which was easily beaten down with no casualties. I might squeeze a story out of it if I hyped the hell out of it, but it's making a mountain out of a molehill when it comes to what's going on in Otjomuise. It won't even make Segment Number Twenty in a nineteen segment newscast! And my editor would send me back to covering the defense budget hearings on the Hill."

"If the action's in Otjomuise, then why are you here?" It was a direct question from Curt that cut right to the heart of the discussion.

"Two reasons, Captain." Spencer was being unusually frank and open for a newshawk, Curt thought, but maybe that was the way this man operated. It was obvious that Spencer was a consumate con artist, able to ease up to people and get their support for whatever he wanted. Curt figured he'd already done that with Alexis Morgan and, seeing that it had gotten him into some difficulty with the company commander, had now started to work on Curt. "First of all, no one could get into Otjomuise with the warbot troops. General Lanrezac wouldn't permit it. Too dangerous, he maintained. He was probably right, but that's never stopped any war correspondent in history! Given the combat situation there plus the fact that the only news bureaus in the town are run by local stringers who are probably busy keeping their heads down right now, plus the fact that we haven't been getting any video feeds out of there tells me that it's an 'after-the-fact' news situation. Secondly, this happened damned fast, and we weren't about to let the Pentagon lock us out of this one the way they did in Trinidad. I pulled in every favor I had in the Outer Ring, and the best I could get was authority to accompany the Washington Greys."

"So we're second best on your laundry list?"

"No, no, not at all, Captain Carson!" The newsman grinned. "Sometimes fate smiles on those who happen to take what they can get and make the best of it! A United States Army regiment attacked from the rear by a South African regiment is one hell of a big story, isn't it? I don't have to make it a big story; it's there to be covered. And that's what I'm here to do: get the big story. And I hope it's going to be the big one of my career."

"You're only interested in the big story, huh?"

Spencer straightened up and looked Curt in the eyes. "Captain, the big point in your career would be the award of the Congressional Medal of Honor, wouldn't it?"

"It's probably in the back of every soldier's mind. But it's not up to me to go out and be a big hero and try to win it, Spencer. It's my job to follow orders as a professional military man," Curt told him, looking him right back in the eyes. "The CMH is a pretty high award. It doesn't come easy to anyone. In fact, no decoration does."

"Well, hell, you've won just about every other medal and decoration the Army has; and with clusters, in some cases. I've checked your bio."

"That doesn't mean that I'm next in line for the CMH."

Spencer picked up his largest bag and slung it over his shoulders as a knapsack. "Captain, the competition to be top dog in the Army is different, and maybe you don't need the Medal of Honor to make it. In my business, it's the other way around. I've won lots of awards and prizes for journalism. But I've yet to get the big one, the one every journalist lusts for, the Pulitzer. And when I get it, I'll write my own ticket from then on. Operation Diamond Skeleton may be the big chance for both of us. We may not get on another merry-go-round like this, so we'd damned-well better grab the gold ring if we can . . ."

"I sort of thought that was what you really had in mind," Curt said. "And I don't guess you'll let anything stop you from getting your big story, right?"

"Oh, don't worry, Captain, I'll get it fair and square; it doesn't mean anything otherwise," Spencer admitted. "Would you have been proud of getting the CMH for that skirmish last night?"

"Hell, no, that was just another fire fight!"

"Soldiers have gotten the CMH for less in the past," the newsman reminded him. "I respect you, Captain. You're like I am: You want to earn your rewards. Well, I hope you get the CMH some day, if not on this operation, then on another one. And I'll help you if I can."

"What did you have in mind?"

Spencer smiled and remarked, "I could have written up that melee last night and made it into something big, and you might have been recommended for a decoration because of it."

"As I asked, what are you suggesting, Spencer?"

"Suggesting? I'm suggesting nothing, Captain! Nothing at all. We've cooperated very well thus far. Let's keep doing it. You scratch my back, and I'll scratch yours. But let's not get in one another's way . . ."

"I wouldn't think of it for a moment, Spencer. You do your job, and I do mine, and we shouldn't find ourselves at odds over that." Curt had this man pegged now. He'd confirmed what he'd only guessed at earlier. Now he had something of substance to talk to Alexis about, to warn her. This newshawk would end up only using her. Curt didn't intend to let that happen, and he didn't intend to let Spencer use him, either.

And the best defense would be to keep Spencer with the Companions where he could keep an eye on the man.

Even though that put Spencer in close proximity to Alexis Morgan.

And now that Curt knew what Spencer wanted, there was no reason to deny it to the reporter if he was indeed good enough in his own field to cut it and be nominated for that Pulitzer. But Curt wanted to be absolutely certain that Spencer understood where Curt was coming from, and this frank and private chat seemed to be the opportunity for Curt to bring up the subject. "I know that your readers—Congress, the American people—have gotten interested in the fact that women are now serving in field combat units where they can be killed. Some are trying to get the Army to withdraw women from the Sierra Charlies, although they seem to have no problem with women operating neuroelectronic warbots remotely in linkage. I know that's part of your story, isn't it?"

"Of course!"

"Whose side are you on?" Curt wanted to know, asking him directly.

"Pardon?"

"Are you for or against women serving in combat roles in the new Sierra Charlie outfits like this one?"

Spencer laughed. "Captain, I'm a reporter. It's my job to be objective."

"Don't give me that bullshit, Spencer! You've got an opinion, and it's going to color your stories no matter what!"

The New York *Times* reporter thought about this for a moment before he replied, "I really haven't made up my mind yet, Captain. Didn't you read my op-ed piece about it in the *Times* about two months ago?"

"Rumor Control said something about it, but I didn't read it, sorry to say," Curt admitted, adding, "We've been pretty damned busy trying to figure out the new doctrine and tactics . . . and then get the regiment trained-up for them."

"Well, let me brief you, Captain. Our culture has always operated on the basis of 'women and children first.' Right?"

"Yeah, that's the basic reason why we fight."

"And you know full well that the art of war hasn't changed right down at the basics," Spencer went on, "but the rest of the world has changed. There are more women in the world than men right now. There's no need to preserve reproductive capacity. In fact, there may be a need to run it through a selection process."

"I don't follow you," Curt admitted. "Are you saying that we need to breed a super-race of warriors by running men *and* women through combat, the survivors take all?"

"Used to be that way ten thousand years ago," Spencer reminded him. "As we scramble up the greasy pole of civilization, sometimes we have to adopt new and different methods to climb higher. We used to use natural systems. If children were born deformed, we didn't have the biotechnology to either help them or save them; if infants couldn't learn to walk on two legs or to talk, they were animals and we ate them; if there were too many children, they were abandoned on the hillsides to die."

"Pretty damned draconian measures, and there were others if I remember my history correctly."

"Had to be draconian; we didn't have control over the forces of nature like we do today," Spencer pointed out. "What do we see now? Any one who wishes to have a child may, and the child will be normal and healthy thanks to the biotechnology of genetic engineering. But we've short-circuited the old natural selection processes, and we didn't know what Mother Nature was selecting for anyway. So we may be retrying some older systems under new circumstances . . . Women served on ships of the Royal Navy until 1841. And few people know that women fought alongside men in the field until the early nineteenth century, especially in colonial America."

"Don't you *dare* mention the Molly Pitcher thing to *any one* in the Washington Greys, male or female!" Curt warned him. "The women don't like it because they consider themselves professionals, not irregulars who happened to step in to help when the going got tough. The men respect the women as professionals and for the same reasons."

Spencer nodded slowly. "I know that, and I wouldn't insult your ladies by using that term."

"Good. But they're not 'our ladies.' We're not possessive. We may seem to be, but that's because of one final matter I need to discuss with you," Curt remarked. "Don't romance the women in the regiment."

"What?"

"In the Robot Infantry, we developed the necessary regulations and protocols to control the sex drive . . . which gets enormously enhanced by combat, I might add," Curt explained carefully.

"Ah, yes! Rule Ten!"

"You know of it? Good! Then I don't have to remind you that it's an automatic dishonorable discharge for both parties caught in violation of Rule Ten." Curt paused, then said emphatically, *"But,* in the inevitable situation of military personnel becoming involved with non-military personnel, we have no such regulation . . . yet. So such relationships pose real problems for commanding officers in a combat situation."

"So, you're worried about the old fraternization problem?"

"Exactly, but it isn't one-way any longer."

"Commanders throughout history have always had trouble with that."

"Except in the case of the Chinese, the Mongols, and the Aryans in India who took their concubines and brothels along with them on campaigns," Curt reminded him. "Needless to say, the fraternization problem is now more complex. We don't have a solution to it yet. In the meantime, your presence in my company quite frankly causes me some problems in maintaining discipline and combat readiness."

"I have no desire to create problems for you, Captain."

"I'm sure you don't. You spoke earlier of cooperation. Your cooperation is solicited here. Don't romance the ladies in this regiment."

"Captain!" Spencer replied with a mixture of astonishment and assurance. "As you pointed out, and as we've discussed, presence of women in combat roles is an important current issue. I intend to get to know the women of the regiment as well as I get to know the men. I intend to talk with them. I intend to become acquainted with them. That's part of my job as a news reporter. However . . . if romance does happen to flower, I don't think there's anything anyone can possibly do about it."

"We'll see," was Curt's cryptic reply because he honestly didn't know what he could do about it other than what he'd already done. But the worst thing he could do at this point was to make an enemy of this man. So he let the subject drop and offered, "Give you a ride back on my ATV."

"Thanks. Getting hot."

"It's going to get hotter."

CHAPTER TWENTY-THREE

"Colonel, we've just lost communications with the Royal Scots Fusileers in Otjomuise." Maj. Gen. Jacob Carlisle didn't look very pleased. In fact, he appeared to be downright angry. Even the interactive flat-screen video link between Swakopmund and St. Helena via satellite couldn't mask his feelings. "Apparently, their satellite link unit was either destroyed or captured."

"Are communications with the diplomatic compound still secure, General?" Col. Belinda Hettrick asked, knowing that if the British unit was out of communications Carlisle could still get some situation reports out of Otjomuise, even though Strijdom was thirty kilometers east of the capital.

"Yes, and the compound is holding out quite well," Carlisle confirmed. "I've still not heard from General Lanrezac. Therefore, I'm continuing to exercise my duties as Deputy Supreme Allied Commander. The Royal Scots may have gotten themselves into the same sort of trouble as the *Legion Robotique*. But I can't know if we have no communications with them."

"Sounds like they learned nothing from our Zahedan operation," Hettrick commented.

"I confirm that. My British deputies say that the French doctrine of massive frontal attacks with the heavily-gunned warbots in the line might have worked reasonably well against Soviet-style armor and motorized infantry tactics. But not against very large numbers of lightly armed guerillas and insurgents."

"France should have sent in the *Legion Etranger* instead. Sending warbots against irregulars and insurgents is like using a sledgehammer to swat a fly," Hettrick mused.

"Well, I can't even get my British deputies to believe it," Carlisle complained. "If the French are overly dependent upon *elan,* the Brits like to fight tidy battles and leave a clean battlefield. In reality, they don't know how to maintain logistics."

"The only workable reserve in modern warfare is a large supply of ammunition," the commander of the Washington Greys reminded him.

"How are you fixed in that regard, Belinda?"

"Fred Benteen managed to loot Diamond Point of everything moveable; he and his people squeezed every round of ammo, pack of food, and liter of fuel out of Fort Lee and Fort Sheridan. We can operate for almost two hundred combat hours without logistical support, more than double our normal duration," she said proudly.

"Major Benteen is a good man, but you've got a lot of good people, Belinda."

"Thank you, General. I anticipated we'd be more involved than originally planned."

"You will be. If you recall, I asked you to be prepared to move to Otjomuise as a reserve force to relieve the French and British if they got into trouble."

"Yes, sir."

"If the French had waited for the British and gone in together, they might have pulled it off as planned because of the element of surprise combined with firepower," Carlisle told her. "The French blew the surprise and didn't have the necessary punch. The British went in with the original plan and haven't been able to relieve the situation. I can't pull the Aussies out of Rehoboth because Intelligence believes the South Africans would indeed try to move into Namibia if I do. I can't move the Assam regiment out of Tsumeb; it's got to cover the Grootfontein airfield build-up for our tacair as well as keep the Ovambos from moving more men into Otjomuise. So it ɔks like the Washington Greys will have to go to ›tjomuise to take the pressure off the warbot troops there ınd relieve the diplomatic compound as well. How quickly can you be on the road?"

"One hour, General."

"One hour? Did you pull out of your guard positions and form up on the road, ready to start engines?" Carlisle asked incredulously.

"No, sir, but we did develop a contingency plan for rapid redeployment, my officers have been briefed already, and my troops are ready to move when the orders are given," Hettrick told him in matter-of-fact tones that masked pride in the outfit. But she added with some concern, "You certainly realize, General, that our redeployment will leave Swakopmund open to what I consider to be a sure and certain occupation by the South African Defense Forces in Walvis Bay."

"Colonel, do you have communications with the South Africans in Walvis Bay?"

"Yes, sir. They do have telephones here, and I know how to contact Colonel van Wijk."

"Then I want you to call him once you're on the road. Tell him that the United States Navy will be offshore very soon—don't let him know it won't happen today—and that the United States Marines will move into Swakopmund to replace you."

"Yes, sir."

"One hour, you said?"

"Actually, General, fifty-nine minutes from now. We've talked another minute."

"Very well! Move out of Swakopmund to Otjomuise by the most expeditious route to reinforce the French and British units already there and relieve the diplomatic compound. Restore order in Otjomuise if possible. But get the people safely out of the diplomatic compound . . . and get anyone else out of that place who wants to leave." Carlisle's phrases were clipped as he gave the orders. He'd seen the maps and satellite images. He knew the sort of country he was sending the Washington Greys into. But he didn't fear for a moment that they wouldn't make it wouldn't arrive in a condition to fight hard.

"Yes, sir!" Even as she said it and the video conference was terminated from St. Helena, she was keying the code words into the terminal and transmitting the redeployment order out to her regiment.

Curt Carson was sitting atop the turret of his ACV scanning the southern horizon for movement. Suddenly, he heard the sound of engines spooling up all around him, including the one in his own ACV. He rolled and called down the turret hatch, "Henry, what's happening?"

"The order to move out just arrived," M. Sgt. Henry Kester's voice replied.

Curt looked at his watch. It was 1134 local time.

The warbots were scurrying back to their transport vehicles all along the line. Curt's jeep dashed up the rear ramp and secured itself for travel.

He dropped through the hatch himself. The first thing he did was check the display screen. Hettrick's order was there with the proper code words. Kester was busy making the final arrangements for the ACV to depart. On the maneuver and travel displays, the outside video views in the visual were up and displayed. The tactical display showed the disposition of all the units and personnel of Carson's Companions. The regimental display showed where the other companies were located on a street map of Swakopmund.

"Where's Len Spencer?"

"Alpha Leader," Kester replied laconically.

Curt punched up the private line to Alpha Platoon. "Alpha Leader, this is Companion Leader. Ready to roll?"

Sgt. Nick Gerard's voice came back, "Alpha has just recovered all warbots. Alpha is ready to roll."

"Where's the lieutenant?"

"Up in the turret where I'm supposed to be, Captain," came Alexis Morgan's voice.

"Spencer with you?"

"Affirmative. He's in the other hatch with his camcorder."

"Roger," Curt said with relief. "Bravo Leader, this is Companion Leader," he called over the general company net. "Ready to roll?"

Sgt. Edwina Sampson's voice replied, "Negatory, Captain! Bravo warbots still on recall; takes a little longer for the Hairy Foxes to move. Be ready to travel in about thirty seconds. Lieutenant Allen is on station."

"Roger! Bravo, lead out when ready; the Companions will file on you according to plan. Do you have the Warriors on the screen?"

"Affirmative! We'll move when they do and will let you know."

"We'll see it," came Kester's voice.

Getting the new Sierra Charlie combat company on the road wasn't as easy as had been thought. Three ACVs, four RTVs, two LAMVs, and the three little ATVs sandwiched in between these hulking monsters was a convoy all in itself. Add three more company units like that, plus all the regimental headquarters and service vehicles, and a modern Sierra Charlie regiment on the road was made up of 106 vehicles of seven types carrying 120 warbots, eighty-seven people, and all the supplies that had been stuffed aboard to keep the regiment running for two hundred hours in combat—longer on just a cross-country mission. What rumbled out of Swakopmund on that bright summer morning was a convoy.

It was not a smooth operation. The Greys had done it only a few times before during field exercises in northern Arizona. It would have been impossible without the artificial intelligence, high speed computers, and high resolution sensors in each vehicle. The master regimental computer, Grey Max, kept track of it all, and its activities were shared on a regimental radio data bus so that any company computer or even the simpler ones in some of the larger manned vehicles could take over and run the whole thing—albeit not without some human help—in case Grey Max went down for some reason. Each vehicle knew where it should be and what vehicle should be ahead and behind it . . . and by precisely how many meters with a tolerance of plus or minus a few meters.

Thanks to the computers and artificial intelligence, there was only one instance of a traffic jam on the way out of Swakopmund, a situation where the slow-down of a lead vehicle amplified down the line into a moving stop-go jam-up typical of a freeway slow-down problem in any urban area. The only difference between the vehicles of the Washington Greys and those which plied the automated freeways was that here there was no autocontrol system in the road itself; the vehicles had to sense where the street or road was, stay on it, and go where it went according to mapped instructions in the computer memories.

This left the human soldiers of the Greys free to monitor tactical displays and to keep a sharp eye peeled for things and patterns that the computers might miss but which might mean trouble.

In less than sixty minutes, the Alpha Platoon ACV of Manny's Marauders cleared the outskirts of Swakopmund and started down the long, straight asphalt highway across the most barren countryside imaginable, the nearly barren flat sweeps of the Namib Desert where only the hardiest succulent plants could survive in clumps and bunches. Fifty kilometers to the east rose the sharp cliffs and ravines of the escarpment.

The regimental convoy was about two kilometers long, and it continued to move at about fifty kilometers per hour until the last vehicle was out of Swakopmund and the speed could be boosted. As planned, Companion Alpha Leader ACV was the last to leave Swakopmund. When that fact was reported to the regimental command post, the computer order went out to increase speed to seventy-five kilometers per hour.

Hettrick was pleased. Using the stabilized satellite antenna atop her vehicle, she reported to Carlisle on St. Helena, then switched to the cellular telephone unit they'd left with the Feldgendarmerie in Swakopmund. She rang up Col. Theo van Wijk in Walvis Bay.

"Good afternoon, Colonel van Wijk. Colonel Hettrick here!"

"A pleasure, Colonel! Why aren't you transmitting video?" came van Wijk's voice.

"Because I'm on cellular from my command vehicle heading up the highway to Otjomuise," Hettrick told him. "I wanted to let you know that the United States Army has temporarily pulled out of Swakopmund but that the United States Navy will shortly put a unit of the United States Marines into the town to provide security."

"Oh, my!" came van Wijk's voice in what Hettrick could have sworn was mock distress. "I suggest that you return to Swakopmund to join your Marines when they arrive . . ."

"Why so, Colonel?"

"A native disturbance occurred last night," came the reply. "The road to Otjomuise was heavily damaged and has been closed by my regiment in order to allow it to be repaired and to prevent injuries . . ."

This set Hettrick back. "Gibbon!" she snapped at her S-2. "Is the highway ahead clear?"

"Yes, Colonel, according to the data from the dawn patrol of my birdbots!"

"Any South African forces out there?"

"If they're there, we didn't detect them, Colonel."

Hettrick returned her attention to the telephone and keyed it. "That's news to me, Colonel. Our reconaissance shows that it's undamaged and clear. And, pray tell, what the hell are you and your forces doing outside your own borders? What you've just told me is that you're blocking the road!"

"That's quite correct, Colonel, if you wish to put it that way," van Wijk's voice replied smoothly. "The situation has changed overnight. A native uprising has taken place in the area. I understand that one of your units was attacked in Swakopmund last night. We don't know the extent of the uprising yet or the level of threat it poses to Walvis Bay. Pretoria has given me the authority to enter Namibia in hot pursuit of the perpetrators, and my forces control the highway to prevent movement of possible hostile forces out of the area . . ."

"Well, I suggest that you instruct your troops to allow us to pass," Hettrick snapped.

"My orders are to prevent by force if necessary any traffic from Swakopmund and Walvis Bay proceeding toward the interior. And, if you are withdrawing your forces from Swakopmund, I may have to enter the town myself to restore law and order . . ."

"Swakopmund was peaceful when we left it, Colonel van Wijk," Hettrick told him, "and United States Marines will soon be there."

"I'll hold it for them until they get there . . . unless, of course, you return to Swakopmund at once."

Hettrick looked at the telephone handset. "How the hell did he manage to move troops out of Walvis Bay and to that highway without me seeing it? Gibbon! Didn't you check the highway last night?"

"Yes, Colonel, at about twenty-two hundred hours. We checked it again at dawn today. We detected no troop movements of the sort that the South Africans must have made to block the highway . . ."

"Yet van Wijk knew about the skirmish last night!" Hettrick said almost to herself. "That was about twenty-three hundred hours. Goddamnit! *Now* I know the reason for it: a diversion! Our total attention was concentrated on Swakopmund while Carson was beating down that assault!" And by the time Gibbon had sent the next recon sweep out at dawn, the South Africans had moved and were stealthed in place.

Hettrick shook her head. *Damn if that didn't take balls!* she thought. Van Wijk could have been caught at any time, but he took a chance and pulled it off! She wished he wasn't on the other side of this one; he would have been a good commander to fight alongside . . .

She keyed the phone. "Good luck, Colonel! Nice move, but I have alternatives! I hope I don't have to shoot at you. Good day, sir!" And she abruptly cut the connection. Even working through the cellular station in Swakopmund, the radio transmission from the cell could be traced to her present position and give van Wijk a targeting coordinate.

"Column halt!" was the next quick order she snapped.

"Roger, column halt!" replied Maj. Ed Canby as he relayed the message. This went out over tight radio beam along the column, hard to pick up without the very best in the way of side-lobe ECM gear . . . which van Wijk might or might not have, but Hettrick was counting on the fact that he probably didn't.

"Get me Companion Leader."

"Companion Leader on the tac net!"

"Curt, Colonel Hettrick!"

"Yes, Colonel. Why the halt?"

"South Africans have blocked the highway," she explained briefly. "More on the tac disposition net shortly. In the meantime, I need you to make one of your famous end runs. Turn south, get off the highway, find a place we can cross the Swakop River, and the rest of the column will one-eighty on the road and follow you! Find that dirt road leading up to Anschluss. We'll outflank these Afrikaaners. If you run into them out there, don't shoot unless shot at and report at once! I'm implementing Plan B. Execute!"

CHAPTER TWENTY-FOUR

"At once, Colonel!" Curt snapped and radioed to his maneuver platoon, "Companion Alpha Leader, this is Companion Leader!"

"Companion Alpha here! Go ahead, Captain!" came Alexis Morgan's voice.

"Take your platoon to the right and find a place to cross the Swakop River. I'll join you."

"Roger, Companion Leader! Looks like there's a lot of vegetation down there. Don't know about the water."

"Stand by on that, Alpha. Companion Bravo?"

"Bravo here!" Lt. Jerry Allen answered.

"Do a one-eighty and follow Alpha Leader and me down the river bank. We're going to search for a crossing. Remain this side of the river until we find a proper ford, then serve as a guide for the Warriors who will be behind you."

"Roger, Companion Leader!"

"Companions all, keep tacomm networked into the regimental freaks. I don't want to have to repeat everything we get down from Regimental. Grey Head, this is Companion Leader," Curt called again to regimental command. "Colonel, what does Doctor von Waldersee have to say about the Swakop River in this vicinity? What can we expect in the way of depth and stream flow?"

"Companion Leader, our guide says that we'll encounter lots of vegetation and a dry, sandy river bottom," came Hettrick's reply. "The river is mainly underground until shortly before it reaches the ocean."

"How about quicksand?" Curt wanted to know.

"He doesn't know of any."

"Good! Where are the Afrikaaners? Can we expect to encounter them during or after crossing?"

"We haven't made contact with the South African forces on the road," Hettrick's voice admitted. "I halted the column before contact was made. I don't want to reveal our exact position to them by making contact, and I didn't want to have to break contact to go back and cross the river. Let them worry about us for a change!"

"What are my instructions if I make contact?"

"Keep moving. If they shoot, shoot back. If the engagement seems to be mainly between foot soldiers, dismount whatever force you feel necessary to engage them and pin them down with fire, but keep your point moving. The chances are that we'll wheel around their left flank undetected because I don't think they could have deployed along the whole river. Van Wijk has only a regiment, and he couldn't have moved a whole regiment out here last night in four to six hours. So we're probably up against battalion strength at the most. Soldiers probably armed with SAR five-millimeter rifles. Maybe some AT rockets, although I suspect they concentrated them along the highway if they have any. I'd be very surprised if we ran into anything in the way of heavy artillery."

"Can I expect any recon reports?"

"Roger, Gibbon has his birdbots up on patrol at the moment. No indication of Afrikaaner forces. Therefore, they must be dismounted with vehicles well hidden. Expect contact with only lightly armed foot soldiers."

"Grey Head, Companion Leader could use a birdbot overhead to spot the best way through the puckerbrush on the river bottom," Curt told her. "Have Gibbon get down low so he can give us best resolution. And if there's an Afrikaaner out there with an anti-vehicle weapon, I want him spotted before he spots me."

"Wilco. But don't forget, we probably know more about the South Africans than they know about the Sierra

Charlies. We're the new kid on the block."

"Yes, Colonel, but Colonel van Wijk scoped us out yesterday when he came over with two of his top staffers. He must have gotten some idea of what a Sierra Charlie outfit was like," Curt reminded her.

"We'll find out . . ."

Curt turned to his first sergeant. "Henry, dismount the jeep and have it trail us. Then join me upstairs." He adjusted his helmet on his head to make sure the neuroelectrodes of the comm/ control system were well seated, then stuck his head through the turret hatch. He felt the rear ramp come down and saw his M30 General Purpose robot, Action Jackson, move down to the ground and take up a following position. Kester joined in the other turret hatch shortly thereafter. They rolled the ACV back down the column toward Alpha's ACV bringing up the rear.

The river bank started right at the edge of the highway, but here it wasn't steep or rutted, just a gently descending slope. Very little rain fell in this part of the world—less than twenty millimeters per year, and often not even that—so the slopes showed no water erosion. But the vegetation was thick at the bottom where the flowing water of the Swakop River was hidden beneath the apparently dry sands.

Curt's ACV joined Alpha Platoon's ACV part way down the slope. "Hello, Alpha Leader, Companion Leader is joining you!" Curt called over the short-range tactical comm unit. "I'd suggest putting Sergeant Gerard and one of your squad leaders in the lead, followed by our two jeeps to test the footing, then a Mary Anne, and finally our ACVS."

Alexis Morgan's voice came back in his head through the neurophonic electrodes, "Welcome to the party, Captain! Sergeant Dillon says he's familiar with this sort of terrain from Montana. So I'm going to dismount him when we reach the bottom of this slope. He says we should be able to find a firm passage through this to the other side . . ."

"It only has to be wide enough to get the ACVs through," Curt reminded her.

"Roger, a four-lane superhighway we don't need . . ."

This was the tricky part, Curt knew. The South Africans could be waiting for them down there in the river bottom underbrush, ready to ambush them. Yet, his tactical sixth sense told him there was no way the Afrikaaners could have guessed at precisely the spot the Greys would pick to move across the river. In fact, the South Africans probably didn't think the Sierra Charlies had enough mobility to move quickly off-road. The United States Army was known as a linkage warbot outfit, and the Sierra Charlies of the Washington Greys would be something new to everyone else.

Regular warbot regiments had larger and heavier vehicles—albeit fewer of them—but lots of warbots. As a result, the ordinary warbot regiment didn't, and couldn't, maneuver as freely or as quickly because doctrine required that the warbot control vehicles containing the human warbot operators take up positions in well-defended, defiladed spots while the warbots were operated out to their maximum linkage range, usually less than thirty kilometers. Once the forward momentum of the advance was obtained by the warbots, half the force was pulled out of action and its command and control vehicles full of warbot brainies was moved up and then put back in action once the operating range was lessened to about ten kilometers. Once this "leapfrog" tactic was set up and moving, a regular warbot regiment could advance about fifty kilometers per day.

Trinidad had proved that the new Sierra Charlie outfits could move a lot faster, and the recent maneuvers of the Washington Greys in Arizona had shown that a Sierra Charlie regiment could move at least twenty-five kilometers per hour.

Unless Colonel van Wijk had carefully studied Operation Steel Band—which was doubtful since the first tactical descriptions and analyses were just beginning to appear in the professional military journals read the world over—he wouldn't suspect the Washington Greys would try to go rapidly cross-country like this.

The most likely spot for an ambush, Curt believed, was when they emerged from the vegetation on the other side and the South Africans could hold the lip of the river bank, giving them the high ground and an opportunity to pick off vehicles, warbots, and people as they emerged from the vegetation.

Provided, of course, that the Afrikaaners hadn't concentrated their forces to block the highway.

When it came right down to gut feeling, experience-tempered combat judgement honed by being both a warbot brainy and the first Sierra Charlie company commander who'd had to work out the original tactics, Curt didn't have to consult a computer to determine the odds. He believed they'd pull this off, be on the south side of the Swakop River, and be moving inland before the South Africans discovered they hadn't retreated into Swakopmund.

Once across the Swakop and onto the desert plain, the Greys could move, and it would be a tail chase if the South African wanted to chase them. He didn't think that Colonel van Wijk would get involved in a tail chase, thus leaving his own rear open when the Navy and the Marines did indeed arrive at Swakopmund. Van Wijk didn't dare take the chance that he could get caught in foreign territory between the Washington Greys and the Marines . . .

There was only one hitch to all of this, and he queried Hettrick about it: "Grey Head, this is Companion Leader. Any aerial recon activity on the part of the South Africans?"

"Negatory. Even if they're pretty well stealthed, we'd pick up their wakes with Gibbon's new Doppler radar."

Any object that moves through the air leaves a turbulent wake of disturbed air behind it, no matter how well it's streamlined. Doppler radar had been used for decades to spot air turbulence at high altitudes and microbursts of violent down drafts near thunderstorms around airports.

But these were large areas of turbulence in comparison to an aircraft's wake. The continuing advance of electronic technology had finally brought Doppler radar to the size, reliability, and resolution that permitted it to be used in the field for detecting aircraft in flight by their wakes. Stealth measures could make any aircraft impossible to detect by radar, and heat emissions could be reduced to the point where an aircraft's infra red signature wasn't much hotter than the background. But there was no way that the aerodynamics engineers could get rid of the turbulence caused by the passage of an object through the air.

"What's the ROE if we spot a recon aircraft?" Curt asked for guidance on the rules of engagement.

"Same as any aircraft. Shoot back if it attacks. Otherwise, take no overt action."

"Roger!" He wasn't very happy about that. Rules of engagement were always such that they reduced a commander's chances of winning.

The Swakop River was less than a kilometer wide at the spot where the Companions had probed it and found a crossing. Curt heard Sgt. Dillon report back to Alexis Morgan, "Companion Alpha Leader, this is Companion Alpha One! It's sandy all the way through with good footing. Haven't run into any quicksand, but I'd stay clear of the sandy spots that look wet. Water level seems to be about a meter down where the sand gets wet. Underground stream for sure. Coming up the other side of the creek here is easy going. I dunno how it's gonna be after we put fifty or more vehicles through here, but I'd say we're okay following this path as long as the ruts don't get dug down to water."

"Can the path be straightened out a little bit?"

"Roger, Lieutenant! I'd say just knock down a few of those trees with one of the heavy vehicles. Roots probably don't go very deep here. Should be easy to do."

"I'll put down the 'dozer blades on the Saucy Cans," Alexis told him. "We'll root 'em out, and we can use the Saucy Cans as temporary bulldozers if we have to."

"Won't have to, Lieutenant. Sand is good footing."

Cole, with his background in the outlands of Montana, knew what he was talking about. Although the landscape didn't resemble Montana—it was far and away more of a desolate desert than the Great Plains—the dry river bed was very similar to those found throughout the American west.

The Companions were over the Swakop in less than thirty minutes, followed closely by Ward's Warriors. By that time, the sandy river bed had been reasonably well packed, especially where it was dampish. No quicksand was encountered.

"Grey Head, this is Companion Leader! We're on the south bank and all is clear," Curt reported. "Even built a good road for you! We oughta get an Engineers' rating for this!"

"We see you, Companion Leader! Well done! I'll forward your request to higher authority. Proceed in column south and east. Try to pick up the dirt road we see on the satellite images and the maps. Shouldn't be more than about five kilometers from the river."

"Companions all, this is Companion Leader! Travel condition Yankee! Companion Alpha, take the point. Companion Leader will join you. Our two ACVs and our two jeeps will run as foragers; the remainder of the company form in column behind. Ground looks good, so come to a forward speed of fifty clicks and to hell with the dust cloud. The Afrikaaners will find us with their recon aircraft soon enough!"

Once they got away from the river, the land became almost flat with no little run-off gullies at all. The soil was sandy and rocky, spotted here and there with clumps of what looked to Curt like creosote bush or mesquite, although he knew this was a different continent with different flora. It was definitely a desert biome; it obviously didn't rain very often here because even the desert plants looked like they were having a hard time surviving.

After ten minutes of travel, Curt had to report back to Hettrick, "Grey Head, Companion Leader here. No road.

Repeat: No road. At least, it isn't where the charts say it's supposed to be."

"Nothing's where it's supposed to be," Hettrick's voice came back. "My inertial positioning unit tells me we're where we're supposed to be, and a satellite location fix confirms the data from the IPU. Take up a heading of one-one-zero and head toward that prominent peak on the escarpment ahead. If we can't find a road, we'll make our own!"

"I've ranged that escarpment with my laser," Curt told her. "We'll never make it into those hills by sundown. Do we intend to attempt penetration of that rough terrain at night?"

"Let's see how rough it is when we get there, Companion Leader. We can't dawdle and fail to move at night. Our guide says we should pick up a canyon into the hills just to the left of the peak. Keep moving . . ."

The entire regiment was across the Swakop by 1800 hours and the low sun in the west was dimmed by the huge dust cloud raised by the movement of more than a hundred vehicles across the sandy, dusty terrain. It was impossible to hide the presence of this large a moving military unit because of this dust. Being on point, Curt wasn't eating anyone's dust although the westerly wind off the ocean tended to make the dust hang with the moving vehicles as they went eastward. But farther back in the column, the maintenance crews of Capt. Elwood Otis found themselves stretched out along the column, cleaning and changing the dust filters on engine intakes on the run.

Curt acknowledged in his mind that Hettrick had chosen the proper alternative. They didn't know where the South Africans were or what they might try to do. Thus far, there was no indication from Manny's Marauders on rear guard that anyone was following them. They might have indeed successfully accomplished the end run around Colonel van Wijk's troops blocking the main highway.

The escarpment loomed higher and higher ahead of them as they approached. It was a formidable wall of sheer cliffs cut with deep gorges. In the lengthening shadows of

ate afternoon, terrain relief began to show up starkly.
1. Sgt. Henry Kester was riding up in the turret with ırt. He scanned the escarpment both visually and ırough his infra red goggles.

"Captain," he said grimly, his face set, "that wall of rock is more than a thousand meters high, and those canyons are pretty damned steep. Just like the Mogollon Rim without the trees. Rough country. Looks like it tapers off a bit slightly to the left. But if you want my honest evaluation of the situation, we sure as hell ain't gonna get through there tonight unless our expert native guide has an ace up his sleeve—"

"All Grey units!" came the call from Hettrick's command vehicle. "Come to Condition Zulu! Two aircraft approaching, bearing two-two-zero, elevation one-five, range five-zero, closing rate four hundred klicks, not stealthed, picking up on single-pulse radar and passive infra red. Three aircraft, bearing two-six-zero, elevation two-one, range eight-zero, closing rate four-five-zero, stealthed, contact only on Doppler turbulence radar, no radar pulse return and no infra red signature."

"Grey Head, this is Marauder Leader." It was Capt. Manny Garcia whose Marauders were running as rear guard now. "I have ground target contact, bearing two-one-five, range five-five, speed twenty klicks. Not closing. Small dust cloud. No IFF. No returns on individual vehicles yet at this range because of the dust cloud."

"Greys all, this is Grey Head! Enable antiaircraft weaponry but do not fire unless fired upon! Repeat: Do not fire unless fired upon!"

"If those are strike aircraft out of Walvis Bay, they'll catch us out in the open here," Kester warned. "And we sure as hell can't stop short of those hills at sundown with someone on our ass. Looks like a showdown for sure!"

CHAPTER TWENTY-FIVE

"Ess-two, get a recon bot up . . . birdbot, anything. I want to find out who or what is following us," Hettrick snapped.

"Grey Head," came John Gibbon's reply. "My C-cubed-I personnel are busy on the radar and i-r. My warbot brainy who was running the birdbot just came out of linkage about thirty minutes ago, and I won't put her back in linkage without expert biotech supervision."

"Ess-two, biotech unit here!" It was Dr. Ruth Gydesen, the major in charge of the biotech unit that would have been called the regimental medical detachment in earlier times. "I'm sending over Sergeant Devlin. She'll be there in two minutes!"

As M. Sgt. Henry Kestler listened to this chatter on the regimental tacomm, he vocalized to his company commander, "Captain, those aircraft will be coming right out of the sun, and we're casting long shadows. We couldn't be better targets!"

"Henry, get below and man the tacair defenses," Curt told him. "Patch into the regimental data bus and use that to track the bogies until we get good data from our own gear. I've got to keep an eye on the terrain. This ACV is smart, but the ground is getting broken up now that we're closer to the escarpment . . . and I don't want this vehicle to go ass over antennas in a gully. Keep me advised on the aerial target data in case we have to start tracking."

Kester just nodded and dropped out of sight into the bowels of the ACV.

Curt turned in the turret hatch and tried to look westward into the setting sun, knowing that he wouldn't be able to pick up the airborne targets as far away as they were but wanting to get an assessment on what the antiaircraft fighting situation would be. The western horizon wasn't clear and sharp as it usually was in the desert; it was hidden in the brownish-yellow haze of dust kicked up by the movement of more than a hundred vehicles across the dry soil. Targeting, aiming, and firing would have to be done by the automatics if radar or i-r could manage to penetrate the dust and discriminate a target. Kester would stay on top of it, so Curt turned his attention back to where they were going.

The talus slopes of the escarpment were now less than five kilometers east of their position, and the ACV was still holding its originally assigned heading, deviating from time to time to maneuver around large rocks and other obstacles. A prominent high peak, their visual guidance landmark, stood slightly to the right. To the south of this, the escarpment rose precipitously from the desert floor, its slopes completely barren of any vegetation. To the left, the terrain began to slope downward . . . or perhaps it was the particular perspective that Curt viewed from his current position. A broad valley appeared to be opening up to the left of the peak, but it wasn't obvious yet, and Curt could see other ridges of the escarpment beyond.

Unless they could find the road, poor as it might be, Curt thought it would be damned difficult to get a whole regiment up into those hills in the dark of the coming night, even with the help of high-resolution, infra red, night vision sensors.

He flipped his i-r goggles down over his eyes to check. All of the terrain around them seemed to be at the same temperature. It was difficult for the i-r sensors to pick out topographical differences because everything out there was at about the same temperature after a day in the unclouded sunlight. He checked the infra red system of his ACV which was supposed to have higher resolution plus better discrimination between small temperature differ-

ces. The result was the same. He could see the sky over the horizon of the ridges, and the rest was a featureless image. Even when he commanded maximum contrast, he couldn't get enough detail. He didn't want to take a vehicle, much less a hundred vehicles, up into that rough country at night under these conditions.

He needed a road if he was to lead the Washington Greys into the hills tonight. And where was the road that was supposed to be there?

His brown study was interrupted by Kester's voice in his head. "Captain, the three stealthed aircraft have altered course and appear to be descending on an intercept with the ground force following us. The two unstealthed aircraft have reversed course and are heading westbound now."

"Roger! Keep tracking!" Curt told him and switched the regimental tacomm net from low-gain to high. He heard the same report from the regimental ACV van carrying the communications and detection gear. But there was additional information, as well.

"Grey Head, this is Sierra Two Drone Alpha, Sgt. Josephine Wheeler in command," another voice reported. "I am in linkage with a birdbot approaching the unknown ground unit. I have visual on the ground target of interest. It appears to be made up of six vehicles. They have the silouettes of the South African Light Reconaissance Vehicle Mark Ten. Certainly not more than company strength. Where are the bogies, please?"

"Airborne targets are in two groups," replied the voice of Sgt. Emma Crawford, Gibbon's top NCO. "First group of two, unstealthed, proceeding westbound toward Walvis Bay, will pass three kilometers to the south, traffic no longer a factor. Second group of three stealthed aircraft should be in your two o'clock position, range two kilometers, will pass below you at high angular rate. We're tracking their wake only. Can you get a visual on them?"

"Looking . . . No contact . . . Wait! There! I have a visual! I have an ident! Three AmerDyne Alpha Alpha

Four Zero tactical strike aerodynes bearing Air Forc markings! They are making a low pass west to east out of the sun over the South African unit . . . Now breaking left and right beyond them! It was only a low pass, Grey Head! They didn't lay ordnance on the South Africans! . . . The Afrikaaner unit has stopped its forward motion . . . The Alpha Alpha Four Zeroes have jinked back sunward and gone to hover . . ."

The USAF tac strike craft must have staged out of Grootfontein, and they provided a bit of nonlethal air support right when it was needed . . . although Curt didn't think Manny Garcia would have had much trouble handling the Afrikaaners had they caught up with the Greys' rear guard. *They've been caught outside the boundaries of Walvis Bay!* Curt thought. *Blocking the highway was one thing; that was just over the border. Moving in hot pursuit of an American regiment in Namibian territory isn't going to make them look real good, especially if Spencer is reporting this data back to New York. Even if the bastards were only on a recon to check us out, Pretoria's ambassador in Washington will have a sweaty time explaining it . . .*

Then he caught himself. *We'll be fighting the Bastaards soon! Can't use that term for anyone else. Could be confusing!*

He turned his full attention back to where his ACV was going.

The sun was about to go down. The terrain was getting rougher and more cut up. Curt had to tell his ACV to slow up and pick its way more carefully. He called Hettrick. "Grey Head, Companion Leader. Once it gets too dark to get visuals, the infra red isn't going to help me drive. And this terrain is getting more difficult. We can't go up that escarpment ahead during the daytime, much less at night. I won't be able to maintain forward movement here for more than another hour at the most. Do you have other instructions for me?"

"Wait one, Companion Leader."

The ACV continued to grind forward, its sensors

ting rocks and ravines and steering the vehicle to ıd them. Nevertheless, the ride was getting a lot ugher. Curt was now forced to hang on to the turret atch lip with both hands to keep from being thrown around.

"Companion Leader, this is Grey Head. Come left three-zero degrees. Doctor von Waldersee says you will come to a dry river bed within two kilometers. Go directly into the river bed and follow it upstream. It will take us around this initial ridge of the escarpment."

"Grey Head, I still wish to inform you of my serious concern about nighttime travel through unknown country like this," Curt reminded his regimental commander. "It would help if we could find that road. Then I'd feel better about traveling at night . . ."

"Doctor von Waldersee believes the road may be around here somewhere and that you may cross it before reaching the dry river bed," Hettrick's voice responded.

"Colonel, it would sure as hell help if the charts and the satellite images matched!" Curt complained.

"I believe we've discussed why the CIA and DMA maps may be inaccurate. But now I'm beginning to suspect the covert hand of the South Africa military intelligence organization," Hettrick told him frankly. "Colonel van Wijk probably could have provided us with a very accurate map."

That was an unsatisfactory answer insofar as Curt was concerned, but he didn't want to push his regimental commander any harder on the issue. It wasn't her fault that the charts were wrong or that Congress penny-pinched the armed services so that the Washington Greys didn't have the capability to pull down real-time satellite images. It had been difficult enough to wrangle through Congress the procurement of a Mexican-designed modern infantry rifle to equip the new Sierra Charlie units; as it was, the Mexican FABARMA M3A2 *Novia* ended up going into initial production in the United States as the M33A2 "Ranger" after Aberdeen Proving Ground people had made their little changes in the design, more to justify the need for US production over Mexican procuren than actual improvements in the weapon. The M3 Ranger was just enough different from the FABARM M3A2 *Novia* that certain critical parts couldn't be interchanged. The Sierra Charlies continued to call it the *Novia* rather than the "Ranger" because it was indeed a sweetheart of a small arm.

"I think you're right, Colonel. Maybe we should have tried to capture that Afrikaaner company that was on our tail. They sure knew exactly where to come looking for us . . ."

"Too late. They turned back to Walvis Bay when the Air Force overflew them. I didn't think General Carlisle would be able to break a flight of aerodynes loose from Grootfontien at this time, but he apparently did."

Shortly after the sun went down and it started to get dark, Curt found the dry river bed right where their guide said it would be . . . but no road. He let Kester slowly maneuver the ACV down the steep bank under manual control; the ACV's inertial reference unit needed for positioning and navigation could be thrown out of alignment by a steep descent, and Curt didn't want to have to go to the trouble of getting everything all lined-up again.

It was indeed a steep descent. Alexis Morgan followed him down and, when her ACV got to the bottom, she called up Curt and said, "Captain, let me send an LAMV down next with its dozer blade deployed. We should try to decrease the slope of that bank a little bit. I can have Sergeant Gerard maneuver the LAMV as a real dozer and cut a shallower roadway for the rest of the regiment to follow."

"Negative. We can negotiate this all right," Curt told her. "We haven't got the time to make a four-lane superhighway out of this. The whole regiment's moving up behind us."

It was reasonably smooth down on the sandy bottom. "Colonel, the bank entrance is steep but negotiable. And the river bottom is smooth and firm. We can make time now," Curt reported.

"Orgasmic!" Hettrick replied. "Von Waldersee says we ould have no trouble moving up this river bed in the ark. He was up this way two years ago and reports he was able to negotiate it without trouble for the next fifteen kilometers with only a four-wheel-drive Ford Cayuse."

"If you don't mind, Colonel, I'd like to keep the forward speed down to about 25 klicks," Curt requested. "This isn't like moving across open country. And it's getting dark."

"Request approved."

It was a good thing the regimental commander had given the slow-down approval, Curt discovered. The river bed ranged from about ten meters in width down to narrow defiles only about three meters wide. And it began to twist and turn as Curt's ACV proceeded upstream into the hills of the escarpment with the regimental convoy behind him.

"Captain," Kester called. "Trouble."

"Report!"

"Inertial reference unit lost alignment. Probably that real steep river bank we went down."

"It shouldn't do that!"

"It did, sir."

"Okay, get an update and realignment from Grey Head as soon as convenient. Right now, we don't need it as much as we need a better night vision system," Curt remarked, peering ahead with his i-r goggles and trying to monitor the ACV's infra red scan at the same time.

It was a very dark night.

Curt decided it would be easier to use headlights even though those bright light sources might compromise security. "Grey Head, Companion Leader requests permission to use lights."

"Grey Head here. Stand by."

There was really no reason to maintain blackout security, Curt decided. The South African company had turned back to Walvis Bay. No reports of any recon aircraft were in hand. Who was going to attack them out here in this desolate place?

"Companion Leader, Grey Head here. Von Walden reports these hills are virtually uninhabited. Permission to use lights granted, but suggest one of you in each vehicle wear red goggles to preserve night vision."

"Roger, Grey Head!" He called to Kester. "Henry, put on your red eyes and light it up!"

The brilliant beams of the ACV's headlamps cut through the night ahead of them. Curt was momentarily dazzled by their brilliance.

After a few seconds, his eyes adjusted . . . and he didn't like what he saw.

"Column halt!" he called on the regimental tac net. "Grey Head, this is Companion Leader. This is as far as we're going to go on this river bed . . . and probably as far as we're likely to get tonight . . ."

Thirty meters ahead of him rose a wall of jumbled rocks fifteen meters high. On both sides, the river bed had cut its way through a deep and rocky defile with rock walls equally as high.

CHAPTER TWENTY-SIX

"We're not going to be trapped and immobile in a river bed all night!" came Col. Belinda Hettrick's firm reply over the regimental tacomm frequency. "Companion Leader, can your platoons get out of the river bed on either side and proceed forward?"

"Colonel, we don't know what's out there, and it's dangerous to move in such rough country at night!" Curt complained.

"Yes, Captain, I know that. But we're going to keep moving," Hettrick maintained with an edge on her voice. "I'll call a thirty minute rest stop here for chow. In the meantime, I want you to get at least a platoon up on both sides of this river bed. I need recon. Companion Leader, can your platoons do it?"

Curt paused and tried to think. He was tired and dirty from the afternoon's trek, and he was feeling the stress of being near combat but not yet in it. Perhaps he was being overly cautious. On the other hand, he thought Hettrick was acting impetuously by ignoring doctrine and continuing to move under these conditions.

But discipline was discipline. And orders were orders. He'd done all he could in warning his superior officer of the potential hazards. Having done that, he knew what his job was: Follow the orders of his regimental commander. "Companion Alpha, this is Companion Leader. Query. My ACV is in a cul-de-sac; rocks ahead and on both sides. As I recall, the river bed was less of a defile about a hundred meters behind me. Can you get up either river bank?" he asked Alexis Morgan, keeping the regimental tacomm on the net.

"Roger, Companion Leader!" Alexis replied at once. "My trailing RTV can get up either bank here. I can wheel the individual vehicles of the platoon and follow. Bravo can go up whatever bank I don't and then carry out recon on the other side."

"Very well, do it! Use standard recon procedure," Curt told her. "Companions all, we're going out of the river bed on recon. Alpha goes to the right, Bravo to the left. I'll do a one-eighty and follow Alpha. Lights are authorized."

"Roger from Alpha!"

"Roger from Bravo!"

"Henry, wheel this humper around and follow Alpha!" Curt called to his master sergeant.

Getting out of the defile wasn't as easy as it looked. The sides of the narrow gorge were much steeper than they appeared to be. It took almost twenty minutes for Alpha Platoon to climb out of the gorge. With its heavier and larger vehicles, Bravo Platoon took almost thirty minutes to grind all the equipment up the bank onto fairly level ground. By the time the Companions were up on either side, the chow-down break was over and Hettrick wanted to move. "Companion Leader, this is Grey Head. Which side do we use?"

"Grey Head, this is Companion Leader. I can't tell you. We've just gotten to the top of the bank on both sides."

"Move out and report!" Hettrick snapped impatiently.

"Yes, Colonel. What does our guide have to say about the terrain we can expect?" Curt asked, perhaps unnecessarily, but he was more than a little frustrated by the fact that von Waldersee had not warned them of the rock blockage of the river bed.

"This is the first defile through the escarpment," Hettrick replied. "Von Waldersee says we've come up to a vertical rock dike. The river cut through it centuries ago. When we get beyond it, the terrain should open out a bit."

It was Alexis Morgan who discovered the root of the problem. "Companion Leader, Companion Alpha has discovered the reason for the river bed blockage . . . and we're blocked ourselves on the right bank. The river bed blockage was caused by a rock slide from the right. Not recent, by the way."

"Bravo, what does it look like on the left?" Curt wanted to know.

"As our guide thought, it looks like a vertical rock dike on the left edge of the river bed coming right up to the river. Apparently, the river once cut its way through here God-knows how many million years ago . . ." Lt. Jerry Allen reported. "I'll go for a closer look at it, but I don't think we can get around on the left bank."

"Captain!" It was Alexis Morgan. "I'm looking down on the river bed blockage at the moment. It's not more than ten meters thick where the rocks spilled over into the gorge. I think we can blast our way through. Let me go back into the river bed with one of my LAMVs, and I'll take out those rocks in a hurry. A couple of well-placed HE rounds from the Saucy Cans should do it. I'll make little ones out of big ones . . . and we should be able to go over the rubble . . ."

"Don't waste ammo," Curt told her. "Let's try positioning some plasticex grenades in there to blow those rocks out."

"Negatory on that plan, Captain!" came Colonel Hettrick's voice. "No one in the regiment knows enough about blasting to figure out where to emplace those grenades so the explosive will do the proper job. And plasticex grenades all by themselves might not have enough energy. Plus, there's the problem of getting them there in the right place and detonating them without having the whole mess fall on somebody. Blasting is an art, and we don't have an engineering battalion attached to the regiment. No grenades. You're authorized to try to blast the river bed blockage with Saucy Can fire. I'll hold the regimental column where it is to stay clear of your heavy fire. Acknowledge, Companion Leader."

"Roger, Grey Head, wilco," Curt responded. "We're heading back. Companion Alpha, I want you to coordinate this effort from the river bed with your Saucy Cans. Back off from the blockage about fifty meters if possible. Companion Bravo, I want you to stand by to take your LAMV down into the river bed only if it looks like Alpha will need additional explosives delivered on target by a salvo. Alpha understand?"

"Companion Alpha, roger!"

"Bravo understand?"

"Companion Bravo, roger . . . and Alpha gets to have all the fun!"

"Knock it off! We're all too damned tired for frivolity!" Curt snapped testily. Insofar as he was concerned, this was a ridiculous exercise to try to carry out in darkness. Maybe he was tired—he shouldn't have been after the relative rest and relaxation of their Swakopmund occupation—or maybe he was getting jumpy because they didn't know where they really were in what might become very hostile territory. Namibia was living up to its reputation as the land God made in anger. "Grey Head, how are we set for Saucy Cans ammo? Will Supply be able to replenish? We've got only a hundred rounds in each LAMV."

The Supply Unit commander, Lt. Harriet Dearborn, replied, "Companion Leader, this is Grey Supply. I've got more than five thousand rounds stashed in reserve beyond what your vehicles are carrying."

It was Lt. Alexis Morgan who replied, "If I can't blow that blockage with less than twenty rounds, I'll buy the drinks."

"You're on!" Dearborn replied.

"And the regimental commander as a witness," Hettrick put in.

Curt kept quiet. He knew that both Hettrick and his lieutenant were very stubborn women. Once they set their minds to something, they didn't exercise the normal perogative of a woman: changing their minds. Well, if they couldn't blast the rock barrier out of the way with point-blank artillery fire, they'd have to wait until morning when Gibbon could put up a birdbot and reconnoiter what was out there ahead of them.

As the Alpha Saucy Cans and ACV started back down into the river bed, Curt told Kester, "I'm transferring to Alpha."

"Yes, sir! Enjoy the fire and smoke, sir."

"Goddammit, Kester, I just want to make sure it's done right!"

"Yes, sir." The older man looked at him seriously, then a flicker of a slight smile played around one corner of his mouth. "Captain, one of the neat things about serving with you is the fact you've always exhibited initiative. Lieutenant Morgan's exhibiting lots of it right now. I just hope you won't lose yours, Captain, because you look a little tired and frustrated . . ."

Curt started to retort but swallowed. He relied on Henry Kester's innate knowledge of the fighting man and woman as much as he depended upon the old soldier's combat-honed experience as both an infantry foot soldier and a warbot brainy. The company commander knew he'd let the Spencer-Morgan affair bother him and perhaps warp his judgement, and he knew he'd probably gotten a bit uptight with his company in the last twenty-four hours ever since the fire fight in Swakopmund. What Henry Kester had said in his flat, midwestern accent amounted to a gentle prodding of his commanding officer, a bit of communication to him that perhaps he should start thinking like a company commander again.

Curt suddenly grinned at his first sergeant. "I'm going to be frustrated, Sergeant, until I get the rocks off."

Kester gave a snort that was a brief laugh.

Curt followed the Alpha ACV down the river bank on foot and crawled up the back of it once it was on level ground. Morgan was in one turret hatch, Spencer in the other. "Joining you, Lieutenant. I want to watch this," he said briefly.

"Captain," Alexis Morgan told him, "you should be behind armor for this. A lot of rocks may be flying around."

Curt looked at both occupied hatches. This was also no time to get Spencer pissed-off at him. "I'll ride the turret of the LAMV."

"I've put Sergeant Gerard in there to make sure everything goes as planned."

"I'll join him." Curt dropped to the ground and walked over to the LAMV.

The Light Artillery Mobile Vehicle was another Sierra Charlie kludge whipped together by Ordnance at Aberdeen in a matter of a few weeks on the basis of preliminary requirements drafted by Curt and Hettrick after Zahedan. It resembled the old Swedish *Stridsvagn* (S)103. Ordnance had taken an existing M888 Robot Recovery Vehicle and simply bolted a French *Canon Automatique de 75mm, Modele 03* to the chassis along the centerline. They'd equipped it with an auto-loader and a magazine for one-hundred rounds of caseless ammo . . . and still had room inside for more. The M888 could tip itself on its suspension to assist in recovering warbots of various sizes, and this feature was used to set the elevation of the gun. Slewing the entire vehicle by computer determined azimuth. The result was a light, highly maneuverable, and rapid-fire piece of mobile automatic artillery that could accompany a Sierra Charlie platoon in action. It had been a lash-up, an improvisation . . . but it had worked. No other army in the world had such a powerful, mobile artillery piece operating at the platoon level. It had worked beautifully on Trinidad, and tests had shown there wasn't a large armored warbot in the world, even those that had layered or Chobham armor, that could withstand the penetrating impact of one of its rocket-assisted AP rounds.

The Sierra Charlies loved having that much heavy supporting firepower right there on the field with them. "Ma'mselle Saucy Cans"—a result of the American vulgar pronunciation of the French words for "seventy-five" or *soixante-quinze*—was a favorite "daughter of the regiment."

Curt clambered over its flat top and dropped through the left hatch. Sgt. Nick Gerard was in the right hatch. The Saucy Cans could and normally did operate unmanned in robotic mode, but like all other roboticized vehicles it had provisions for human on-board monitoring and even control. "Thought I'd join you for the fun," Curt remarked.

"Welcome aboard, Captain. How does this position look?" the Alpha Platoon sergeant wanted to know.

The pile of rocks was only about twenty-five meters in front of them. "Little close, isn't it?" Curt said in a concerned tone.

"Can't get any further back," Gerard pointed out. He was right. The river bed took a sharp bend to the left behind them.

"Point-blank range. What's your aim point?"

"Two meters below the top of the pile," Gerard explained. "It's mostly pretty dense but breakable granite-like stuff. Volcanic, I guess. Some marble-like rock mixed in with it. Ought to be able to shatter it with ordinary HE rounds. So I think we ought to work it down to rubble from the top."

"Wish to hell we had a demolition expert with us," Curt muttered. "Impact or delayed detonation?"

"Going to use delayed, Captain. I want the round to be inside the pile when it blows. Get the most shattering effect from it. They taught me to blow bridges with warbots that way; plant the charges deep to shatter the concrete. Since we can't position shaped charges, we'll have to let the round slam deep and then blow."

"Okay, button down and let's try it," Curt growled. "Time's a wastin', and I've got a colonel on my back."

Gerard keyed the command computer and wiggled the aiming joystick. The Saucy Cans wiggled its tail as he nudged it onto the proper azimuth. Its rear suspension came down, pointing the gun near the top of the rock pile.

"Stand by!" Curt called on the regimental tacomm. "One round, HE, delayed fuse, into the top of the rocks. Ready on the left?"

"Ready on the left!" came the call from Sgt. Edie Sampson who was monitoring the operation from Bravo's location on the bank.

"Ready on the right?"

"Ready on the right!" was Sgt. Jim Elliott's reply.

Morgan was behind them around the curve in the river bed.

"Fire at will!" Curt snapped.

In spite of its long barrel and flash hider, the muzzel blast from the Saucy Cans lit up the night.

The muzzle blast itself was loud and sharp in the confines of the gulch, but the explosion of the shell inside the rock pile was a muffled boom.

"Jesus Christ!" Nick Gerard exploded, too.

The air was full of rock shards that peppered the front of the LAMV.

"Took out our headlamps," Gerard noted, peering into the dark dust cloud that boiled down the gully toward them in the light of the vehicles on both sides of the gorge.

As the dust cleared, Curt saw that only the top few meters of the rocks were gone, but there was shattered rock and rubble scattered in the river bed. "You aimed too high, Nick," he told the Sergeant. "Put the next one into the bottom of the pile about two meters up."

"Right, Captain! We'll be here all night blazing away at this if we just take a meter or so off the top each time . . ."

Curt felt the LAMV jack up its ass-end to lower the gun's elevation.

"I'll put a little more time delay on the fuse this time," Gerard remarked. "Ready to fire."

"Ready on the right?"

"Ready on the right!"

"Ready on the left?"

"Ready on the left!"

"Fire at will!"

Again the muzzle flash and brisant blast of the 75 mm gun.

The armor-piercing, high-explosive shell bored its way into the pile of boulders and then detonated.

The world was suddenly full of flying rocks.

As the cloud of dust boiled down the river gorge toward them, Curt saw large rocks and even boulders, some of them three meters or more in diameter, propelled outward by the blast and rolling rapidly down the river bed toward them.

There wasn't time to do anything about it.

Something big and heavy hit the LAMV . . . hard.

Curt remembered only that he was tossed about, slammed against the interior of the lash-up mobile artillery vehicle, and finally hit hard on his helmet.

CHAPTER TWENTY-SEVEN

The world was full of noise—mostly the roaring and whining of engines, the heavy booms and bangs of huge loads being moved around, and the sound of many people talking and shouting.

The world was also dark, but spots of light focused in front of Curt, pinning him in a bright circle of illumination.

He hurt all over.

"Captain? Captain Carson? Do you hear me?"

Two faces formed in front of him. It was hard to recognize them with the light shining behind them.

"Yeah . . . yeah . . . I hear you. Get the light out of my eyes!"

"Move the light around," the voice said.

Hovering over him, Curt saw Capt. Tom Alvin, a medical doctor with the Biotech Unit and the Companion's biotech, Sgt. Shelley Hale.

He was flat on his back on the ground.

His head hurt the most.

He felt like he'd been beaten with a club.

"Sergeant, he's conscious!"

"Thank God! Damned miracle we got 'em out of that Saucy Can alive!" There was no mistaking the voice of M. Sgt. Henry Kester.

". . . The Saucy Cans . . . What happened?" Curt suddenly remembered that final round fired from the 75 mm high-velocity gun on the LAMV.

"Written off, Captain." said Henry Kester.

"What the hell—?"

Tom Alvin shone a small flashlight into Curt's eyes, then held up a finger. "Look at my finger. Follow it," he ordered. Curt did so. "Good! No sign of head injury. Possible mild concussion, however. That had me worried for a bit. And no broken bones. Couple of minor cuts. Some bruises and contusions. Captain, you're lucky. Can you sit up?"

It hurt Curt to do so, and he was a little dizzy from the effort, but he decided the doctor was right and that he didn't have any broken bones. Mostly, he felt thoroughly beaten to a pulp. "As I said, what the hell happened?"

"You and Sergeant Gerard were trapped inside that crushed LAMV for more than thirty minutes," Sgt. Shelley Hale told him. "We were afraid it was going to catch fire. Then we were afraid you'd been crushed in there." She gave him something to drink. It might have been water, but it might have had something else in it. Curt didn't know and he didn't particularly care. His mouth was dry, and the liquid helped his raspy throat and made it easier for him to swallow and speak.

"When Nick put that second round into the rocks," Henry Kester explained, "it was one of them new Comp-H rounds, and it went deep before it detonated. Comp-H has a lot of bang per kilo. Lot more than we're used to. The explosion blew rocks all over hell . . . including two big ones that came down the river bed and clobbered the LAMV. Bent the shit out of it. Like Hale said, took us more than half an hour to cut the two of you out of it. We had to drain the fuel out so it wouldn't catch fire when we used a cutting torch—and that heavy composite armor on the Triple-Eight is goddamned tough to burn through! Only thing that saved your ass was the heavy composite hull. It was designed to carry the loads of picking up damaged warbots."

"Sure blew the hell out of that pile of rock, though," Alvin remarked.

"Gerard! Where's Nick Gerard?" Curt suddenly remembered.

"Just stay put," Tom Alvin told him, putting a hand on his shoulder. "You took a hell of a bang. Ruth Gydesen and Denise Logan are both working on him."

"Lieutenant Morgan's with them," Kester added. "Lieutenant Allen's got temporary command of the company. So don't worry, Captain. The company's okay—except we lost an LAMV—and Gerard's getting the best help available . . ."

Curt tried to get to his feet. He had trouble. He was pretty bruised and battered. When Alvin put his hands on Curt's shoulders and forced him back down, Curt exploded, "Goddammit, Tom, if one of my sergeants is hurt, I want to know how bad and—"

"Sit down and shut up," Captain Tom Alvin told him, "or I'll squirt you full of tranquilizer and *keep* you quiet for your own sake! Give me a chance, and I'll tell you what I know . . ."

Curt sighed and tried to relax. It helped the hurts. "Okay, tell me."

"Broke at least one leg, maybe the other. Busted some ribs. Maybe some internal damage and bleeding. Maybe a ruptured spleen . . . We don't know it all yet. He may have some head injuries although that's highly improbable because his helmet wasn't crushed," the doctor explained. "He was unconscious when we got him out of the LAMV, and he's now back in the surgical van with two good trauma doctors and two of the best biotechs working on him. My job is to make sure you didn't get hurt badly enough to be put on the sick list . . ."

"Shit," Curt muttered. "I should have known better than to try to do a demolition job. We aren't trained for that sort of thing . . ."

"Wasn't your fault, Curt," Alvin told him.

"Maybe, but it was my responsibility in any event. Lemme try standing up now."

As he did so, he noted that Len Spencer was there with his camcorder running. That was the least of Curt's worries right then. He could stand without help, the dizziness had gone away, but he was still sore. "Tom, return me to duty status," he told the doctor.

"Tomorrow morning," Alvin promised. "You're in no shape for duty right now. You need to rest and relax for about six to eight hours—"

"Rest and relax? With one of my NCOs in surgery? And God knows what the rest of the situation looks like? Bullshit! Where's Colonel Hettrick?" Curt demanded in a loud voice.

"Look, Curt," Alvin told him in formal tones, "I understand your concern for your troops. But I'm concerned about you. You took a hell of a beating inside that vehicle. I want to keep my eye on you for a day or so."

"I haven't got a day or so, Tom," Curt snapped. "Do you find anything seriously wrong with me now?"

"No, you survived the accident in surprising condition. Might have some badly sprained neck or back muscles, but—"

"I've been hurt worse playing football! Unless you officially sign me into sick bay and put me aboard the Biotech Support Vehicle," Curt told him in no uncertain tones, "I'm reporting back to duty with Hettrick . . . *now!"*

Capt. Tom Alvin shrugged. Maybe he was being medically conservative without reason, but it had been a long time since medics had had to treat infantrymen in the field. Maybe he was overly concerned. So he said, "Okay, but no strenuous activity. Take it easy. Check in with the colonel, look after your company, then turn in and get some rest. Understand?"

"Yeah. Sure. Sergeant Kester, let's go find the colonel."

"Remember: rest and relax," Alvin reminded him, knowing full well that he couldn't stop this man short of sedating him, which really wasn't indicated and couldn't be justified.

"You bet—"

"Hale, stay with him."

"Yes, Doctor."

Belinda Hettrick was standing on the edge of the river channel looking down while stationary vehicles on the lip flooded the area below with light and the heavier vehicles equipped with dozer blades scooped and scraped away rocks in the river bed.

He and Gerard had indeed blasted a path through the barrier with a high-velocity shell loaded with powerful Comp-H explosive that had detonated deep within the rubble. Some large boulders remained, but they were being pushed away or to the side by the big RTVs.

The regimental commander turned when Curt stepped up. "Good evening, Captain! Glad to see you're not badly hurt . . ."

"Hurt, yes, Colonel, but not badly. And fit for duty."

"What did Captain Alvin say?"

It was Sgt. Shelley Hale who replied, "He didn't actually return the captain to duty, Colonel. Told him to rest and relax until morning. But this captain of mine is sort of stubborn . . ."

"That he is," Hettrick agreed. "Captain Carson, I'm officially and temporarily relieving you of command—"

"*What?* May I ask why, Colonel?"

"The doctors haven't confirmed that you're fit for duty at this time, and you didn't seem to pay attention to them . . . but you'll have to pay attention to me," Hettrick told him gently but firmly. "Look, we're going to be another couple of hours clearing the path down there. We don't need you for that. You did a good job even if you aren't a demolition specialist. But you and Sergeant Gerard were too close. Never mind; you got the job done. As I said, good work. I don't need you right now, and I won't need you for many hours yet. The regiment will function without you. Turn over your company to Lieutenant Morgan and—"

"Morgan's back with Gerard," Curt pointed out.

"She can't do much of anything for Sergeant Gerard except be the official worrier . . . and Gydesen doesn't need one," Hettrick went on. "Curt, I know you'd like to be with Sergeant Gerard, too. Both you and Morgan are concerned about your troops, and that's natural. But you've got to get over that banging around you took, so you're officially off duty for the next six to eight hours—we'll see what Alvin says later. Let Morgan take over Carson's Companions. Sergeant Kester, go get her and tell her that her duty is with her company as second in command. Curt, go to your ACV and climb in the sack. I'll talk to you in a few hours and we'll see then if Captain Alvin thinks you've recovered well enough to lead your outfit again."

"Colonel, I—" Curt started to complain.

"Dammit, Captain, *that's an order!*"

"Yes, Colonel."

"Sergeant Hale, take Captain Carson to his ACV and make sure he starts logging some sack time. Rock him to sleep with a rock if you have to."

"Yes, Colonel." Shelley Hale put her hand firmly but gently on Curt's arm. "Captain, let's get started, sir. Your ACV is down in the river bed."

"How did it get there? I left it on the other bank—"

"Sergeant Kester brought it down," Hale explained. She started to lead Curt away.

Curt shrugged her off only to turn and salute Hettrick. "By your leave, Colonel." Field and combat conditions or not, protocol was part of discipline, and Curt wasn't about to let that slip. Although he often relaxed discipline and operated informally in his own company, it was discipline that kept military units together when the going got tough . . . and the going had gotten tough.

"Good night, Captain. And thank you."

"Part of our efficient and effective service, Colonel. Good night," Curt quipped and turned to join Hale.

CHAPTER TWENTY-EIGHT

Unnoticed by Colonel Hettrick, Len Spencer had accompanied Curt and his two NCOs to see her. The newshawk had stayed discreetly in the background, listening and watching. His videocam wasn't running, but his little audio recorder was. As Carson, Kester, and Hale walked off toward the bottom of the river bed and the Companion Leader's ACV, Spencer decided to stay with the regimental commander. He saw no need to trail Carson and possibly bother him now; the man needed rest after the shaking up he'd gotten when the rocks bowled over and nearly crushed the LAMV . . . a dramatic sequence that Spencer had gotten on videotape. Carson needed rest at the moment. So Spencer shifted his attention to Belinda Hettrick whose only job at the moment was watching her regiment clear out the river gorge so the convoy could proceed. He stepped up beside her and remarked, "Took guts for Carson to go down there in that artillery vehicle with his sergeant, didn't it?"

Hettrick glanced at him and returned her attention to the work going on in the river bed. Offhandedly, she replied, "Captain Carson is an outstanding officer." She wasn't certain she really wanted to talk about it right then.

But Spencer persisted in a gentle way. "Looks like he's one of those officers who'll never let any of his people do something he won't do himself."

Hettrick nodded. "Usually he's out in front leading them."

"A very brave man."

Hettrick shook her head this time. "No, it's part of what makes a good leader. What Carson did tonight wasn't really bravery. He was courageous, yes, because courage involves something you do because you feel in your heart that it's right."

"Courage comes from the French word for 'heart,'" Spencer reminded her.

"I didn't know that. German was my foreign language at the Military Academy," Hettrick admitted. "But bravery is different from courage. Bravery is when you do something without witnesses that you might do with the whole world watching."

Spencer patted his camcorder. "The whole world was watching. And I think the quote about bravery comes from Duc Francois de La Rochefoucauld . . ."

Hettrick shrugged. "Could be. I guess you'd know more about French literature than I."

"About quotations, maybe, but not about bravery . . ." Len Spencer admitted, seeing that he was beginning to get this laconic woman to talk a little more. "Commanding a combat regiment, you've seen a hell of a lot more bravery than I have."

"I suppose so. Yes, I guess you could say I've seen my share of it. Lot of the battle and campaign streamers on the regimental colors were hung there since I joined the Greys."

"How long ago was that?" Spencer asked her gently. He was getting fantastic human interest stuff here, material that the general public didn't often know and that would make these robot infantry soldiers less mechanical and a lot more human than the public perceived them to be. Ernie Pyle and Maggie Higgins stuff. The material that Pulitzer prizes were made of.

"Twenty-two years . . . less the time I spent on temporary assignment in the war colleges and staff schools."

"Twenty-two years in the same regiment?"

"The Army stopped transferring people around like they used to," Hettrick explained then started to ramble. She was growing weary, and it sort of helped to be able to talk to someone who wasn't a subordinate. She needed to talk. She was the most senior officer around, and radio conferences with General Carlisle were strictly official business. Command is indeed a lonely job. That's why she'd enjoyed the luncheon with Colonel van Wijk, even though she'd had to be very careful about what she said for security purposes. Spencer was a good man to talk to; he listened well and seemed to understand what the military profession was all about. She knew he was probably recording, but she didn't care. She'd say nothing that wasn't doctrinaire in the first place. If he'd really wanted to dig for it, he could have found it in the various Army manuals and handbooks anyway.

"Army units are all smaller today—divisions, regiments, companies, platoons—because of warbots and automation," she went on to explain. "So we have to work together more closely as teams. And once you get a good team working—like they're doing right now down there cleaning up that rubble in the river bed—you don't break them up. That was a hard lesson from Korea and Southeast Asia and a couple of skirmishes after that which the Army chose to ignore. When the neuroelectronic warbots came in about twenty years ago, we found we had to hold the combat teams together. Spencer, have you ever experienced robot linkage . . . extending your senses and powers out through a machine that may be kilometers away?"

"I've been in the simulators a couple of times," he admitted, "but I didn't have the time to undergo the six months' basic training it requires to do deep linkage work."

"Well, it's like sex: Until you've done it, you don't know anything about it," Hettrick admitted. "Probably the closest thing we'll get to real mental telepathy is when you're in warbot linkage and tie in with someone else through a warbot. You can get right inside their mind. When that happens you either get to know and like them very much—like marriage, I understand—or you discover you can't stand them. We have our petty little likes and dislikes in the regiment; some officers and NCOs don't like others. Capt. Joanne Wilkinson, my personnel officer, does her best to balance out the assignments and put people where they'll work best with others. So once our good combat and support teams were formed in the robot infantry, they tended to work better if they stayed together. That policy sloshed over into the Sierra Charlie outfits because it works so well—"

"What happens when someone comes along and everyone in the outfit hates their bloody guts?"

"Oh, they get shipped out early in the game, and the Army tries to find a unit they'll fit into or a slot that works for them." Hettrick didn't mention that these people tended to clump into companies like her perennial problem, Kelly's Killers. She smiled. "You might say we're a horticultural organization . . ."

"Eh?"

"We weed out people."

"I asked for that. How's the new Special Combat doctrine going to affect this?" Spencer asked, having read up on everything he could about the Sierra Charlies and watched the Companions in Swakopmund.

Hettrick shrugged. This man was easy to talk to, and she could still keep an eye on the work in the river bed. "I don't think it's going to have very much effect on what we've learned about each other in the course of developing the robot infantry. In the process of learning how to work with these fantastic machines that are extensions of ourselves, we've learned a little more about ourselves, too. We're still warbot brainies, you know; we can get back into linkage with very little refresher training. Sort of like riding a bicycle, something you never forget once the neural patterns are established. Okay, the new warbots won't change that very much because they're just dumb mechanical infantry riflemen."

"Some Pentagon spokemen explained that these new warbots have an IQ of about seventy-five," Len mentioned.

"Not a fair comparison," the Colonel told him. "Their

circuits work faster than ours, and they don't forget anything, and they follow orders *exactly* . . . which took my troops some getting used to. But they can't make decisions like we can and they aren't anywhere near as versatile as we are."

"And they don't care . . ." Spencer added.

"You know, Spencer, you're right. A machine doesn't care if it wins or loses. We do," Hettrick admitted. "So I guess that's why we're managing to keep most of the closeness of our former roles as warbot brainies. We've rediscovered something of the earlier cameraderie of old-time infantry units."

"Seems in a close group like your regiment you'd lose a lot of your men and women to marriage," Spencer observed, probing down a new tack. And all of this was absolutely new; no newshawk had ever really gotten head-to-head with the warbot brainies; they preferred to write gee-whiz stories about the warbots and the technology. This was real human interest material he was gathering . . . and from the boss lady herself!

"Surprisingly not," she told him. "At least, not in the combat companies. The support companies are something else, just like the various support and non-combat Army branches. Non-combat people get transferred around more, and they tend to marry and raise families, especially if they're not assigned to one of the combat regiments."

"What happens if two of your combat soldiers get married? Do they get transferred out to non-combat outfits?"

"Men and women in the combat teams sometimes get married, but they gain no special privileges by doing so. Rule Ten is Rule Ten. If it happened in my regiment, I'd pay a little more attention to what's going on in their company. But as long as it didn't adversely affect the combat team, I'd be damned dumb to mess with the situation." Hettrick thought a moment, then went on, "After all, Spencer, you've got to realize that this regiment is just one big family . . ."

"You've never married?" It was part question, part statement from Spencer.

Hettrick shook her head. "Nope. Not that I haven't had plenty of opportunities, mind you. And not that I don't enjoy the intimate companionship of male members of the opposite sex. But that's getting a little too personal, and I should keep personal matters out of this. In a mixed-gender warbot outfit, it's one big family. First your platoon that's your initial assignment and responsibility. Then the company. Now, for me, the Washington Greys regiment, a family of more than eighty people."

"Miss having children?" It might have been a delicate question. Spencer hoped it wasn't.

Hettrick looked at him with a surprised expression; he thought he'd blown it until she replied, "My God, Spencer, I've got over eighty children here! Besides, I'm too old now to have natural kids, even with modern biotechnology. Doesn't bother me. I decided long ago there were too many people in the world. So my life has been devoted to the military service of my country. I like military life."

"What do you particularly like about it?" Spencer probed.

"The people," Hettrick answered without hesitation. "Quite frankly, I like the men, and I like the 'equal but different' policy. Sure as hell has come a long ways since the days of Deborah Gannett . . ."

"Sorry, but who was she?"

"Len Spencer, with your knowledge of military history, I felt sure you'd know!" Hettrick chided him gently.

"Remind me," he asked her.

"In the Revolutionary War," she explained. "Deborah Gannett masqueraded as a soldier for two years. Don't ask me how she did it! But she fought alongside men and did it very well."

"You said you liked the men," Spencer returned to an earlier subject that Hettrick had mentioned but apparently glossed over quickly. He was again probing for that elusive tidbit or quote that would make a story great, especially since many civilians secretly believed the modern mixed Army was often a taxpayer-financed orgy. "Is there something different about them?" He was looking for a sexual angle.

But he didn't quite get what he was probing for because Hettrick told him, "Yes. Definitely. Not all of them, but most of them. At the Military Academy, we learned duty, honor, country. The men and women who go through four years of having that philosophy pounded into them day and night are men and women who will do their duty, cherish personal honor, and love their country—"

"Ah! 'My country, may it always be right, but my country, right or wrong!'"

"No. *You can depend upon these people!* We have our disagreements. Often, we don't like our orders. We can make our objections known, and a good commander will listen carefully and consider the opinions of subordinates. But when the orders come, we march. Dependability, Len, dependability. I've come up against a few shitheads, male and female, in this man's Army, but they don't last long. The remainder are good people. Man and woman, they are *ladies and gentlemen,* and I refuse to use a scrambled gender word here because I consider 'man' to be a contraction of the word 'human.' Do you know what a lady or a gentleman is, Len?"

"There are many definitions," Spencer reminded her.

"Only one definition counts: 'A lady or a gentleman is a person who is never unintentionally rude.' I like people in this Army because they're ladies and gentlemen . . ."

"Uh, Colonel, haven't you just presented me with a paradox: A military establishment of people who are never unintentionally rude but who are also trained in the application of physical force and violence . . . ?"

Hettrick smiled sweetly at the newshawk. "Len, I'm a violent person who's learned to be gentle. All of us are that way, military and civilian alike. But we military people admit it. Right at the moment, I'm being gentle with you. However, I assure you that if I should ever have to kill you, I'd do so in a pleasant manner accompanied with great regret . . . Don't worry! Thus far, you've been a gentleman and given me no reason to do that. If I were given orders to do it, I'd lodge the most persuasive objection possible with my superior officer. One does not kill without very good reason. But, sir, I would never be rude to you while I did it!"

Len Spencer exhaled long and slowly. "I'm not at all sure," he said slowly, "that I'd want to have you as an enemy, Colonel. On the other hand, I'd feel most secure with you at my back in a dark alley or a barroom brawl . . ."

Col. Belinda Hettrick inclined her head. "Thank you, sir. Although I doubt that either of us would get into such a situation, I couldn't have received a greater compliment from a man. And the other ladies in my command would feel the same way."

"I've noticed. You've taken female equality to its absolute limit, haven't you?"

She nodded. "Of course! Where else did they believe it would lead when Abigail Adams started it all? But, Spencer, don't *ever* confuse equality and difference! Or the ladies of the Washington Greys are likely to take you to pieces in their own inimitable way . . ." She paused, having noted as a good commanding officer should have noted the growing triangle between Curt, Alexis Morgan, and Len Spencer, then added, "And God help the man who thinks he can love 'em and leave 'em."

"Uh, Colonel, I—" Spencer began, at a loss for words for once.

"Enough said, Mister Spencer. Now, please excuse me, you've got your human interest story and I've got a military mission to accomplish. Several hundred people are in deadly danger in Otjomuise . . . and we've *got* to get there!"

CHAPTER TWENTY-NINE

Live shot from New York of the world-recognized news anchor staring seriously into the camera. "The *Times'* Constant News Channel has been trying to get reports out of the besieged embassy compound in Windhoek, the capital city of Namibia. But the native rebellion there, reminiscent of the recent Colour War in South Africa, has resulted in the shut-down of all communications with the outside world save those systems in various embassies which utilize satellite communications to maintain contact with their home capitals. However, the *Times* is always on top of world events, and our correspondent Leonard Spencer is one of the few reporters allowed to accompany the troops of the United States Army into that part of the world. We go now direct to Len Spencer live via his own miniature satellite station with United States forces in Namibia. Good evening, Len."

Live shot via satellite showing Len Spencer standing in the darkness illuminated by moving lights from vehicles around him with lots of noise accompanied by the voices and shouts of people. "Good evening, Walter. Len Spencer here, reporting to you live from somewhere in the southwest African country of Namibia, that unfortunate nation now being racked by a rebellion that has trapped nearly a thousand people in the diplomatic compound of the capital city of Windhoek. We've learned through military command channels that British warbot troops failed earlier today in their attempt to relieve besieged French forces that had landed in the capital city on a rescue mission yesterday. As a result of this military blunder on the part of the French and British, American troops who had been landed in the seacoast town of Swakopmund as a reserve force yesterday were ordered to move to Windhoek shortly before noon, local time. We've been on the road now for well over fourteen hours, and progress is slow in this barren, rocky desert country that's very much like Nevada or Arizona.

"If you've been following my reports—and I'm sure the Channel has been rebroadcasting them all day long to keep you up to date—you'll remember that I joined the American contingent—the Washington Greys robot infantry regiment—on the British-held island of St. Helena, our jumping-off point. The British and French military commanders running this joint multinational operation ordered the Washington Greys under the command of Colonel Belinda J. Hettrick to land in the seacoast town of Swakopmund, which is a pleasant summer resort dating back to German colonial rule in the nineteenth century. Well, it's summertime here in the southern hemisphere although many of you in America have to bundle up warmly before going outside these days.

"The Washington Greys were to hold the town of Swakopmund to keep the South Africans at bay while the French and British pulled off the rescue mission in Windhoek—which is a lot easier to say than Otjomuise, the native name for the town. For little more than twenty-four hours, this guard duty in Swakopmund seemed like a vacation to our troops."

Cut to videotape showing Carson's Companions deployed along the Swakop River with their vehicles and warbots.

"The American officers I got to know were keenly disappointed that the United States didn't get a more active role in the rescue operation. The Washington Greys are one of the new Army regiments dedicated to Special Combat missions. This regiment, under Colonel Belinda Hettrick, played a major role in the recent invasion of Trinidad."

Cut to a shot of Hettrick with the Germanlike buildings of Swakopmund behind her. The tape had been shot early on the second morning after landing. Without her battle helmet and wearing her campaign beret, she looked too feminine to be a military officer in command of a regiment. Squinting into the morning sun because Spencer had told her to remove her sunglasses, she speaks, "Mr. Spencer, of course we're disappointed that we aren't seeing the major action in Operation Diamond Skeleton. We're the first Army regiment to convert to the Sierra Charlie doctrine . . ."

"What's that, Colonel? Some people at home don't follow Army slang easily," Spencer voice off-camera asks her.

"'Sierra Charlie' are the phonetic alphabet initials for 'Special Combat,' Mr. Spencer," Hettrick replies somewhat impatiently. She flicks her eyes to one side; it's obvious she'd rather be off taking care of some regimental military matter than talking to this newshawk, and it's equally obvious that she knows she has no other choice. "We've been letting machines do the fighting for the last two decades or so; seemed cheaper than getting people killed. Warbots come off assembly lines and, although they're not cheap, you can make 'em quicker than you can make a soldier; a human being requires months of training to become a soldier . . . after you've spent eighteen years before that letting them grow up. Warbots were big and powerful. Still are. But warbots can't do everything. The French and British are now learning that in Otjomuise. We learned it during the rescue of the hypersonic airliner passengers in the Iranian town of Zahedan."

Len Spencer's off-camera voice asks, "Do you think your Special Combat regiment should have been sent into the Namibian capital instead of two crack French and British robot infantry units?"

Hettrick shrugged. "The French organized this; they were the ones who had their ambassador killed by the *bleep* who started the *bleep* rebellion. We go where we're ordered and we do what our civilian government leaders tell us; that's the American military way. Yes, we're sitting on our duffs here in Swakopmund at the moment guarding the coast and keeping the South African troops in Walvis Bay over there from getting ideas about taking Namibia back again as a result of the *bleep* rebellion. It isn't all R-and-R, Mr. Spencer; we had a little fire fight last night when some native terrorists or guerrillas snuck in from the north of Namibia and tried to ambush one of my companies. We took care of them in short order without harming any of the civilians here. So we can fight hand-to-hand if we have to."

"Your regiment contains twenty-six women. Most of them are left over from its organization as a warbot unit," Spencer asks in a pointed manner. "Do you expect them to fight hand-to-hand?"

"Damned right! And they aren't 'left over,' as you put it! They're part of the Washington Greys right along with the men. They fought right along with the men in Trinidad and during the little fracas we had when we came in here yesterday morning . . ."

"What happened during that shoot-out in the town square where one of the local policemen was killed, Colonel?" came Spencer's off-camera voice.

"Just exactly what I told you yesterday when you quizzed me about it."

"The women get trigger-happy in the crunch?"

"It was my only all-male combat company that was involved, Spencer, and—" The tape was edited right there to take out the rest of Hettrick's rather scathing and profane reply about his over-emphasis on the women of the Washington Greys.

Cut back to live shot of Spencer with the bright lights of the river bed clearing operation still going on behind them. "At about noon today, local time—we're seven hours ahead of New York—Major General Carlisle of the United States Army, the Deputy Supreme Allied Commander of Operation Diamond Skeleton, ordered the Washington Greys to proceed overland to Windhoek.

Their plan to go via the main highway was frustrated by South African troops who closed the road and were attempting to locate the native terrorists who had infiltrated into Swakopmund the previous night. Of course, this is totally against all the United Nations' rules, but one must remember that the French, British, Indian, Australian, and American troops are in Namibia today in violation of the principles of the United Nations as well. Technically, I'm told this isn't a military invasion or the use of military force in an armed conflict. It's a rescue operation because the government of Namibia is itself powerless to protect the foreign nationals in its capital city.

"As a result, the American regiment had to move directly across country without the benefit of roads . . ."

Long shot on tape of the dusty convoy of vehicles crossing the barren, hot, sun-drenched Namib Desert earlier that afternoon.

Spencer's voice over a medium shot of Doctor Paul von Waldersee which Spencer got on tape shortly after talking with Hettrick that morning. "Colonel Hettrick hired a local explorer as a guide to help the regiment make the trek to Windhoek. Doctor Paul von Waldersee is a native-born white Namibian who has lived in Windhoek all his life. He's a professor of anthropology at the University of Windhoek and claims to know the country . . ."

The anthropologist began to talk on the tape. "I've been into these mountains between Swakopmund and Windhoek for years. They're rather barren and rugged, but I don't foresee any difficulty in guiding the regiment overland to Windhoek if necessary. Of course, the maps aren't very good because hardly anyone but myself ever goes into the hills, but I think I know the land well enough to guide the Colonel on the basis of prior knowledge of the area. I'm particularly interested in the various native tribes that inhabit this part of Africa . . ."

"Any particular dangers involved from these native tribes, Doctor?" Spencer's voice asked off-camera.

Von Waldersee shook his head. "No, just rugged

country, that's all. Some snakes and scorpions, but they're no real problem."

"No possibility of hostile natives attacking the Americans like they attacked the whites in Windhoek a few days ago?"

Von Waldersee laughed. "Hardly! The hills of the escarpment haven't been populated by small tribes of Bushmen since prehistoric times. The Germans first and then the South Africans resettled most of the native tribes in their own homelands in far better locations in Namibia. Even if we were to run into a few isolated Bushmen, these people are basically friendly. I speak their language, and I've gotten along well with the various tribes for years. I'm their friend, and they know it. Those mountains out there are basically uninhabited. The Bastaard homelands are located far south of us, and we shouldn't run into anyone except perhaps a few isolated hunting parties . . . and I doubt even that because game is so scarce now in those mountains . . ."

Cut back to Spencer live alongside the brightly illuminated river bed. "Shortly after night fell, the regiment was proceeding up the dry river bed you see behind me. All the rivers around here are dry; any water in them flows underground. The lead vehicle encountered a rock slide that had blocked the river bed. An attempt was made to blast the rocks out of the way with mobile artillery . . ."

Cut to tape showing Curt and Nick Gerard in the LAMV firing their second round into the rocks. The rock slide erupts in smoke, dust, and flying debris. Two huge boulders roll down the sandy river bed and smash the LAMV.

Spencer's voice over: "Two men were trapped there. One is still in serious condition in the regiment's mobile surgical van. The other, Captain Curt Carson, escaped without serious injury but has been sent to rest for the night by the medical team."

Cut back to Spencer on the lighted river bank. "The demolition was otherwise a success, and the rubble is being cleaned out of the river bed to make a path for the rest of the convoy to proceed toward Windhoek. Colonel Belinda Hettrick tells me we'll be underway again in less than an hour. I'll keep all of you up to date as the American rescue mission proceeds across landscape that deserves its local name as the 'land God made in anger.' Leonard Spencer reporting live from somewhere in Namibia . . ."

The anchor in New York fired a question at Spencer. "Len, how long before the Americans get to Windhoek to relieve the people in danger there?"

"Walter, I'm told we have only about a hundred-forty kilometers yet to go. But they are one-hundred-forty very rough kilometers. The regiment managed to cover about a hundred and twenty kilometers in the first twelve hours of this trek, but they were easy kilometers over fairly flat desert scrub land. With any luck at all, and if Doctor von Waldersee can indeed pilot us through these endless rugged mountains, we might be in Windhoek by tomorrow night . . ."

"Len, how are the women soldiers holding up?"

"Walter, whoever once called women the 'weaker sex' was dead wrong! The twenty-six women in the Washington Greys are trim, tough, trained, and certainly not weak! They're professionals who performed professionally in Trinidad, and the American people need not worry about them. They can certainly take care of themselves! I have several upcoming special reports on this unique American regiment and its people. Stay tuned for a special segment at eleven—which will be about five o'clock in the morning here. I'll be sending some live shots of this very beautiful and desolate country showing the Americans who are making a do-or-die effort to get through it to help the people under siege in Windhoek . . ."

"Any problems with the military equipment, Len?"

"Well, Walter, soldiers always find something to gripe about. If it isn't their food, it's their equipment. But this food isn't bad if you don't mind the sort of grub you have to eat on a camp-out in the woods while hiking. And this regiment is very well-supplied indeed. They've got food, ammunition, and other equipment stuffed into every nook and cranny of their vehicles. They came into Swakopmund yesterday prepared for anything from a long siege there to this desolate trek to Windhoek. Colonel Belinda Hettrick—who is a dedicated officer and West Pointer, by the way—told me the Washington Greys can operate up to two hundred hours on their own. Thus far, they've been on the road a little more than fourteen hours . . . and they've lost only one vehicle due to the accident blasting through the rocks in the river bed. Other than that, there have been no breakdowns that I'm aware of. As taxpayers, we can be glad that we've gotten our money's worth . . ."

"Thank you, Len," the anchor intoned. "Leonard Spencer, long known as one of the top military journalists, will continue to report to us as this incredible story unfolds in far away Namibia. With his satellite link system, he'll feed pictures and prerecorded tape to us as often as he can, and you'll be able to follow his unedited video coverage on the *Times* Constant News Channel as it comes in to us. By special pool and sharing arrangements, CNC will also continue to broadcast video and audio coverage as it comes in from Reuters, the London *Times*, the French news services, and the Nippon World Watch. Hard-copy printouts, graphics, and video frames will also be available to *Times* subscribers as this native rebellion in Namibia grinds toward its climax with the American military force approaching Windhoek. Will the French and British troops be overwhelmed in Windhoek before the Americans can get there? How soon will the airbase at Grootfontein be fully capable of establishing air superiority over Windhoek? How long will the hundreds of people trapped in the diplomatic compound be able to hold out against the hordes of native warriors storming the walls? These and a hundred other suspenseful questions come to mind as the story unfolds. Dan, our viewers want suspense and excitement, they don't have to tune to an adventure series tonight!"

"Right you are, Walter! Now for other news . . ."

CHAPTER THIRTY

The sandy defile of the dry river bed leading up into the hills of the Namibian escarpment finally got too narrow for the vehicles of the Washington Greys to negotiate.

Curt was back in the turret hatch of his ACV again, feeling somewhat better after six hours of sleep. He could have sworn that Shelley Hale had slipped a mickey into whatever she'd given him to drink because he'd been able to sleep through the sounds, bumps, and pitching motion of the ACV making its way up the river bed during the night.

He had a plethora of black and blue spots on his body, including one on his thigh that looked ghastly yellow but which Hale said was really only a bruise. He had no broken bones, although his back felt like it had been wrenched, he had a sore neck, and one of his ankles hurt.

He looked around at the terrain with a mixture of disdain and disillusionment. The hills were steep and barren. There were some scrub-like trees here and there that reminded him of the pinion pines and junipers south of Payson in Arizona, the Sonoran Desert plant biome that ran from about 1,000 to 1,700 meters in altitude with very little rainfall and lots of summer heat.

There was no sign of life anywhere.

And the regiment was travelling under X-ray Alert, the lowest of all possible combat readiness levels. Curt continued to wear his battle helmet primarily to keep the hot sun off his head and to use the neurophonic communications gear built into it. Guns were stowed in travel position and no one was required to wear body armor.

The river bed walls weren't very high now, but the river canyon sloped steeply away from both banks of the dry stream.

By mid-morning, Lt. Alexis Morgan reported back from her ACV in the lead, "Companion Leader, this is Companion Alpha. I've got to get up out of the river bed. It's becoming too steep and narrow."

"What does von Waldersee have to say about it?" Curt asked. The guide was now riding in Morgan's vehicle.

His voice came back through the neurophonic transducers of Curt's helmet. "If we can follow this river to its source up there in the hills about three kilometers ahead, we should go over a saddle rise that will put us in a fairly flat but somewhat rocky area that we can traverse until we have to tackle the next ridge which is about fifteen kilometers beyond that, if my memory serves me rightly."

"Doctor, your memory had better be serving you rightly," Curt reminded him. The inertial positioning unit in his ACV had not kept its alignment through the night. In fact, even the master IRU in the regimental command van had tumbled twice, forcing Sergeant Crawford of S-2 to get a realignment from the SkyNav satellite system. The latitude and longitude numbers from SkyNav didn't match their position on the map, judging from the hills and other landmarks they could see. In short, either the SkyNav satellite system was wrong—which was a very low probability—or the maps were wrong, which had a higher probability.

"Oh, there's no question about it, Captain," von Waldersee replied easily. "I was in here about nine years ago. Nothing much seems to have changed."

"You could have forgotten a lot in nine years, Doctor."

"Not bloody likely either. I'll prove it in a few minutes after we get out of this river bottom and move along past the base of those cliffs up ahead."

"Which bank do you recommend we use?" Curt asked directly.

"I was through here on foot, Captain. I don't know what's best for your vehicles."

Curt called up regimental headquarters. "Grey Head, this is Companion Alpha. The river bed is becoming too steep and narrow for our larger vehicles. I'm sending scouting parties up ahead—squad leaders mounted on ATVs. In the meantime, we'll pick the best looking side of the river and proceed."

"Roger, Companion Alpha. Approved. Proceed." Colonel Hettrick's voice sounded tired.

"How's Sergeant Gerard doing?" Curt asked with concern.

"Call up Major Gydesen yourself and ask her."

"Roger, will do." First things first. "Companion Alpha, go up the bank that looks easiest and that might have the lesser slope," Curt ordered his platoon leader. "Send Sergeant Koslowski up ahead of you in an ATV as a scout ranging five hundred to seven hundred meters ahead . . . but not out of sight. I want Sergeant Elliott up on the other bank in another ATV ranging about five hundred meters ahead of us as a scout, too. Elliott can work on his own better; he's from Appalachia where the land stands on end like this."

"Yes, sir. He just said to tell you that where the land stands on end, it helps the local economy there; they can sell both sides of the same acre . . ."

"Yeah, but who wants it? Like this place. No wonder there's no habitation around here!" Curt observed.

He put in a call on the discreet regimental net to the Biotech unit, intending to speak with Major Gydesen. But he got Chief Biotech Sgt. Helen Devlin who'd been his personal biotech back in the days when the regiment was operating neuroelectronic warbots. With the shift to the Sierra Charlie doctrine, the bio-medical technicians had had to shift from a concentration on the biological effects of linkage to trauma medicine intended to treat wounds actually suffered in combat. Helen Devlin, who'd been an outstanding linkage biotech because she was also an R.N., was one of the few support personnel who'd managed to adapt to the change not only because she was very good at what she did but because she liked the Washington Greys and had worked very hard indeed to reacquire the trauma medicine expertise needed by the new regiment. She was loyal, she was cute, and she and Curt had had a lot of fun together before the incredible pressure of the conversion work had occupied all her time. That she'd made the change successfully was evidenced by the fact that she was now Chief Biotech Sergeant, in effect the Chief Nurse of what had become, in reality, a mobile regimental hospital.

"Biotech Leader, this is Companion Leader, requesting to speak with Major Gydesen . . ."

Devlin's voice came back, "Hello, Captain! Remember me?"

Curt had to smile. "How could I ever forget you, Sergeant?"

"It's been known to happen . . . not by you, but by other warbot brainies who don't appreciate the outstanding physiological and psychological services I can provide!" There was always a brightness in Helen Devlin's voice.

"Please put Major Gydesen on the net, Sergeant."

"My, aren't we all official business this morning?"

"I got banged around last night, I still hurt all over, this scenery is boring me out of my skull, and I've got a platoon sergeant in your surgical unit who was in pretty poor shape when they pulled him out of that crushed LAMV last night," Curt complained.

"We spent four hours working on Nick Gerard last night," Devlin told him. "Major Gydesen and Captain Logan are resting right now. I was the scrub nurse. I was told that if you called about Gerard, I was to field your questions."

"Okay, you'll do . . ."

"Haven't I always?"

"Sergeant, I'm bounding around up here in the turret of an ACV wondering when the damned thing is going to hit a gully and go ass over cannon," Curt snapped, "and I hurt all over. So let's get to the point please. What's Gerard's condition and prognosis?"

Devlin immediately became all professional business. "Sergeant Gerard is resting well and in guarded condition," she reported stiffly. "His left leg was crushed, but the doctors rebuilt it. He has four broken ribs and had a ruptured spleen, which was repaired by surgery. His left collarbone was also fractured and has been internally cuffed with a degradable splint. The Sergeant has come through the post-op situation well and is currently resting."

"When will the major return him to duty, Sergeant?"

"I don't know, Captain. Major Gydesen has requested a medical evack aerodyne for him, but I don't think it can get here before noon," Devlin admitted.

"Great! That makes me short a platoon Sergeant! Helen, how's Nick's attitude? It may be a while before I can get back to visit him."

"He's still recuperating and pretty weak. Hard to tell. He's been out of surgery less than six hours at this time."

"Thank you, Sergeant. I'll call from time to time to get an update on his condition. Thanks for your help."

"Any time, Captain. Just give the word. How are *you?*"

"Unfortunately, I may survive in spite of all the aches and pains."

"You were lucky you didn't get caught in that collapsing LAMV like Gerard was."

"Just happened to be on the side that didn't get clobbered. Thanks, Helen."

He switched off as he watched Morgan's ACV grind up the right bank. He heard her swear at something.

"What's wrong, Companion Alpha?"

"Lost my IPU again!"

"Forget it!"

"Pardon, sir?"

"Forget it, Lieutenant! We're going to have to proceed without maps and IPUs and all the other high-tech crap that wasn't designed for this high-temperature environment in mountains where we get very large pitch angles," Curt told her. "By the way, the Biotech Unit reports that Sergeant Gerard will be evacked whenever an aerodyne can get here today. Better put one of your squad leaders in charge of Gerard's platoon."

Alexis was very diplomatic. She knew damned good and well who she wanted for that job; she'd thought about it all night. But she wanted her Captain's input. "Do you have any suggestions, Captain?"

"Koslowski."

This seemed to surprise Alexis. "Really, Captain?"

"Really. As I recall from his one-oh-one, he got busted once by the cops in Michigan for leading a street gang into a pretty good fight . . . which they won, I understand. He's an aggressive midwestern Pollack . . . but don't ever tell him I said that!"

"I won't, Captain."

"Elliott's your frontier scout; he can operate out there on his own. I have the feeling that Koslowski could run two warbot squads if he had to, but out on patrol by himself he'd get lost in five minutes."

"Captain," Alexis remarked," "how come you seem to know about as much about my people as I do?"

"Because I'm the company commander, Lieutenant. That's my job. And I'm glad you know them, too, because if something had happened to me last night in that LAMV, you'd be leading Carson's Companions right now . . ."

"Yes, sir," she replied somberly. "I did lead the Companions last night when Sergeant Hale put you down for six hours. Uh . . . I didn't really like the idea."

"Alexis, some day soon you're either going to get this company or another one of the Greys' combat companies," Curt reminded her.

"Yes, sir. But I've got a little bit to learn first."

"Look," he told her in a friendly, confidential tone, "Alexis, there are two kinds of commands in the Army. The first is the one you sweat for years to get, and sometimes you don't get it. The other is when something happens—as it can and does in combat, to say nothing of the service itself—and you've suddenly got a command that's a whole handful, a lot bigger than anything you think you can handle. We're a combat outfit, and we're facing combat, so keep the latter in mind . . ."

"I . . . uh, I don't like the idea of anything happening to you, Curt."

"Neither do I. And the feeling's mutual . . . in spite of our recent problems with Len Spencer—"

"Please keep him out of this!"

"I can't. You won't."

"What am I supposed to do, turn on the deep freeze?" Alexis was suddenly defensive. "The man likes me, and I find him interesting, and if he writes up anything about me it could not only help my career but also help alleviate some of the public and political concern about women in combat roles."

"Alexis, beware of the news media," Curt tried to warn her. "Their job is to get a good, juicy story . . . and that's all that Spencer is trying to do."

"I think he has a genuine concern and liking for me."

"Just don't get so involved that you end up with a big disappointment, Alexis."

She told him coolly, "As I said before, Captain, I shall take my commanding officer as my model."

Curt sighed. "Zeenat Tej got the Legion of Honor for what she did at Sangre Grande."

"She also got *you* when no one else who cared about you *could* because of Rule Ten," Alexis reminded him. "Captain, I am perfectly capable of handling my personal affairs in full accordance with Army Regulations! And I shall do so. However, I appreciate your concern."

"Just doing my job, Lieutenant. Now please get your scout moving."

He switched to regimental tacomm and called, "Grey Head, this is Companion Leader. We're moving out of the river bottom. I've got mounted scouts out on both sides of the river ahead of us, and Companion Alpha has gone up the right bank. Also reporting that we've lost Alpha's IPU again!"

"Very well, Companion Leader, proceed!" Hettrick's voice replied. "Forget about the IPU. This Army got along without it for a long time. So we'll go back to using compass headings, dead reckoning, and following the easiest terrain with the assistance of a local guide."

But there was no "easiest" terrain as both Koslowski and Elliott reported back from their advanced forays on ATVs. The country was all rough and rugged with heavy slopes cut by gullies from rain that must have fallen decades or even centuries ago. The erosion wasn't as stark or sharp as that encountered in the American southwest because thermal erosion had softened the ancient gullies, making them somewhat easier for the vehicles to negotiate.

The convoy was down to the fantastic speed of about 10 to 15 kilometers per hour.

And it went on like this for hours as the blazing sun climbed higher in the sky.

The only break in the monotony of the trek was the sudden halt of Alexis Morgan's ACV.

"Companion Alpha, this is Companion Leader. What's wrong?"

"Doctor von Waldersee has located something," Alexis reported. "He's found some Bushman petroglyphs on the cliff here. Fantastic stuff!"

"Lieutenant, keep moving. The Doctor can come back and photograph them later! We're not on an archaeological expedition here!" Curt reminded her.

"But he says some of them are new since he last saw them about nine years ago."

"So let him dismount, snap a few photos, and I'll pick him up in my ACV when I go past him."

When Curt's ACV drew abeam of the cliff, he noticed the scrawlings and scratchings in the rock, primitive artistic depictions of people and animals, some in fading color. He stopped the ACV for Doctor Von Waldersee who clambered aboard with great reluctance.

"Amazing!" the anthropologist bubbled. "Down there near the bottom, see it? That's a new glyph! And another one over to the right! I don't know how they could have gotten there. This part of Namibia is no longer inhabited by Bushmen or any of the Koishan peoples . . . yet those are Koishan glyphs!"

"I hope you got photos," Curt replied with condescension. "You can come back here once this trek is over."

"Only if I can get the coordinates!" von Waldersee said, securing his camera and looking at the color prints he'd just taken.

"Well, our inertial positioning unit is out, but I'll have Colonel Hettrick get a fix from the navigational satellite system . . ."

"Thank you! Thank you very much! This is indeed a great puzzle! These Bushman petroglyphs appear all over Namibia. I have photo documentation on all of them. But this one has some new rock carvings that are impossible!"

"If you want me to transfer you back up to Lieutenant Morgan's vehicle, I'll have one of my ATVs made available to you," Curt offered.

"Not necessary, my dear sir. We'll top the ridge here in less than a kilometer, and the land beyond is a relatively flat basin in between ranges. Some rock outcroppings—mostly excellent marble, by the way—and a great deal more vegetation than we've seen before. Going should be much easier and require far less moment-by-moment direction."

"Doctor, if you believe no native tribes exist in this area, where did those recent rock carvings come from?" Curt wanted to know.

Von Waldersee shrugged. "A mystery. A great mystery. No Bushmen tribes have been in these mountains for over a hundred years. I'm not sure what this really means . . ."

They found out very quickly.

One by one, the vehicles of the Washington Greys crossed the saddle of the ridge at the head of the valley. Sure enough, before then opened out a huge plain at least thirty kilometers wide with another range of mountains on the far side. The landscape was covered with rocky outcrops and clumps of pinion-like trees. Some thin grass now grew along the ground. But it was still very dry terrain.

"Now we move," Curt called to Alexis Morgan. "Take it

as fast as feasible, given the ground condition."

"I can't move too fast. We keep running up against these dikes and ridges about a meter high that cut directly across our course," Morgan replied.

"The rock is mainly pumice," von Waldersee pointed out. "It's not very hard, and it pulverizes easily."

"And is liable to grind right into the mechanical working parts of our vehicles," Curt added. "Take it slow, Lieutenant. Let's not let the terrain demolish our vehicles."

About ten kilometers from the ridge saddle through which they'd entered this plain, the column had to wend its way through defiles in rock outcroppings.

And when the Washington Greys found themselves in a position where they couldn't maneuver very well and were prevented from spreading out and utilizing their firepower to the utmost, that's when it happened.

The convoy suddenly came under fire.

But it was a hail of spears and arrows.

CHAPTER THIRTY-ONE

The horde of well over a hundred little brown men dressed only in animal skin breech clouts stormed silently out of the nearby rocks and shrubs, moving quickly and furtively in and out of eyesight. Armed only with short bows and unfletched arrows, throwing sticks, and wooden spears with fire-hardened points, they carried out an incredibly sudden silent assault on the armored vehicles and the exposed personnel of the Washington Greys.

The assault came in complete silence and with total surprise. Since no one had *ever* attacked a regimental convoy of robot infantry with such primitive weapons and apparently fearless zeal, it was unbelievable. The Washington Greys, taken completely by surprise, didn't react immediately. The few seconds required for the Sierra Charlies to realize that they were indeed under attack by primitive spear-carrying warriors in this desolate and supposedly lifeless landscape caused an inordinate number of quick casualties.

The ambush caught more than two dozen Greys riding outside their vehicles in the hot sunshine, a somewhat cooler place to be than inside the vehicles because the vehicle air cooling systems had been cycled back to conserve precious turbine fuel.

Furthermore, in X-ray Condition, none of the Greys were wearing body armor. Some of them were even without their battle helmets. Most of them had their personal small arms either slung or holstered.

The small brown attackers appeared to be fearless.

Certainly, they were expert hunters because they'd cautheir quarry in a place where it was difficult for t.
Americans to fight back.

They swarmed up the vehicles, thrusting with their spears. At short range, their unfletched arrows were remarkably accurate. Their throwing sticks allowed them to launch short spears at very high velocities from somewhat greater range.

The first alarm went out from regimental headquarters five seconds after the ambush began, by which time these brown warriors were all over the vehicles. "All personnel, Zulu Condition! We're under attack!"

In that five seconds, the attackers skewered more than a dozen Greys, including Squad Sgt. Tracy Dillon who'd been outriding as a scout on one of the Companion ATVs about fifty meters ahead of the point vehicle.

In Ward's Warriors bringing up Number Two slot behind the Companions, only one person got hit. Cpl. Ernest Johnson who was riding on the aft deck of Warrior Alpha's ACV was killed instantly when a sharpened throwing stick hit him directly in the eye and penetrated into his brain.

But it was regimental command and the headquarters company following the Warriors who took the worst initial beating. Not completely combat trained or experienced, some of these specialist headquarters people reacted in a way that would later seem to be stupid but was typical of the manner in which most people respond when surprised: they freeze, then they look around and gather data about what's happening.

Maj. Edward Canby didn't duck down into the regimental command vehicle quickly enough. He took an unfletched arrow in the fleshy part of his chest, the pectoral muscle just below his left arm, where it penetrated deeply without being deflected by one of his ribs.

Regimental S. Sgt. Forest L. Barnes was hit in the stomach by a throwing stick as he reached to grab his Hornet submachinegun.

One of the intelligence NCOs, Sgt. Josephine Wheeler, grappled hand-to-hand with one of the brown warriors and managed to throw him off S-2s combat support vehicle, but not before the attacker drove a spear into Wheeler's leg.

Lt. John Gibbon stuck his head and shoulders out of the top hatch, Hornet submachinegun in hand, and was the first Grey to open fire. But he didn't watch his minus x, and another brown warrior hit him from behind with the butt of a spear, then stuck the pointed end through the back of Gibbon's neck . . . but not before Gibbon shot him with the Hornet.

There was no time for battle planning. There was no time to give orders. There was only time to react to the ambush.

Capt. Martin Kelly of Kelly's Killers bringing up the rear of the column, was still in a position to back out of the defile through the rocky outcrop and gain some mobility. Instead, Kelly ordered the Killer warbots out and all his men to dismount and fight outside. The Killers were the first to deploy their warbots . . . and they didn't have any targets for their heavy 25mm and 50mm weapons. Kelly's men had their M33 *Novias,* and in close quarters the fantastic field qualities of the rifle were severely hampered. A major fire fight developed in the rear guard.

"Companions all, forward! Move it! NOW!" was Curt's immediate order as he realized what was happening. When he'd seen Dillon get hit, he'd buttoned up and closed hatches. It wasn't his intention to abandon the rest of the regiment, especially the headquarters and service companies that were now under such intense attack, by moving rapidly forward. He wanted to gain manuevering space. He wanted to clear the way so that Capt. Joan Ward could move her Warriors out of the rocks and gain open ground, too.

She did. As Curt's vehicles moved, festooned with little brown attackers hanging on for dear life, some of them dropping off, he called to Hettrick on tacomm, "Colonel!

Clear out of these rocks! They give the attackers the advantage of concealment and surprise! I'm going for open ground and I'll try to sweep around to either side and see if some of our heavy stuff can't pick them out of the rocks."

"Roger!" was Hettrick's hasty and curt reply.

Curt knew she was up to her armpits in alligators. What he didn't know was that Col. Belinda Hettrick had taken an arrow in her left side just below her rib cage as she'd tried to roll into the open hatch of her OCV.

The Washington Greys had developed *no* contingency operational plan to handle an ambush by guerrillas *without firearms!* No one had ever thought that they would ever come up against such a situation!

As Curt slipped and slithered into his soft body armor, he decided several hundred natives must have attacked. One thing for certain, they either had a hell of a lot of guts to ambush an armored warbot column or they were damned stupid and didn't know any better. However, thus far they'd done very well simply because their ambush was totally and completely unexpected.

He had his ACV scan the area visually while it ran for open ground. Then the sensor went dead.

Kester, who was manning another display, remarked, "One of those sonsofbitches heaved a damned rock right at the sensor!"

"My God, that thing is supposed to be hardened against A-T fire!" Curt objected.

"Rock was big enough; it busted the whole damned sensor platform right off the chassis!" Kester explained.

They hit the open plain about two hundred meters away. Curt snapped on tacomm. "Companions, report!"

"Alpha here! We're okay!" Alexis Morgan's voice came back.

"Bravo here! We lost Dillon. Sergeant Hale went after him," Lt. Jerry Allen reported.

"Get her back!" Curt yelled. "These savages don't know what the hell a red cross stands for!"

"Too late! She unloaded off my ACV when we went past

re Dillon was lying," Allen reported.

Give her covering fire!"

"She's out of sight now."

"Warrior Leader, do you read Companion Leader?"

"Roger, Companion Leader! We're behind you, and we have your man and the biotech in sight and under covering fire," Capt. Joan Ward's voice came back, strangely calm and well-modulated. "Got a plan, Curt?"

"Yeah. Have your Bravo Platoon join my Bravo Platoon. I want to swing to the left out here. That looks like the best bet. I want all our Hairy Foxes and Saucy Cans to fire into those rocks on both sides of the defile," Curt told her. "If they have any reinforcements hiding up there, I want to make sure they don't get the chance to attack. Overshoot our forces in the defile. Allen, did you get that?"

"Roger, Captain. Davy, let's go!" Jerry Allen addressed his Warrior counterpart, Lt. Dave Coney.

"I'm riding your minus x, Jerry!"

"Companion Alpha, we're going around the other side with Warrior Alpha," Curt went on. "Dismount your Mary Annes and jeeps. We can't fight these people inside these vehicles, and the armament on the warbots is too heavy for this kind of fighting. We've got to take them on in person. Dismount following the warbots, and follow the warbots back into the defile. Secure your vehicles and *move!*"

"Roger!" came from Alexis Morgan.

"We're with you," was Joan Ward's reply.

"Where the hell is Manny Garcia?" Curt asked openly, hoping someone knew.

"This is Grey Major," came a new voice, "Sergeant Major Jesup speaking. Captain Kelly's behind us, sir, but he isn't talking to us. Looks like a hell of a fire fight back there. His troops are shooting up a goddam storm. Captain Garcia ordered all his personnel to button down inside their vehicles; he's deployed his warbots trying to use radio-linked verbal commands!"

"Sounds like Manny forgot to put on his winter boots

today," was Joan Ward's acidic comment. "Sonofa[illegible] has cold feet when it comes to personal combat . . ."

"Knock it off!" Curt commanded. "Joan, the Warri[illegible] ready with their Mary Annes and jeeps?"

"Right!"

"Alexis?"

"Let's move it!" was the excited reply.

"Everyone in body armor?"

"Damned right!"

"Allen, you and Coney coordinate fire between the two of you. Watch for our combat beacons on your displays," Curt told him. "I don't want to have to worry about your fire, too."

"Gotcha, Captain!"

"Henry, let's do it," Curt told his master sergeant. "Dump the ramp!"

The rear ramp came down, and Curt's jeep hurried out, swivelling its head sensors to search for targets. Curt and Kester followed, and the ramp came back up.

On a hunch, Curt turned and looked at his ACV. A small brown warrior with a spear sat atop the hatch, looking somewhat surprised at the action of the ramp and the sudden appearance of two men and a warbot. It was obvious he'd never seen a warbot before. And he didn't get the chance to look very long, either. Companion Action Jackson swivelled its 7.62mm automatic weapon and shot the tribesman off the top of the turret with one accurately placed round. Curt got his chance to outshoot his warbot when a small head topped with curly, fuzzy black hair peered around the other side of the turret; Curt got him right between the eyes with a round from his *Novia*.

Kester and Action Jackson were by that time busy shooting natives off the top of the other Companion vehicles.

The native guerrillas were smart. They rolled and dropped off the top of vehicles and began to hide around them. Working together, the Alpha Platoons of the Companions and the Warriors managed to clean up the place. Those natives who didn't get shot managed somehow to make it back into the rocks. But an amazing number of them got away. *Sneaky little bastards,* Curt thought.

Allen and Coney had apparently gotten into position because the top and sides of the rocky outcrop began to erupt with the explosions of heavy fire.

"Back up the road!" Curt ordered. "Stay behind your warbots. Use them as fire bait. Don't try to be a hero by killing the most brown fuzzies."

On his right, he was accompanied by Lt. Alexis Morgan, her two platoon sergeants, and her twelve Mary Annes leading the way. On his left was Capt. Joan Ward, Lt. Claudia Roberts, the Warrior Alpha Platoon, and its twelve Mary Annes. The warbots would have to remain on the more or less level and regular stretch of the rocky ground because of their larger size and inability to work in and around the boulders, but the human troops immediately dispersed into the rocks.

The "brown fuzzies" were slick and fast. They moved among the rocks in such a way that it was very difficult to aim and fire at them. They had a well-developed system of visual signals—hand motions, mostly—but occasionally Curt heard a yell in a strange language full of what sounded like tongue clickings.

After about a hundred meters, the combined combat force made contact with the beleaguered main body of the regiment. The fuzzies had managed to roll enough rocks in front of the vehicles to prevent them from moving forward or backward. Although they didn't know how to enter the vehicles and seemed to be aware of the lethality of small arms, they were apparently baffled by the warbots. Their primary weapon against the jeeps and Mary Annes was an accurately-thrown rock which didn't penetrate the warbot armor but could, and did, simply wipe out sensors and their mountings as well as antennas and some of the exposed mechanical parts. For example, one warbot had been stopped by the idiotically simple expedient of jamming a rock in its track drive system.

The personnel in the headquarters and supply companies carried M26A4 Hornet submachinecarbines, a li[illegible] personal weapon with limited range and accuracy. T[illegible] Hornet had been intended more as a "scare" weapon t[illegible] make the enemy keep heads down while one of the combat companies moved in to help. Because their mission was to support the Sierra Charlie companies, the headquarters and service companies had no warbots. Outside of their vehicles, their only protection was body armor which most of them disliked wearing.

And headquarters and service personnel were not trained in personal combat as the Sierra Charlie company people. As a result, they'd taken losses because they'd been caught outside, hadn't reacted in the same manner as the combat Sierra Charlies, and had tried to fight from inside their vehicles.

Curt was appalled by the number of bodies lying on the ground. Far too many of them were Washington Greys. And two of them wore the white tabard with the red cross front and rear, the identifier of combat trauma biotechs who were usually immune from being attacked by people who knew what the Geneva and Manila Conventions were. The fuzzies didn't. They'd assaulted everyone.

"Mary Annes, direct your fire toward the attackers on either side of the main body," Curt ordered when he saw the situation. He didn't want that heavy fire going into friendly troops and vehicles. "Sierra Charlies, use your *Novias* to pick off the natives . . . but make sure you shoot only at natives! Don't worry about hitting our vehicles; their armor will stop a *Novia* round!" This last remark was unnecessary, but in the heat and haze of battle no one was keeping score whether or not orders followed protocol; here, the only thing that mattered was whether or not the order was understood and followed.

"Grey Head, this is Companion Leader," Curt called for Hettrick. "Is that professor around? Does he understand the language these fuzzies speak? Can he talk to them?"

Sgt. Maj. Tom Jesup's voice came back, "Companion Leader, this is Grey Head! Been trying to raise you, sir!"

Curt suddenly realized that something was terribly

wrong. "What's the problem, Sergeant Major? Where's Colonel Hettrick?"

"She took an arrow," Jesup reported.

"Oh shit!"

"Not to worry, Captain," Jesup's voice came back confidently. "Captain Logan and Sergeant Devlin are with her. She's in no danger, but she's out of it for a couple of hours. That's why I've been trying to raise you. You're in command now!"

"What the hell? Where's Major Canby?"

"He bought it, Captain. Took an arrow in the chest. Bled to death before the biotechs could get to him. Sergeant Colter was killed tyring to get to him, and Sergeant Molde was wounded."

Regulations required that the second-in-command—the late Maj. Edward R. Canby, the headquarters company commander—be a combat-rated officer. Canby had been; he'd opted to keep his warbot brainy MOS. The chief of staff, Capt. Wade Hampton, was theoretically next in the chain of command, but Hampton's MOS had been changed two years ago as a result of a general Army-wide policy of upgrading the speciality rating of high-standing War College graduates to keep them out of actual combat.

As a result of all of this, the command of the regiment resided in the senior combat company commander.

"That can't be! Kelly's senior to me," Curt reminded Jesup, aware of the fact that the regiment would be in deep shit with Kelly in command.

"Captain Kelly's wounded and out of action," was Jesup's reply. "Captain Carson, you're the senior officer present. You're in command of the Washington Greys. What are your orders, sir?"

CHAPTER THIRTY-TWO

Four years at West Point and seven years of active service in the Robot Infantry of the United States Army had prepared Capt. Curt Carson for this. But when it actually happened, he didn't feel he was ready for it. He'd wanted the command of a combat company and worked hard for his second bar. But getting command of a regiment under combat conditions because all the qualified senior officers in the chain of command had been disabled wasn't the way he really wanted it to happen.

But it had to be done.

A headless regiment in action would die.

He knew what he had to do.

Keying his tacomm, he snapped, "Companion Bravo, this is Companion Leader. Assume command of the company!"

Alexis Morgan's voice came back with uncertainty in it. "Very well, Captain! What's going on?"

"Grey Head is disabled. Grey Two is out of action. Killer Leader is disabled. I've got to take Grey Head," Curt explained briefly.

There was a moment of silence, then Alexis' voice came back. "Yes, sir! Good luck! I'm with you! Count on me, Curt!"

"I do and I will. Thanks." Curt shifted freaks. "Jesup, this is Carson! I'm out in the open now. I'll try to get to Grey Head vehicle. In the meantime, where the hell is von Waldersee?"

"He's listening, Grey Head."

"Does he understand the brown fuzzy language?" Curt wanted to know.

Dr. Paul von Waldersee's voice came into Curt's head with a strange quality to it that told Curt the man was using a microphone and not neurophonic pickups. "Captain, this is Doctor von Waldersee. I haven't heard much of the language of the Bushmen who attacked us. Somewhat muffled inside this vehicle. But I suspect they probably speak or at least understand Bushman San."

"Try it! Get Jesup to put you on the external speakers. Broadcast to these people in that language. Ask for parley." Curt instructed him.

"Captain, I don't think—"

"Doctor, please do as I ask!" Curt fired back. "I haven't got time to argue. And I want to stop this senseless slaughter if I can. We're taking losses but they're taking worse losses. Why are they doing it? Why did they attack? It doesn't make sense! Let's see if we can't get them to stop before I have to order the regiment to wipe them out. We can do it but that will also create more losses of our own . . . and we've taken too many already. I'd like to see if I can't stop it instead."

"Very well, Captain, but I have my doubts. Bushmen—if these indeed be Bushmen, and they look like Bushmen even though I don't know of any tribe in this area—Bushmen have a code of valor. They tend to fight to the death if they fight at all—"

"Give them an alternative," Curt ordered. "Request a truce and extend my offer to treat their wounded. If they keep this up, there won't be any of them left an hour from now, and we'll lose more people, too. We didn't come here to fight them. We've got another job to do in Otjomuise."

"Very well, Captain, I'll try. But these Bushmen seem to be exceedingly vicious—"

"Goddamit, stop farting around and *do it!*"

"My, you Yanks are certainly testy about getting the impossible done, aren't you? Very well. Sergeant Major, can this microphone be connected to an external Tannoy?"

Curt suddenly felt a sharp blow to his back. An unfletched arrow bounced off his soft body armor and fell to the ground. He turned and fired, blowing away the fuzzy-headed Bushman who'd managed to fire from behind one of the big Combat Support Vehicles of Headquarters Company. Unlike Marty Kelly, Curt didn't like to kill needlessly, and he didn't like to see the little brown man be picked up by the impact of the 7.62mm *Novia* round and tossed several meters through the air like a limp rag doll. But he wasn't squeamish about having to do it when necessary. He slipped a fresh clip of caseless ammo into his *Novia* and armed the weapon again.

Von Waldersee's highly amplified voice came from the regimental OCV. It spoke a strange language full of tongue clicks and guttural stops.

Curt had an idea. The opponent here was a group of primitive people, and he remembered the date grove outside of the Iranian town of Zahedan where modern high-tech fireworks had created a display of magic that caused a group of religious fanatics to cower in wonder. "Jesup, order all units to launch flares, signal rockets, smoke, whatever they've got that's not CB or heavy firepower," he ordered the regimental sergeant major. "Tell von Waldersee to explain to these idiots that we've gotten our magic working now and that if they don't stop fighting us, we'll have to unleash even more evil spirits . . ."

"The Doctor says he'll do the best he can," Jesup's voice came in Curt's head.

There was a pause in von Waldersee's announcements in the strange language, then he went on.

And the deep blue afternoon sky over the rocky outcrops suddenly filled with eye-searing bright flares as well as the rumble and black smoke of signal rockets. Arcs of colored smoke appeared as warbots, vehicles, and Sierra Charlies launched or threw smoke cannisters and grenades. The air was still torn with the sound of firing from warbots, *Novias,* and Hornets. But the fireworks display was spectacular even in the bright sunlight of late afternoon.

Low in the rocks, a small brown man suddenly stood up and held two spears crossed above his head. He shouted something in his strange tongue-clicking language. Curt couldn't hear what he said because of the din of battle.

"Von Waldersee says that must be the chief and he's giving the sign for a truce," Jesup reported.

"Suspend firing!" Curt ordered. Different from a "cease fire" command, it meant that warbots and Sierra Charlies would stop firing but maintain their weapons at the immediate ready.

As the racket subsided, Curt stepped out into the open and held his *Novia* aloft in both hands, hoping that the Bushman chief and his cohort would understand that it was the best Curt could do with a rifle in his hands. Curt could have been hit by arrows or spears, but he felt reasonably confident that his soft body armor would stop most of them. Most of them. There was always the chance . . . and his mouth was dry as he walked toward an open space about ten meters from the Bushman.

But the little man didn't come out from behind the rocks.

Curt suddenly realized that he must look like something from another planet to this primitive man. So he put his *Novia* on the ground, straightened up, and removed his helmet, stripping himself of his communications, his battle management visor displays, and his sensors. But this was neither the time nor the place where they'd be particularly useful. What *was* useful, insofar as Curt was concerned, was to appear to be reasonably normal to this primitive man. Curt wasn't wearing cammy grease; there hadn't been time to apply it. So the Bushman chief saw Curt as he was.

That was the right thing to do. The chief sprang gracefully from behind the rocks and came up to within two meters of Curt.

Curt towered above the little man, but the chief didn't appear to be intimidated by size.

Curt turned his head and shouted back over his shoulder, "Anyone hearing me, relay to Grey Major! Send von Waldersee out here at once!"

"I hear you, Captain!" It was Platoon Sgt. Edwina Sampson. Curt suddenly saw that his Companions had been right with him and were standing quietly alongside vehicles nearby. "Relayed!"

"Sampson, would you be willing to sling your *Novia,* step out, and take your helmet off?" Curt asked her. He wouldn't give her a direct order to expose herself.

"Sure!" Sampson quipped. She'd seen her Captain walk unprotected into the clear and remove his helmet, and she knew he would never ask any of the Companions to do anything he wouldn't do first.

He saw her remove her helmet, and it was apparent to him—and hopefully to the Bushman chief—that she was a woman. Curt wanted to reveal that he had women in his command. He didn't know what effect this might have on the chief, but he was hoping it would put the little man somewhat off guard because of the revelation that the Washington Greys were more than just a little different from the soldiers that the chief might have encountered in the past.

The chief noticed Edie Sampson. Curt could tell from the quick double-take the little man did indeed see her, but the chief tried to hide his surprise at learning one of the soldiers was a woman. Women in his tribe didn't fight, they were too valuable to a tribe of hunter-gatherers where survival was of primary importance and where men were less important to the tribe than women because one man could make babies in many women.

The chief said something, and Curt held up both open hands. "Wait one," he said unnecessarily, knowing that the chief probably didn't understand English. "I don't understand or speak your language. My interpreter is on the way."

"Your interpreter is here," came Paul von Waldersee's voice. It had an excited ring to it. "This is damnably unusual, Captain! I don't know of this tribe of Khoisans. This isn't Bushman homelands. They shouldn't be here!"

"Well, they are," Curt reminded him. "See if you can

talk with him. Greet him for me."

Von Waldersee stepped up beside Curt and spoke in the tongue-clicking language.

The chief replied.

"Strange dialect of Khoi," the anthropologist remarked. "Central Bushman group with some southern sounds mixed in. But it's generally basic Khoisan Bushman language. I can make talk with him."

"Good! Do it! You can make your scientific analysis later, Doctor. Offer a truce, treatment of his wounded, and an exchange of gifts," Curt said. Maybe he could get this whole thing stopped and turned to his advantage instead.

"I'll do my best," von Waldersee remarked and began a long exchange with the chief.

After a few minutes during which animated conversation took place, von Waldersee looked pensive as he paused and tried to collect his thoughts and express in English what had just been said between them.

"Well?" Curt finally asked.

"Shouldn't be. Just shouldn't be at all. They shouldn't be here," von Waldersee muttered.

"Give with the story, Doctor. Who is he? How do I address him?"

"He's called 'Ba' which is a general word meaning 'father,'" von Waldersee explained. "Ba is literally the father of this band. The old father, actually, but they have no words to describe that. Just call him Ba."

Curt looked at the little man with the reddish-brown skin who stood only about 150 centimeters tall and whose face and upper body were covered with scarification marks. "Ba, I'm Curt. We don't want to fight with you." To von Waldersee he said, "Tell him that."

The anthropologist did. The reply was brief.

"Ba says that only by fighting you can his band be protected," von Waldersee explained. "I don't know how many are in the band; the language has words only for 'one,' 'two,' and 'many.' I would estimate between fifty and a hundred. Big for a Bushman band. They're a tribe of fighters, and they've never surrendered to anyone, especially whites. They have refused contact. Captain, this is a 'lost tribe,' if you will."

Curt shook his head. "I don't get it. Why do they refuse contact? Why did they attack us?"

Dr. Paul von Waldersee was inwardly excited but was doing his best to hide it. "Ba tells me that this is the first group of white soldiers the band has not been able to destroy. For generations, they've kept their privacy and way of life by simply slaughtering everyone who found them. No wonder I haven't heard of them!"

"Tell Ba that I think his warriors are brave, valiant, and good fighters," Curt remarked. Which they were; few people, including the Pentagon, were going to believe that a group of about a hundred Bushmen armed only with spears and arrows had the balls to take on a whole Sierra Charlie regiment and strike with such ferocity and surprise that the regiment suffered a considerable number of casualties. Curt knew that the Bushmen had taken casualties, too, and probably in greater numbers and percentages than the Washington Greys. The ambush had been a lesson to the Sierra Charlies: Never proceed through strange territory without staying at least at Yankee Alert status. He figured that a later analysis of who got hit and when would show that the casualties had all been taken in the first minute of the engagement. After that, it had been the Bushmen who had suffered casualties as the Sierra Charlies and their firepower had come to combat level.

Given another hour or so, Curt knew that the Greys could wipe out the Bushmen. But Curt didn't want to do that. These little men were not the enemy. Curt had to conserve the regimental strength for the relief of Otjomuise.

"He thanks you for the compliment," von Waldersee translated. "And he wants you to know that this is the first group of outsiders they haven't been able to destroy. He wants your medical help, although he doesn't really understand the 'magic' of your biotechnology. And he's willing to offer a truce and a deal."

"What sort of a deal?"

Von Waldersee engaged in several minutes of conversation with Ba.

"We may go on our way if we will give our word that we won't reveal the existence of the band. Otherwise, he will order the assault continued until one of us is totally annihilated. He has no choice. Tribal policy, it seems . . ."

Curt nodded. "I know all about high-level policy," he remarked darkly. "Tell him it's a deal. Tell him we'll give his people medical treatment. And that we'll exchange gifts to seal the bargain."

Something seemed to pain von Waldersee. "I am rather caught in a dilemma here, Captain. These people are the only known example of what an original Bushman band must have been like before the Europeans got here. I want to study them, to come back and live with them if I can. But if we accept their terms, I can't. If we don't accept their terms, you'll destroy them and I won't have anyone to study. If I had my way, I'd stay here with them if they'd let me under the proviso that I not report their location to the world. If I did that, I would not be able to carry out my agreement with you to guide you to Windhoek. So . . . I can't advise you on this, Captain. But you should be made aware of my feelings in the matter."

The regiment had taken serious losses. It had been a hard fight. Proceeding at night right then might be too much. The Greys needed an overnight rest. So Curt replied, "I'll meet you halfway, Doctor. We'll stay overnight here and throw a party for them. Tribes like this always like to party. That will give you a chance to study them for twelve to eighteen hours, at least. Given those constraints, I'll bet you can do a hell of a lot of studying in a damned short time. Right?"

"It's better than trying to study dead Bushmen . . . or to continue the remainder of my professional life knowing that I missed what might be the one golden opportunity I had as an anthropologist," the scientist remarked, then added, "Let me see what Ba thinks of the deal . . ."

Another several minutes of conversation between the

Bushman and the anthropologist.

"Ba agrees," von Waldersee reported. "It is an armistice. You will treat his wounded. He will share fire with us tonight."

"Good! The fire's on him. The food's on us. We don't fight each other, and we don't squeal on him and his band," Curt said with great relief. "How do we seal the bargain. Doctor? Do they know what a hand shake is? Can I depend on Ba's word?"

"You can depend on Ba's word of honor," von Waldersee replied. "Bushmen have a very simple code of conduct, but it includes the principle of personal honor. As for a hand shake, they might understand it. They touch hands. Give it a try."

Curt extended his right hand, palm partly up.

Ba did the same and the two men, separated in social time by millennia, touched one another.

The old Bushman's hand felt strangely leathery but warm to the touch.

Curt smiled. "Tell him to locate his wounded. Edie, relay to Grey Major. Get the biotechs to work. Everyone else, prepare for overnight bivouac here. Put away the weapons, get out of body armor, and take off the helmets. Time for chow when the wounded are treated. Then we'll share a little social time with some goddamned courageous and somewhat insane warriors. If we could all manage to get along with Kelly's Killers, we can manage to get along with these crazy Bushmen!"

CHAPTER THIRTY-THREE

Col. Belinda Hettrick was flat on her back in one of the bunks of her Operational Command Vehicle. She was pale. "I'll be all right, Curt. Gotta get over the shock," she muttered sleepily. "Belly hurts like hell—"

Curt turned to Maj. Ruth Gydesen, the doctor in charge of the regimental biotech unit. "I'm surprised a simple arrow could do this, Doctor," he remarked. "Did you have to take it out surgically?"

Gydesen shook her head. "It had no barbed tip, and it hit no vital organs. But I had to go in surgically to clean out the wound. It was full of gooey black stuff from the arrow." The doctor held up the shaft. Curt could see that the front ten centimeters of the stick were coated with some sort of blackish tar-like substance.

"I want to show this to Doctor von Waldersee, the anthropologist. He's an expert on the Bushmen," Curt said and reached out for the arrow.

Gydesen gave it to him. "Maybe he knows what that black goo is."

"What do you think it is?"

She shook her head. She was a middle-aged doctor who'd kept herself in good shape so she could serve with a front line warbot outfit, but Curt could see from her dark eyes that she was tired. The biotech unit had been busy. Far too many casualties had been taken by the Greys because of the Bushman assault. "I don't know," she admitted candidly. "Could be poison, but I can't identify it."

"Has it had any effects on the Colonel?"

Gydesen shrugged. "Blood work came out negative for the sort of chemical and biological warfare agents we might run into and have to treat in combat conditions. But I'm not equipped to run a full analysis for poisons. I wish I had the facilities; I feel I need to check some enzymes and other blood factors because the colonel's suffering from some strange side effects that I wouldn't anticipate a simple arrow puncture could produce."

"Yeah . . ." Hettrick said sleepily, the effects of the anaesthetic still clouding her mind. "Goddamned arrow shouldn't have bothered me at all. But my fingers are all tingling and I can't feel my toes . . ."

Gydesen turned to the regimental commander. "You didn't tell me that before."

"Just noticed it," Hettrick muttered.

"Could be after-effects from the anaesthetic," Curt suggested, realizing that he had no damned business trying to second-guess the doctor.

Gydesen shook her head and didn't take issue with the new regimental commander. She knew he was under terrific pressure, too. "Not a chance! But I do suspect poisoning. Can we get the Bushman expert to look at this arrow?"

"I'll check it out with von Waldersee right away," Curt promised, then said to Hettrick, "Don't worry about a thing, Colonel. I've taken over command of the regiment while you're recovering, and we've negotiated a truce with the Bushmen."

"That's good. You'll do a good job, Curt. But I'll be up and riding the command seat in the OCV later today . . ." It was patently obvious that the Colonel wasn't with it. She also didn't seem to notice that Curt hadn't mentioned anything about Major Canby assuming command, which would have been normal if the Major hadn't been killed in the assault.

"She may be up and around tomorrow morning," Gydesen forecast.

"Unless this arrow was poisoned, in which case we've got problems." Curt observed, turning the crudely aped, unfletched shaft over in his hands. It might have een a very primitive weapon, but, like a simple rock, it was a lethal one . . . as lethal as a warbot if not as technically advanced.

"Yes," Major Gydesen admitted, "Because we'll have the same problem with everyone who took an arrow."

"How many casualties?"Curt wanted to know.

"Three dead, twelve wounded."

"Oh, Christ!" Curt breathed. "Get me a casualty list, will you, Doctor? And get Wade Hampton—he's running Headquarters company, I assume—to set up a burial detail. Deliver the bodies to him, and we'll conduct services at dawn before we get underway." He promised himself that he'd have the graves well-marked and precisely located by the inertial systems so the Washington Greys could come back after this was over, collect their dead, and see to it that they are buried at Arlington as they should be.

"Who was killed?" Hettrick wanted to know. She tried to sit up and had trouble doing so. But it was obvious she was disturbed by what she'd heard. Curt realized he'd made a mistake even discussing the subject with Major Gydesen in Hettrick's presence.

Gydesen leaned over and gave her an injection with a pressure syringe. "I'll get the list and let you know, Colonel. Right now, you need rest." She'd injected her commanding officer with a sedative; she had no intention of letting Hettrick become upset at this critical point.

"Yeah, I do feel damned sleepy . . . bushed . . . but pain's gone away . . ."

Curt got out of there. He had a real aversion to sick and injured people, and to see his colonel in that condition bothered him. He couldn't allow his emotions to affect his temporary command. He had to lead the Washington Greys out of this and into combat at Otjomuise. He faced a rough and tough task, and he could give no excuses if he screwed the pooch.

The sun was just beginning to set over the hills to the west as Curt exited the OCV. In the cloudless sky, the sun was perfectly visible over the starkly etched profile of the Khomas Hochland. If the situation had been different Curt might have enjoyed the view; it was very much like the clear, cloudless sunsets of Arizona, halfway around the world and in another hemisphere entirely.

Well-clear of the vehicles, the Bushmen had started a huge bonfire. T. Sgt. Ray Wolf of the maintenance unit had given them some quiet and discreet help by adding a bit of fuel to the wood which had been laboriously gathered and carried by the women of the band. Where they'd gotten the wood, Curt didn't know. Except for some scrubby trees that looked like pinion and juniper higher up on the slopes of the hills, he hadn't seen a tree all day. And even the bushes were small and stunted by the dry climate.

But, thanks to the Wolf's magic liquid otherwise known as "fuel, turbine, TF-4," the fire was well under way. About eighty Bushmen—men, women, and children—had gathered around. They were accompanied by some of the Greys. Both were clustered in their own groups looking somewhat suspiciously at the other. Paul von Waldersee was busily translating.

Curt walked up and showed the blacktipped arrow to the anthropologist. "Doctor, the Bushmen shot a lot of these at our people. Almost a dozen of my troops were wounded by these arrows. Their reactions aren't normal for a simple penetration. I think the arrows were poisoned, but our chief medical doctor hasn't any information about poisons other than the normal ones we might encounter in chemical or biological warfare."

Von Waldersee had only to glance at the shaft. He nodded. "Poisoned, of course."

"Do you know what the poison is?"

The anthropologist took the arrow in his hands and looked at it. He nodded. "No name for it. It's used only by the Bushmen, as far as I know."

"What do they make the poison out of?" Curt needed information.

Von Waldersee gave him information in great abunance in a very pedantic and academic manner. "The band's women search for and collect the pupae of the *Diamphidia simplex* beetle. They store the pupae in jars they make of clay. Before a hunt, a warrior takes several pupae and rolls them between his palms, crushing them. When it turns into this black, viscous material, the warrior smears the compound on the first hundred millimeters or so of the shaft. It will remain viscous and potent for days. When the shaft punctures the skin of an animal, the poison enters the body and causes a slow paralysis. It appears to work on the nervous system. When a hunter shoots a shaft into a wildebeest, for example, it doesn't kill the animal at once. The hunter then tracks the animal for about a day before it becomes totally paralyzed and can be finished off by a spear thrust. Then the band cuts up the animal and eats the meat—"

"Good God Almighty!" Curt breathed. "Doctor, we've had several people, including Colonel Hettrick, who were hit with poisoned arrows."

"Belinda? Hit?" von Waldersee asked incredulously.

Curt caught a new note in the tone of von Waldersee's voice. It was one of serious concern, the sort of reaction one would give when a loved one is hurt. Had something been generated between the two in Swakopmund? Curt knew that Belinda Hettrick was a very normal woman, but he didn't know and didn't really care right then what the two had done in the seacoast resort town. He, too, was concerned about Hettrick as a result of von Waldersee's description of the Bushman poison. "Doctor, I want you to see Major Gydesen at once. Give her all the information you can, especially about the antidote—"

"There is no known antidote," the anthropologist told him gravely.

This caused Curt to pause for a moment, then he blurted out, "Bullshit! There's *got* to be an antidote!"

"We know of none."

"That's probably because no biotechnician has ever had the opportunity to analyze this stuff in a lab and study how it attacks the nervous system," Curt guessed.

"You're right, it's never been studied. I've already told you everything I know, and that's everything anyone knows about it. Poisoned Bushman arrows aren't found very often these days since the rest of the Bushmen people took to agriculture and herding instead of gathering and hunting. In fact, this is the first poisoned arrow I've seen in twenty years, and the first one I've *ever* seen out in the field," the anthropologist admitted. "In my opinion, I doubt that your medical people can save—"

"The hell you say! I don't give up that easy, Doctor!" Curt snapped in irritation at the response of the scientist. "I've got communications and access to the world's data base. We can draw upon the expertise of the best medical and biotech facilities available—Walter Reed, Bethesda Naval Hospital, Brooks Air Force Base, even the Mayo Clinic if we need it. Dammit, they'll find it! In the meantime, I'm going to get all our wounded the hell and gone out of here by airlift so they can get better treatment. Now, I want you to see Major Gydesen and tell her everything you know—"

"I'll talk with the Major if you wish, Captain. However, it will take me away from my translation work here, and that may be critical, too."

"The Colonel's health is a pretty critical item to this regiment," Curt reminded him.

"True, but there isn't very much that I can do about it other than worry, which I'm already doing," von Waldersee pointed out.

"Okay," Curt told him impatiently, "I'll tell Major Gydesen what you told me and get her on the dish with Walter Reed. How do you spell the name of that beetle?"

Von Waldersee spelled it out for him.

Curt took the poisoned arrow back to the OCV, told Major Gydesen what he'd learned, and got in touch via satellite link with the 17th Iron Fist Division's master computer under Diamond Point in Arizona.

Georgie, the familiar name given to the computer, tapped several data banks before telling Curt exactly what the anthropologist had.

Curt wasn't happy with what he learned.

But he had to do something to save the wounded people, especially Col. Belinda Hettrick. If he didn't, they'd die before he could get the regiment to Otjomuise.

So he had the communication unit put him on the satellite dish so he could talk to General Carlisle in St. Helena.

He didn't like many of the answers he got from that, either.

It wasn't going to be easy to do what he had to do.

CHAPTER THIRTY-FOUR

When Curt got back to the bonfire, it was dark except for the bright firelight that was casting strange, moving, flickering shadows on the sides of the hulking light tan vehicles of the Washington Greys. Night came quickly in the desert hills. He found that the Greys were now sharing their field rations with the Bushmen. The little yellow-brown people reacted at first with suspicion until they saw the Americans eating the food, whereupon they began to try it on a very tentative basis first, finally gorging themselves on it.

They were a strange people, Curt decided—not very large with yellow-brown skins deeply wrinkled like old parchment or an overripe fruit that had sat out in the sun too long. They were all rangy without much fat on them except for enlarged buttocks.

Lt. Jerry Allen came up beside his company commander. The young lieutenant was eating from an expendable camouflaged biodegradable plastic container. He looked out upon the assemblage and remarked. "Great place for an ass man. Leg man, no. Tit man the same. But asses, wow!"

"Where do you fit?" Curt asked him.

"I'm an ear lobe man, Captain."

"Ear lobes? Goddamn, some people get turned on by the strangest things! You must have had a rough time at West Point."

"Problem is, Captain, when I try to pull your leg, it always comes right off in my hand," Allen explained.

That caught Curt just the wrong way after a couple of hours of having to deal with dead and wounded. "Don't joke about that sort of stuff, Allen. We've taken too many casualties today. Far too many."

Allen nodded. "Yeah, sorry, Captain. I know. Dillon's wounded. So's Gerard. I've lost a good squad leader. Unless he can get back on his feet pretty quick."

"And Ward's Warriors lost Johnston," Curt said, then added in frustration, "On top of which, Sergeant Shelly Hale was wounded with a spear because these Bushmen didn't understand what the red cross tabard means. So the Companions lost their biotech, and we're short-handed all around . . ."

"How's the Colonel?"

"Not good."

Alexis Morgan came out of the darkness with Leonard Spencer in time to overhear Curt's last remark. "The Colonel took one of the poisoned arrows, didn't she?"

Curt nodded. "Alexis, you've got to run the Companions until Hettrick gets back on her feet and I can turn the regiment back over to her . . . if she gets better at all. That Bushman beetle poison is probably a slow paralyzer if von Waldersee is right about it."

"Oh, no!" Alexis breathed. "Tracy Dillon got hit with one, too."

"Along with about ten others," Curt pointed out.

"Damn! What a story this is turning out to be!" Spencer exclaimed. Curt could sense the word "Pulitzer" practically written on the man's face.

"It damned well better be, Len," Alexis remarked, "after all the time I've spent giving you background."

"Don't think I don't appreciate it, Allie," Spencer told her. "I wish all my research work could be as pleasant . . ."

Curt caught the diminutive of Alexis' name that Spencer had used. He looked askance at Alexis and simply asked, "Lieutenant?"

She replied, "Captain?"

"Please check all company personnel and equipment tonight. Correct any shortages or deficiencies, and take care of any maintenance and repair needed on the warbots and vehicles," Curt told her levelly. "Please contact the other company commanders at once and tell them I want them to do the same. I'll expect a status report from each company commander when I meet with all of you in the regimental OCV at oh-five-hundred hours tomorrow morning."

"Pretty early in the morning, Captain. We'll have to work most of the night," Alexis reminded him.

"I know. But I want the regiment ready to roll right after the interment ceremonies for our dead comrades at dawn," Curt pointed out.

"We're going to bury them *here?* Out in the middle of nowhere?" Alexis Morgan was shocked. The idea of dead comrades still hadn't become part of her reality in spite of losing Capt. Samantha Walker on Trinidad. That was almost universally considered within the regiment as having been a fluke, one of the fortunes of war. A regular warbot unit—which the Washington Greys had been only a short time before—never anticipated anything worse than a warbot operator suddenly losing all warbot contact and suffering traumatic mental disruption. Termed "killed in action" or KIA, it didn't mean that the human operator was actually killed because therapy could return the warbot brainy to duty six months to a year later. The idea of a human being *actually* being killed in combat was relatively new to the Robot Infantry.

"Can't take them with us, Lieutenant Morgan," Curt reminded her. "When this is over, we'll come back for them and take their remains to Arlington."

Alexis nodded glumly. She didn't like the idea of having to spend all night inspecting the Companions. She'd had other plans with Len Spencer that were out the window now. She suspected that was behind Curt's request for a shape-up inspection and report.

She was only partly right. Curt was taking regimental command quite seriously. And he knew the regiment had suffered losses of personnel, equipment, and ammo in the ambush. "Very well, sir," she told him formally. "Glad to hear we'll come back and get them. I'll take care of the inspections. Can we get to Otjomuise soon enough to get our wounded to proper treatment?"

Curt shook his head. "Afraid not. The medical data bases have no information on this beetle juice poison, and we don't know how effective it is against human beings. According to von Waldersee, it causes paralysis and death in animals in about twenty-four hours. The best and most optimistic estimate the intelligence unit can make indicates we're about thirty-six hours out of Otjomuise if we get rolling shortly after dawn tomorrow . . . providing there aren't any serious topographical barriers in the way. The lousy charts and maps are next to useless in my opinion, so they're relying on the data in the inertial positioning systems. Even with no problems, we'd be in Otjomuise twelve hours too late . . . if the poison time factor is right."

Len Spencer asked incredulously, "You mean you're going to have to let them all die of paralysis?"

"Len, we have communications with Walter Reed, and they have access to all the biological data available in the DC area . . . or the world, for that matter," Alexis tried to explain to the newshawk. "If they can find an example of that beetle in the national biological collections, they may be able to analyze the poison."

"And maybe not," Curt told her. "I can't count on it. And I won't."

"Captain, why not call in an air lift to take the wounded out?" Alexis suggested.

"Good idea. I have," Curt replied. "But the earliest the Air Force can get evack aerodynes to us is shortly after dawn tomorrow."

"What?" Alexis exploded, nearly overturning her plastic plate. "Why can't the bloody Air Farce get here any sooner?"

"They're busy," Curt pointed out. "They're up to their assholes in resupply missions and medical evack flights already."

Len Spencer jumped on that right away. "Are they

getting in and out of Strijdom now?"

Curt made a rude noise. He didn't like the way the French had messed up the whole operation. He explained, "No, the *Legion Robotique* and the Royal Scots are still pinned down there. The various air forces are replenishing them at Strijdom by air-drop. Heavy Bastaard ground fire has made a combat mission out of a simple air drop there, and General Carlisle reports that we've lost some aircraft. And the Indian First Assam Regiment is catching hell up near Tsumeb from the Ovambo tribesmen they're blocking out of Otjomuise. They're taking casualties, too; they're not a warbot outfit. Down at Rehoboth, the First Kokoda Aussies are running short of rations; they hadn't expected to be there more than a day or so—which is all that Operation Diamond Skeleton would have lasted if the French hadn't jumped the gun. So the air units are resupplying the Aussies by air-drop, too. Carlisle is trying to round up more air units, but it will be tomorrow at the earliest before they can be deployed to St. Helena and Namibia. Right now, Grootfontien is the only operable air base for pouring supplies into Namibia to support Operation Diamond Skeleton and evacuating wounded to St. Helena."

"Carlisle's got his hands full, doesn't he? The whole operation has turned into a can of worms," Len Spencer observed.

"Yeah. As originally planned, Operation Diamond Skeleton might have worked, and we'd all be home by now. But the French made it a nightmare by trying to salvage their national honor." There was no hiding the bitterness in Curt's voice. "But . . . we'll have our wounded picked up sometime shortly after dawn tomorrow. We'll have to keep our fingers crossed. I hope to God the beetle juice poison doesn't work very well on human beings. We're going to need everyone we've got when we go into Strijdom and Otjomuise. Especially the colonel." Curt knew he was probably engaging in wishful thinking, but he really didn't feel he was ready to take the Washington Greys into combat. He could handle a company of twelve people and twenty-four warbots; he wasn't sure he was capable of running an outfit with many times that many troops, warbots, and assorted vehicles. "Where's some chow? I've got to get something in my belly."

"I'll have someone get some for you, Captain," Jerry Allen volunteered, deliberately not asking who Curt's aide de camp might be; with the confusion in the regiment—only now beginning to be sorted out and put back in order—everyone had to pitch in to help. "How do you like your steak?"

"Barely dead. Don't stick it in that fire."

"I'll make sure it's microwaved right," Allen promised and disappeared.

"Well, that must be a load off your mind, Captain," Len Spencer suggested.

"What? Chow? No, we've got plenty," Curt replied, watching people around the fire consuming Army field rations voraciously. "I don't know how long it will last if these Bushmen keep it up. Damn! They're probably starved! Look at them put it away!"

"I think," Spencer put in, "it's probably because we've given them more food than they've ever seen in their lives. I checked up on Namibian background while we were sitting on our butts in Swakopmund. My researchers in New York fed me back a complete dossier on Namibia, including stuff about the Bushmen and other tribes I thought I'd never use. I recall reading that Bushmen are typical hunters; between hunting kills, they eat lightly—mostly nuts and tubers. When they do kill a large animal, they have to gorge themselves because they can't preserve the meat. Real Stone Age people."

"Have you filed a story on this ambush yet?" Curt suddenly wanted to know.

Spencer shook his head. "When have I had time?"

"Good. Don't do it."

"Oh? Why?"

"I promised this Bushman band that we'd honor their desire to remain isolated and unknown," Curt explained.

"Really? Well, the world needs to know about what's happened here," Spencer pointed out. "How are you going to explain three deaths and twelve wounded people? Snakes and scorpions?"

"I don't have to explain anything to the public," Curt reminded him. "I'm a professional military officer doing what I'm told to do within the Nuremburg protocols. I simply report to my boss, General Carlisle. It's not necessary that I justify any of this to the world. We came under attack. We defended ourselves. I negotiated an armistice before one of the two outfits was annihilated. What the hell did you want me to do, Spencer? Turn tail and run? To where?"

Spencer didn't say anything. He knew better than to argue. He wasn't about to allow this young Captain to infringe upon the freedom of the press. He had his own satellite terminal in his suitcase back in Alexis' ACV. He could contact New York any time. He'd file whatever report he wanted, any time he wanted to do it. He was on to one of the hottest stories of the century here, one that could make his career forevermore. He wasn't about to let it slip between his fingers. But he didn't tell Curt that.

He didn't have to. Curt already guessed what was going through the newshawk's mind. The new regimental commander wouldn't take any action until necessary, but he knew what to do about Len Spencer and his satellite terminal when and if he was forced to do it. In the meantime, no sense in irritating and alienating the newshawk; Curt had enough to worry about already.

Sgt. Tom Cole from the Companion Bravo Platoon showed up with a covered and camouflaged disposable plastic mess kit and a "Container, liquid, disposable, tea, 500 milliliter, Mark 311 Model 5."

"Thank you, Cole," Curt told him. The plastic kit was hot.

"Sure thing, Captain! Cole said brightly. The tall, lanky sergeant reminded Curt of pictures of the old Indian fighters; the robot squad leader wore his battle gear and carried his slung *Novia* with obvious ease and familiarity . . . and Curt knew that he wouldn't be caught out in the open here without personal weapons. Cole had been one of the few who hadn't been surprised by the Bushman ambush and had been among the first to open fire.

Curt turned to Alexis Morgan. "Lieutenant, I believe you have plenty of work to do . . ."

"Yes, sir, I do. And I'll get right on it." She started to go, and Len Spencer began to follow her.

"Spencer," Curt called out, "the Lieutenant's going to be pretty busy and won't have time for your questions. Stick with me. You might learn something about how we *might* pull this thing out of the manure pile."

Spencer came up short and turned around. Curt was right; Alexis was going to be busy the rest of the night, and his Pulitzer-winning coverage might well be improved by getting some inside background information on what this new regimental commander, a mere captain, could do to bring off what was turning into an almost impossible mission. He sauntered back and remarked to that effect, "I was wondering what you planned to do, Captain. You're down to about seventy people or so, aren't you? And about a hundred or so warbots? I'm curious about how the hell one regiment is going to make a dent in what seems to be going on in Otjomuise. Have you got a tactical plan yet?"

Curt shook his head. "The maps are lousy; I don't trust them. I'm hoping we can get an overview of the area when we get there and swing south along the Auasberg to Strijdom. I won't know until we get some recon data. I'll put out some birdbots when we get within range of the city. We can't afford to make any mistakes."

"From my own experience in covering a couple of reduced intensity conflicts, I'd say you're somewhat shy on manpower and warbot power to tackle the relief of Strijdom and the diplomatic compound in Otjomuise," Spencer observed. "You certainly didn't anticipate taking losses on this overland trek . . ."

"No one knew about this Bushman tribe," Curt told him, "not even Paul von Waldersee . . ."

"True, and no one anticipated they'd fight the way they

did. Damn, they're the most fearless fighters I've ever seen!" Spencer exclaimed. "I've covered a lot of brushfire wars and guerrilla operations, and these Bushmen are either downright stupid or had lots of balls to take on a regimental-strength armored column. I've never seen such ferocious people. Yet, look at them now! They're friendly and polite. I can't figure that one out."

"Mutual respect," Curt said.

"Huh?"

"We're the first outfit they've come up against that's been able to fight them to a standstill and threaten to wipe them out," Curt told him. "Von Waldersee has interrogated Chief Ba pretty thoroughly. This band has a history of taking on intruders—Dutch, Germans, English, and even South Africans—because intruders don't suspect the band is here. They've been tracking us for about a day, ever since we drew their attention with the explosions in the river bed. They weren't about to attack us. Chief Ba would just as soon have melted back into the hills undetected . . ."

"Then why did he?"

"Simple, according to von Waldersee. We stumbled right into their current camp here in this rock outcrop. Ba had to protect his women and children. When we didn't run but stood and fought back, he knew damned good and well it was either root hog or die. Chief Ba won't say so, but von Waldersee gets the impression Ba is damned glad I stepped forward and proposed an armistice. Von Waldersee—when he isn't being teutonically pedantic—has some real insights into human behavior," Curt pointed out.

"He damned well ought to. That's what an anthropologist is supposed to know something about.

"I'd think an experienced reporter such as yourself would also have such an insight," Curt said without rancor.

"I do," Spencer snapped back, hiding his irritation with this officer. "I wanted to get your viewpoint. How the hell do you think a newsman works? I can't report only my own observations and opinions. I wanted to get yours, and

I did."

"What are yours?" Curt asked suddenly. He, too, was interested in what the newsman might have sensed. Curt was in a position where he could use all the data he could get his hands on.

"Well, I've talked to Chief Ba, too . . . through von Waldersee; I don't speak or understand this click language. Too rough on the tongue," Spencer pointed out. "Chief Ba wanted to know why we were here, so von Waldersee told him what's happened in Otjomuise. The chief is worried about it."

"Worried? Why?"

"If the Bastaards and Ovambo win," Spencer explained, "Ba is worried that more foreign troops like us will come through here. The band will be discovered again, and Ba knows now that he can't win a fight against soldiers with modern warbot technology that's 'magic' to him. If we can put down the Bastaard Rebellion, things will go back to 'normal' for him—maybe under the current unstable Namibian government, maybe under the South Africans again, the Chief doesn't care because they don't know about his band and he's left alone. Do you know what really impressed Chief Ba about you?"

Curt shook his head.

"You agreed not to reveal the existence of this band to the outside world. Otherwise, he would have fought until his entire band was anihilated."

"Does it impress you enough so that you won't report it?"

"Oh, I'll report it, Captain. Rest assured of that," the newsman emphasized. Then he added quietly, "But . . . I don't have to tell it *exactly* like it is to make it a good story. All newsmen slant their reports."

"Yeah, I know that," Curt told him with distaste. "That's one thing I don't especially like about you newshawks. I can't anticipate what you'll say."

"Well, I can't report *everything*, so I must be selective. I tell the truth and nothing but the truth, but I can't tell the *whole* truth. Not enough time, not enough space. Even in a book. Besides, you and the Washington Greys are the central figures as far as I'm concerned; my readers and viewers can identify with you. A lost tribe of Bushmen detracts from the main thrust of my story. The way I intend to report this, no one will know about Chief Ba's band of Bushmen. We're close to the homelands of the Namas and Damaras, so I'll say that's what they are if I have to identify them. No one will know the difference except maybe a couple of anthropologists. And who's going to listen to them?" Spencer explained. "Be that as it may, the Chief feels obligated to you beyond the cease fire and the food. He told me that he'd take the risk of helping put down the Bastaard Rebellion if you asked him to do it—"

"What?" Curt was having trouble believing what he heard.

"Ask the Chief," Spencer suggested. "Chief Ba will leave the women and children here. He has about forty good warriors. He'll take them into Otjomuise with the regiment. They can probably get into the Bastaard or Herero or Ovambo positions a hell of a lot easier than you and your warbots. Go ask him, Captain. You're short of manpower and firepower. You need an ally at this point. Otherwise, you're likely to get clobbered the same way the French and the Brits have been . . ."

CHAPTER THIRTY-FIVE

It was a lonely, desolate place in the rocky outcrop where they'd fallen in battle, the only place where the ground was maleable enough to dig three trenches. The dawning sun struck the Stars and Stripes where it flew on a makeshift flagstaff fabricated from a length of flexible whip antenna and carried by Chief Supply Sergeant Manuel P. Sanchez; the Sierra Charlies of the Washington Greys had no wood to make a standard. The rays of the rising sun also caught the rocky outcrops above.

Three bodies lay wrapped in sleeping bags covered with the national colors of the United States of America. There were no coffins; there wasn't enough wood around to make coffins, and the Sierra Charlies were so new that the Supply Company didn't carry any plastic coffins; nobody really believed they'd be necessary. Death was something that happened to soldiers in movies and TV.

Eight platoon sergeants and squad leaders stood in a line next to the bodies, their *Novia* assault rifles held at port arms.

The entire regiment was there to say farewell to three of its members who'd fallen in battle the day before.

The Bushmen of Chief Ba's band watched these strange religious rites from perches on the surrounding rocks. Their customs required that they, too, bury their dead, but their protocols were different. None of them showed contrition; they'd already buried their own casualties, and to them this was all a consequence of battle and, in fact, of lives lived much closer to a world of sheer survival.

The service was well under way. It wasn't exactly as prescribed by the regulations or by the church books. But the Greys didn't have a church out here in the desolate wilds of Namibia, and they didn't have many of the niceties required for a completely proper burial. They made do, knowing that they'd come back for their fallen comrades, take them home to America, and give them the proper farewell then. Now they did what had to be done.

Just before the bagged bodies were lowered into the graves, the flags were removed, folded, and carefully put away. As the bags were slowly lowered into the ground, they were sprinkled with dirt by Capt. Curt Carson, Maj. Ruth Gydesen, and Capt. Joan Ward, the immediate commanding officers of the slain. The regimental chaplain, 1st Lt. Nelson Crile, intoned, "For as much as it hath pleased almighty God in his wise providence to take out of this world the souls of our deceased comrades, we therefore commit their bodies to the ground; earth to earth, ashes to ashes, dust to dust; looking for the general Resurrection in the last day . . ."

When Father Nelly Crile had finished, Lt. Jerry Allen who had been placed in command of the firing squad, gently barked the commands and three volleys were fired over the graves.

The sun broke over the last rocky ridge and cast its blood red illumination on the assembly.

Curt softly said into his portable tac comm unit, "Georgie, play 'Taps.'"

His command was relayed by satellite to the other side of the world. There were no buglers in the Army now. But the 17th Iron Fist's divisional computer, nicknamed "Georgie," sitting under Diamond Point, Arizona, synthesized perfectly the sound of a bugle playing Taps. Back across time and space came the signal, finally to be broadcast into the silent dawn air of the Namibian hills. Taps was once the last bugle call a soldier heard at the end of a long day; tradition required that it be played over a soldier's grave to mark the beginning of the last, long sleep and to express hope and confidence in an ultimate reveille to come.

"Burial detail, complete your work. Regiment, return to your vehicles," Curt ordered. He'd made sure that the graves would be carefully marked so they could be located again.

The Washington Greys didn't march away in formation; the Army didn't march any longer. But they filed back to their vehicles in columns, each person alone with private thoughts.

As Curt was about to enter the regimental OCV, he heard the unmistakable sound of aerodynes approaching—the low-frequency pulsing rumble and swish of moving air accompanied by the muffled whine of turbine blowers. "Captain Carson," came the voice of Regimental Intelligence Sergeant Emma Crawford in his helmet receiver, "the evack aerodynes are less than a kilometer out and requesting vectors for landing."

"Have them hold in hover until we can get someone out of this outcrop and direct them to a landing point," Curt replied. "Captain Wilkinson, get someone out to the east where the terrain is flat enough for aerodynes and vehicles. Let's get our wounded out of here."

"Yes, sir!" came Joanne Wilkinson's voice. Curt saw one of the other OCVs of Headquarters Company move out of the rocky defile to the flat ground beyond where Curt had rushed the Companions yesterday and begun his counterattack.

Col. Belinda Hettrick was sitting up in her bunk in the regimental OCV, eating breakfast. She looked better. When she saw Curt, she spoke up, "Dammit, Curt, I told you I wanted to be present at the burial ceremonies!"

Curt shook his head. "Major Gydesen said no, Colonel. When the doctor says no, I can't and won't override that order. You're still on the wounded list. How do you feel this morning?"

"Better. No pain in my gut," Hettrick responded. "Still got tingling in my hands, and I can't feel my toes. Having a little trouble moving them, too. Toes, that is—"

"That was a poisoned arrow that went into your side yesterday," Curt told her. "Ruth Gydesen doesn't know what the poison is or what the antidote might be. And we can't get any information from the world data bases, either. So," he paused before he went on, "we've got to get you out of here to a place where you can get better treatment, Colonel. We don't know how long it will take for the poison to do its work—"

Hettrick lowered her head and glowered at him. "The hell you say, Captain," she growled. "I'm not going—"

"The hell you say, Colonel, you're going," Curt replied. "Medical orders."

"Screw medical orders," Hettrick snapped in irritation. "I'm not sick enough to be evacked!"

"Ruth Gydesen thinks you are."

"I'm the one who knows how I feel. I've still got a lot of piss and vinegar in me. That'll help neutralize the poison—"

"Maybe, Colonel, but that poison may be long-acting and you may not really begin to feel the effects until later today. No one knows, but you could end up being completely paralyzed . . ." Curt didn't want to withhold that information from her any longer.

"I'll burn that bridge when I come to it," Hettrick maintained. "How long does it take to get an evack aerodyne in here if I suddenly go limp?"

"About thirty minutes from Grootfontein . . . if one is available. I pulled every string I could from Carlisle on down, and it took the Air Force damned near twelve hours to schedule evack aerodynes for us. They've just landed outside. Come on, I'll help you," Curt offered.

Hettrick shook her head and slowly and shakily got to her feet. Holding on firmly to an internal brace, she replied, "So? Others probably need to be evacked worse than I do. I'm assuming command, Captain! Return to your company!"

"Get back on the bunk, Colonel," Curt told her. "I'll be right back." He intended to seek out Maj. Ruth Gydesen because he wasn't getting anywhere with this stubborn woman.

"If you're going to get Ruth Gydesen, good!" Hettrick

anticipated him. "Send her in here because I want to talk to her. Then report back youself because I want a full rundown on what you did while I was on my ass in here. I need a full sit-rep from you, so get it together! That's a direct order, Captain!"

Curt shook his head. "I'll do what you tell me, Colonel, but you'll have a hell of a time arguing with Gydesen."

"We'll see!"

He couldn't help but admire her stubborn persistence. Guts might be a better word. Or plain stupidity if the Bushman poison was indeed at work inside her body. "Goddam, Colonel, but you're sure one grand battle-axe . . ."

"Thank you, Captain! Not often I get such a compliment. Now scat your ass over to biotech, get Gydesen, then report back here on the double!"

Curt did as he was ordered.

Maj. Ruth Gydesen didn't have any better luck with Colonel Hettrick. Finally, she told the regimental commander, "I'll have to report this over your head to General Carlisle. And I'm going to request that an evack aerodyne be diverted to us on an emergency basis if you start to deteriorate."

"Good thinking. That's the way I like my officers to approach problems. As for the deterioration, Ruth, that started setting in about ten years ago, and there's nothing can be done about it except for me to take six month's leave and check into a biocosmetics center . . ."

"I want you to let me know at once if you lose muscular control of your arms, legs, or *any* part of you," the chief medic instructed her.

"Hell, I have a tendency to pee in my pants every time I get shot at anyway. Does that count?"

"No, but you know what I mean, Colonel."

"Yes, I do. And I'll let you know. I do have a strong attachment to this body, and I'm a devout coward when it comes to dying," Hettrick admitted in a serious tone of voice.

Once the major had left, Hettrick wanted a full briefing

from Curt. She got it.

"Three dead and eleven wounded?" she asked in disbelief.

"Twelve wounded," Curt corrected her.

"I don't count."

Curt told her about his deal with the Bushmen. He thought she'd probably blow her top over that, but again she surprised him.

"Damned good thinking, Curt! I'm going to put you in for a commendation for exposing your ass the way you did and talking the Bushmen into quitting. And with fifteen of our Greys out of action, we can use all the help we can get!"

"I was hoping you'd see it that way," Curt admitted, pleased and surprised at her response.

"I want to see this Chief Ba as soon as possible. How far are we from Otjomuise?"

"Wade Hampton says thirty-six hours at the speed we've been travelling."

"We'll do better than that. Two regiments and about a thousand people are in deep yogurt in Otjomuise. Every hour we can cut from that schedule means more people we'll get out of the muck." She looked around, noticing that the OCV wasn't moving. "When did you tell this outfit to get on the road?"

"Right after the burial services."

"That was thirty minutes ago! Goddamit, Curt, when you're running a regiment, you've gotta keep on their ass all the time. An outfit this big doesn't move unless it gets kicked in the butt constantly. Now get the hell back to your Companions and take the point. Move it right along . . ."

"Yes, Colonel." Whether Colonel Hettrick was feeling the effects of the poison or not, she certainly wasn't letting it show, Curt decided.

As he slung his *Novia*, Hettrick suddenly asked, "Before you shove off, tell me: What the hell happened to Manny Garcia?"

Curt paused before he told her. "Just between you and

me, Colonel, Manny Garcia isn't going to cut it as a Sierra Charlie. His instincts are to go for cover and button down under attack. He assumes the defensive. As a result, his company damned-near got clobbered if it hadn't been for the fact that Marty Kelly was right behind him in the column and made up for Manny's cold feet by sheer balls in the counterattack . . . as you might expect from Marty."

"What do you suggest I do about it?" Hettrick asked.

"Team the Marauders and Killers as the Second Tactical Battalion," Curt proposed. "Marty was wounded here and so was his first sergeant, T. V. Slaughter. Lt. Russ Frazier's in charge now. Put Russ in charge as batt commander even though he's only a first looie. Manny will be pissed, but he *knows* he can't cut it and won't admit it. We can't transfer Manny now. In the meantime, Russ will kick Manny's butt hard enough to goad him into the offensive, and Manny will act as a damper on the Killers' balls-out tiger blood."

"I think you're right. Thank you. Curt, one of these days, you're going to make a good regimental commander."

"Well, I did have a regiment for about eighteen hours, Colonel."

"You did all right. Good show. Now get out of here and let's get our ass in gear. Otjomuise awaits!"

CHAPTER THIRTY-SIX

"Len Spencer of the *Times'* Constant News Network reporting to you live via satellite from somewhere in the African nation of Namibia. I'm with the United States Army Third Robot Infantry Regiment, the Washington Greys, and we're trekking across the barren Namibian wilderness on our way to the Namibian capital city of Windhoek, locally known as Otjomuise."

Spencer had set up his camera and portable satellite transceiver station alongside the ACV now manned by Lt. Alexis Morgan and M. Sgt. Henry Kester. The column had stopped for a rest break and lunch. His talking head appeared on the TV screen monitor. The read-back panel flashed its comforting lights to him that indicated his signal was going out and being received in New York from a satellite bounce over the Atlantic Ocean.

"Those of you who saw my reports last night and this morning at dawn, local time, know that the Washington Greys were ambushed yesterday afternoon by a native tribe of Stone Age warriors armed only with arrows and spears. Because of the sudden and unexpected nature of the attack, the Greys were caught unprepared and had three of their number killed and a dozen others wounded in the first minute of the attack."

Cut to some fantastic video tape that Len Spencer had managed to shoot during the Bushman attack. It was jerky. The camera moved rapidly and without the care he usually took in aiming and framing. But Spencer had been checking his minus x during the entire time he was taping to prevent a Bushman from sneaking up behind him and driving a spear into the back of his neck. It was extremely realistic coverage, and it showed Sgt. Tracy Dillon taking the poisoned arrow and Sgt. Shelley Hale being clubbed down with the butt of a spear as she tried to succor him.

Back to Spencer's talking head. "We don't have a full list of the dead and wounded yet. The Pentagon is withholding names until the next of kin can be notified. Of course, since I've gotten to know the people of the Washington Greys, I know who was killed or hurt. But out of respect for their families I'm withholding their names as requested by Col. Belinda Hettrick, commanding officer of this regiment."

Cut to tape of Capt. Curt Carson stepping into the open, slinging his rifle, being joined by Dr. Paul von Waldersee, and parleying with Chief Ba. "If it hadn't been for the courage of Captain Curt Carson who stepped forward and, with the help of anthropologist Paul von Waldersee, negotiated an armistice, this fierce native tribe would have continued fighting until it had wiped out the regiment or been obliterated itself . . . more likely the latter because of the firepower of a warbot infantry regiment. So many different native tribes and bands occupy Namibia that I can't keep them straight, and my research staff has been unable to identify the tribe that attacked us. But it seems we blundered into one of their campgrounds in a rock outcrop, and they attacked to protect their women and children against the strange intruders. The cease-fire and armistice was celebrated last night by a roaring bonfire provided by the tribe and some of the food the Washington Greys brought along in abundance."

Cut to a shot of the bonfire surrounded by dancing Bushmen accompanied by the beating of gourds and the shaking of rattles by their women. The Washington Greys stood obviously amused in the firelit background.

Cut to a head shot of Lt. Alexis Morgan.

"Unlike the natives who don't allow their women to fight, the women in the Washington Greys were an intimate part of the battle. One of the ones in the forefront was First Lieutenant Alexis Morgan, a West Pointer from Burlington, Iowa. Lieutenant, how did you feel about fighting these natives?"

"Scared, surprised," Alexis replied candidly. "Everyone was. It was an ambush. Actually, I don't think I had time to be scared. I had to respond damned fast because one of those *bleep* was crawling up the back of my ACV with a spear. He'd already put an arrow into a Sergeant, so I blew his *bleep* off before he did something like that to me."

"Any qualms?"

"Sure. No one likes to kill. Sometimes you have to. Like this afternoon."

"Sounds rather bloodthirsty. Do they pick warbot soldiers on that basis, or is it trained into them?"

"I'm not sure what you mean," Alexis replied candidly. "The Army wants aggressive people, even for pure robot warfare. In other words, we'll fight hard if we have to, although we often ask ourselves ahead of time what the hell we're doing and why we're putting our pink bodies in danger. But we're not belligerent."

"Oh? There's a difference?"

"Len, you're supposed to be a wordsmith. You should know the difference."

These last two remarks were edited from the tape before transmission.

Cut back to Len Spencer's head. "Lest viewers think that the women officers and soldiers of our Army have been brainwashed into being cold-blooded killers, let me point out that I've met and gotten to know most of the women in the Washington Greys since I joined the regiment on St. Helena several days ago. Frankly, to use an old cliche, they're like the girl next door when they're not in combat. Lieutenant Alexis Morgan, for example, is indeed an officer and a lady. Twice I've seen our women Sierra Charlies or Special Combat forces in action—once in Swakopmund and again yesterday afternoon. They're certainly the equal of men when it comes to modern combat, and they may have greater endurance and staying power. After all, women like Lieutenant Alexis Morgan have breached the last bastion that stood in the way of total female equality: The right to voluntarily place themselves between their loved ones and the war's desolation, serving in personal combat alongside men with all the physical and mental stress this intense activity has demanded since time immemorial. This reporter's hat is off to them!"

Cut to tape of the burial scene at dawn with regimental chaplain Nelson Crile reading the service, the three volleys of rifle fire over the graves, and the computer-synthesized sounds of a bugle playing Taps. "The three Washington Greys killed in yesterday's ambush were buried at dawn today with as many military honors as the regiment could muster under these conditions. It was a touching ceremony, as a military funeral always is."

Cut to tape of Capt. Curt Carson announcing somewhat emotionally but without his voice breaking, "They were our friends and comrades. We're going to come back and get them when this rebellion is over. We've carefully located the graves so we can find them. They don't deserve to lie here forever in this desolate land far from their friends and family. If I have anything to say about it, they'll be re-interred in Arlington . . ."

Cut to tape again, this time showing the aerodynes being loaded with wounded and taking off in a cloud of sand and dust.

Voice-over from Len Spencer: "The wounded were evacuated shortly after the burial ceremonies. When I asked why the dead weren't taken out as well, I was told that the air forces involved in Operation Diamond Skeleton are so short of equipment and manpower that first priority is given to evacuation of the wounded while second priority is given to the resupply of the French and British forces at Strijdom Airport and the people trapped in the diplomatic compound in Windhoek. Apparently, these operations absorb nearly all the capabilities of the air units here, and there is neither the time or the fuel or the lift capability right now for evacuating the dead."

Cut back to Len Spencer standing beside the Companion's ACV. "Which brings up the question I've asked before: Why do we always seem to get into military situations of all sorts, deadly and otherwise, with our forces short of manpower, short of equipment, short of supplies, and short of time? Some will say it's been that way since the Revolutionary War. I have to agree with the historical record. Americans have always distrusted and disliked keeping large military forces in peacetime. So maybe it's impossible to maintain and deploy American military forces as strong as they should be. And there's probably a reason for this. The British still remember the military coup that brought Cromwell into power, and our American forefathers wanted to keep something similar from happening in America. But the billions we spend every year on defense plus the professional dedication and zeal of our officers and soldiers are often wasted or even squandered because of this."

His editorial opinion voiced, Spencer cut to tape showing the regimental column moving through the rugged Namibian hills that morning. Each vehicle had two or three Bushmen riding atop it. "We got under way again shortly after the aerodynes picked up the wounded. When the natives learned that other native groups were causing trouble in Windhoek, the Chief volunteered the men of the band to act as guides and reserve forces around the capital. Why? Let's let Namibian anthropologist, Doctor Paul von Waldersee, explain it for us."

Cut to head shot of von Waldersee taken last night with the huge bonfire burning in the background. "These natives have lived here in self-imposed isolation for centuries. They don't want to be bothered. They want to live their lives as they please. The Chief told me that if the rebellion succeeds, he's afraid that other foreign military forces will come through here and disturb them. He'd rather see an unstable national government or even a continued occupation by the South Africans because that's a situation he knows how to handle and can live with. These people just want to be left alone. Helping us in Windhoek will, in his belief, help them continue to live in their Stone Age manner . . ." Von Waldersee had been very careful what he'd said and how he'd said it. He was vexed with Curt's agreement to respect the secrecy of the band's existence, but he was a man of honor and would respect the agreement. The Chief's decision to accompany the Greys to Windhoek had given him precious additional time to study this lost tribe. He knew he had a golden opportunity as well as an exclusive; he was going to make the best of what he could get because even that would help make him a leading anthropologist. Only in his personal papers, to be locked up and revealed fifty years after his death, would he reveal the truth about this Bushman band. But he said nothing about that then and many things happened before he was able to write those reports and studies.

"This is the twenty-first century, and the Washington Greys will be going up against opponents armed with modern weapons," Spencer pointed out. "How can a group of about fifty Stone Age tribal warriors armed only with spears and arrows help the Washington Greys in Windhoek, Doctor?"

"I don't know," von Waldersee told him. "I haven't asked Captain Carson. Apparently there's a plan, but I don't know what it is. I'm not sure he'd want me to talk about it in any event."

"So we're on the last leg of the trek to Windhoek," Len Spencer concluded as his round face with its twinkling little eyes filled the screen again. In the background, the Washington Greys were mounting their vehicles and it was obvious that the column would begin moving shortly. "For security purposes—which I intend to honor because the survival of everyone in this column depends on it—I won't reveal our expected arrival time in Windhoek. More news when and as it happens, however. This is Len Spencer reporting from somewhere in Namibia with the United States Army Washington Greys regiment approaching Windhoek . . ."

CHAPTER THIRTY-SEVEN

"Column halt!" came the command from Lt. Alexis Morgan's ACV on point as it topped the slight rise ahead.

The command was passed back down the two kilometer line of Washington Grey vehicles.

It woke Curt up. He'd been resting in his ACV's bunk, trying to make up for a night of lost sleep after serving as temporary regimental commander following the Bushman ambush, a previous night during which he'd been battered about as a result of trying to blast a boulder out of a creek bed, plus the continuous days of trekking across the desolate, rugged Namibian wilderness toward the capital city of Otjomuise somewhere beyond the hills ahead. He got to his feet, put on his helmet, and slung his *Novia* over his shoulder.

M. Sgt. Henry Kester was up in the turret hatch. "What's up, Henry?" Curt called.

"Lieutenant Morgan stopped her point ACV on the ridge ahead, called for a halt, and is now backing down to the military crest," the old soldier reported.

"Companion One," Curt addressed his ACV auto-pilot computer, "pull out to the right of the convoy, move ahead, and stop next to Companion Alpha One."

The vehicle didn't answer. Curt had deactivated its voice reply, a redundant feature intended to make the lifeless machine a little more human and to reassure its occupants that it was indeed working properly. Curt didn't care right then. He was far more concerned about his troops, their robots, and their weapons working properly than he was in hearing a vehicle talk back to reassure him. He felt the ACV swing right and speed up.

He popped up in the turret's aux hatch. In the light of the low afternoon sun, the shadows of the scrubby trees and bushes were long, and the terrain relief stood out starkly. It reminded him of the terrain in Bloody Basin, Arizona, where the division conducted maneuvers when the U.S. Forest Service would let them. The sky was still a cloudless blue, and the disk of the sun was sharply etched in the sky. It would be another sudden sunset with the sun slipping behind the Khomas Hochland behind them.

The form in Alpha One's turret turned and motioned to Curt to join up. It was Lt. Alexis Morgan, and she was indicating for him to come forward. He crawled out of the turret, grinned and waved at the two Bushmen riding the aft deck, and dropped to the ground. The Bushmen followed, joined two others who slipped off Alpha One, and disappeared quickly into the underbrush.

"Come up here and have a look!" Alexis called to him. "I don't believe this!"

Len Spencer had dismounted from Alpha One and was taping with his video camera, first getting a shot of Curt approaching the ACV, then panning right to show what Alexis had seen.

Curt clambered up Alpha One and looked where Alexis indicated.

Just over the lip of the ridge from which Alexis had backed away to get her ACV off the skyline was a four-lane divided asphalt highway.

It was empty. No traffic zipped past in either direction.

Crossing the highway on a double-span plate girder bridge was a railway.

Beyond the highway and railway was a dry river bed.

"Autoroute One," Alexis guessed, "and the railway between Otjomuise and Marienthal."

"Christamighty!" Curt exploded, checking the inertial position unit readout on the turret lip below Alexis. "We're too far south!"

"Check your helmet visor tactical display," Alexis

suggested, activating a control on the panel below the turret lip. Curt did so and saw the Namibia map projected there with a point of flashing light indicating their position. Sure enough, the map showed the railway crossing the autoroute with the river on the far side.

"We're twenty-seven kilometers south of where we should be!" Curt observed from the chart.

"Lucky to hit it that close with the charts and satellite data not matching," Alexis said. "Damned maps! The South Africans deliberately distorted them! They've got access to satellite positioning just like everyone else but they made inaccurate charts for security purposes."

"And we copied them," Curt reminded her. "And didn't square them with the satellite photos. Well, what would you do if you wanted to keep someone from using lat-long coordinates to program a missile to land on your town? I sure as hell wouldn't give them the right coordinates to read off a map!"

"You're right as usual."

Curt noticed a sharp tone in her voice. "Sorry you had to give back the Companions. But I had to give back the regiment, too."

"My time will come, Captain."

"Damned right . . . if I have anything to say about it," he told her. He turned and tried to get his bearings. "Okay, that's the Auasberg ahead and the Eros Mountains down to the left. Otjomuise must be beyond the pass where the highway and the railway go through the hills. We've come to a decision point, even though we're twenty-seven klicks south of position and a day ahead of schedule."

"I'd rather be ahead of schedule," Alexis admitted. "That was a long haul up from Swakopmund."

"Agreed," Curt muttered, then told her," Okay, park it here and stay put. I'm going back to my ACV and get on a tight lasercomm link to Grey Head. We're within thirty klicks of Otjomuise, and I don't want to take the chance that anyone can snoop our freaks and discover we're here. We've still got the element of surprise on our side, which makes up for being somewhat short-handed."

"You don't think the Namibians have that sort of sophisticated electronic warfare capability, do you?"

"I don't want to take a chance on it. Maybe the Angolans are snooping with Soviet gear up north, or even the South Africans with surplus stuff our arms merchants have sold them." Curt dropped back to the ground and made his way to his ACV.

He managed to set up a lasercomm relay through Capt. Joan Ward's ACV to the regiment's Operational Command Vehicle. Sgt. Maj. Tom Jesup's voice responded to Curt's call-up.

Curt reported what had happened, then said, "Ask the colonel what she wants to do: stay put for the night, cross the highway and deploy in the Auasberg, or turn south and go for the Eros airport and Otjomuise?"

"Captain, you'd better get back here, sir," Jesup's voice told him gravely. "The colonel's been up in the turret hatch all afternoon. When the column stopped, she tried to get down and complained that her legs were paralyzed. She fell, and I think she broke her leg . . ."

"Oh, shit!" Curt muttered. "Get Major Gydesen there on the bounce!"

"I've already called her, sir."

"Good! And if it's that bad, get on the dish to St. Helena and request that evack aerodyne they promised," Curt instructed.

"That's done too, sir. I recorded a message from Major Gydesen to General Carlisle earlier today and stored it for possible transmission."

Curt wasn't upset that Gydesen had gone over the Colonel's head to Carlisle, but he wondered what good it would do in getting a scarce aerodyne, even though the message had come from the chief regimental medic. "No wonder the colonel counted on you, Jesup. I guess now I'll have to do the same . . ."

"Yes, sir. You can, sir."

"I will, starting now. Get back on the dish to St. Helena. Request a teleconference with General Carlisle and his staff on St. Helena and all the unit commanders of Operation Diamond Skeleton here in Namibia. Then pass the word that I want all officers and NCOs down to platoon level to meet in the OCV in fifteen minutes. I want them to sit in on that teleconference, by the way."

"Yes, sir!"

Curt switched to his company freak. "Companion Alpha Leader, this is Companion Leader."

"Go ahead, Companion Leader."

"The colonel's worse. Her legs are paralyzed, and she fell out of the turret of her ACV and broke her leg."

"Oh, my! . . ."

"You've got command of the company, Lieutenant. Transfer to Companion One when you get the chance. Right now, get on your ATV and head for regimental command. As you pass Companion One, stop and pick me up."

"Can I bring Len Spencer?"

"No."

"He'll come anyway, even if he has to walk," Alexis pointed out. "If he walks, he'll be pissed at us. If he gets pissed at us, it'll affect the way he reports all this in his evening segment, especially Hettrick's accident."

"I could care less about his report and public opinion right now," Curt growled. He cleared the frequency and turned to Kester, "Take good care of things, Henry. I've got a frigging tiger by the tail again."

"Yes, sir! Good luck, sir!"

"I'm going to need more than luck . . ."

Len Spencer was with Alexis when she stopped her ATV to pick him up. Curt scowled but said nothing. In fact, no one said anything during the trip back down the column to the hulking Operational Command Vehicle of the Washington Greys.

Maj. Ruth Gydesen met him as he entered the OCV. "She broke her leg when she fell," the chief medic reported.

"So I was told by Jesup. He also said her legs were paralyzed."

Gydesen nodded. "We've got to get her out of here. The evack aerodyne will be here from Grootfontien in eighty minutes. Sorry, Captain, but I went over your head and got

General Carlisle on the satellite dish. He got a long-range aerodyne that will lift her straight from here to St. Helena. She'll be in Walter Reed in twelve hours."

"I know all about it. And for that sort of thing, you can go over my head any time, Doctor. I believe it's called medical privilege. By the way, how'd you manage to get through to General Carlisle?"

"Well, General Carlisle and I are . . . good friends. I called in a few favors."

Curt just nodded. He didn't give a damn whether or not there was anything between the General and the regiment's chief medic, although this confirmed what had come through Rumor Control at the Club several weeks back.

"She knows she's got to relinquish command now," Gydesen went on. "She's upset about it, but she's taking it well. She's resting pretty well considering. I'm using acupuncture to control the pain of her broken leg; I didn't want to risk using chemical pain killers with her body full of that Bushman beetle juice."

"Any report on what the poison is?"

Gydesen shook her head sadly. "But the neurophysiologists at Walter Reed will be able to figure it out once she's there."

"Will she last twelve hours?"

"Are you kidding? She's as tough as they come, Captain! Well, I shouldn't be so positive about that because I don't really know. But I'll make book on it anyway. Besides, once she's aboard that medical evack aerodyne, they've got the equipment to keep her alive even if she's totally paralyzed." Gydesen stepped to one side. "She wants to see you."

Col. Belinda Hettrick was lying under a blanket on the OCV's bunk. Curt tried not to look at the acupuncture needles in her neck. She seemed alert although she looked tired and somewhat pale.

"'Evening, Colonel."

"Good evening, Curt. Have you taken command of the regiment?" Hettrick wanted to know.

"Yes, Colonel. But I don't like the circumstances under

which I had to do it."

"I don't either, but don't bitch about it. And don't worry about how you'll handle it, either. You'll do fine."

"Do my best."

"I know you will. If the procedure hadn't been in the regs and I'd been asked about it, I would have named you anyway. I'll let you tell me about it back at Diamond Point when this is all over. In the meantime, don't forget what we learned: Hold 'em by the nose with fire and kick 'em in the ass with maneuver."

Curt nodded. "That's the Sierra Charlie tactical doctrine we worked out together, Colonel."

"Swiped it from Patton," Hettrick admitted. Then she began to brief him on the regiment. "Wade Hampton's doing a good job picking up Ed Canby's responsibilities. Joanne Wilkinson's filling in for John Gibson. You won't have to worry about Headquarters Company. But keep an eye on Manny Garcia and try to keep Manny's Marauders out of critical spots where they might have to go into combat. Use the company as reserves or as a fire base."

Curt nodded. "I've noticed that. I'm also planning temporary realignment of the regiment for the Strijdom operation. I may catch hell for doing it . . ."

"What do you have in mind?"

Curt told her. "It may cause some heartburn in the regiment."

Hettrick shook her head. "Curt, the Greys are good people. Tell them why you're doing it, and they'll be right behind you."

"Or an epileptic fit on St. Helena."

"Carlisle will support you."

"I hope so."

Hettrick smiled. "I've talked with the General. He knows what's going on. And he seems to know where the bodies are buried when it comes to the Supreme Command. Hate to check out and leave you holding the bag at this particular point. I was looking forward to breaking the Bastaards at Strijdom."

"We'll do it. I'll tell you how it went later. Just get to

Walter Reed ASAP so they can take care of that paralysis."

Hettrick shrugged. She put her hand on his arm and told him confidentially, "It may have gone too far already. I didn't want to let on how bad it was until it finally got the best of me. It was important to get the Greys this far in a rough trek. I've got no complaints and no one to blame but myself. And, well, if they can't fix it up with some sort of antidote, they might be able to jump-start the nerve trunks electronically so I can walk again. If not, I'll learn how to pilot a wheechair. I don't have to be able to walk to sit behind a terminal as a staff stooge. But I sure as hell don't intend to resign my commission and retire before I've got thirty on the books. What the hell would I do with myself? Quilting? Needlepoint?"

"You could always write a book," Curt suggested. "Other officers have."

She shook her head. Then stopped and looked pensive. "Maybe I will. But not the usual memoirs. But with the public preoccupation with Rule Ten, women in combat, and the continual sexual orgies we're supposed to have, maybe I'll write military pornography! What do you think? Could I do it?"

Curt grinned. "I think you might have enough experience, Colonel."

"Thank you, my young buck. So don't worry about me, see? Earn your pay. Make me proud of the Greys. Make your name to shine!"

Curt knew damned well that there was a chance he'd never see her alive again. But he restrained himself from leaning over and kissing her on the cheek. That would have embarrassed both of them. Instead, he just squeezed her hand. And said nothing in reply.

"And until the evack aerodyne arrives," Hettrick went on, "I've still got all my marbles upstairs. I want to sit in on your teleconference, if you don't mind."

"What the hell, Colonel, it's your OCV," Curt reminded her.

"No, Curt, it's yours now."

CHAPTER THIRTY-EIGHT

Gen. Jacob Carlisle's image filled the two-dimensional video screen. Behind him could be seen several members of the Supreme Allied Command staff. Carlisle looked tired. But, after several days of the intense activity of Operation Diamond Skeleton, every officer on the screen looked tired.

So did everyone crowded into the large interior of the Washington Greys' regimental Operational Command Vehicle. All officers and the lead NCOs were present. On the screens in addition to the image of Maj. Gen. Jacob O. Carlisle with his allied command staff gathered around him was Gen. Franchet Lanrezac, the Supreme Allied Commander, who was trapped at Strijdom International Airport with Col. Charles Henri Mangin of the *Legion Robotique* and Col. Douglas McEvedy-Brooke of the Royal Scots Fusileers. On voice-only channels were Col. Alymer Birdwood of the 1st Australian Kokoda Regiment in Rehoboth, Col. Siraj Mahadaji of the 1st Assam Regiment in Tsumeb, and the military attache of the French embassy in Otjomuise, Capt. Charles Peguy Portales who had been assigned to the Otjomuise legation because he'd had the temerity to question the dependence of the *Armee de l'Terre* on neuroelectronic warbots in the face of the American experience in Zahedan and Trinidad.

Carlisle began, "I've called this teleconference because we have what may well be the last opportunity to do what we were sent here to accomplish. We have units in position now to relieve the Strijdom Airport and the Otjomuise diplomatic compound. But, for the first time in Operation Diamond Skeleton, *everyone* is going to have to work together as a team. We need good coordination, surprise, mass, and firepower. Judging from what I've seen of the tactical situation, we may have one and only one more chance to pull this operation out of trouble. If *any* of us screws up, we could lose our units and even our lives."

"I am very happy that you have called this conference, General Carlisle," General Lanrezac interrupted from the *Legion Robotique* command vehicle at Strijdom. "It has been difficult to exercise overall command from here. But with the new units in place, I will give orders that will result in a massive attempt to break out of Strijdom. The American regiment en route from Swakopmund is to attack the aerodrome in a massive frontal assault from the foothills of the Auasberg mountains at dawn tomorrow with their mobile warbots in the van and supported by a heavy rolling barrage from their heavy fire warbots. The Royal Scots Fusileers will provide crossfire from within our perimeter. With this frontal assault on the Bastaard lines, we shall break the ring around the aerodrome so that the *Legion Robotique* may proceed at once toward the city in a victorious advance . . ."

Curt cringed. It was the typical French doctrine of massive frontal assault under heavy artillery fire. Lanrezac understood nothing about Sierra Charlie tactics and probably didn't realize that the Washington Greys were a Special Combat unit of mixed human and warbot troops.

"General Lanrezac, with all due respect, sir," Carlisle replied formally and carefully, aware that he was dealing with an allied organization made up of officers most of whom he considered to be prima donnas, "the burden of overall command fell upon me as your deputy when you went into a tactical situation with the *Legion Robotique* at Strijdom. The nature of your situation precludes your ability to obtain or possess adequate C-cubed-I, and you have no staff to evaluate it or to process parallel orders to the supporting units. Under these conditions, General, I as your deputy respectfully request that I be allowed to continue as *pro tem* Supreme Allied Commander until we have the opportunity to put you back in an overall command environment—"

"Impossible!" Lanrezac exploded. "France has been wronged, France initiated Operation Diamond Skeleton, and France shall continue to command it!"

"General, at the moment, you have nothing to command but two surrounded regiments," Carlisle reminded him. "Furthermore, *you can't exercise overall command from where you are!* Allow me, as your deputy, to continue to work with the staff you brought together for this operation. We'll resolve the stalemated situation, whereupon I shall gladly relinquish the command back to you."

Lanrezac sputtered, but Col. McEvedy-Brooke of the Royal Scots put in, "Please excuse us for a moment, General Carlisle. I should like to speak privately with General Lanrezac." Whereupon he leaned over to the French supreme commander and, with his mouth hidden from videocamera view by his hand and in a voice too low to be transmitted by the microphone, said something quietly to Lanrezac. The old French general who should have been put out to pasture several years before responded twice with brief exclamations, then quieted down.

Only later would Curt learn from discreet private sources what the British colonel had said to the French general. Basically, it amounted to, "Get out of the way, *mon Generale,* and accede gracefully to this magnanimous offer to save your ass—and ours—or the Royal Scots Fusileers will do what is necessary to cooperate with the Americans and break out of this sticky wicket . . . and the *Legion* will then have the option to follow or be left behind to fight this your way."

Colonel Mangin of the *Legion* must have overheard because he also said something privately to Lanrezac. Apparently from Lanrezac's expression, Mangin supported McEvedy-Brooke.

General Lanrezac relaxed and accepted the inevitable. After all, if he didn't make too much of a fuss now, he could later resume the supreme allied command and take credit for what his subordinates were going to do anyway, with or without him. He may have been an old fool, but he was not foolish. He turned to face the video pickup and told Carlisle brusquely, "Very well, General. What are the plans?"

"I believe it depends upon the Washington Greys regiment," Carlisle observed. "They're our ace in the hole, so to speak. Furthermore, the Washington Greys is a mixed soldier and robot unit, the first United States Army 'Special Combat' outfit. They operate with a tactical doctrine that is totally new and may be unfamiliar to many of you. Therefore, I'd like to hear the evaluation of the tactical situation by their commanding officer. Colonel Belinda Hettrick was in command but has sustained wounds; therefore, the regiment has been taken over by the senior combat officer, Captain Curt Carson. Captain, what's your estimate of the situation?"

It was right out of the textbooks at West Point. But Curt was a little hesitant. He'd hoped as a result of a previous conversation with Carlisle a few minutes before the teleconference that Carlisle himself would do what Curt had just been asked. The new regimental commander felt somewhat out of place leading a discussion of general officers and senior staff people. It was highly unusual for a mere Captain to be making suggestions to such high brass. But Curt knew he'd asked for it by accepting command of the regiment, he was Johnny-on-the-spot, and he'd better come through. Furthermore, the regimental OCV was filled with his fellow officers and lead NCOs; he'd invited them to listen so they'd get the full picture.

So he began, "General, the Washington Greys, the Third Robot Infantry Regiment of the United States Army, is prepared to attack tomorrow morning. We're bivouacked twenty-seven kilometers south-southwest of Otjomuise in the Eros Mountains on the west side of Autoroute One and the railway between Otjomuise and Rehoboth. I've transmitted our location coordinates so you should have them on your tactical displays. By the way, the coordinates do *not* match the maps. We can move into position tonight for an assault at dawn. But, because we are *not* a regular warbot outfit and will be putting our pink bodies in the line of fire with tactical doctrine we've developed and tested, I want to make damned certain we have a planned operation here.

"We do *not* have the strength or firepower to carry out a successful frontal attack. We suffered fifteen dead and wounded in a native ambush yesterday," Curt went on. "We're shorthanded. Even when we're at full regimental strength, we're small and lean, and we depend upon surprise and mobility. The extent to which this has been degraded by our losses is unknown, but I believe we can continue to perform as specialists in maneuver and shock action. If you want the nearest historical analogy, we're the modern light cavalry. Unlike the armored forces with their big roboticized tanks, our voice-commanded, artificially intelligent warbots can be considered as very small, very light tanks mounting light, fast-firing antipersonnel and heavy anti-armor weaponry. We can screen and recoinnoiter fast and stealthy. Our best mode for action is to hit the flanks or the rear of the enemy. Within the regiment itself, we're organized to make contact with the enemy, pin him down with fire, and then move around his flanks to take him from the rear. We can also work with existing warbot units that provide the suppressive fire to pin down the enemy while we move around the flanks and strike.

"We have with us about fifty native warriors who are stealthy, maneuverable, and deadly, even armed only with spears and arrows. They won't fight in the city of Otjomuise; they don't know how to fight urban warfare because they're open-country warriors. So they'll be handy in the terrain around Strijdom because they'll be a contingent of native shock troops fighting other natives . . . and they *hate* the Bastaards and Hereros."

Curt paused, then added, "With that as a background, I recommend that we be allowed to use our strengths. The first of these is surprise; the Bastaards, Hereros, and

Ovambos have shown they can overwhelm warbot units, and they know about the non-warbot First Assam and First Kokoda . . . but they don't know about the Sierra Charlies. We can take them by total surprise. And we will.

"But, before I can give you a reasonable estimate of the situation or recommend a suitable assault plan, General Carlisle, I need to know the current tactical situation. Can you download the present unit locations and strengths? Where is everyone, and how strong are you?"

"Is this a secure conference net?" asked Col. Birdwood of the First Kokoda.

"No communications net is secure, Colonel," Carlisle pointed out, "but it would take some highly sophisticated gear to tap this one. Maybe the South Africans are eavesdropping. Or maybe the Soviets have the capability up in Angola. But whether or not they can do anything about what they hear is something else. If they try to relay data to the Bastaards, our ECM jammers will get on top of it within a second of the time the transmissions start. So you can consider this net to be about as secure as feasible."

"Very well," Colonel Birdwood replied. "No need to use a digital response. We're sitting on our asses in Rehoboth at full regimental strength and no South Africans to be found by our reconnaissance within two hundred kilometers. In short, the Afrikaaners are sitting tight and so are we."

"I certainly wish we could say the same," was the verbal report from Colonel Madhadaji in Tsumeb. "The Grootfontien airfield is now secure, but we've taken about nine percent casualties and we're in constant action with Ovambos who are trying to stream south to Otjomuise. We have our hands full, but we can handle the Ovambos."

Captain Portales reported from the diplomatic compound, "We're reasonably well secure in the legation compound. The Namibians built this place very strong. Nothing short of artillery or a concentrated air strike could breach these walls. We have water from internal wells and several weeks' stockpile of food. We'd like to get out of here, but we can hold quite well until you break through to us. We have perhaps fifty diplomatic guards and another hundred armed civilians manning the ramparts in shifts, and we have the firepower to hold out because we've concentrated it along avenues of approach. All noncombatants are sequestered in well-protected temporary bunkers out of the fields of fire and beyond the possibility of injury if the Bastaards should attempt to mine or shell the walls . . . which, of course, is classical medieval siegecraft . . ."

The *Legion Robotique* and the Royal Scots had taken about eight percent human casualties and lost about twenty-three percent of their warbots. They were surrounded by an estimated 4,500 native rebels. "No heavy artillery," Colonel Mangin reported, "but they have lots of old Soviet AK-74s, American M-16s, and South African SAR-16s, plus some light machine guns probably commandeered from the Namibian arsenals in Otjomuise. More important, however, is the fact that they have ample manpower to simply overwhelm the warbots to the point where our warbies cannot handle the overload."

Curt and the other Washington Greys knew exactly what he was talking about even though he'd used the British slang for a warbot operator. He'd found himself in the same situation when the Greys were still a full warbot outfit and had come up against the Jehorkhim hordes at Zahedan. Massed waves of human soldiers would overwhelm neuroelectronically controlled warbots if the enemy didn't worry about taking casualties in the process. In many ways, massed regular infantry horde tactics against warbots were like the old World War II Soviet tank-rider tactics. It was a classic example of the verities of combat which stated that the side with greater numbers usually wins and that any attacker determined to pay the price can overcome the best defense and the most modern weaponry. The French and British warbot units at Strijdom had confirmed that the hard way.

"Colonel Mangin, we know what you're up against; we've been there ourselves," Curt told him, then stopped.

After a pause of about ten seconds—it seemed an eternity

in the tension-filled conference—General Carlisle broke the silence by saying, "Well, Captain Carson, what is your evaluation of the situation?"

Curt was studying the tactical display in the OCV's projection tank. "We can break the Bastaards, General Carlisle."

"How?"

"Do you want a proposal, sir?"

"I do."

"Look at your displays," Curt instructed and unlimbered a laser marker to illuminate what he was talking about. "First of all, I'd leave the First Assam regiment where it is but change its orders so that it's prime function is to protect Grootfontein which is the critical air base for both tactical air support—which we'll want a great deal of tomorrow—and the evack operation, which will start tomorrow night, if everything goes well."

"You assume an optimistic schedule, Captain," was the remark from Colonel McEvedy-Brooke of the Royal Scots. "Such optimisitc schedules can be far removed from reality, as we found out—"

"Yes, but we won't make the same mistakes all over again, Colonel," Curt told him candidly. "We don't gain anything by moving slowly and deliberately; we'll win by hitting hard and fast with lots of opportunism. Which is what I'd suggest we do. I'll get to my general outline in a moment, ladies and gentlemen. But next I would move the First Australian Kokoda Regiment out of Rehoboth *tonight* and bring them quickly up Autoroute One . . ."

"But that would leave the southern flank open to the South Africans," Colonel Birdwood objected.

"Colonel, you've reported no South African units within two hundred kilometers," Curt reminded him. "Therefore, no South African Defense Force units will follow you tonight. By tomorrow at dawn, you can be here where we are, astride the highway and railway where it cuts through the Auasberg. If necessary, the Kokoda can protect the southern approaches to Otjomuise from here quite well—"

"Well, yes, but not if the Afrikaaners move in with an airborne unit right behind us."

Curt shrugged. "They won't. They've got to find you first. And they'll waste some time in recon activities . . . and I suspect some of the unit commanders on the teleconference tonight would like the chance to either spoof their recon or have a slight accident which eliminates it in a regrettable incident. We're doing the unexpected, remember? It will take time for them to react to the Kokoda pulling out of Rehoboth. By the time they might drop an airborne unit into the town, what difference will it make? We'll be in the process of evacking people out of the compound by the time they could possibly be a threat to us . . . and they'll also have their hands full fighting the Bastaards and the rest just like we've done. The Afrikaaners aren't well-liked in Namibia, Colonel. And our first job is to get the people out of the Otjomuise diplomatic compound, not to defend Namibia against an invasion. If we do this right, we can relieve the compound by sunset tomorrow. By dawn the following day, we're either out of here as we've been ordered . . . or we're in the catbird's seat for whatever occupational duty our politicians and diplomats decide they want us to perform. And I refuse to take bets either way on that one, gentlemen. Besides, Colonel Birdwood, the Kokoda is going to be the reserve force in the Otjomuise battle."

"Very well, I'll buy off on that. I'll have my troops on the road in one hour."

"Good. Now here's what I'd recommend to break the *Legion* and the Royal Scots out of Strijdom and get the people out of the diplomatic compound. It's a general plan that won't work if it's micromanaged from headquarters. Objectives are straightforward. We'll need air support with ground-fire suppression missions to keep the air environment reasonably sanitary and with tactical targets of opportunity called out by forward observers on the ground. As for the tactics, let them be flexible in response to objective barriers. Let your own field units down to the company level determine their own tactics for achieving the objectives. Leave things to the initiative of your troops, and they'll probably surprise the hell out of you with innovative reactions. Don't strap them, but don't try to make it too easy for them, either. No guts, no glory. Although the overall plan is quite simple and not overly time-critical for the most part—the haze of battle and the friction of war always make things run slower than planned—we can't afford *any* massive screw-ups by anyone who thinks that a minor diversion to an unrelated objective would be justified for personal honor or ego building. Here's the overall picture. You work out how your own regiment is going to fit in, then let General Carlisle know . . . and keep the rest of us clued-in while you're doing it. So listen up . . ."

CHAPTER THIRTY-NINE

"In order to carry this off," Curt addressed the officers and NCOs of the Washington Greys after the supreme command teleconference concluded, "I'm going to have to make some changes in the T-O, but only for the Strijdom assault. Once we break the Bastaards, we'll go back to normal organizational configuration. First off, in breaking the ring around Strijdom, we won't be dealing with any armor or fortifications, just native irregulars armed with old assault rifles and some light machineguns. So our heavy weaponry would be less than useless and may even cause problems for the *Legion* and the Royal Scots if we overshoot. Now, everyone in the combat companies has been cross-trained in all warbot equipment, so you shouldn't have any trouble working Mary Annes if you've been running Hairy Foxes, for example. Anyone have a problem with that?"

Capt. Joanne Wilkinson raised her hand. "No one in the Headquarters Company can run anything but the jeeps, and we're not very experienced with them."

Curt nodded. "I know that. I have something else in mind for Headquarters. I'll get to that in a minute. First of all, I want to transfer all M60 Mary Annes to the Companions, the Warriors, and the Killers. All M44 Hairy Foxes and the LAMVs with their Saucy Cans will be under control of the Marauders and the maintenance unit of the Service Company. Elwood, your people know the workings of all the various warbot types in the regiment; do you think they'll have any trouble commanding the heavy-fire warbots?"

This was a surprise to Capt. Elwood Otis, head of the Maintenance Unit of the Service Company. Other than being shot at on Trinidad and learning how to handle the M26A4 Hornet submachinecarbines for personal protection, none of his "grease monkeys" was combat-trained. "I don't see any problems with what you've said thus far, Curt. But if my people have to go into combat, be advised they aren't trained for it. They may not be psychologically fit for it, either."

"I'm aware of that," Curt replied. "But don't get antsy about it. You probably won't have to fire a shot. In any event, the heavy-fire equipment won't be in the front line. At best, you may be called upon for some supporting fire if tacair doesn't do its job. Now the big question: We're in a manpower situation where the whole damned regiment is going to have to fight—*everyone* including staffers, supply people, even the Old Man himself, me. Everyone except the biotechs and the chaplain, but they'll probably be plenty busy anyway if the people on the line get stupid or try to be heroes. Captain Hampton, I know Headquarters Company is basically a supporting staff unit not intended to be involved in personal combat. But the regiment is short-handed. You saw and heard what I suggested we do and you know the approved plan based on that. We desperately need second-wave armed troops to follow the Companions, the Warriors, and the Killers with their Mary Annes and jeeps. We need the secondary wave as insurance to finish off what the assault wave misses or to plug any holes that occur in our assault lines. I can give you some backup in the form of the empty Robot Transport Vehicles with their fifteen-millimeter automatics. But I won't ask your non-combat people to go into combat without their consent. This is highly unusual. By the book, I would simply give the order to do it. But I don't work that way. I may be new at regimental command, but even on the company level I don't demand that my people do things they never expected or haven't trained for unless they express their willingness to do it. We are, after all, a volunteer army. On the other hand, this should be no worse than Rio Claro or Sangre Grande. Will you meet with your staff people and get their consensus, please?"

"What's the alternative, Captain?" Hampton wanted to know.

"More casualties. The ultimate possiblity that this critical assault may fail," Curt told him candidly.

Otis thought for a moment, then replied, "As you said a while ago, no guts, no glory. If anyone in Headquarters Company ever thought they'd never get shot at, they should have accepted slots in a Robot Armor or old Robot Infantry regiment where they'd always be safely in the rear echelon. They've had their chances to transfer out to other units since we converted to a Sierra Charlie outfit. Captain, I commit the Headquarters Company. If some individuals can't hack it, that will be their decision. But I don't think we'll have any no-shows. Just don't forget that we'll be a green combat outfit, Captain."

"It's my job not to forget anything, and it's Captain Hampton's job to make sure I don't," Curt remarked, looking at the man who was now his chief of staff. "Now, I've got to run this show, and the best way I can figure out to do it is this. Hensley," he spoke to Lt. Hensley Atkinson, S-3 Operations who had had to take over S-2 Intelligence as well, "I'll be in the Intelligence unit's Combat Support Vehicle. Who's your best warbot specialist?"

"Sgt. Bill Hull," she replied.

"All right, I'll want Sergeant Hull to assist me. Both of us will be in full neuroelectronic linkage with as many recon birdbots as we can put aloft and keep aloft. If conditions warrant, I'll do a quick delink and join the trouble spot in person."

Major Gydesen shook her head. "Captain, you haven't been in linkage for months. Too damned dangerous. Especially your plan for a quick delink."

Curt grinned. "I'm going to shave this nice, bushy head of hair tonight," he told her, running his hand through the hair he'd allowed to grow back since Zahedan. "And I want Biotech Sergeant Helen Devlin standing by. Devlin has worked with me before, and she knows how to handle me in emergency situations such as a rapid delink."

"Why couldn't you have decided to take the safe and easy way?" Lt. Alexis Morgan asked him. "Damned risky for you to go into linkage without recent practice."

"We're all taking risks. That's what combat is about."

"Yes, but one Golden BB into that birdbot, and you're KIA," she reminded him. "That puts you out of action for months. Who's your second in command?"

"Captain Joan Ward," Curt informed everyone. He knew she wasn't the senior combat officer below him. Captain Manny Garcia was. But he wasn't about to name Manny as his replacement. He knew that the quiet nickname for the officer was now "Gutless Garcia."

There was a silence among the officers and NCOs of the Greys. They all knew exactly why Curt had done that.

Capt. Manny Garcia wasn't happy about it.

"Very well, here's how I want you to deploy," Curt went on. "Grey Head Computer, project the tactical plan for Operation Strijdom."

On the chart table, the computer immediately generated a holographic topographical map of the area with colored overlays showing the locations of various units.

"You all know the objective: Cut off the path of retreat of the Bastaards from Strijdom to Otjomuise, break the Bastaards' noose at the highway, let the Royal Scots get into the break so they and the *Legion* can do their thing, then turn and proceed westward into Otjomuise," Curt summarized the plan. "Tonight, we'll move eastward then northward over the Auasberg ridge. At dawn, the Companions, the Warriors, and the Killers will occupy the positions called for in the overall plan here. The Companions will be under the command of Lieutenant Alexis Morgan. Captain Ward will lead the Warriors as usual. The Killers will be commanded by Lieutenant Russ Frazier. With Captain Ward's permission, I've detached Lieutenant Ellie Aarts from the Warriors to command the Headquarters support company. Company commanders, talk directly to your heavy tacair support on the discreet freaks already given you. Call in your own strikes as needed. Marauders and Service, use tacair to supplement your own heavy fire and to hit targets you can see but can't reach. Doctor von Waldersee, I'm going to give you a tactical communications handset so we can talk to each other, and I want you to accompany Chief Ba's contingent over to the east flank where they're going to provide the initial diversionary attack."

Curt looked around. "Any questions?"

Silence.

"Very well. Let's move out."

Dr. Paul von Waldersee came up to Curt immediately. He was upset. "Captain, I was retained as a guide, not as a combat soldier."

Curt looked directly at him. "I'm not asking you to fight, Doctor."

"You're putting me in a command position with the San Khoisha band," the anthropologist pointed out.

"Not at all. Chief Ba retains command. You've got to be there as a translator."

"I could do that just as well from here," von Waldersee pointed out.

"Do you think Chief Ba can operate a radio?"

"No, but—"

"Tell you what, Doctor, would you feel better if I sent a couple of armed Greys along with you?"

"It would help."

"I haven't got any combat qualified people I can spare," Curt pointed out. "You know we're short-handed. I can spare Master Sergeant Georgiana Cook and Staff Sergeant Emma Crawford to accompany you and see that you get back safely."

Von Waldersee hesitated. He didn't quite know what to say, but he finally blurted out, "But they're *women!* And one of them is *black!*"

Curt had done that deliberately. He'd long suspected the man's basic prejudices. "I hadn't noticed," he quietly and calmly replied to the anthropologist. "But both of them have something you apparently do not: guts."

"Give me the radio," von Waldersee suddenly demanded. "I'll do your dirty little job for you. Quite honestly, Captain, I was distressed to see Colonel Hettrick deposed as regimental commander. We got along a lot better than you and I seem to be doing. And she seemed to understand—"

"I suspect, Doctor, that she was an outstanding leader of people and that you were the one who didn't understand," Curt said. "And, whether you like me or not, I'm counting on you to pass the word to Chief Ba when it's time for him to attack the east flanks of the Bastaard ring around Strijdom. If you do it too early, the Bastaards will have time to intensify their counterattack on you. If you don't do it at all, we have ways of dealing with traitors . . ."

"Are you implying—?" von Waldersee bristled.

Curt shook his head. "Not at all, Doctor. But you're not one of us. And you've just given me cause to doubt you. And that deposit into your Swiss bank account that Colonel Hettrick told me about hasn't been made yet."

Doctor Paul von Waldersee drew himself up imperiously. "Sir, I am a man of honor. The money means nothing to me, as I remarked several days ago. If I say I will do something, you may count on me."

"Very well, Doctor, I shall."

"And we'll talk no more about potential dishonor."

Curt's visible angry behavior suddenly subsided. Levelly, he replied, "Agreed. Sergeant Crawford will provide you with your tactical radio, Doctor. I suggest you and the band get moving as soon as possible. You've got about sixty kilometers to cover before dawn. Stay in touch. I'll be monitoring your radio frequency. And good luck." Curt extended his hand.

Von Waldersee looked at Curt's proffered hand, hesitated, then took it and shook it. "Good luck to you, Captain. I hope you can break the Bastaard ring and get your people out of Windhoek." He acted as though he never intended to see Curt again.

As he left the OCV, Capt. Manny Garcia appeared in the

doorway and rapped on the frame. "Captain Carson, I'd like to see you."

Curt turned. "Come in, Manny." He'd been expecting this. "Have a seat. Cup of coffee?" Curt popped the top from a plastic mug and put it under the hot water tap. He reached down to get another mug from the storage bin.

"No thanks, Curt."

"What's up?"

"I think you know."

"Inform me."

"Two things are bothering me."

"Well, unload, Manny. What are they?" Curt sat down with the tactical display base between them. "Sit down and tell me."

Garcia remained standing. "First of all, why did you give second-in-command to Joan Ward? I'm senior to her."

"That you are. What's the second thing?"

"I'd like an answer to the first one," Manny said.

"Tell me the second. The two may be related."

"That's what I suspected. Okay, *Captain,* why did you put the Marauders in the rear echelon as the base of fire? We're a combat company, not the regimental artillery unit."

Curt warmed his hands around the mug. "Sit down, Manny."

"I'd just as soon stand."

"Goddamnit, Manny, I asked you to *sit down!*" Curt told him sternly.

"Is that a direct order, Captain?"

"Yes."

Manny Garcia sat down. There was no hiding his hostility.

Part of it, Curt knew, was caused by the tension and anxiety that precedes going into battle. Different people express it in different ways. Curt knew it had probably triggered something that had been building up in Capt. Manny Garcia for months. Its first manifestation had been during the maneuvers in the snow up on the Rim before they'd been yanked into action.

"Do you want me to declare you unfit for combat at this time and turn the Marauders over to Josh Rosenberg?" Curt suddenly asked.

"I'm *not* unfit for combat!" Manny snapped. "By the way, you sure as hell put a big fucking hole in the Marauders by reassigning Ellie Aarts to lead your rump Headquarters combat outfit!"

Curt straightened up and looked the man in the eyes. "First of all, Captain Garcia," he said with icy coldness in his voice, "get it through your head right now that you're talking to your regimental commander and not just another company commander like yourself. I didn't want this job. I'd a whole hell of a lot rather that Colonel Hettrick was sitting here instead. But she isn't. Fortunes of war. So I've got to do the job. And I will. I'm easy, but I'll be damned if I'll allow familiarity *or* dissatisfaction to destroy the discipline that Colonel Hettrick maintained in the Washington Greys! Especially on the night before a major action. We've had a meeting to discuss and plan our tactics. I called for comments. I listened to the ones I got and took them into account if I could. I heard none from you. I got my orders from above, and I've passed on orders to the regiment. The time to bitch and moan about them is over. *I now expect my orders to be carried out, Captain!* Respectfully. Eagerly. And on the bounce. I will not tolerate dissension, objections, cricitism, or second-guessing, regardless of the causes. And, although I don't have to explain my orders, I try to back them up with rationale because I don't expect the Washington Greys to blindly follow orders without knowing why they're doing what they're doing. Do you understand your orders, Captain?"

"Yes . . . Captain."

"Then carry them out."

"Yes, Captain."

"And, Captain, Garcia, if you really want to know why I didn't name you as second in command and why I put you in charge of the supporting fire base," Curt went on with considerably less coldness, "it's because you're my friend and my comrade in arms whom I've known since West Point. I did it for many reasons, not the least of which was the fact that I didn't want to order you to your death."

"What?"

"Manny, you're a good warbot brainy," Curt complimented him honestly. "You can handle neuroelectronic warbots with the best of them. And you did a hell of a job in Trinidad supporting my brand-new Sierra Charlie company. Running a warbot and a warbot company, you're second to none. You've been courageous, and you've been where you're supposed to be when you're supposed to be there. You've even pulled my ass out of trouble more than once with your warbots."

"So?" Capt. Manny Garcia asked, inviting more although he knew he wasn't going to like what Curt was going to tell him.

"But even though you haven't admitted it, you know and I know that you're not the type of person who can become a good Sierra Charlie officer," Curt told him quietly and personally. "You have a lot of trouble putting your body out where it can be hit, and you have a great reluctance to order the Marauders to do it, too. Because of this, you've had problems on maneuvers and left other units in deep shit. When we got hit by the Bushmen yesterday, you buttoned down inside instead of coming out to take them on one at a time like the rest of us did. Well, tomorrow is going to be too damned critical, Manny. I've got to put the few people I've got left in positions where they'll do the best job. And I think you can do the best job commanding our fire base." He stopped and waited for a response from the man.

Garcia relaxed just a tad. He looked down and said, "Captain . . . Curt, thank you for talking about it. I can't. I couldn't."

Curt knew that the man's *machismo* prevented him from doing it. Which is why Curt had to do it, much as he disliked it.

"I'm not a coward," Garcia muttered.

"I know you're not. And I don't want to put you in a

position where you might be perceived as one," Curt admitted. "Maybe experience will change things. Maybe you'll grow into a Sierra Charlie's shoes. Maybe you've got what it takes to command a regiment. I don't know. That's up to you. I can't try to haze you to change like I could at West Point. Right now I've *got* to apply your strengths where they'll do the most good. This is not a war game. This isn't a maneuver. And we don't always get what we want in the Army."

Curt stood up. "I can't bullshit all night like we used to do. I've got lots of work to do before dawn. And you've got to integrate a whole new regimental fire team. You'd better get on it, Manny. Dismissed."

CHAPTER FORTY

It was a strange feeling for Curt to be back inside a warbot, seeing what it saw, hearing what it heard, feeling what it felt, yet knowing that it was only an extension to his own senses made possible by computers, artificial intelligence, intelligence amplifiers, and other electronic gadgetry.

It was also very lonely.

He'd never noticed the loneliness before. But since he'd fought in the field alongside other people, he'd learned that people in combat relied on one another far more than they did when operating neuroelectronic warbots. He now felt that the bird-shaped reconnaissance warbot had detached his mind from the real world. He *knew* his body wasn't a thousand meters in the air in the cold dawn over Strijdom International Airport. In reality, he knew—although he couldn't feel it—that he was instead reclined on a sensor-lined couch in the Combat Support Vehicle of the Washington Greys' C-cubed-I unit in the foothills of the Auasberg mountains just south of the airport.

But he had an outstanding view of the terrain below, still shrouded in pre-dawn darkness. From the birdbot, he'd be able to concentrate on the battle below and direct the Washington Greys with the sort of battlefield perspective that Wellington, Grant, or Patton never had. The autocontrol circuits of the birdbot kept its wings beating and its flight straight and level; he didn't have to devote any of his conscious effort toward the flight dynamics of a bird.

He could switch at will to any of three recon birdbots automatically circling in the dawn twilight sky over Strijdom under computer control.

He was doing fine, even after about a year of no linkage experience. As far as he was concerned, linkage was like riding a bicycle: Once you learned how to do it, you never forgot it. Curt thought that Major Gydesen had been overly conservative in her estimate of Curt's ability to carry out neuroelectronic warbot control.

In the infra red wavelengths, he could see the *Legion Robotique* and Royal Scots regiments on the Strijdom Airport below. The French and British warbots weren't stealthed in the infra red; it had been deemed unnecessary by the Supreme Allied Command because intelligence reports had indicated the warbot troops wouldn't come up against any sophisticated weaponry such as heat-seeking shells or missiles. Intelligence had been correct in that regard but certainly not in the estimate of how many native irregulars would be arrayed against the warbot forces. A-2 had simply not believed the intensity of xenophobic feeling among the natives of Namibia, the hatred of foreigners that would break loose, and the sheer mass of natives that would gather to vent the pent-up emotions of centuries of European and South African dominance and exploitation.

The Bastaard, Herero, and Ovambo hordes ranged through Strijdom were also visible to Curt's birdbot, although their individual infra red signatures weren't as strong. He located individual groups by their open fires still smoldering from the previous evening and now being brought up to flame again to prepare the morning meal and give warmth to native bodies huddled around.

He saw his own Washington Greys poised below the Auasberg ridge off the dawn skyline and ready to attack.

To the east, the sky was clear and bright in the visual spectrum. Swinging his view to the west, Curt actually saw the shadow of the Earth, a dark dome of sky that was slowly dropping toward the hills on the starkly clear horizon.

"Grey Major, this is Grey Head," he transmitted, although what he "said" was in thought terms which the computer on the CSV converted into voice signals heard by Sgt. Major Jesup. "Checking communications. How do you read?"

"Loud and clear, Grey Head. How me?"

"Roger, the same. Let's do a swing-around. Grey Companion Leader, this is Grey Head. Comm check."

"Grey Head, Grey Companion Leader, loud and clear," came Alexis Morgan's voice. "Sorry you had to shave, Captain. I was getting used to that head of hair!"

"It'll grow back," Curt reassured her. "Grey Warrior Leader?"

"Grey Warrior Leader here. I agree with Companion Leader," was Capt. Joan Ward's comment.

"Knock it off! Grey Killer Leader?"

"Loud and clear, Grey Head. I couldn't care less about how much fuzz you've got topside, Grey Head," was Lt. Russ Frazier's quip.

"Grey Marauder?"

"Grey Marauder Leader here with the big bang."

"Grey Stopper Leader?" Curt called, using the new code word for the Headquarters Company reserve unit.

"Grey Stopper here," was Lt. Ellie Aarts response.

"Ba Head communicator?" Curt called for Doctor Paul von Waldersee with the Bushman tribe.

"We're ready," was the terse reply.

"Checking other units," Curt went on. "Diamond Head?"

"Diamond Head is reading you, Grey Head," was the calm voice of General Carlisle from St. Helena.

"Thank you. Sedan Head?"

"Sedan Head, loud and clear," came the reply with the twinge of accent from the *Legion Robotique*.

"Loch Head?"

"Loch Head standing by," the clipped British accent of the Royal Scots' communications officer replied.

"Windmill Head?"

"Windmill Head on the line," came the reply from the

diplomatic compound in Otjomuise.

"Air Head?" Curt called up the master air controller in Tsumeb. He could just detect the shadowy forms of the i-r stealthed tactical strike aerodynes hovering in defilade behind a low ridge of hills to the north that had already been used for masking inbound flights of tacair strike ships, the "mud pounders," and had therefore received the approbation of "Mud Ridge."

"Air Head standing by and ready at Mud Ridge," the American voice replied.

"All stations on line," Sergeant Major Jesup observed.

"All stations please stay on line," Curt requested. "This is going to be difficult enough as it is. Without communications, it will be nearly impossible." Because Curt had been the one who'd suggested the general plan for the Strijdom operation and had been willing to go into a recon birdbot to overwatch it, he'd also been given the task of coordinating the initial actions of the various elements and directing forces to trouble spots if required.

The upper limb of the sun's disk broke over the top of the far eastern ridge of hills. However, it was still dark below.

Curt waited until half the sun's disk was visible from his birdbot's alititude of a thousand meters.

"Ba Head, this is Grey Head," Curt called out, moving over to a birdbot that was circling the eastern side of Strijdom. "Code Zulu. Code Zulu. Engage! Engage!"

"Grey Head, Ba Head. Confirming Code Zulu and engaging," von Waldersee replied.

Two minutes later, the eastern loop of the Bastaard ring was in turmoil. Shadowy infra red images that looked like people began to move around. Two minutes after that, Curt detected a general movement of people in the encircling ring to the point of trouble.

"Sedan Head, this is Grey Head. Code Juliet. Code Juliet. *Avant! Avant!*" Curt called.

"Grey Head, Sedan Head. *Alors!* Code Juliet! *Pour Dieu et France! Commencer fusillade!*"

The flash of a hundred heavy warbot guns and dozens of

rocket trails erupted from Strijdom in two trajectories headed for both sides of the eastern disturbance.

"Air Head, this is Grey Head. Code Foxtrot. Code Foxtrot. Execute Strike One! Play ball!"

"Air Head, coming over the plate!" A gaggle of aerodynes began to move fast from behind Mud Ridge toward Strijdom.

"Air Head, this is Grey Head! Come right five degrees. Target ahead," Curt advised from his vantage point at a thousand meters.

"Roger! Tally ho! We have a lock-on!" Squadron Leader Barker of the RAF 222 Squadron replied.

As the morning sun touched the tops of the remaining trees and the ragged stumps of what had once been trees on the western marge of Strijdom International Airport, ten tacair strike aerodynes rolled in on their infra red targets, the morning fires of the Bastaards blocking the road to Otjomuise. Their approach was met with intense ground fire. "They've got a couple of old Soviet ZSU-twenty-threes!" came the call as streaks of tracer fire reached up from the ground toward the strike craft.

"Black Anvil, burn 'em out!" the call went out to the electronic fire suppression aircraft still loitering behind Mud Ridge. The heavier and slower Wild Weasles of the American 55th Tactical Fighter Wing rose vertically upward and flung out their unseen beams of electromagnetic energy. "Okay, two of them now!"

"That's Herbert and Inglebrook," another aerodyne driver called. "They haven't moved since yesterday. And Herbert's stopped transmitting."

"Okay, I got a fix on him from his last burst. Stand clear. A Torch Fire is on its way. There goes a second one for Inglebrook. Damn, that isn't a ZSU with a Gun Dish! It's an Eagle Ka-band!"

"Must have retrofitted it."

"Rolling in, chaps."

"Howdy, Torch Fire! Just went past. Oh, nice! Goodby, Herbert! Right between the eyes!"

"Hold it in there, Reggie! I do believe you've got him!"

"I'm hit! I'm hit! Rolling back! I'll try to make it out of here!"

"Don't eject right yet, pal! Yer in my way!"

Curt tried to get past this melange of sound by busting in on top of them and hoping the higher transmitter power of the Grey Head OCV would smother the tacair transmissions. "Air Head, Grey Head here! Time! Time! Get the aerodyne jocks off the net. Patch a monitor channel through to Diamond Head just in case. Hold Strike Three on the deck. Time out for Strike Three."

The excited chatter of the tactical strike pilots abruptly stopped. "Roger, Grey Head. Strike Three, time out."

"Companion Leader, Warrior Leader, Killer Leader, this is Grey Head. Code Oscar. Code Oscar. Execute! Execute!"

Three quick "rogers" came back almost atop one another.

The Washington Greys moved into combat from their camouflaged jump-off positions south of the Airport. But they didn't try to take on the Bastaard ring in a frontal assault. They moved to the left or west of the rear echelon of the native irregulars surrounding Strijdom International Airport. They moved fast, still in their OCVs and RTVs. They didn't fire. They just moved. Within a few minutes, they'd crossed the highway between Strijdom and Otjomuise without incident. Curt had been counting on this. The Bastaards and other native irregulars had their attention occupied by the tacair strike coming in from the north and the sudden and unknown fuss that was taking place on the eastern side of the Airport between Chief Ba's Bushmen and the irregulars there. Curt could discriminate nothing out of the confusion on the east side. It seemed that the Bushmen had infiltrated quite deeply, probably because of the irregulars' inability to discriminate the Bushmen from their own kind in the semi-darkness. The situation on the east edge was further confused by the intense warbot fire pouring into the irregulars' ring on either side of the sector where the Bushmen were attacking.

It was high time to give the Bastaards something else to confuse them. "Marauder Leader, this is Grey Head. Code India. Code India. Commence firing!"

"Grey Head, Marauder Leader. Opening fire now!"

The 75mm shells from the Saucy Cans sped into the concentration of Bastaards camped across the Otjomuise highway while 50mm fire from the Hairy Foxes bit into the rear of the southwest segment of the encirclement.

"Break off the Saucy Cans, Marauder Leader! Some rounds are overshooting by about fifty meters!"

"Roger, Grey Head! We're just getting round-following radar data here now. We see it, too," Manny Garcia replied.

"Diamond Head, this is Grey Head," Curt called the General. "Pick up my birdbot's infra red and visual. Looks like we achieved surprise!"

"I'm monitoring, Grey Head! About time to initiate Code Romeo?"

"Give them another minute or so to get more confused and disorganized before we turn Loch Head loose on them," Curt advised. "Looks like a Chinese fire drill down there. The Bastaards weren't prepared to be hit from the rear in several sectors."

"Their big mistake was failing to press the advantage during the first twenty-four hours," Carlisle pointed out. "As you pointed out, Carson, without unity of command, they lost momentum pretty fast. With each tribal chief running his own little show down there and trying to make points for his own outfit, they couldn't help but be ground to a halt by the French and British, who did exactly the right thing by holding their attention until you could get there."

"Well, it's about time to let the Scots show their stuff. Loch Head, this is Grey Head. Code Romeo. Code Romeo. Wake up your pipers and move out!"

"Roger, old chap. Pity you Yanks don't fight to music. But I dare say you scare the hell out of your enemy because you attack silently! Pipers, sound 'Scotland the Brave!' By the front quick . . . *Harch!*"

"Tell me honestly, Loch Head," Curt asked, his curiosity getting the better of his battle discipline, "do you *really* have pipers down there?"

"Of course not, old chap! Computer synthesized, unfortunately. Best we can do under the circumstances. A platoon of pipers would be dead meat with all this automatic fire going on around us. Excuse me, we have a bit of work ahead of us . . ."

"G'day, mytes!" a new voice broke in. "Colonel Birdwood reporting in! The First Kokoda is in the slot astride the highway and railway to the south of you. Can we take ten for coffee and buns, or do you need us somewhere first?"

"Good day to you, Colonel! Grey Head here! Your call sign is Slaughter Head." Curt replied. "Do you have the tactical plan downloaded?"

"Slaughter Head? I like that! Roger on the tac plan, Grey Head. We'll break for a bite and keep an eagle-type eyeball peeled to the south."

"Anyone on your tail, Slaughter Head?"

"Not likely, Grey Head. Our rear guard would have handled them rather neatly. But we spotted some air activity over Rehoboth on a visual about thirty minutes ago. Bloody clear air and low sun angle made them stand out. Could be an Afrikaaner airborne unit."

"Diamond Head here! I'll check into that and make some nasty noises toward Jo-berg," Carlisle cut in.

"Grey Head, Companion Leader here!" came the urgent call from Alexis Morgan. "The Bastaards have broken to the west along the highway! They're in retreat!"

"Retreat, hell! This is Killer Leader! It looks like a rout!"

"Okay, Greys. Do your thing. Put in the cork!" Curt told them. "Air Head, Grey Head. Code Bravo. Code Bravo. Pitch Strike Three!"

"Pitching Strike Three. Care to give us coordinates so

we don't mash your people?" asked Colonel Phil Glascock of the USAF 55th Tactical Fighter Wing.

"Get your strike coordinates on the appropriate tac channel, Air Head. Our ground units will work directly with your aerodyne drivers," Curt reminded the tac wing commander. "Just don't mid-air the RAF chaps; they're on the way out to Groot to refuel and rearm now."

"We'll check all quadrants for them, Grey Head. Okay, Double Nickle is starting to roll in!"

Curt jumped to another birdbot, looked around, then hopped to a third one.

What he saw was pure confusion. The *Legion* had smashed the eastern flank and was pouring out of the Strijdom pocket, splitting into two thrusts north and south to work around behind the irregulars' encirclement.

Where was von Waldersee and Chief Ba's band? Curt couldn't find them in the melee below. Nor would von Waldersee respond to repeated radio calls.

Curt couldn't waste his time worrying about them. Chief Ba had shown himself to be a smart fighter. Hopefully, he'd gotten his men in fast, done the necessary dirty work of diversion, and gotten out again before the *Legion Robotique* broke through the confusion they'd created.

The north and south sectors of the Strijdom encirclement had collapsed in confusion. Curt could see even on visual that groups of natives were hightailing it for the Auasberg or toward Mud Ridge on the north. There was no order in their retreat just as there had been little order, only numerical superiority, in their assaults and entrapment. Hit from the rear, their forces shattered. Without a unified command, they couldn't reassemble before the allied troops did what they'd come to do.

On the west, the retreating irregulars had been caught between the erupting Royal Scots and the Washington Greys Sierra Charlies already in place covering the highway retreat route.

"Grey Head, this is Companion Leader! Hey, this is a turkey shoot, Curt!" Alexis Morgan called. "You oughta get a piece of the action! Come on down!"

Curt chuckled to himself and ordered the birdbot to swoop low over the retreating Bastaards. "Let me get a final look at this, then—"

The birdbot's visual and i-r sensors suddenly caught something, and the computer signalled to Curt. He had the chance only to get a quick look. The birdbot was being fired on by the retreating column. Only old assault rifles, but he was about fifty meters up and flying slow.

The recon birdbot suddenly came apart around him.

CHAPTER FORTY-ONE

Curt's first reaction was, "I'm hit! Gotta get the hell out of here before I'm KIA!"

Other than having the warbot control van captured by the enemy, being KIA or "killed in action" was the worst thing that a warbot brainy could suffer. The nearly instantaneous cessation of electronic signals representing sight, sound, and kinesthetic or limb position information was something like being actually, physically killed, it was said. The shock to the mind and nervous system was profound. The warbot brainy usually snapped into a catatonic state. It often took six months or more of careful therapy to return a KIA warbot brainy to the real world.

It had happened to Curt once before. He knew what it was like. He didn't want it to happen again.

He tried to jump to another birdbot.

Too late.

But he wasn't confronted with the total absence of data from his senses that had happened before.

Strangely, he was suddenly in a dream world.

It was indeed like a dream.

A wet dream.

Everything he could sense around him was pleasurable.

He was warm and comfortable.

He had plenty of food and drink.

He had companionship in the form of erotic visions of women he knew. Incredibly sexy images of Alexis Morgan and Joan Ward. Dr. Rosha Taisha from Zahedan. Zeenat Tej from Trinidad. The dead Capt. Samantha Walker.

Sexy little Biotech Sgt. Helen Devlin. Patti Kirtland, the first girl with whom he'd had sex those long years ago. And, strangely, an image that somehow combined the attributes of his own mother and Col. Belinda Hettrick.

Curt knew it all had to be in his head. These were images drawn from his own beautiful memories. His mother was long dead. So was Capt. Samantha Walker, killed on Trinidad.

What the hell is going on? he asked himself because there was no one else to ask. *If this is KIA, it wasn't this way before!*

Being KIA before had been total sensory deprivation which had led to hallucinations of the worst sort where the demons trapped deep in his mind were turned loose to create pure mental hell.

But this was lovely! It made him want to get back to the real world right away because *he couldn't reach or touch any of the sensual female images.*

The spartan interior of the regimental Command Support Vehicle housing the recon birdbot neuroelectronic linkage equipment suddenly took form around him. He was lying on the linkage couch sweating profusely.

Kneeling beside the couch was Biotech Sgt. Helen Devlin. "Welcome back," she said in a low voice.

Curt focused his eyes. "What the hell?"

Devlin looked up to where Sgt. Bill Hull was monitoring the neuroelectronic warbot linkage terminals. "You snatched him okay, Bill."

"I didn't have a damn thing to do with it," the technical sergeant remarked. "Computer and intelligence amplifier acted a hell of a lot faster than I could. It was over almost before I knew it."

Curt reached out and grabbed Devlin's arm. "Look, I asked you, what the hell went on? I should have been KIA! What the hell happened?"

"You're okay," Devlin observed, checking his vital signs on her biomonitor. "Headache?"

"No! *What the hell happened?*" he repeated.

"How long since you've been in linkage?"

"I don't know. A year. Maybe more. Ever since we got back from Zahedan."

"The state of the art has progressed a little bit since then, Captain," Devlin explained. "A few new wrinkles in the programming. Since the master computer has a new forty-ninety-six-bit system running at a hundred megaHertz with a couple of gigabytes of ROM and RAM, it caught the loss of birdbot downlink signals long before your mind could. Then the artificial intelligence unit recognized the situation as a pending KIA and acted before you even knew anything had happened. The new program uploaded, and you were pulled out of the birdbot automatically before you lost all downlinks. The warbot sensory signals were replaced by your own subconscious memory signals to provide you with ersatz sensor inputs. Put you in a dream state, so to speak. Then you woke up, just like coming out of REM sleep. Looks like it worked fine! You're in much better shape than I've ever seen you, even when you delinked normally. Tell me, Captain, were they sweet dreams?"

"Damned right!"

"Tell me about them . . ."

"Some other time. You were in them," Curt admitted. "I think you knew damned good and well you would be! Well, let me get a battle fought and a campaign won, and then I'll have some time to describe and demonstrate in great detail . . ."

"Good!" Biotech Sgt. Helen Devlin was pleased. One doesn't serve as the biotech specialist to a handsome young officer like Curt Carson for several years without getting to know him well . . . very well. She'd been happy to help Curt get back into linkage this time; since his company and then the regiment had converted over to the Sierra Charlie doctrine, she hadn't seen as much of him as in the past. She hoped that would now change after Operation Diamond Skeleton was over and Rule Ten wasn't in effect.

Curt rotated on his butt and put his feet on the deck, sitting up. Whatever the new programming for delinkage was, it sure worked! He had no headache or fatigue at all. "Am I cleared for duty?" he asked.

"Unfortunately, yes. Now you're going to go out there and get shot at," Devlin complained. "Try to come back without getting something important blown off, will you?"

He stood up and looked down at her. "Sometimes I think I'd like to take six weeks in the hospital and do absolutely nothing."

"I wouldn't let you do absolutely nothing."

"That's what I'm afraid of. Check with you later. I've got a goddamned regiment to worry about right now . . ." Curt crawled into soft body armor, then pulled sand-and-shit cammies over the armor. His helmet, sized to fit his head with his former haircut, now flopped on his shaven skull. But the neuroelectronic sensor pads made much better contact. He slipped into his equipment harness and picked up his *Novia*. "Where's the regimental OCV?" he asked Sgt. Bill Hull who was the one to know.

"Outside the rear ramp, turn right, twenty meters under a bunch of trees, Captain. You can't miss it."

"Sergeant, judging from your accent and your use of the phrase, 'You can't miss it,' you're from New England."

"Craftsbury Common, New Hampshire, sir! Heart of the Northeast Kingdom!" Hull replied proudly.

"Thought so. Well, I'll look real carefully for that OCV. Chances are, I'll miss it," Curt told him and stepped out into the bright sunlight.

The smell of war was everywhere. It was the stink of smoke, burning equipment, expended explosives, hot oil, reeking hot metal, and death. The command post was far enough back from the fighting areas so that no small arms fire was overhead, but Curt ducked and dodged as he ran in the direction of his OCV.

Once inside, he went up to where Sergeant Major Jesup was studying the tactical display board. "Situation report, please, Sergeant Major," Curt snapped.

Jesup looked at him then turned his attention back to the board. With a laser pointer, he indicated as he spoke.

"The Strijdom pocket is demolished. The *Legion Robotique* broke out and turned west. They joined with the Royal Scots on the west side of Strijdom where about four thousand Bastaards are trapped between those two regiments and the Washington Greys. We're astride the road, dug in, and forcing the Bastaards to attack us."

Curt nodded. "Just what I was hoping. Defensive offense. Move offensively to gain a defensible position which forces the enemy to attack."

"Clausewitz and Moltke would have been proud of you, Captain!"

Curt looked quizzically at him.

"Well, Captain," Jesup explained, "people besides officers read Clausewitz and Moltke, you know."

"How long have the Greys been engaged?" Curt asked, noting the unit dispositions.

Jesup checked. "Thirty-two minutes, sir."

"And they haven't gotten a surrender of the irregular forces in that time? Shit, how much fire can those Bastaards take? Any casualty estimates?"

"Sergeant Kester reports about four hundred Bastaards . . . and three Greys."

"Greys? Who?"

"Corporal Bill King of the Marauders, Corporal Frank Blunt of the Killers, both severely wounded. Platoon Sergeant Clyde Ingle of the Warriors killed."

"Damn!" Curt swore mildly, but it was the intensity behind the word that gave it stronger force. "Has the *Legion* or the Royal Scots closed on the new west pocket yet?"

"Negatory, Captain. They're both following standard warbot doctrin: Leapfrog, throw in heavy fire, then leapfrog again."

"Too slow. And I don't want to exhaust the Greys. Time to call in the reserves. Let's let the Aussies do a little fighting," Curt decided. He reached up on the frequency selection panel and punched up the channel to St. Helena. His helmet comm unit was picked up by the OCV system which relayed through the roof dish to the satellite and thence to St. Helena. "Diamond Head, this is Grey Head. Request Slaughter Head be turned loose on the west pocket. I want to withdraw the Greys before they get fought out; they've already taken three more casualties, and I want to have enough manpower left to get in to Windmill."

Maj. Gen. Jacob Carlisle on St. Helena had the same display in front of him that Curt did. He knew better than to try to micromanage the battle from more than two-thousand kilometers away, and he was counting on such recommendations from his on-the-scene commanders. "Approved, Grey Head. Move Slaughter Head into position to hit the pocket from the south side. When contact is made, you can execute a retrograde maneuver with the Greys and break contact. Then proceed to Windmill. As quickly as Sedan Head can disengage, he'll follow for heavy fire support."

"I'll need tacair in the city," Curt advised.

"Air Head here. Double Nickle is tasked for that. Trey-Duece will continue to support the west pocket," came the voice of Air Vice Marshal Moorhouse from Grootfontein.

"Roger, Diamond Head," Curt finalized. "Grey Head is now moving to the road west of the Grey fire point. We'll disengage when Slaughter arrives and engages. Maybe those goddamned idiot Bastaards will surrender by then!" Curt added this last comment hopefully.

"Unlikely," was Carlisle's comment. "A-2 reports that native tribes normally don't request terms. They fight to the last."

"Great! Some day I'd like to get into a war that runs by the rule book so it isn't so goddamned deadly!" Curt muttered, but the comment went out on the net anyway.

"Let me know when you find one, Captain." The reply came from a source that didn't identify itself. Curt suspected it was McEvedy-Brooke of the Royal Scots.

As Curt led the regimental command post vehicles northwesterly toward the road to Otjomuise, the Australian 1st Kokoda Regiment went around him. The Aussies were exposed in their vehicles, standing up, and singing at the top of their lungs to be heard over their engine noises. Curt first thought this was crazy. Why reveal yourself to the enemy before contact? On the other hand, singing—or bagpipes as used by the Royal Scots—had a psychological effect on both the regiment and on the enemy. Nothing could be a blood-curdling as the raspy skirl of pipes or the full-throated and confident singing of troops. The Americans had learned their frontier-style of fighting more than two centuries ago in the Indian Wars; stealth and surprise had always been their specialty. On the other hand, the Brits and other Europeans tried to intimidate their enemies by sounding like they were many times their actual numbers.

There was no mistaking the sound of battle as Curt swung the regimental command vehicle convoy around to the west to get behind the Greys where they straddled the highway. He worked his way in behind the Companions on the south edge of the road, always keeping in communication with Alexis Morgan so she knew who and what was coming up behind her.

The need for heavy fire into the irregulars' ring no longer existed, so Curt gave the necessary orders for Manny Garcia to move west behind the Aussies and join up with the command post.

He also called in the Headquarters and Service troops that he'd positioned as a reserve.

It took about an hour before Curt had all the Greys—with the exception of the three combat companies still engaging the Bastaards astride the highway—in position to the south of the road, ready for the sweep into Otjomuise once the Aussies had completed their final assault on the Bastaards attempting to escape into the city.

By that time, the Bastaards, Hereros, and Ovambos were trapped between the Greys and the Royal Scots and assaulted from the flank by the Aussies. Both the Greys and the Scots had to cease heavy fire for fear of overshooting the continually shrinking group of irregulars and putting fire into one another instead. Most of the action was in the hands of the Aussies who were earning their code name, Slaughter. Most of the action facing the Greys amounted to sporadic attempts by groups of ten or fewer irregulars to break out along the highway.

So Curt debouched from the OCV and went to join Alexis Morgan.

Capt. Joan Ward and the Alpha Platoon of her Warriors were deployed along the highway west of where the Companions held the north side and the Killers the south. Ward's twelve Mary Annes were positioned to cover the road at an angle and one would occasionally fire a burst from its 25mm automatic cannon at some target picked up by its sensors through the dust and haze caused by the sun being straight over the road to the east. Joan Ward noticed Curt come up from the rear, hailed him, and told him, "Turkey shoot, Captain!"

"You're in a good position for it," Curt observed. "But it doesn't look like you're getting much action now."

"You should have been here half an hour ago," Ward told him with a grin. "The Bastaards were running down the highway. Alexis and Russ would let them get between their two companies, and I'd open up on them. Got first pickings. Then the Companions and Killers would catch them in a crossfire from both sides of the road. Bastaards must have made five or six tries to break through before the Aussies hit them from the south flank. I tell you, it was deadly out there! Thank God for these *Novias;* they'll reach out with just as much punch and accuracy at a couple of hundred meters as the twenty-fives on the Mary Annes! Little bit neater kill than having a twenty-five splatter a guy!"

Curt was beginning to believe that the females were indeed the deadlier of the species.

"Why haven't the Bastaards tried to get around us?" Ward continued.

"Lack of organization . . . or maybe they're just confused and disoriented by all the fire we poured in on them. The effect of fire should never be discounted . . ." Curt began.

He was interrupted by a call from Alexis Morgan. "Grey Head, all Grey units, this is Companion Leader! We've got an assault on our hands from the left flank! Must be a hundred irregulars trying to slip around us! Killer Leader, pick targets from my coordinates! Warrior Leader, I could use some back-up here!"

Curt saw it immediately on his helmet visor's tactical display. "Give me six Mary Annes!" he told Ward. "I'm going forward on the left to re-inforce the Companions!"

"Warrior Alpha Six, Warrior Alpha Seven, Warrior Alpha Eight, Warrior Alpha Nine, Warrior Alpha Ten, Warrior Alpha Eleven!" Joan Ward snapped a verbal command to six of her Mobile Assault warbots. "You are to obey the commands of Grey Head! Here is Grey Head's voice!" and she nodded to Curt to take over.

"This is Grey Head," Curt announced to the six warbots verbally and by radio link. "I am identifying my beacon for your information. I am leaving Warrior Leader. Proceed along the north edge of the road toward Companion Leader. Follow me!" He got up and started forward about twenty meters north of the highway, dodging back and forth through clumps of stunted trees and bushes.

Six Mary Annes went with him.

"Companion Leader, this is Grey Head!" he called to Alexis somewhere ahead. "Ident so I can locate you! I'm coming up the north side of the highway with six Mary Annes from Warrior Leader!"

"Grey Head, move along the highway, please, and take up my previous position to cover the highway!" Alexis' voice told him. "I'm redeploying to the north to engage the flanking assault! You'll also be able to give me covering fire from my right flank!"

Curt saw how and where she was moving and headed toward where she had been at the top of a rise on the north side of the highway. As he gained elevation on the rise, he could see the Companions and their warbots in action to his left. They were under heavy assault by a literal mob of irregulars trying to use their standard anti-warbot tactics of overwhelming one warbot at a time. This wasn't very successful against Sierra Charlies because Alexis, Elliott, and Koslowski were picking off the irregulars as they attempted to overwhelm warbots. Alexis' Mary Annes were taking a beating, but she was holding the assault of the irregulars.

Curt moved his Mary Annes into position, designated targets for them, and had them commence flanking fire to help Alexis.

He was suddenly joined by Len Spencer with his video camera on his shoulder. "Thought you were back at the regimental command post, Captain."

"Got a battle to run. Not easy to do by remote control."

"Still a combat company officer . . ."

"Get the hell down! That videocam is bright and shiny. You'll give away my position! In addition, it makes a good target!" Curt warned him.

"It's my job to get coverage, not to hide," Spencer snapped. "Just don't shoot me; I see a great visual from a good angle." Suddenly the newshawk was running off to the north directly toward Alexis Morgan. He took up a position with his camera to cover the assault of about ten irregulars on Alexis, her jeep, and a Mary Anne covering her.

"Grey Head! Give me some covering fire!" Alexis suddenly called. "I can't stop all these Bastaards! Give me some flanking fire!"

There was no way Curt could shoot toward the irregulars charging up on Alexis without hitting the newshawk. "Spencer, get the hell out of the fucking line of fire!" Curt called to the man.

"Screw it!" was Spencer's reply. "I'm taping!"

"They'll clobber Alexis!"

"And I'll cover it!" The newshawk was deliberately putting Alexis Morgan in jeopardy because he was more interested in getting an exciting piece of videotape.

There was only one thing Curt could do.

He brought his *Novia* to his shoulder, aimed, and fired at Len Spencer.

CHAPTER FORTY-TWO

The high-velocity 7.65mm bullet with its high-density depleted uranium core neatly homed on the reflection of the sun from Len Spencer's videocamera. It ripped the device off his right shoulder and shattered it into pieces as it carried it away. The high-density battery blew up as the bullet passed through and shorted it out, but the videocamera was by that time almost a meter off Spencer's shoulder. Tape went everywhere. Pieces of clear plastic from its multi-lens sparkled in the sunlight as they sprayed forward. The camera was junk before it hit the ground two meters in front of Len Spencer.

Spencer himself was thrown forward by the force of the bullet tearing the videocamera off his shoulder. He fell on his face in the sandy soil.

Curt reset his *Novia* to three-round-burst mode and opened fire on the irregulars attacking Alexis Morgan, firing directly over Len Spencer. He didn't give a damn about the newsman now. Spencer had confirmed what Curt had known all along: He was more interested in a good, prize-winning story than he was in the health and well-being of Lt. Alexis Morgan whom he'd romanced for days. "Warrior Alpha Six, Warrior Alpha Eight, targets ahead! Aim on my rifle fire!" Curt told the two Mary Annes closest to him, knowing that their millimeter radar could track the bullets from his *Novia* and therefore designate the proper targets for their laser range finders so the 25mm automatics could be accurately fired.

Curt kept firing and was joined by the Mary Annes. If

Spencer tried to get to his feet now, he'd probably be killed by the bullets from Curt's *Novia* and the 25mm rounds that were going about a meter over his prostrate form. Again, Curt didn't care. If Spencer were stupid enough to get up with rounds snapping over him, the man deserved to die.

Most fire fights are short and incredibly intense. This one was a textbook example. It was all over in less than a minute. The ground to the east of their position was littered with bodies of irregulars. There were no screams or moans from wounded men. No attackers had been wounded. The fire from the Companions and their Mary Annes had been true and on the mark. It hadn't been intended as wounding fire. Wounding one of these irregulars wouldn't tie up a dozen of more irregulars to help him, remove him from the battlefield, treat him at an aid station, and transport him back to a mobile field hospital. The irregulars had no such biotech support.

Curt leapt forward and jumped over Spencer's prostrate form while noting that the man's eyes were opened wide in terror, that he was still breathing, and that he didn't seem to be hurt. He got to Alexis Morgan. "Are you all right?" was his anxious question.

Alexis was breathing hard. "Damned altitude. Makes me short of breath. I'm all right, Curt. Thanks to you. You saved my life. I'll pay you back . . ."

That was almost a standard response from a soldier who'd been rescued under fire by a buddy. "Don't want to lose you. Couldn't run the Companions without you." He suddenly grinned at her. "Want to pay me back?"

"Said I would."

He gave her an old Army cliche. "Some time you can give your last pair of clean, dry socks!"

Alexis laughed, a release of pent-up emotion. "Maybe that works for men, but I'll give you more than that!" She looked like she wanted to grab him and hold him, but they were both on a battlefield . . . or what had been a battlefield moments before.

One of the Mary Annes suddenly gave the alarm:

"Unidentified targets, bearing zero-eight-zero magnetic, five-five meters range, in motion, closing rate one meter per second!"

Curt whirled with his *Novia* at the ready. "Warrior Alpha Six, Warrior Alpha Eight, Warrior Alpha Nine, take range and bearing from Warrior Alpha Seven, but hold fire until my command!"

A warbot whose camouflage was broken only by a band of Scot's plaid running diagonally around its body churned through the stunted trees and bushes, followed by another.

"Hold fire! Friendlies!" Curt called out verbally.

The warbot spoke to him in a typically clipped British accent, "Hallo there! We've made contact with the Yanks! I say, Captain, the two of you make a smashing couple. Pity we don't have birds in our ranks! I'm Captain Wallace Heatherstone, His Majesty's Royal Scots Fusileers. And you might be?"

"Captain!" Curt replied, throwing a casual salute which he knew would be seen by Captain Wallace Heatherstone who was operating the warbot by linkage from some distance to the rear. "I'm Captain Curt Carson, commanding the Washington Greys regiment, United States Army. May I present First Lieutenant Alexis Morgan, commanding Carson's Companions?"

"Charmed, Lieutenant! I hope we have the opportunity to meet under somewhat different circumstances when this foray is all over and done with!" the warbot replied.

"We'll buy you a drink at the Club somewhere sometime," Curt promised.

"Were you right behind those Bastaards that just attacked me?" Alexis asked.

"Right-o! Chasing the buggers as fast as we could."

"You chased them right into me!"

"Well, I daresay we can't run as fast as those Bastaards when they decide to retreat," the warbot replied. "But we managed to hold them off at Strijdom until you got there."

"Captain, if we've done our job here and cleaned up the irregulars around Strijdom Airport, it's time to get into

Otjomuise," Curt said. "I'd like to meet as soon as possible with both the British and French commanders as well as Colonel Birdwood of the Australian regiment. Please give my respects to your commanding officer and ask him to come to my regimental command post either in person or driving a warbot. If he'll come in person, I'll serve some hot tea. Otherwise, I'll try to find some silicone lube for his warbot."

"Right-oh! Done, Captain! Half-past the hour be acceptable?"

Before Curt could reply, he was accosted by Len Spencer. "You filthy, goddamned, motherfucking son of a bitch!" Spencer shouted at the top of his lungs, his round, pudgy face livid with rage. "You shot my camera off my shoulder! You could have killed me, you sonofabitch! Goddamit, you also blew away ten thousand dollars worth of camera *and all the tape I shot this morning!* Do you know what this does to my coverage? How the hell can I expect to get the Pulitzer if you shot away my best stuff? Goddamit, I ought to punch out your—" He suddenly stopped as he felt something hard pushing against his backbone.

"Captain," said the warbot being controlled by Captain Heatherstone, "is this unruly person causing you trouble?"

"Back off, Captain Heatherstone," Curt advised the warbot. "I'm sure you can handle newshawks on your own. I certainly can."

"Of course, but if I may be of help, don't hesitate to let me know. We've been bothered by his counterpart from the London *Post* syndicate who sneaked aboard our aerodyne and was unfortunately trapped with us at Strijdom. Tiresome chap."

Curt looked down at Spencer. "First of all," he told the newsman, "you were in the field of fire. Sorry I hit your videocam, but it was a choice between doing that and getting you the hell out of the way, or letting Lieutenant Morgan come under attack from those ten Bastaards . . ."

"That was the best damned visual I'd taped all day! Ten of those fuzzies attacking a woman officer!" Spencer was no longer quite as livid. Discretion and disappointment had replaced diatribe.

"She could have been killed," Curt pointed out.

Spencer shook his head. "No. Not at all. She would have fought back! Goddam, it was going to be a *wonderful* shtick!"

Alexis was coming to a slow boil. She didn't often lose her temper; she'd been trained not to do so. She'd been taught that an officer had to keep a cool demeanor, especially when commanding troops. "You would have just stood there with your camera running and let those ten men attack me?"

"Hey, it's your job to fight, Allie. It's my job to cover it and report it."

"That isn't what you told me about being a team in gathering the best of all possible coverage of Operation Diamond Skeleton," she reminded him. "I put you in positions you wanted for coverage. I arranged for interviewing my NCOs and with other officers I knew. I even put myself into jeopardy a couple of times to help you out. And you just stood there taping while ten men attacked me?"

Spencer shrugged. "Hell, it doesn't make any difference now. Captain America here destroyed my videocam and all the tape in it. Get him to take you to the Press Club and share a penthouse with you the next time the two of you are in New York!" He turned away from her abruptly and scurried over to where the remains of his videocam lay scattered on the ground. "Jesus, maybe I can collect enough pieces of tape here to splice something back together. It'll be ragged and noisy, but that will just make it all the more realistic, especially when I report that the tape was put together after the camera had been shot off my shoulder during the fighting. Come to think of it, no other newsman has been shot at this closely thus far. If that Brit was talking about Herbie Wilson at the *Post*, that wimp wouldn't stick his bald head anywhere it might get shot at . . ."

Alexis Morgan walked slowly over to where Spencer was on his knees on the ground, trying to salvage a Pulitzer prize. She looked calmly at the demolished camera and the scraps and strips and tangled piles of videotape scattered around. Slowly, she brought her *Novia* to her hip and fired ten rounds into the tangled and torn tape, an action that didn't improve Spencer's chances of ever getting it back together again. Spencer knelt there with a shocked look on his face, then clasped his hands over his ears, too late to muffle the blast of the gun. He rolled quickly to one side in an attempt to get out of any possible spray of additional bullets.

But Alexis then merely slung the *Novia* over her left shoulder, turned, and calmly walked back to where Curt and the Royal Scots warbot were standing and watching. In a pleasant voice with a smile on her grimy face, she said to Curt, "Sorry for the delay, Captain. I had to take care of a rather unsavory personal matter." Then her voice got hard as nails as she looked squarely at Curt and growled, *"No one toys with Alexis Morgan and gets away with it!"*

She brightened again. "Captain, please don't let me keep you from your command conference—"

"I ought to charge you for those ten rounds, Lieutenant," Curt remarked. "I didn't notice that you expended them in combat—"

"You cad! You wouldn't!" Captain Heatherstone's warbot erupted.

"Damned right you wouldn't, *Captain,"* Alexis told him firmly. "That was the final shot in the war between the sexes insofar as Leonard Winston Spencer of the New York *Times* syndicate is concerned. And I don't give a damn what he writes about us girls in the combat arms."

"Come to think of it, expended under combat conditions in the war between the sexes is enough justification for me," Curt quipped. "Just don't shoot at me; I charge when I'm wounded. Very well, carry on, Lieutenant. Please join me for lunch if you can break away from company duties."

"Drat!" Captain Heatherstone burst out. "I was preparing to ask the Lieutenant to join the Royal Scots for a bite . . . after I get out of linkage, of course."

Capt. Curt Carson shook his head slowly. "Afraid I couldn't authorize the Lieutenant's visit to the Royal Scots, Captain. You don't have the equivalent of Rule Ten in the British Army . . ."

CHAPTER FORTY-THREE

Maj. Gen. Jacob O. Carlisle had had a great deal of previous experience in urban combat. Since most officers now served in the same unit for as long as possible—a policy adopted in order to assure high morale and thorough knowledge of a given outfit—Carlisle had been in command of various units of the Washington Greys or the 17th Iron Fist Division (RI) when the battle streamers for Sfax, Tyre, Munsterlagen, and Trinidad had been added to the regimental colors.

But, although he'd done the overall planning of the assault on Otjomuise with his staff on St. Helena, he was wise enough to present the plan to the allied forces now ready to move into Otjomuise, then stand back and let the people in the field run the show. He didn't micromanage the operation.

(General Franchet Maurice Lanrezac, the actual Supreme Allied Commander of Operation Diamond Skeleton, received the official credit for the assault although he'd been airlifted from Strijdom International Airport to St. Helena and on to Paris on the first evack flight that came out of the previously surrounded airfield. The French military history books tend to cover the Strijdom incident rather lightly while at the same time praising Lanrezac for being in the heat of the battle with the *Legion Robotique* and leading the final breakout. However, the Australians recognize Carlisle as the master planner of Otjomuise with their own First Kokoda Regiment as being in the front line alongside the Americans. Few people anywhere—other than professional military historians—know who did what in the Washington Greys. On the scene reporters such as Leonard Spencer of the New York *Times* tended to concentrate on Carlisle's contributions while the British and French newspapermen reported primarily on the achievements of their own national forces in the final assault.)

On the ground and in the air, the allied forces victorious at Strijdom didn't waste any time moving on Otjomuise. They regrouped west of Otjomuise, had a rapid command meeting, and got under way shortly after 1200 hours local. More Ovambos were moving down from Tsumeb because the First Assam Regiment had concentrated its resources on defending Grootfontein's critical air base.

Curt was bushed. So were most of the Greys. They'd pushed hard for days. Curt remarked about this to Carlisle, who gently reminded his temporary regimental commander, "I'm tired, too, Captain. But there are more tired division and regiment commanders than there are tired divisions and regiments. This is where training, physical fitness, and morale pay off."

"Yes, sir. I understand. We'll try to do the difficult immediately; the impossible will take a few hours longer," Curt replied.

"We haven't got a few hours," the General pointed out. "The Bastaards are in confusion right now; tomorrow, they'll have reinforcements in the form of about seven thousand Ovambos and Hereros pouring into Otjomuise from the north. We don't have the manpower or warbots available to defend the city as well as to break the siege of the diplomatic compound. It's got to be done this afternoon, then reform everyone tonight into defense lines for the city. Let the Ovambos run up against our defenses. I don't think they'll be willing to pay the price to break our defense."

"Understood, General. Will do!" Curt assured him. He, too, knew that a defensive offensive plan was workable in their current situation where they could be greatly outnumbered and would have to depend upon their firepower.

The main assault was made by the *Legion Robotique*, of course. The French insisted upon it. The *Legion* drove its warbots directly down the thirty kilometers of highway into Otjomuise accompanied by a parallel column of the Royal Scots Fusileers moving down the railway line. The two regiments met immediate resistance from the native irregulars who'd anticipated this and established a line of defense in the outskirts of the city.

Because of their greater mobility, the First Kokoda Regiment and the Washington Greys were deployed on the north and south flanks respectively with the task of sweeping around the city and coming in from the west. It wasn't an easy trek. Otjomuise is sheltered by the Auasberg and Eros mountain ranges and the Khomas Hochland. Although the city itself was at 1,700 meters elevation, some of the mountains around it soared up to 2,400 meters.

But speed was demanded. And Curt pushed the Greys hard with everyone riding vehicles in order to save strength. Ammo and food were still in good supply, but fuel threatened to get low because of the high speed to which the Greys were pushing their vehicles. Curt advised the regiment to ignore fuel economies; if a vehicle ran out, personnel and warbots were to transfer to another vehicle or, if worse came to worse, proceed on foot.

It was a forty kilometer swing by the Greys. They did it in two hours. By 1430 hours, the regiment stood ready in the western suburbs of Otjomuise and were in communication with elements of the First Kokoda that had swung around the north side of the city.

Curt found a small rise from which to have an actual look at the city. The visuals and other computer-generated displays of the street plan told him a lot, but he wanted to get a *feel* for the place. He'd learned the hard way in previous engagements. He wanted to see the potential battlefield with his own eyes.

A greyish-brown haze hung over the city in the calm afternoon air. Curt could smell the stench of burning buildings, untreated sewage from disrupted waste management systems, and unburied bodies. Mixed in with this was the acrid ordor of expended high explosives, mostly from the smokeless powder of the old brass-cased ammo fired by the Soviet AK-74s and American M-16s.

Surprisingly, Otjomuise looked to Curt to be a fairly modern city in many respects. Certainly it wasn't as quaint as the German-like Swakopmund. It was evident that the South Africans had tried to modernize the capital city before the Colour War forced them to withdraw from Namibia. The consequences of millions of rands of subsidized construction were obvious. The center of the city had been completely torn out, the streets realigned and widened, and new high-rise buildings erected in a cluster around the Centrum. Elsewhere, it was a low-profile city with buildings that seldom rose more than three stories high and a street layout that was almost European in its randomlike pattern except for broad boulevards reminiscent of Paris and Berlin.

Munsterlagen all over again, Curt thought, although he'd been only a green second lieutenant warbot brainy in that operation which had cinched the German Reunification.

He couldn't see the diplomatic compound although the displays and maps showed him where it had to be.

His company commanders were with him for a final briefing before entering the city itself. He turned to them and asked, "Everyone reorganized back to normal T-O-and-E insofar as losses thus far permit?"

"We'll never get back to normal, Captain," Joan Ward observed. "We've lost too many people, and even the wounded will be absent for months."

"I know. But that's an aspect of combat we should have recognized as a result of Trinidad," Curt replied, referring to the fact that the Greys had lost several people there as well, especially the lady whose company Joan Ward now led. "So don't take chances this afternoon. Most companies are down two or three people trying to handle a dozen warbots. We can't take many more losses without losing platoon and company integrity and command. Any problems?"

"Captain, I'd like to have Lieutenant Aarts reassigned

to the Marauders," Capt. Manny Garcia requested.

"Manny, I was just saying that the Greys are, in effect, short of manpower. We're marginal in all combat companies," Curt emphasized. "Headquarters Company under Wade Hampton here is going to be goddamned busy on C-cubed-I, and I won't operate under urban combat conditions without decent C-cubed-I! Service Company *must* be used as a reserve even though they don't have any warbots. Major Benteen's people have agreed again to serve as a fire support regular infantry company, although they've only had basic personal protection training with their Hornets. Incidentally, I want you to know that the Service Company did an *outstanding* job at Strijdom; they were where they were supposed to be when they were supposed to be there, and we were just fortunate that we didn't have to use them until right at the last during the mop-up. Major Benteen, well done, sir!"

"Thank you, Captain," said the commander of the Service Company, normally a non-combat unit in the Greys. "My tech and supply people aren't trained fighters like the rest of you, but I can certainly report that they're now seasoned. . . ."

"Grey Head, this is Diamond Head," came the call in Curt's helmet comm unit. "Code Mike. Code Mike. Play ball!"

Curt gave the thumbs-up signal to his commanders. "Diamond Head, this is Grey Head! Batter up!" He addressed his Greys. "You've all got your ops plans and understand them? Good! Let's go!"

Everyone took off at a run for their OCVs and ACVs.

The warbots were dismounted from the RTVs. The vehicles, including the OCVs and ACVs, might be too large to maneuver down narrow streets. As a result of Zahedan, urban combat doctrine now required that large vehicles be left where they could be maneuvered and serve as rallying and reassembly points. Or where they might be called to come in and get troops and warbots out if necessary and if possible. The occupation of Rio Claro on Trinidad had confirmed the validity of the doctrine. The only vehicles that accompanied the Greys and their warbots were the LAMVs with their 75mm Saucy Cans and the ATVs which were to be used only if rapid transportation were required in order to reach a critical location fast or to get wounded out.

And, according to doctrine, the Mary Annes of each company's Alpha Platoon preceded the officers, NCOs, and squad leaders down the streets. Bravo Platoon with their heavy-fire Hairy Foxes followed.

Curt accompanied the Companions rather than remain in the regimental command post with Sgt. Major Jesup and Captain Wade Hampton. He believed that a regimental commander should be in the field with the troops. Hampton and Jesup had tried to dissuade him of doing this, pointing out that doctrine called for the regimental commander to stay in the command post to direct the operation. Curt merely pointed out that he had excellent communications with the command post and that he felt it was his duty to lead the regiment, not manage it. Sgt. Major Jesup had been quite candid, reminding Curt that leading a regiment was somewhat different than leading a company. Curt had put a stop to the discussion by stating he would lead the Greys in his own way, right or wrong.

Off to their left, the First Kokoda Regiment moved in totally on foot without warbots. Insofar as Curt was concerned, that sort of operation required real guts, which the Aussies seemed to have in abundance.

Each company followed its own course through the city streets. They had only about two kilometers to go before coming up against what was believed to be the rear of the enemy surrounding the diplomatic compound.

Hovering low in the sky behind them were hordes of tactical strike aerodynes. The Greys and the Kokoda were to be supported by the USAF 55th Tactical Fighter Wing as required and requested by ground commanders.

Curt was surprised. The streets in this part of Otjomuise were reasonably wide and lined on both sides by huge old homes with verandahs. It was apparent that the Greys had achieved the element of surprise because in the midst of what must have been fierce fighting a short distance away around the diplomatic compound, people were out in their front yards tending flower beds, mowing lawns, and generally puttering around. Some of them ran into their homes when they saw the strange parade of warbots and helmeted soldiers proceeding down the center of the street. Others, including many children, came up to the curb, shouting and waving to the passing troops. Apparently, none of the populace had ever seen a warbot except on television; they were curious and somewhat awed.

It was unreal to Curt. He tried to warn them to get back in their homes because fighting could erupt at any moment. Some listened to him. Others pressed flowers into his hands. "Alexis," he called out, "instruct your people and warbots to exercise extreme caution if they have to open fire. I don't want these good people to be hit."

"Captain, if everything suddenly goes to slime, I don't know how they can help but be hit!" Alexis replied with concern in her voice. She, too, was carrying an armload of flowers and was being followed by about a dozen children. "Go home! Get out of here! Shooting could start at any instant, and you'd be shot! Scat! Scram! *Raus! Allez!* Dammit, Captain, how do you say it in Afrikaans?"

Curt didn't try to talk to the children. Instead, he called to the people on the sidewalks, "Get your children out of here! Get back in your homes! Now! It's very dangerous to stand out here!"

No one paid the slightest bit of attention to him.

Fortunately, nothing happened until the Companions drew closer to the diplomatic compound. The change in the appearance of the streets was striking. As the column progressed toward the compound, it could be seen that the homes and stores had suffered an increasing amount of damage of gunfire. If the stores didn't have stout steel shutters or lattices across their fronts, they'd been looted.

Nothing happened until the Companions came within two hundred meters of the high wall that appeared across the street—the diplomatic compound.

A heavy solid metal gate in the wall was closed.

The flags of several nations flew atop the wall. They were the national colors of the countries whose legations were in the compound.

Squad Sgt. Charlie Koslowski and his two Mary Annes literally blundered into action.

Koslowski was in the van, following his two warbots. He was moving slowly and cautiously now that he was so close to the compound. In addition, he was from Detroit where he'd grown up in the inner city, had been a member of a street gang, and knew how to fight in an urban environment. Caution and experience saved his life because he knew what to do.

Three dark-skinned men carrying AK-74 rifles stepped out of a building's doorway into the street behind the Mary Annes that had already passed. These men were joking and laughing among themselves and paying absolutely no attention to the compound wall less than a hundred meters down the street. Apparently, they felt they had fire superiority over that street. But when they saw Koslowski, they froze.

Koslowski didn't freeze. He was primed and ready. "Mary Annes!" he yelled. "Target five o'clock, three humans! Commence firing!" And he opened fire with his *Novia* braced against his hip. There wasn't time to raise the weapon and aim. And the range was only about fifteen meters. He couldn't help but hit something with the *Novia* on full auto.

The Mary Annes were fast but Koslowski was faster that day. By the time the warbots had slewed their 25mm guns to bear, Koslowski had finished off what was left of a fifty-round clip and three dead men lay on the sidewalk.

"Take cover!" Alexis Morgan called. She knew what would be coming next.

The brief fire fight alerted the Bastaard forces emplaced in the buildings around the compound.

Now the attack of the Washington Greys on their rear was known.

CHAPTER FORTY-FOUR

Curt could now see how the Bastaards and other irregulars had been able to lay siege to the diplomatic compound:

They'd taken over the houses and buildings that surrounded the walled compound and had used those structures as locations for snipers, riflemen, and a few machinegunners to cover all gates and other openings in the wall as well as the perimeter road between the wall and its surroundings.

In order to break the siege ring around the compound, Curt saw that it wouldn't be necessary to send troops into every house and building to clear out the Bastaards. He only had only to clear a salient near one of the gates.

Curt figured there were several ways this could be done.

His first impulse was to send his warbots and troops against the houses and buildings on both sides of the street leading up to the compound's west gate. But he knew from previous experience that warbots couldn't get into those structures and root out the irregulars. Warbots made lousy house fighters; they were too big, too clumsy, and designed for operations in the open.

The only way to get the irregulars out would be to send the Greys into those buildings. He wasn't going to do that.

Buildings were expendable. True, they were homes and businesses that had either been there long before the Namibian government had ordered the diplomatic compound walled off, or the buildings contained businesses serving the needs of the diplomatic compound.

But this was war, whether it was called that or not. And Curt's alternative was to destroy the buildings, move in to occupy the rubble, and bring the flanking buildings and irregular outposts under fire. Then he could get through the compound's gate and establish a sanitized corridor for the occupants to get out.

Obviously, there was no place in the compound where an aerodyne could land or this technique would have been used days ago to evacuate the place. No one had thought about an aerodyne landing pad on any of the buildings which either had sharply peaked or slanting roofs liberally covered with communications antennae and satellite dishes.

He called up the local street map on his visor display. Apparently when the South Africans had rebuilt the city, they'd cut a broad boulevard from the City Centrum to the west suburbs. This was a wide parkway with a fifty-meter green strip down the middle. There were some trees; but Curt knew that trees could be demolished rather quickly and removed as an obstacle to aerodyne vertical landings and takeoffs. The West Parkway was only about a kilometer to the south of the compound.

"Sedan Head, this is Grey Head," Curt called the *Legion Robotique*. "I'm at the west gate of the compound. I can open the ring at this point, extract the refugees out the west gate, and create a sanitized corridor for their escape to the West Parkway for aerodyne pickup. What is your position and situation? And can you cover this withdrawal operation from the west gate?"

"Grey Head, this is Sedan Head," came the reply from the French warbot regimental headquarters. "Hold your position and pin down the enemy forces in the vicinity. We are fighting our way through the City Centrum. We anticipate reaching the main gate of the compound in about two hours. You are to provide a diversion at the west gate so we may effect the rescue and extraction from the main entrance . . ."

Two hours? That would put the French unit at the main compound gate no earlier than 1635. It would be unlikely that they could clear out the ring of irregulars, get into the compound, and organize a rescue before darkness.

Curt didn't relish the idea of urban fighting at night. He wanted to get this thing over and done with in the next four hours while he still had sunlight.

He switched displays and projected the tactical situation in the city. The *Legion* had a long way to go. The Royal Scots were moving too slowly through the main rail marshalling yards and hadn't yet even reached the Centrum. They'd be in poor position to support the *Legion*. On the other hand, the Royal Scots could form an effective defensive line against Ovambo forces coming from the north.

"Diamond Head, this is Grey Head," he called Carlisle on St. Helena.

"Go ahead, Grey Head."

"General?"

"I'm on, Carson. Problems?"

"Yes and no. I'm in a position where I can probably break through the west gate within an hour and sanitize a corridor to the West Parkway for the evack. Sedan Head wants me to hold and provide pin-down fire for the irregulars already here," Curt explained. "I don't see the French request as a viable plan. So I'm going to take out the Bastaard forces in this sector and get those people out of the compound. Alert the evack aerodynes for pick-up along the West Parkway."

Curt knew he had his neck out a long, long way. And he'd deprive the French of the honor of the refugee extraction. But the French *Legion Robotique* might not be able to pull it off because they were an all-warbot unit. Curt *knew* the Washington Greys with the help of the First Kokoda could get it started before sundown. Carlisle had promised that he would not micromanage the operation. But Curt would be treading on the tender toes of some very high French and British brass if he did what he knew he could do. In addition to looking for some support from Carlisle, Curt wanted to make sure the General knew what he was planning to do. Carlisle always had the option of halting it before Curt started it.

"You're in the field. You know your situation. If you can do it, don't sit on your ass. When do you need the evack aerodynes?" Carlisle replied with directness, not giving Curt an order but also not directly approving of what Curt proposed. Curt knew the General was in a command van on St. Helena surrounded by French and British staff officers. Carlisle would be taking his own amount of heat from them no matter what he said or did.

But Curt surmised that was one of the nasty little problems that general officers often had to deal with. On the other hand, Curt had to deal with the reality of combat facing him. So he replied, "I'll ask the First Kokoda to sanitize the corridor and protect the West Parkway evack area after they back up our assault. And I'll coordinate my actions directly with Windmill Head. Have the evack aerodynes on the Parkway by 1600, and I'll provide them with tactical cover to handle any forces the irregulars might manage to concentrate in that area."

"Keep me advised, Grey Head, and don't hesitate to ask for help if you need it." That was all Carlisle had to say. That was all he could say. Curt Carson was obviously in charge of the operation. All that Supreme Allied Command on St. Helena could do at this point was to provide the necessary support.

"Windmill Head, this is Grey Head. Do you read?" Curt called Captain Portales inside the diplomatic compound.

"This is Windmill Head. We see you outside the west gate."

"Good! We're going to break the Bastaard siege ring here and open a corridor to evacuate the compound down to the West Parkway for pickup. Get everyone ready to move in the next hour. We won't have much time. And stand by to open the west gate for us when we get the Bastaards cleared out of their positions."

"The *Legion Robotique* said they'd be at the main gate in a few hours," Captain Portales interjected. "We were planning to let them evacuate us then."

"Captain, we're already at the west gate and about to

clear it of Bastaards. You've got your choice. You can let your countrymen try to bring you out if they can get there before sunset—which is doubtful; they're bogged down in the center of town—or you can get ready to move out under our cover in about an hour."

"I'll have to check with my *charge d'affaires* and the other ambassadors . . ."

"Captain, it's my understanding that you're in charge of the diplomatic compound under these siege conditions," Curt snapped at him in an irritated tone. "We've trekked a couple of hundred kilometers through the wilderness and fought a couple of battles to get here. If a committee is running the compound, we haven't got time to screw around with it. We'll blow the damned gate off its hinges and herd the people out ourselves because we're running out of time and people and supplies. And we've got a couple of thousand Ovambos coming in from the north. Now are you in command, or do I have to blast through that gate and rescue the people you've supposedly been defending for the past several days? Make up your goddamned mind because I'm about to get shot at out here and I haven't got time to screw around with protocol!"

There was a brief silence during which Curt just about figured he ought to tell Portales to get out of the way because his Saucy Cans would blow the gate apart. Then the reply, "I'm standing by to evacuate out of the west gate, Captain Carson. Let me know what you want me to do."

"Just open the gate when I tell you to, Captain Portales."

Alexis Morgan had deployed the Companions according to the urban combat procedure they'd worked out for Sierra Charlies. She'd used her own initiative to modify it on the basis of intelligence data which indicated the Bastaards had no heavy weapons. She moved the warbots into covering fire positions in the open and ordered the troops to take cover. The Mary Annes were located where they'd have the best fields of fire into the houses and buildings next to the wall while Jerry Allen's Hairy Foxes had zeroed-in with their 50mm automatics on the more substantial buildings. The LAMVs with their Saucy Cans were almost useless in the close-range situation of the streets, but Alexis had them back where they could fire point-blank into buildings most likely to contain irregulars.

It was apparent that the Bastaards hadn't expected or planned for an assault from the rear. There was some sporadic firing toward the Greys from windows but little else. Apparently, those in each house were trying to figure out a way to defend themselves from this new threat to their rear. Or how to get out of a trap.

"Warrior Leader, this is Grey Head," Curt called. "Stop the Warriors about five hundred meters from the wall and take cover to your left. Do not engage the irregulars but keep your street under surveillance for possible irregular reinforcements coming across from the right. And protect your right flank."

"Wilco, Grey Head."

"Killer Leader, this is Grey Head," Curt spoke to the company on his left flank. "I want you to stop the Killers where they are and take cover to your right. Keep your street under surveillance and open fire on any irregulars trying to cross it between your position and the wall. Protect your left flank."

"Do we return fire?"

"Affirmative. But don't charge in there like Kelly used to do," Curt told the temporary Killers' commander, 1st Lt. Russ Frazier. "Grey Support, this is Grey Head. Major, your job is to cover our rear back there and keep me advised if any irregulars move to cut us off from the parkway. Any problems?"

"Not at all, Grey Head. No irregular forces appear to be behind the Greys," Maj. Fred Benteen reported.

"Marauder Leader, Grey Head. Cut to your right at the first side street, move to your right flank, and join the Companions. Deploy as support to the Companions."

"Roger, Grey Head. What are your plans, Captain?" Manny Garcia wanted to know.

"The Companions will take out the remaining irregular riflemen and you'll mop up behind them," Curt told him. "Let me know when you're deployed behind the Companions."

"Roger, we're moving now. We should be over there in about five minutes."

"That's what I estimated. All Grey Leaders, this is Grey Head," Curt snapped on the regimental freak. "Stand by. I'm going to ask the Aussies to come in from the left flank and be ready to provide us with manned ground support if we run into any trouble. Slaughter Head, this is Grey Head. Copy?"

"G'day, myte! Roger! Heard you! We'll slide through some side streets here and make contact with your left flank," was Colonel Birdwood's immediate reply.

"Thank you. Slaughter Head, I believe we have an opportunity here to break the siege cleanly. We can do that if we concentrate our forces to provide maximum mass at this one point. The irregulars can be pinned down so they can't move to their flanks once we hit. Thus far, they don't seem to know what's going on and they're not prepared to handle an enemy in their rear."

"So I gathered, Captain. We'll be prepared to take them on under fire."

"It may not be as intense as you think," Curt told him. "I intend to soften them up more than just a little bit. Stand by and keep your heads down. I'm calling in a surgical air strike."

Curt switched freaks and called, "Air Head, this is Grey Head. Double Nickle, are you there?"

"Read you loud and clear, Grey Head. Need us to lay some ordnance on someone?"

"Would appreciate it. Who's this?"

"Ripper Leader."

Curt's visor display told him that "Ripper Leader" was Maj. Red Reilly, commanding officer of the 313th Tactical Fighter Squadron of the 55th Tactical Fighter Wing, otherwise known as "Reilly's Rippers."

"Okay, Ripper, this is Grey Head. Does your digital uplink read the coordinate designators I'm indicating?

Surgical strike, please. Take out those designated buildings," Curt requested.

"Got it. Just a couple of buildings and houses along the road facing the compound on either side of the west gate. Grey Head, can you confirm it by laser designator?"

"Negative, Ripper Leader. We're afoot down here. No ACV available."

"We gonna take any ground fire?"

"You may encounter small arms fire from positions north or south of the target area," Curt estimated. "We'll locate that and try to suppress it."

"Roger, as long as I don't get the Golden BB, I won't sweat it," the airman replied. "So we'll approach to minimize the Golden BBs. We're coming up from hover now! First flight will use smart iron bombs. Second flight will use rockets homing on bomb bursts."

"Hit the buildings. Don't hit the wall."

"Captain, I can put a smart bomb through the middle second story window of the house on the left side of the street!" Red Reilly's voice came. "Do you want the humper to go through the top or bottom half of the window?"

"Your option, Ripper."

"Okay, Reilly's Rippers rolling in now! First flight has the target. Okay, keep your heads down so you don't get hit by any flying debris! Here we go!"

The strike aerodynes came in from behind them at tree top level and began launching and firing as they passed directly overhead. The down blast from the aerodynes raised dust and dirt, and the din of the discharging weaponry was deafening. They pulled out of their attack run over the diplomatic compound.

The houses along the street running parallel to the compound wall erupted in smoke and flame.

The second strike flight was hot on the heels of the first, and they launched their rockets directly overhead. The rockets streaked into the erupting flames and smoke of the bomb explosions.

"Ripper Leader, good work! You knocked those buildings flat! Thanks much!"

"Any time, and we'll stand by in your rear if you need anything else."

"Companion Leader, have your Hairy Foxes put some rounds into the target as well," Curt ordered. "Marauder Leader, I want some Hairy Fox fire into those buildings on the right. And some of your Saucy Cans fire into those on the left. Let's knock down any possible resisting fire so the Companions can get in there and secure the two corners. Then send your Alpha Platoon in behind the Companions to help secure the street that runs along the wall. Companion Leader, forward! Take those two corner buildings or what's left of them, and stand by to enter the compound once I get Windmill to open the gates . . ."

"Grey Head, this is Killer Leader! We're taking some fire from our left flank! Some irregulars have apparently abandoned their siege positions and are moving in on our flank!" came the call from Russ Frazier.

"Grey Head, Slaughter Head intercepted that message!" Colonel Birdwood's voice interrupted. "We're moving in to cover and suppress that. We're behind whomever is firing on your lads."

Curt almost corrected him until he realized that Kelly's Killers was the only Grey company that had no women.

It was only a matter of time now because Curt had concentrated so many people and warbots and firepower into a small area before the west gate. They'd be able to swat down any resistance from the irregulars because, for a change, the allied forces enjoyed superiority of numbers in addition to their mobility, firepower, and unity of command.

Curt was right with Alexis Morgan and Jerry Allen as they moved with Platoon Sgt. Edie Sampson and the three remaining squad leaders into the rubble of the demolished houses. No one was left alive who'd been in them. Reilly's Rippers had done their job.

They picked up some flanking fire from houses and buildings on either side, but it wasn't very accurate. The Hairy Foxes suppressed most of it.

Manny Garcia and the Marauders moved forward into the perimeter street, looking and firing in either direction along it while the Companions moved up to the west gate.

"Windmill Head, this is Grey Head! We've got the west gate approaches secured. Open up!" Curt broadcast.

But as the gates slowly started to swing, all hell broke loose on the perimeter road.

To the left, the street was filled with running men charging at a full run toward them, old assault rifles being fired from the hip or being waved in the air so that their old bayonets glistened in the afternoon sun.

"To the left!" Curt yelled. "We're under assault! Commence fire! Warriors, Killers, give us heavy fire to our left flank!"

"We see 'em! We've got them on their flank!" came the call from Russ Frazier.

"Windmill! Can you give us any fire from the wall?" Curt wanted to know.

He never got an answer because it all happened so fast.

Not even concentrated *Novia* automatic fire plus the auto fire from the Mary Annes and jeeps stopped the attack wave. When the front row went down under fire, the next wave stumbled through their bodies and continued the assault.

When the onrushing tide of human bodies hit the strung-out Companions and Marauders in front of the gate, it was a melee. Manny Garcia and his company took the brunt of the attack. Warbots were totally useless in such close-quarter, hand-to-hand fighting. Curt dodged bayonets and fired point blank. When he didn't have time to shoot, he swung his *Novia* and clubbed Bastaards. His body armor saved him. He took at least one 7.62mm round on his body armor and something glanced off his helmet.

But Kelly's Killers under Lieutenant Russ Frazier took the assaulting horde from the flank.

And then elements from the Aussie's First Kokoda waded into the flank and rear. The Aussies had never given up their bayonets, a weapon considered by most modern military experts to be an obsolete holdover from the days when infantry was armed with pikes. And they hadn't been spoiled by high-technology warbots. They were fighters.

It was over in a few minutes.

And the west gate of the Otjomuise diplomatic compound was open. The embassies therein didn't have extensive military guard details, but what they have poured out to help finish off the melee.

The ones the Aussies didn't account for were targeted by murderous fire from the rest of the Washington Greys who'd moved up in response to the sound of battle.

The surviving irregulars, seeing that they couldn't break the backs of the Americans and Australians, tried to run when the compound's military units sallied forth.

Breathing hard, Curt looked around.

Alexis Morgan was standing next to him. She, too, was breathing hard. And there was blood on the butt of her *Novia*. Jerry Allen had had his helmet knocked off and bore a bleeding cut on the side of his head, but he looked grim and squeezed off a three-round burst toward a fleeing Bastaard . . . who was clubbed down by an Aussie. M. Sgt. First Class Henry Kester looked as though he were ready for a retreat ceremony; his uniform wasn't even mussed, and he was standing in the midst of a pile of seven dead irregulars.

Sgt. Edie Sampson looked at Curt, brandished a small automatic pistol, and said, "I kept my Beretta, Captain, in spite of what you told me. You're right; it ain't accurate. In these close fights, it may not kill 'em, but it sure scares the shit out of them."

The Companions had fought and survived.

The same could not be said for the other companies of the Washington Greys.

A dapper Captain wearing a French *kepi* stepped up and said, "Captain Carson, Captain Portales! Nice work! We're ready to evacuate!"

Curt saluted briefly and said, "Stand by a moment, Captain, while we get this mess cleared out." He looked around and didn't like what he saw. He was suddenly tired, very tired, and happy that his Companions had made it through that wild and violent Bastaard assault. But he saw other things that caused him to grit his teeth. Keying his helmet comm, he saw it was still working in spite of whatever had hit his helmet. "Captain Hampton, Captain Carson here. Bring in the vehicles; I want you to take charge of the evack while we tend to some other things. Major Gydesen, please get your biotechs to the west gate fast. We've taken casualties! I want everyone to move . . . fast! Allen, you were right: This goddamned place is the land God made in anger. Let's get the hell out of here!"

CHAPTER FORTY-FIVE

Sixty-five people arrayed themselves in formation on the open field atop the Diamond Point Casern.

It was nearly sundown.

Capt. Curt Carson found himself standing and facing the Washington Greys regiment. He knew what to do; he'd participated in this ceremony daily for years, but always as part of the formation, not in front of it. Standing on one side of him was his adjutant, Capt. Joanne Wilkinson. On the other side was Regimental Sgt. Maj. Tom Jesup.

This was the first regimental Muster and Retreat ceremony since the 3rd Infantry (Special Combat) regiment, the Washington Greys, had returned from Namibia over a week ago.

Curt still felt tired. There had been so much to do. The days had been busy. But his work as temporary regimental commander involved administration; Curt hated administrative duties, in spite of the fact that he had a staff equipped with computers to do it. The work tended to take him away from people, and he was still people-oriented. He wasn't sure he was ready for regimental command yet. But he was the senior combat rated officer, and he had to do the job.

"Adjutant, muster the regiment!" Curt snapped the order.

Wilkinson stepped forward and to her left, then faced the regimental formation. It was a small one with fewer people than an infantry company of a hundred years before. Although machinery, especially warbots and computers, had taken over a lot of the military activity formerly done by people, no warbots were present with the formation. The regimental adjutant consulted a hard-copy print out and called out in a clear voice, "Attention to muster! Hettrick, Belinda J., Colonel."

"Wounded on the field of battle! I answer for her!" Curt called out clearly. He'd talked with her at Walter Reed. She'd make it in spite of the fact she was paralyzed from the waist down. He didn't understand all the biotechnology involved, but the biotechnicians had determined the nature of the poison and had gotten to her in time to arrest its spread through her nervous system. Some of her nerve trunks would need to be regenerated, and it would be more than a year before she'd be able to walk again. But there was promise; she'd walk again, even though she'd have to drop out of the line of command because of the extent of her therapy. Hettrick was unhappy about that but took solace in the fact that her combat leadership experience would be very useful to the Army in other positions. She spoke of the possibility of a slot at the Army War College. Or of a position at West Point. But she knew she'd never get the Washington Greys back, and that bothered her as much as it bothered Curt.

"Canby, Edward Robert, Major!"

"Fallen in service in Namibia! I answer for him!" Curt announced again. Canby's body had been recovered. It was scheduled for Arlington next week.

"Gibbon, John Steven, Captain."

"Wounded on the field of battle," was Captain Wade Hampton's reply. "I answer for him."

"Garcia, Manuel Xavier, Captain."

"Wounded on the field of battle! I answer for him," came the call from Lt. Russ Frazier.

"Kelly, Martin Clarence, Captain."

"Wounded on the field of battle! I answer for him!" Again, it was Frazier who replied.

"Rosenberg, Joshua Micah, First Lieutenant."

"Fallen in service in Namibia! I answer for him!" was the clear call from Lt. Ellie Arts.

The names of the dead and wounded continued to be read by Capt. Joanne Wilkinson, the regimental adjutant. A superior officer or colleague responded to each name, confirming in principle that the people killed or wounded were still considered to be on the regimental roles until interment or recovery from wounds. The response to each name of the killed or wounded brought the clear response, "I answer for him!" Or her, as the case might be.

When it came to names of Carson's Companions, it was Lt. Alexis Morgan who responded. There were two names: Platoon Sgt. First Class Nicholas Gerard, and Sgt. Terry Dillon, both wounded and recovering.

Curt couldn't help feeling more than a little grim about it. Operation Diamond Skeleton had been expensive for the Washington Greys.

Twenty-two people had been killed or wounded.

This was the greatest percentage loss taken by a regiment since the Vietnam War.

Curt knew now that it was an inevitable consequence of re-introducing people on the battlefield in spite of such high-tech protection as body armor and the superior firepower of the new warbots. The Sierra Charlies had a long way to go before reaching congruence between weapons and tactics. And a lot of learning to do. In both Trinidad and Namibia, the regiment had been rushed into action long before it was ready.

And the last Bastaard assault before the west gate of the diplomatic compound had been costly. It had been a senseless suicide attack carried out with little leadership and no coordination. A mass of humanity charged into the enormous firepower of a Sierra Charlie regiment assisted by a regular infantry regiment. Capt. Manny Garcia and his Marauders on Curt's left flank had taken the brunt of it. Manny had been wounded by a bayonet thrust that caught the seam of his body armor at his shoulder; Josh Rosenberg had been killed by the impact of an AK-74 rifle butt to the side of his head below the helmet line.

After the siege of the diplomatic compound had been lifted and the people therein led out to the West Parkway, the sporadic attacks of the Bastaards, Herero, and Ovambos acting singly or in small groups had harassed the Greys, the Kokoda, and the Royal Scots as they'd maintained the evacuation corridor while the *Legion Robotique* had pinned down other irregulars in other parts of Otjomuise. In these final skirmishes, no one was immune from action. Even the Service Company had taken unexpected casualties because the irregulars attacked everywhere.

Grim as it seemed, the roll call of casualties was necessary. It was official notification of losses to the regiment. Nearly everyone knew who had been hit, but the muster made it official.

That done, it was then necessary to officially account for the rest of the regiment. "Companies, report!" called Wilkinson, to which Alexis Morgan, Joan Ward, Ellie Aarts (temporarily in command of the Marauders), Russ Frazier, Wade Hampton, and Fred Benteen sang out in turn, "All present or accounted for!"

Wilkinson did an about-face, saluted Curt, and reported, "The Washington Greys, Third Regiment, Special Combat, Seventeenth Iron Fist Division, Robot Infantry, all present and accounted for, sir! Nine fallen in service and sixteen wounded in action, but their whereabouts are spoken for, sir!"

"Post," Curt told her. Then he sang out, "Attention to orders! All personnel, stand-to at eighteen hundred hours at the Club!" Then he did an about-face because Maj. General Jacob Carlisle was standing behind him. Saluting, he said, "Sir, the Washington Greys have been mustered!"

Carlisle returned the salute. He turned to his aide, Capt. Kim Blythe, and took a bit of folded cloth from her. Raising his head, he announced, "The President of the United States has authorized me to present to the regiment a battle streamer bearing the legend 'Namibia' which is to be attached permanently to the regimental colors. Captain, please do the honors."

Curt stepped over to where the regimental colors stood

in their standard alongside the national colors. Slipping the staff from its support, Curt dipped it so he as regimental commander could reach up and remove a black burgee that had been previously affixed to it. The honor of the regiment, sullied in Swakopmund, had been restored by subsequent actions. Then Maj. Gen. Jacob O. Carlisle attached yet another battle streamer to the ones already affixed to the top of the staff with its gleaming eagle cast from Mexican silver wine goblets captured at the Castle of Chapultepec in 1847. Thus done, Curt replaced the standard in its holder.

Carlisle went on, "This streamer shall serve to indicate to all personnel now and in the future that the regiment served with valor, gallantry, and honor in Namibia during Operation Diamond Skeleton. The actions of the regiment were instrumental in the safe rescue of one thousand two hundred and three men, women, and children from forty-six countries including the United States. This streamer should be considered by the personnel of the regiment to supplement the individual awards and decorations for bravery and heroism in action that shall later be presented. Personally, I want to express my gratitude for your outstanding performance. It was in the tradition of the regiment which extends back more than two hundred and fifty years." He saluted the colors, then returned Curt's salute.

Curt turned and ordered, "Sound Retreat!"

The retreat gun boomed, its report echoing off the pine-covered slopes. The US Model 1857 "Napoleon" twelve-pounder might have been a museum piece and was fired that day by computer control, but it spoke as it had for almost two centuries.

The bugler wasn't present, but Georgie's computer-synthesized bugle call was as pure and perfect as if sounded by an accomplished musician.

At the end of the "Retreat" call, Georgie's synthesized bugler sounded "To The Color," and the flag was slowly raised from half-staff to the peak, then slowly lowered, again by computer control although Sgts. Geraldine

Wendt and Larry Jordan stepped out of ranks to receive the flag and fold it.

The Retreat ceremony had bothered Curt for many years, even after he'd left West Point. The concept of simulating retreat every evening and lowering the national colors didn't make much sense to him. Retreat signified failure. But that afternoon, standing on the formation field above Diamond Point, he suddenly sensed what it was all about.

Even though protocol requires the national colors to be lowered at night unless illuminated—unlike the French who fly a tricolor day and night until it's in tatters—the only time Old Glory is lowered is to signify a retreat. To the military forces, the formal retreat ceremony conducted in garrison reminds everyone of the many times in history when the nation's military forces have had to retreat and abandon their possessions, lowering the flag before leaving. But Americans had always returned to raise their flag another day. The ceremony was intended to jog military people into remembering that they serve a tenacious nation. To the individual, it was like the funeral ceremony Chaplain Nellie Crile read in a far away Namibia: the new day always follows the long night.

"Sergeant Major, dismiss the regiment," Curt told Tom Jesup when it was all done.

The Club was much warmer, cozier, and less formal.

Curt had ordered the stand-to although he was ambivalent about it. All he really wanted to do was log some sack time and perhaps take several days' leave. But he was the regimental commander, albeit temporary, and the regiment needed the informality of the stand-to in order to let off steam, relax, bitch about things, and mingle in a social situation of equality that had been impossible in Namibia. And especially so that evening because Curt had called for *all* personnel, not just officers.

The Washington Greys were special. As a robot infantry regiment, they'd been few and highly specialized. As Sierra Charlies, they were even more special with a developing unique *esprit de corps* that hardly existed—and perhaps could not exist—in regular warbot regiments. Now the uniqueness was even more pronounced because they were the only unit in the Army that had actually been shot at in recent times. That fact created a unique bond of companionship of "them what has been shot at," as Henry Kester once put it. Curt felt very close to all these people in a way that resembled his loyalty to the members of his West Point class; they had all gone through something together that no one else could ever share.

Besides, Curt was a maverick with respect to the separation between officers and enlisted. Insofar as he was concerned, the only real difference was a matter of responsibility and level of education. Beyond similar distinctions that existed in other professions—between medical doctors and biotechnicians, engineers and technicians, pilots and mechanics, for example—Curt had never felt elitist about his commission.

The Companions knew that, and the Greys were discovering it.

And Curt couldn't sequester himself in a private room with his Companions now. He had to mingle with the entire regiment. At least for an hour or so.

He heard bitches about lost personal equipment in the airlift in and out of Namibia.

He listened to gripes about screwed-up equipment, but he was damned glad that the tacomms, which had been giving so much trouble during maneuvers, had worked and were rapidly repaired when they didn't.

Surprisingly, there were even complaints about the food, but Army people have *always* complained about the food.

He got several discreet requests for both passes and leaves, and he promised he'd look into those in the next few days.

During the evening, he remarked to Capt. Joan Wilkinson about this, "Feel free to grant weekend passes to anyone. Matter of fact, personnel with more than four weeks' accumulated leave should get a couple of weeks, Joan. Wish I could get a week's leave myself . . ."

She looked at him and reminded him, "Captain, you're the regimental commander. You're authorized to grant passes and leaves to anyone, including yourself!"

"Well, I'll be damned! So I can!"

"You just haven't started thinking like a regimental commander yet, Curt."

"No, and I don't want to," he admitted to her. "The regiment's only been loaned to me. I've got to give it back some day soon. Any word on Hettrick's replacement?"

Wilkinson shook her head. "Not even a rumor, but the new commander will have to come from another outfit. I don't think there's any way that even General Carlisle can buck you up from captain to lieutenant colonel in one jump. Not in today's Army. But I'd sure like to see that!"

"Flattery will get you a lot of things," he reminded her.

"Well, I must admit that I studied the regs pretty carefully trying to find a loophole," she admitted without revealing that General Carlisle had asked her to do just that. "Long time ago I learned there are two types of adjutants in the Army. The first type can always find a regulation to keep someone from doing something. The second type can always come up with a reg that lets people get what they want."

"What type are you, as if I didn't know."

"For some people, the first. For most, the second."

Lt. Hensley Atkinson asked him at one point, "Captain, what happened to Doctor Paul von Waldersee?"

"I don't know," Curt told her. "I thought you might have some information."

She shook her blonde curls. "No, sir. He never reported back from the east side of Strijdom."

Curt thought a moment, remembering the man's obsession with finding the lost tribe of Bushmen and his frustration at Curt's agreement with them to honor their desire for isolation. "Hensley, I'll bet he got permission from Chief Ba to study them. He's probably living with them out in those barren hills right now."

"Oh, that's great!" Atkinson said in dismay.

"Problems?"

"Yes. He never got paid, and I've got some money for him. And I'm on the hook for the radio transceiver he took with him!"

"Put his money in a bank savings account somewhere; if he ever shows up, he can claim it. As for the comm unit, Harriett Dearborn will write it off as destroyed in action and I'll initial it. So quit worrying about it. Have fun tonight. You've earned it . . ."

By tradition and custom, the stand-to lasted only as long as Curt wanted it to last. Once he departed, it was the signal it was over. He let it last for about two hours. By that time, drinks had relaxed everyone and relieved most of the tensions of the last few weeks. And it was time for other things.

M. Sgt. Henry Kester met Curt as he was about to step out the door. "Begging your pardon, Captain, but someone wants to see you."

"Henry, I'm heading for the latrine and then the sack. Who is it?"

"I was asked to be discreet, Captain."

"Henry, I'm too pooped to piss, but let me do that first and I'll go along with you. You've whetted my curiosity," Curt admitted. And he wasn't about to argue with Henry Kester. The master sergeant was many years older than Curt and somewhat smaller, but he was hard as nails and experienced. One did not argue with a man who had rockers on the rockers of his chevrons accompanied by hash marks marching up his sleeve in company strength.

"Yes, sir. I'll tag along, sir, to make sure in your condition that you don't fall in," the old soldier told him. "Then with all due respects, I've been given a direct order to deliver you."

Curt knew there was only one person who could give M. Sgt. First Class Henry Kester a direct order.

Kester showed him to a private dining alcove that had been set for only two and left. Lt. Alexis Morgan was there alone. It wasn't a totally unpleasant situation to be delivered into.

Curt thought he knew why this had been set up, but he

really didn't know how to break the ice. But as an officer he was supposed to appear to be able to handle any social situation with aplomb. So he told Alexis, "It's good to be back. And you're looking great!"

"Thank you. You didn't give me time to change out of this Army Green Pantsuit into something more social," she told him levelly. She looked him up and down. "And you confirm what I suspected during the evack of Otjomuise. You haven't been taking care of yourself."

"Try running a regiment some time," he told her.

"Running Carson's Companions shorthanded in combat was no joy ride, either," she retorted.

"Oh, I thought you did pretty well once you told Len Spencer to shove it," Curt told her bluntly.

"I knew that was going to come up, and I'm glad you mentioned it early in the evening so I can dispatch it forthwith and get down to serious stuff with you," she said with level tones and a sweetness in her voice that warned Curt. "I gave him his story. That's what he wanted."

"That's all you gave him?"

Alexis looked at Curt haughtily and proclaimed, "Variety is the spice of life . . . as you discovered on Trinidad!"

"I also discovered—and I think you did too—that it's often here today and gone tomorrow."

"Ah, yes! Well, he called me from New York today to apologize and tell me he might get a Pulitzer—he won't know for a couple of months—but he's been nominated for the Ernie Pyle Award."

"That make you happy?"

She nodded. "He worked hard . . . especially for my cooperation, I might add. Anyone who would put up with what I insisted upon deserves some public recognition. Besides, he did do a pretty good job of accurately portraying the role of women in combat. In some ways he's a jerk, but he's as much a professional in his line of work as we are."

"Sounds like it was fun while it lasted," Curt remarked.

"It was, as you also know." Alexis reached down to the

table where a bottle of Bordeaux stood next to two glasses of the red wine. She handed one glass to Curt and took the other, raising it as she spoke. "Let's drink to lost loves, all of them. Here today and gone tomorrow, but the Army goes on forever!"

He entwined right arms with her in the old Slavic drinking fashion. Looking her right in the eye at a distance of only a few centimeters, he said, "Ah, Rule Ten, you'll be the death of us yet!"

In a low voice, she asked, "Forgiven?"

"Of course! Forgiven?"

"Months ago, remember?"

"How could I forget?"

"Let your hair grow back, will you? It's all prickly right now. Very poor velcro factor . . ."

"I didn't think you cared."

"What do you mean? Damned right I care! I don't want the other girls to think I'm hooked on a perpetual warbot brainy!"

"Is that what they think?"

"They think, sir, that you are about the best goddamned officer they've ever seen . . . and most of them are green with jealousy . . . and I'm glad! Now that we've gotten that matter settled, I'm hungry."

"I'll order for us," Curt remarked, reaching over to key the terminal.

"Not that kind of hunger, you dummy!"

"Well . . . yes . . . but—"

"And why here? Let's escape into town."

Curt nodded and grinned. "Why not? I'll write us both a three-day pass right here and now while I'm still a regimental commander . . ."

APPENDIX ONE

Fallen In The Line of Duty

Canby, Edward Robert, Major
Rosenberg, Joshua Micah, First Lieutenant
Ingle, Clyde Warren, Platoon Sergeant
Schultz, James Zebulon, Platoon Sergeant
Twombly, Charles Smith, Sergeant
Colter, Donald Baker, Biotechnical Sergeant
Johnston, Ernest Rogers, Corporal
Blunt, Frank Norwood, Corporal
Norton, Roy Thomas, Corporal

Wounded In The Line of Duty

Hettrick, Belinda Jane, Colonel
Gibbon, John Steven, Captain
Garcia, Manuel Xavier, Captain
Kelly, Martin Clarence, Captain
Messenger, Phillip Barnes, Second Lieutenant
Slaughter, Taggart Victor, First Sergeant
Gerard, Nicholas Peter, Platoon Sergeant
Barnes, Forest Lee, Staff Sergeant
Miller, Willa Pauline, Technical Sergeant
Ireland, Mariette Worshame, Supply Sergeant
Wheeler, Josephine Winona, Sergeant
Timm, John Tait, Sergeant

Molde, William Banes, Sergeant
Hale, Shelley Christine, Sergeant
Dillon, Tracy Carlin, Sergeant
King, Billy Ed, Corporal

APPENDIX TWO
ORDER OF BATTLE
OPERATION DIAMOND SKELETON

Supreme Allied Commander—
General Franchet Maurice Lanrezac,
Armee de l'Terre, France

Deputy Supreme Allied Commander—
Major General Jacob O. Carlisle,
Army of the United States

Deputy Supreme Commander, Land—
Major General Sir John Herbert Maitland-Hutton,
V.C., K.B.E., D.S.C., British Army, Great Britain

Deputy Supreme Commander, Sea—
Vice Admiral Sir John William Unwin,
D.S.O., K.B.E., Royal Navy, Great Britain

Deputy Supreme Commander, Air—
Air Vice Marshal Sir Alan Kenneth Moorhouse,
O.B.E., D.F.C., Royal Air Force, Great Britain

Legion Robotique, Armee de l'Terre:
Regimental Commander—
Colonel Charles Henri Mangin

Groupe Cigognes, Armee de l'Air:
Group Commander—
Colonel Etienne Jean Millerand

Groupe Transport de Pasteur, Armee de l'Air:
Group Commander—
Colonel Jean Alexandre de Cary

Royal Scots Fusileers, British Army:
Regimental Commander—
Colonel Douglas McEvedy-Brooke, D.S.C.

No. 222 Squadron, RAF:
Squadron Commander—
Squadron Commander Guy Gibson Barker, D.F.C.

No. 525 Air Transport Squadron, RAF:
Squadron Commander—
Squadron Commander A.G. "Jack" Percival

Task Group Number 4, Royal Navy:
Group Commander—
Vice Admiral Sir Ian Spicer Simpson, K.B.E.

1st Australian "Kokoda" Regiment:
Regimental Commander—
Colonel Aylmer G. Birdwood

1st "Assam" Regiment, Army of India:
Regimental Commander—
Colonel Siraj Kasim Mahadaji

Task Force 44, USN:
Task Force Commander—
Vice Admiral Warren G. Spencer

55th Tactical Fighter Wing, USAF:
Wing Commander—
Colonel Philip C. Glascock

60th Tactical Airlift Wing, USAF:
Wing Commander—
Colonel William James Barnitz

375th Aeromedical Airlift Wing, USAF:
Wing Commander—
Colonel Geraldine Janice Carr

3rd RI "Washington Greys" Special Combat Regiment, 17th Iron Fist Division RI, Army of the United States:
Regimental Commander—
Colonel Belinda J. Hettrick

1st Company, "Carson's Companions"—
Captain Curt C. Carson
Master Sergeant First Class Henry G. Kester
Alpha Platoon—1st Lieutenant Alexis M. Morgan
Platoon Sergeant First Class Nicholas P. Gerard
Sergeant James P. Elliott
Sergeant Charles S. Koslowski
Bravo Platoon—1st Lieutenant Jerry P. Allen
Platoon Sergeant First Class Edwina A. Sampson
Sergeant Tracy C. Dillon
Sergeant Thomas C. Cole

2nd Company, "Ward's Warriors"—
Captain Joan G. Ward
Master Sergeant Marvin J. Hill
Alpha Platoon—2nd Lieutenant Claudia F. Roberts
Platoon Sergeant Corinna Jolton
Corporal Ernest R. Johnston
Corporal Vernon D. Esteban
Bravo Platoon—1st Lieutenant David F. Coney
Platoon Sergeant Clyde W. Ingle
Corporal Michael E. Nalda
Corporal Thomas G. Paulson

3rd Company, "Manny's Marauders"—
Captain Manuel X. Garcia
First Sergeant Carol J. Head
Alpha Platoon—1st Lieutenant Joshua M. Rosenberg
Platoon Sergeant J. B. Patterson
Corporal Lewis C. Pagan

Corporal Edwin W. Taylor
Bravo Platoon—1st Lieutenant Eleanor S. Aarts
Platoon Sergeant Betty Jo Trumble
Corporal Billy E. King
Corporal Roy T. Norton

4th Company, "Kelly's Killers"—
Captain Martin C. Kelly
First Sergeant T.V. Slaughter
Alpha Platoon—1st Lieutenant Russell B. Frazier
Platoon Sergeant J. Z. Schultz
Corporal Walter J. O'Reilly
Corporal Robert Lee Garrison
Bravo Platoon—2nd Lieutenant Phillip B. Messenger
Platoon Sergeant Isadore Beau Greenwald
Corporal Frank N. Blunt
Corporal Harlan P. Saunders

Headquarters Company—
Major Edward R. Canby
Regimental Sergeant Major—
Sergeant Major Thomas S. Jesup
Staff Unit Commander—
Captain Wade W. Hampton (chief of staff)
Regimental Adjutant—
Captain Joanne J. Wilkinson (S-1)
Regimental Staff Sergeant—
Master Sergeant Georgina Cook
Regimental Operations—
1st Lieutenant Hensley Atkinson (S-3)
Regimental Operations Sergeant—
Staff Sergeant Forest L. Barnes
Staff Sergeants—
Staff Sergeant Andrea Carrington
Sergeant Sidney Albert Johnson
Intelligence Unit Commander—
2nd Lieutenant John S. Gibbon (S-2)
Regimental Intelligence Sergeant—
Staff Sergeant Emma Crawford

Intelligence Sergeants—
Sergeant William J. Hull
Sergeant Jacob F. Kent
Sergeant Josephine W. Wheeler
Regimental Chaplain—
1st Lieutenant Nelson A. Crile

Service Company—
Major Frederick W. Benteen (S-4)
Regimental Service Sergeant—
Master Sergeant Joan J. Stark
Regimental Maintenance Unit Commander—
Captain Elwood S. Otis
Chief Maintenance Sergeant—
Technical Sergeant First Class Raymond G. Wolf
Maintenance Specialists—
Technical Sergeant Kenneth M. Hawkins
Technical Sergeant Charles B. Slocum
Technical Sergeant Willa P. Miller
Sergeant Charles S. Twombly
Sergeant Geraldine D. Wendt
Sergeant Jamie Jay Younger
Sergeant Robert H. Vickers
Sergeant Louise J. Hanrahan
Sergeant Richard L. Knight
Sergeant John T. Timm
Sergeant Robert M. Lait
Sergeant Gerald W. Mora
Supply Unit Commander—
1st Lieutenant Harriet F. Dearborn
Regimental Supply Sergeant—
Chief Supply Sergeant Manuel P. Sanchez
Supply Specialists—
Supply Sergeant Mariette W. Ireland
Supply Sergeant Lawrence W. Jordan
Sergeant Jamie G. Casner
Biotech Unit Commander—
Major Ruth Geydesen (M.C.)

Biotech Professionals—
Captain Denise G. Logan (M.C.)
Captain Thomas E. Alvin (M.C.)
Captain Larry C. McHenry (M.C.)
Chief Biotech Sergeant—
Biotech Sergeant Helen Devlin
Biotechnicians—
Biotech Sergeant Donald B. Colter
Biotech Sergeant Laurie S. Cornell
Sergeant Clifford B. Braxton
Sergeant William B. Molde
Sergeant Shelley C. Hale

APPENDIX THREE
GLOSSARY OF ROBOT INFANTRY TERMS AND SLANG

ACV: The Armored Command Vehicle, a standard warbot command vehicle highly modified for use as an artificially intelligent, computer-directed command vehicle in the Special Combat units.

Aerodyne: A saucer- or frisbee-shaped flying machine that obtains its lift from the exhaust of one or more turbine fanjet engines blowing outwards over the curved upper surface of the craft from an annular slot near the center of the upper surface. The annular slot is segmented and the sectorized slots can therefore control the flow and, hence, the lift over part of the saucer-shaped surface, thus tipping the aerodyne and allowing it to move forward, backward, and sideways. The aerodyne was invented by Dr. Henri M. Coanda following World War II but was not developed until decades later because of the previous development of the rotary-winged helicopter.

Artificial Intelligence or AI: A very fast computer with large memory which can simulate certain functions of human thought such as bringing together or correlating many apparently disconnected pieces of information or data, making simple evaluations of importance or priority of data and responses, and making decisions concerning what to do, how to do it, when to do it, and what to report to the human being in control.

Biotech: A biological technologist once known as a "medic."

Bot: Generalized generic slang term for "robot" which

takes many forms as *warbot, reconbot,* etc.

Bot flush: Since robots have no natural excrement, this term is a reference to what comes out of a highly mechanical warbot when its lubricants are changed during routine maintenance. Used by soldiers as a slang term referring to anything of a detestable nature.

Cee-pee or *CP:* Slang for "Command Post."

"Check minus x": Look behind you. In terms of coordinates, *plus x* is ahead, *minus x* is behind, *plus y* is to the right, *minus y* is left, *plus z* is up, *minus z* is down.

Down link: The remote command link or channel from the robot to the soldier.

FABARMA: The 7.62mm M3A4 *Novia* caseless ammunition assault rifle designed by Fabrica de Armes Nacionales of Mexico and used by the Special Combat units as the M33A4 "Ranger."

Fur ball: A complex and confused fight, battle, or operation.

Go physical: To lapse into idiot mode, to operate in a combat or recon environment without robots; what the Special Combat units do all the time.

Golden BB: A lucky hit from a small caliber bullet that creates large problems.

Greased: Beaten, conquered, overwhelmed, creamed.

Hairy Fox: The Mark 60 Heavy Fire warbot, a voice-command, artificially intelligent war robot mounting a 50mm weapon and designed to provide heavy fire support for the Special Combat units.

Humper: Any device whose proper name a soldier can't recall at the moment.

Idiot mode: Operating in the combat environment without neuroelectronic war robot support; especially, operating without the benefit of computers and artificial intelligence to relieve battle load. What the warbot brainies think the Sierra Charlies do all the time.

Intelligence Amplifier or IA: A very fast computer with a very large memory which, when linked to a human nervous system by nonintrusive or neuroelectronic pickups and electrodes, serves as a very fast extension of the human brain allowing the brain to function faster, recall more data, store more data, and thus "amplify" a human being's "intelligence."

Jeep: Word coined from the initials "GP" standing for "General Purpose." Once applied to an Army quarter-ton vehicle but subsequently used to refer to the Mark 33 General Purpose voice-commanded, artificially intelligent robot which accompanies Special Combat unit commanders in the field at the company level and above.

KIA or "killed in action": A situation where all a soldier's neuroelectronic data and sensory input from one or more robots is suddenly cut off, leaving the human being in a state of mental limbo. A very debilitating and mentally disturbing situation.

LAMV: Light Artillery Maneuvering Vehicle, a computer-controlled robotic vehicle used for light artillery support of Sierra Charlie units; mounts a 75mm "Saucy Cans" weapon originally designed in France.

Linkage: The remote connection or link between a human being and one or more neuroelectronically-controlled war robots. This link or channel may be by means of wires, radio, laser or optical means, or other remote control systems. The robot/computer sends its data directly to the human soldier's nervous system through small electrodes positioned on the soldier's skin; this data is coded in such a way that the soldier perceives the signals as sight, sound, feeling, smell, or the position of a robot's parts. The robot/computer also picks up commands from the soldier's nervous system that are merely "thought" by the soldier, translates these into commands the robot can understand, and monitors the accomplishment of the commanded action.

Mary Anne: Slang for the Mark 44 Maneuverable Assault warbot, a voice-commanded, artificially intelligent warbot developed for use by the Special Combat forces to accompany soldiers in the field and provide light fire support from its 25mm weapon.

Neuroelectronic(s): The electronics and computer technology that permits a computer to detect and recognize signals from the human nervous system obtained by means of nonintrusive, skin-mounted sensors as well as to stimulate the human nervous system with computer-generated electronic signals through similar skin-mounted electrodes for the purpose of creating sensory sensations in the human mind—i.e., sight, sound, touch, etc. See "Linkage" above.

"Orgasmic!": A slang term that grew out of the observation, "Outstanding!" It means the same thing.

Pucker factor: The detrimental effect on the human body that results from being in an extremely hazardous situation such as being shot at.

Robot: From the Czech word *robota* meaning work, especially drudgery. A device with humanlike actions directed either by a computer or by a human being through a computer and a remote, two-way, command-sensory circuit. Early war robots appeared in World War II as radio-controlled drone aircraft carrying explosives or used as targets, the first of these being the German Henschel Hs 238 glide bomb launched from an aircraft against surface targets and guided by means of radio control by a human being in the aircraft watching the image transmitted from a television camera in the nose of the bomb.

Robot Infantry or RI: A combat branch of the United States Army which grew from the regular Infantry with the introduction of robots and linkage to warfare. Active RI divisions are the 17th ("Iron Fist"), the 22nd ("Double Deuces"), the 26th ("R.U.R."), and the 50th ("Big L").

RTV: Robot Transport Vehicle, a highly modified artificially intelligent, computer-controlled adaptation of a warbot carrier which is used by the Special Combat units to transport their voice-commanded, artificially intelligent Mary Annes and Hairy Foxes (which see).

Rule Ten: Slang reference to Army Regulation 601-10 which prohibits physical contact between male and female personnel while on duty other than that required for official business.

Rules of Engagement or ROE: Official restrictions on the freedom of action of a commander or soldier in his confrontation with an opponent that act to increase the probability that said commander or soldier will lose the combat, all other things being equal.

Saucy Cans: An American Army corruption of the French designation for the 75mm "soixante-quinze" weapon mounted on a LAMV.

Sierra Charlie: Phonetic alphabet derivative of the initials "SC" meaning "Special Combat," the personnel trained to engage in personal field combat supported and accompanied by voice-commanded, artificially intelligent warbots.

Sierra Hotel: Shit hot. What a warbot brainies say when they can't say, "Hot shit."

Simulator or sim: A device which can simulate the sensations perceived by a human being and the results of the human's responses. A simple toy computer with an aircraft flight simulator program or a video game simulating a human-controlled activity is an example of a simulator. One of the earliest simulators was the Link Trainer of World War II that provided a human pilot with the sensations of instrument or "blind" flying without leaving the ground.

Sit-guess: Slang for "estimate of the situation," an educated guess about the situation.

Sit-rep: Short for "situation report."

Snake Pit: Slang for the highly computerized briefing center located in most caserns and other Army posts.

Spasm mode: Slang for killed in action (KIA).

Spook: Slang term for either a spy or a military intelligence specialist.

Staff stooge: Derogatory term referring to a regimental or divisional staff officer.

Tacomm: A portable, computer-controlled, frequency-hopping tactical communications radio transceiver once used primarily by rear echelon troops and now generally used—in a ruggedized version—by the Sierra Charlies.

Tiger error: What happens when an eager soldier tries

too hard to press an attack.

Up link: The remote command link or channel from the soldier to the neuroelectronically-controlled war robot.

Warbot: Abbreviation for "war robot," a mechanical device that is operated remotely by a soldier, thereby taking the human being out of the hazardous activity of actual combat.

Warbot brainy: The human soldier who operates war robots, derived from the fact that the soldier is basically the brains of the war robot.